GIRL GENIUS

AGATHA H AND THE
CLOCKWORK PRINCESS

ALSO AVAILABLE FROM TITAN BOOKS

Agatha H and the Airship City

GIRL GENIUS

AGATHA H AND THE CLOCKWORK PRINCESS

PHIL & KAJA FOGLIO

TITAN BOOKS

Girl Genius: Agatha H and the Clockwork Princess
Print edition ISBN: 9781781166499
E-book edition ISBN: 9781781166505

Published by Titan Books
A division of Titan Publishing Group Ltd
144 Southwark Street, London SE1 0UP

First edition: January 2013
1 2 3 4 5 6 7 8 9 10

This is a work of fiction. Names, characters, places, and incidents either are the product of the author's imagination or are used fictitiously, and any resemblance to actual persons, living or dead, business establishments, events, or locales is entirely coincidental. The publisher does not have any control over and does not assume any responsibility for author or third-party websites or their content.

A CIP catalogue record for this title is available from the British Library.

Printed and bound in Great Britain by CPI Group Ltd.

Did you enjoy this book? We love to hear from our readers.
Please email us at readerfeedback@titanemail.com or write to us at
Reader Feedback at the above address.

To receive advance information, news, competitions, and exclusive offers
online, please sign up for the Titan newsletter on our website:
www.titanbooks.com

GIRL GENIUS

AGATHA H AND THE
CLOCKWORK PRINCESS

PRELUDE

The sun had set, the sideshows had closed, and now the crowd waited expectantly. The wooden stage with its heavy fabric hangings was dark, but from behind the curtain, lights flickered. Squeaking, clanking, and slow, rhythmic thumps could be heard.

Suddenly, with a roar, a great plume of steam erupted upwards. Lights set high on poles flared to a golden brilliance. The curtain itself vanished in a ball of flame, through which strode Master Payne, unscathed. On the backdrop behind him could be seen the shadows of a great set of gears, slowly turning.

The circus master raised his hands with a flourish, and a swarm of electric blue lines burst to life, glowing in the empty air above him. They looped and swirled in intricate patterns, writhing like flying serpents.

Payne's voice boomed over the crowd, silencing the gasps and squeals erupting from the more excitable members of the audience.

"Welcome ladies and gentlemen—to a show like no other! It is true that we bring you the usual amusements, sleight of hand, thrills, jokes both cheap and witty! Ah, but these can be had from any ragtag troupe or two-penny dreadful, and I can see that you are an audience that demands more! *And we shall provide it!*"

Another small explosion punctuated this speech, and easily half the audience shrieked as the surrounding light poles bowed gracefully toward them. Payne produced a glowing orange whip from within his voluminous coat and whirled it about his head before lashing out. After three explosive cracks, the poles flinched, then hastily straightened back up. Payne tossed the whip into the air—where it vanished with a bang.

"For tonight—" he roared, "we bring you a story of The Heterodynes! A story of brave heroes! Dastardly villains! Monsters both human and non! All set against a background of blood and thunder, tragedy and subterfuge, revelations and true love, laughter and tears, noble sacrifice and base betrayal, science and magic!"

The lights went out. Before the audience could panic, Payne reappeared, floating several meters above the ground and glowing brilliantly. He spread his hands and the lights came up, revealing the stage, now filled with fantastically costumed characters arranged in a magnificent tableau.

"For before you tonight is that glittering company known throughout the World—and beyond!—*as Master Payne's Circus of Adventure!*"

PROLOGUE

TWO HUNDRED AND SIXTEEN
YEARS AGO

Andronicus Valois, Leader of the Coalition, Savior of Europa, known to the people as The Storm King, rested his chin upon his folded arms, leaned against the chilly stone battlements of Sturmhalten Castle and allowed himself a moment of loathing.

He loathed this cold, miserable mountain air, as opposed to his beloved Provence.

He loathed this raw pile of rock he'd had to hastily erect as his base of operations. It was hard and sharp, so unlike The Palace of Enlightenment he'd built over the last eight years, with its magnificent gardens and its ten thousand windows.

He loathed the mud and the grime and the blood and the smoke he'd lived with for the last three years. At night he dreamed of the Grotto of Ruby Pools where he'd had his last decent bath before he rode out.

He loathed this... well, to be honest, he actually preferred the clothing. The simple linen shirt and leather pants were ever so much more comfortable than the traditional royal regalia, what with its starched collars and multiple layers of waistcoats. It had been a revelation the first time he'd been able to remove his trousers without having to start unbuttoning himself a half an hour previously.

He sighed. A trap of his own making, that. If he was to keep his courtiers and their pet monsters preoccupied with harmless trivialities like fashion, than he had to be willing to be the exemplar they tried to imitate.

He thought about it, and decided that on the whole, he'd wear the damned clothing in exchange for peace.

He would have to do something about those trouser buttons though.

On the eastern plain below, he could see the assembled forces of the Heterodyne. Now them, he could loathe without reservation. In the dim, pre-dawn light, several thousand campfires sparkled off of armor, weapons and engines of war.

Suddenly, one of the Heterodyne's great war mammoths shrieked, its call reverberating between the mountain peaks. That would probably set the rest of them off.

It was said that one of the Heterodyne's allies was trying to breed the beasts down to the size where they could be ridden like horses. An intriguing thought.

Sure enough, several dozen of the brutes began screaming. Andronicus wondered if it was true that the things really were part rooster. Well, it's not like anyone in either camp was sleeping.

Even now various units of the Heterodyne's armies were performing some odd form of close order drill, and the great furnaces and alchemical pavilions were still roaring and sparking, sending up billows of sickeningly sour smoke.

Some would consider that a bad sign, since the two sides were supposed to formally sign a treaty declaring an end to the fighting this day. But, ever since the Thinkomancer Bludtharst Heterodyne and his army of monstrosities had boiled up out of the East, he had played a heavy-handed game, psychologically. He relied on fear and the stories of atrocities he'd visited upon those who had dared to defy him to weaken his enemy's resolve. Often to good effect, although this time, he had overplayed his hand.

The ruined ground between the Heterodyne's camp and the castle walls showed ample evidence of the last few years of fighting. Craters, torn earth, and the twisted remains of destroyed engines littered the ground. When the horns announced the dawn and twilight cessation of battle, clearing them had been deemed unimportant compared to removing the dead and the wounded.

Even that seemingly obvious courtesy had been hard fought for. The Coalition had learned the hard way that you didn't allow The Heterodyne to collect your dead. Towards the end, the battlefields had been all but swept. Even so, Valois noted that there was evidently still sufficient material to draw the interest of a vast flock of ravens, which covered the battlefield like a dark blanket, feeding.

Without conscious effort, he again analyzed the all-too-familiar terrain as well as the size of the forces before him—until, with an impatient shake of his head, he dismissed the calculations. After today, he'd no longer need them.

He allowed himself a small smile. Oh, no doubt, there'd be… difficulties. There always were with alliance marriages, and the Heterodynes had been unchecked for centuries, rampaging over much of Eastern Europa. He suspected they would not knuckle under smoothly.

The problem was that he had been a bit too successful in his campaign to domesticate the Thinkomancers of Western Europa. As a result of his efforts, everyone had known that a relatively cushy position for them and their patrons could be easily found at the Palace of Enlightenment, and they had flocked to him.

It had even been easy finding ways to keep them busy. Building roads and ports, designing sanitation and communication systems sounded deadly dull, but when presented in the right spirit of competition, and lavishly rewarded for success, the results were amazing.

Of course there was the expected percentage of grotesque errors of judgment, but they were usually put to good use, just not as they were envisioned.

A good system. But it had never been designed for the Heterodyne. He didn't want trinkets, respect, and a fancy title, he was already a ruler of his own empire.

He didn't want to just conquer the neighboring village, he wanted to conquer *everything*, and then dance on the bones. He was bad for business.

But the Heterodynes had done too good a job of letting people know just how terrible they were. Once it was obvious that their armies were crossing the Carpathian Mountains en masse, it had been relatively easy to assemble forces to fight them. The trick had been convincing the fat merchants in Brussels and Amsterdam, who thought they had all of Western Europa to hide behind, that they were in more danger than they dreamed.

Tricky, but displaying a few of Bludtharst Heterodyne's captured troops had been an exciting and effective visual aid, especially when they had "accidentally" escaped, and torched a few warehouses before they were taken down.

After that, the governments, and even more importantly, the great financial houses of the West, had given their support. With their backing, he'd been able to gather almost every fighter between here and the Atlantic, as well as the madboys they controlled.

Thus, even the Heterodynes, after throwing everything they had for over two years against the fortress Andronicus had ordered built here in Balan's Gap, had realized that they could not win.

It had taken another year of negotiation, punctuated with assorted treachery and attacks of opportunity of course, but those had been expected, and Sturmhalten had held firm. So had Valois, who had not risen to the bait and tried to counter-attack.

He snorted in amusement, certainly the final terms were ones he had never dreamed of when he had first sat across from the Heterodynes' negotiators, but the enemy was not the only one to grasp an opportunity.

The particular opportunity he had in mind was Euphrosynia, the beautiful daughter of Clemethius Heterodyne, and Bludtharst's own sister.

Andronicus had first seen her by accident at an early parlay meeting. He had been struck by her appearance and her obvious intelligence even before he had known who she was.

In the year since then, the two had carried on a covert correspondence, aided by discreet diplomats. As a result, when Valois had added the taking of Euphrosynia in marriage as the final part of the treaty, he had been confident that she would come willingly.

Oh, there had been screams of rage from her father, of course, accompanied by a brief rain of burning tar. Apparently the girl had been promised to one of the Heterodyne's allies, and he didn't have many to spare.

But eventually the Heterodynes had relented, old Clemethius gave his blessing, and the treaty was approved.

And today was the day of the wedding, at which the Treaty of Sturmhalten would be signed, formally ending the conflict, and everybody could go home in time for the spring planting.

This was why Andronicus was up this morning, after a sleepless night, watching and waiting.

He realized that he felt... jumpy. He'd felt more and more like that lately. Usually he was only nervous like this during the actual fighting.

Once oafs started running at each other screaming, they could take the most simple battle plan and make a hash of it within thirty seconds. But the whole point of it all was to make things so bloody, unpleasant and pointless that even a crazed despot would be willing to negotiate in order to make it stop.

That's what he lived for. Strategy, diplomacy, negotiating. The delicious art of the back room deal. But lately, it had all felt... wrong somehow.

If this was what *love* did to one's head...

A soft scraping sound behind him caused him to spin, his hand going to his sword—

He stopped short. He hadn't even heard them arrive, and they had undoubtedly made the noise just to let him know they were present.

Arrayed before him were The Muses. It was unusual to see all nine of them in one place, in a motionless, glittering tableaux.

The King scowled. He'd been avoiding them for weeks. They stared back at him silently. A wind began to rise along with the sun, ruffling the great feathers of Otilia's wings.

Damn van Rijn! Why hadn't he built the blasted things with a way to shut them down that didn't entail taking them apart? The old fool had made such a damned spectacle about it when he presented them, that now, whenever Valois opened his mouth, everyone looked to see if they agreed with him!

They were supposed to be these fabulous, mechanical advisors, but bugger him sideways if they made *sense* half the time. Granted, when they did, they were usually spot on, but all too often they just spun pointless stories, or played music, or showed him one of those devilish cards.

They'd been... clearer when there was fighting to be done. Orotine's maps had made developing strategy seem like child's play. But these days, when he was juggling a hundred and a half treaties and coalitions—if he spent too much time with them, his head just started to ache. Their latest pronouncements had been the final straw.

As if reading his thoughts—which he wouldn't put past them—the non-twins, Mawu and Liza, stepped forward and spoke in perfect unison. "Storm King. You are about to make a great mistake. This marriage will not cement your alliance, but rather, will destroy it." They then stood silent, their black and white robes fluttering in the breeze.

Andronicus blinked. What they had said was hardly a surprise, but the way they'd been hinting, and suggesting and being so damned subtle and oracular about it for so long—

Andronicus was surprised that they could just come out and *say* it plain and simple.

Maybe he *could* talk to them like normal people. Clanks. Whatever. "You don't *know* that. You're just guessing."

They all turned to the Muse, Prende, who had, as always, been examining the large, hypnotically intricate, gold wire sphere she carried. Andronicus sighed. Not another obtuse parable about courtly love—

With a smooth movement, the Muse brought her hands together, collapsing the sphere down to the size of an orange. "Euphrosynia Heterodyne is not in love with you, my King. She is working as her father's cat's-paw to sabotage the coalition."

Andronicus felt like he was dreaming. These were the same blank porcelain faces staring back at him, but they were actually talking sense.

"What proof do you have?"

Prende paused, and glanced at the other Muses. "No physical proof, your Majesty."

Valois slammed his hand down upon a parapet. "Then this is useless! I cannot refuse to marry her for no reason! Especially after *I* insisted I marry her in the first place! This marriage is the lynch-pin of the whole treaty!"

"Indeed it is," said Artimo, closing her book with a thump, "And whose idea was that?"

Andronicus opened his mouth and then paused. The negotiations at that point had been delightfully complicated, but surely *he* had wanted...

All of a sudden he could understand things that had not been clear before... He had been manipulated. He could feel it.

Suddenly there arose the moan of hundreds of horns and the

16

pounding of the great saurian skull drums from the Heterodyne camp. Andronicus looked down and saw the wedding procession emerging from Bludtharst's easily spotted tent.

He turned back to the Muses. "I can't refuse the marriage. Even if you are correct. I can't!"

Artimo nodded. "But at least you are now aware that caution is required."

Andronicus snorted. "I'll be bedding a Heterodyne. Caution goes without saying." He sighed. "But I'll take little enough enjoyment from it now." He glared at the assembled clanks. "Damn you! Damn you all! *Now* you have to talk sensibly! If you'd explained this to me weeks—*days* ago—I might have been able to *do* something!"

"We could not!" Otilia said flatly. "We would have... damaged ourselves by speaking this plainly before now."

"Otilia is correct," Artimo agreed. "We were designed to teach you, to inspire you, to help you make the correct decisions. We cannot lead you. We cannot force you. We cannot rule you."

Andronicus thought about this. "That's... good to know, I suppose. So why tell me this now?"

Suddenly, there was a clattering upon the stairs and a squad of Storm Knights, led by Hugomont, his aide-de-camp, were there. The man shrugged apologetically. Valois waved it off, the old fellow had done wonders, Andronicus had easily had almost fifteen minutes to himself.

Hugomont spoke. "Your Majesty! The Heterodynes are approaching! You must prepare!"

The Storm King nodded, squared his shoulders and allowed himself to be led away to his destiny.

The Muses watched him leave, and then, as one, swiveled about to look down upon the approaching procession.

"Because, my King," Artimo said softly, "It is too late to change anything."

ONE

SCENE: A small cottage. Table. 3 Chairs. Shutters on the windows. Sturdy door. Princess Vonia & Her three servants are center stage.

SOUND EFFECT: KNOCK KNOCK KNOCK

PRINCESS VONIA: Now who could that be?

THE FIDDLER (softly): Please let me in. I want your light.

PRINCESS VONIA: My light? How peculiar!

THE SERVANT MADE OF ICE: Princess! Remember! These are the Wastelands! Don't open the door!

THE FIDDLER (softly): But I'm so dark. I need your light.

PRINCESS VONIA: But he sounds so weak.

THE SERVANT MADE OF ICE: Princess! We were warned! These are the Wastelands! Don't open the door!

THE FIDDLER (softly): Please. You are using so very much. I need it. Just open your door.

PRINCESS VONIA: Why, surely a little light couldn't hurt.

19

THE SERVANT MADE OF WHEELS: Princess! There is something
wrong here! These are the Wastelands! Don't open the door!

ALL THREE SERVANTS: Don't open the door! Don't open the door!

(TO THE AUDIENCE) Help us before it is too late!

SERVANTS AND AUDIENCE (louder each time): Don't open the door!
Don't open the door! Don't open the door!

PRINCESS VONIA: Surely a peek will not hurt. (OPENS DOOR) Oh!

(LIGHTS GO OUT)

—ACT 1/SCENE 1, *THE HETERODYNE BOYS AND THE
MYSTERY OF THE THRICE-DARK CITY*

The little airship was losing altitude fast. Agatha could
see the wild pine forests and mountain outcrops
growing ever closer, and this worried her. She had
guessed that her quick patch-job wouldn't hold for long, but
she *had* hoped it would last long enough for the stolen ship to
get her over the mountains before nightfall. Now, she wasn't
so sure. She aimed toward a promising gap in the peaks, then,
locking the wheel so the course would hold, killed the engines.

She turned to the center of the gondola and tugged at a likely
ring in the floor, stumbling backward slightly as the heavy hatch
first stuck, then swung open as if spring-loaded. She quickly
scanned the mechanism it revealed, humming softly to herself.
Then, she dragged a leather roll of tools to her side, flipped it
open with a deft movement, and began to work.

She wasn't even sure what mountains they were[1], or where

---

[1] As any serious student of the life of Agatha Heterodyne must be aware of by now,
hard facts about things like geography are frustratingly difficult to nail down. As
far as we have been able to ascertain, the mountains referred to here were probably
part of The Balkans, but could easily have been part of the Transylvanian Alps.
All we know for sure is that they were flat on the bottom, pointed on the top, and
had ears.

she was, exactly. She knew she was traveling east, toward the sun rising behind the peaks.

Agatha had been insensible on the trip from her home in the University town of Beetleburg to the great airship city Castle Wulfenbach.[2] She now realized, with some annoyance, that in all the time she had spent on Castle Wulfenbach, she had never bothered to discover the present location and route of the gigantic airship as it continued its endless patrol of the Wulfenbach Empire. This morning's escape could have begun practically *anywhere* over Europa.

Well, she thought, as she slammed the hatch and re-started the engines, it hardly mattered at the moment. Putting the mountains and their turbulent air currents between herself and any pursuit seemed like her best shot at escape. Once on the ground, she could worry about where she was. For now, anywhere but Castle Wulfenbach was her goal.

"Krosp—wake up." She called to the gondola's other occupant, a large white cat who yawned and stretched.

"What is it, Agatha? Pursuit?"

"No, but we're starting to lose altitude." She tapped a fingernail against a dial face. The needle within flicked briefly, then continued in its slow decent. "Pretty quickly, too, thanks

[2] See our previous textbook, which, due to unfortunate market forces is entitled *Agatha H and the Airship City.* We had suggested *The Life of Agatha Heterodyne; Part One—Leaving the University. An Examination of the Causes and Tribulations Leading to the Restoration of the House of Heterodyne, A Reexamination of the Storm King Mythos and Some Clues as to the Underlying Troubles Within the Political Structure of the Wulfenbach Empire* . We will concede that this was a bit dry. However we *were* able to prevent it from being titled *Agatha's Electrifying Orbs of Scientific Seduction!* So we must take our victories where we can.

to that hole Othar[3] shot in the envelope."

"Yeah, I didn't think that patch would hold long." The two of them scanned the ground. Dense forest covered a jagged landscape that occasionally revealed rocky spires. Patches of late snow still clung to the higher, more shaded dells. A multitude of streams and small rivers coursed through the numerous valleys. It looked like an absolutely terrible landscape to travel on foot.

"Can we at least clear that?" Krosp stopped licking one paw long enough to gesture toward an especially craggy mountain that loomed to one side of the gap.

"I think so." Agatha said. "I'm going to try. I've made some changes to the ship's engines—they'll give us more speed for about twenty minutes."

"Twenty minutes? Then what?"

She considered this. "Then, they'll start to explode. But don't worry. The envelope doesn't have that much time left anyway, from the look of it."

Krosp gazed at her for a long moment. "I'm reassured. Thanks."

Agatha continued, oblivious to the sarcasm in the cat's voice.

---

[3] Othar Tryggvassen, self-styled Gentleman Adventurer, was an important figure in the life of Agatha Heterodyne. Obviously overly influenced by the legends of The Heterodyne Boys, he was, at this time, an adventuring do-gooder. Unknown to most people, he was determined to eradicate all Sparks, as he was convinced that they were the source of all the evil and madness in the world. This was an attractive theory, and even most Sparks had to admit that he had a point, in his own tiresome way. This task was complicated by the fact that Othar was, himself, a very strong Spark. It is hypothesized that a young Othar had something to do with the eradication of the city of Oslo, which would explain a lot of the evident guilt and self-loathing. However, Othar had resolved this inner dichotomy to his own satisfaction by declaring that once he had destroyed all the other Sparks, he would finish the job by killing himself. As far as Sparks go, this is actually a fairly well thought out plan.

"But it *should* get us over the mountains before we're scraping the tops of the trees. That's assuming that the winds here don't tear us to shreds, of course."

Krosp's ears twitched. "...Of course."

The wind certainly *tried*. Krosp's voice was drowned out by a sudden, screaming blast that hit the tiny airship from the starboard side—knocking the cat off his feet and sending him tumbling across the deck. He landed hard against a roughly carved trunk and grasped frantically at the netting that held it firmly lashed in place. As she lunged for the ship's wheel, Agatha spared a glance backward, reassuring herself that Krosp hadn't been blown over the side. There was nothing she could do for him in any case. She would have to trust in the cat's own terror and claws to keep him safely on board through the worst of it.

The airship bounced to and fro. The wind first tossed it dangerously close to the sharp mountain crags—now nearly level with the ship's engines, then picked it up and flung it even higher into the air. For a couple of sickening seconds, the gondola was blown fully sideways as the ship shot upward, just missing the cliff below.

Through all of it, the modified engines roared in protest, driving the ship ever faster ahead. Agatha hauled on the wheel, fighting to keep the ship—not steady, that was impossible—but at least pointing in roughly the right direction through the madness. If she could keep the ship above the tearing rocks below and pointed toward the gap in the mountains ahead, there was a chance she could get them through alive.

The winds whipped her hair into tangles across her face,

tearing it from the strip of greasy rag she had used to tie it back while working on the engine. At least the flight goggles someone had left hanging from the dirigible controls fit over her glasses, but vision was still difficult. There was moisture in the morning air, and a cold mist was continually forming on the goggle lenses, then streaking away as the droplets condensed and blew aside.

The air above the mountains was icy. Agatha's gloveless hands were growing raw and numb, making it difficult to hang on to the wheel. She grit her teeth, braced her feet, and tightened her grip. Whenever she flew higher, vicious blasts of air—full of tiny particles of ice—stung her cheeks painfully. She winced and hung on, as the winds finally seemed to cooperate, driving the airship hard forward.

Suddenly, they were on the other side, the ground below dropping away as the rocky peaks turned to scrubby, bracken-blanketed slopes, then wooded, boulder-strewn foothills.

The wind was less ferocious here, but now the engines had nearly given out. The ship was roaring along—still forward, but now heading toward the ground at an alarming rate.

A quick glance upwards confirmed that the high winds over the mountains had torn out the patch and enlarged the hole in the ship's envelope. The little craft would not remain airborne much longer. Agatha squinted at the landscape ahead: the glare of the newly risen sun made her eyes water, but as she looked out across the approaching valley she could see fields here and there between the trees, and light flashing on the surfaces of streams and ponds. She shut down the engines, allowing the ship's forward momentum to carry it on its course.

"Aim for that field!" Krosp shouted. He had been hiding

under a blanket during the worst of the trip over the mountains, but had now returned to Agatha's elbow.

"I'll aim for that pond!"

The ground was approaching faster now. Too fast. Mentally, Agatha paged through the manual she had studied, then glanced down, and kicked hard at a pedal on the floor beneath the controls. A series of jolts ran through the entire vessel—the emergency chutes had engaged. With luck, they would slow the ship to the point where its passengers might have a hope of surviving a crash landing.

Her concentration was broken by Krosp's scream of anguish. "No! Anything but that! Land in the field! The *field*!" He grabbed the wheel with his small furry hands, and with his full weight, dragged it to the left.

"What are you doing! Stop that!" Agatha screamed as the ship lurched sideways. She jerked the wheel back, disengaging Krosp, who fell off with a furious yowl. The sudden lack of thirteen kilograms of frantic cat-creature dragging on the wheel caused Agatha to spin it much too hard in the opposite direction.

The ship missed the pond, skittering, bouncing, and then juddering through scrub bushes like a giant sled before coming to a rest neatly among the rocks on the pond's bank.

After some minutes, Agatha realized that she was still alive and no longer moving. This was good. For several more minutes, she lay still, clutching the edge of the wrecked gondola and noting with a detached interest how long it took for her breathing to return to normal.

Gradually, she became aware of her surroundings, and the voice of Krosp somewhere nearby. "Agatha? Agatha! Hey! Agatha! Are you okay?"

Agatha moved her head. "Uhhh... yes... I think so..."

"Can you move?" Krosp's voice sounded close. Where was he? She answered. "Ughr... yes, I think so..."

"Then get *off* me!"

The tumbled heap of the gondola's contents shifted beneath her as she hastily rolled to one side, and Krosp, grumbling, hissing, and slightly flatter than before, clawed his way out.

Agatha sat up and gingerly swung her legs around until she was sitting on the edge of the battered craft. She eyed the chaos with chagrin. Debris was smeared across what looked like almost a hundred meters, bracketing a huge scar that had been carved into the ground. It was obvious the airship wouldn't be going anywhere.

She glared at her companion. "Look at this! It's completely destroyed! There's no way I can repair all this. We're lucky we're even alive! Why didn't you let me land in the pond?"

Krosp glared at her, then his green eyes narrowed and he turned away to lick one paw. "Jeez. Then I would have gotten wet."

Agatha rolled her eyes weakly, and let it pass. After a few long breaths and a quick self-examination, she realized that she was mostly unharmed. True, her clothing was torn and singed, she was covered in small cuts and bruises, and a large scrape on her leg was still bleeding, but none of that mattered. The important thing was that she could, she discovered after some wobbly experimentation, walk. Good. When the inevitable pursuit from Castle Wulfenbach arrived, she would be long gone.

Somewhat unsteadily, she got to her feet and watched Krosp. The cat had already shaken off the panic of the crash, smoothed his fur, and was now rummaging through the remains of the airship.

"Well, so much for traveling easily." She said in disgust.

Krosp flicked an ear. "Yes, yes, mistakes were made. Now we should see what we've got to work wi—hey *hey*!" He sounded triumphant. "You know that chest we couldn't open? Weapons locker!"

He pulled a decoratively etched metal cylinder out of the demolished box. It was connected by bare wires to a piece of unidentifiable machinery that had been housed in a now-shattered glass casing, and another ornamental piece that looked like it had once been an inlaid wooden grip. He held it up for inspection, its damaged parts dangling forlornly from his paws.

Agatha frowned as she leaned past Krosp to examine the rest of the stash. "They all look pretty messed up. I think something in here exploded. See? This box was smashed open from the inside."

Krosp glanced at it again. "I'll take your word for it. Can you fix them?"

Agatha looked at him askance. "Are you serious?"

Krosp nodded. "Absolutely. You *do* understand that we're in the Wastelands, right?"

Agatha swallowed. It was true. Lost though she was, she could see *that* plain enough. After all, "The Wastelands" was simply a convenient, catch-all term for the parts of Europa that were not under direct human control… and there was a lot of that.

At their best, the Wastelands were simply vast stretches of untouched forest and wilderness, places where humans had never held sway. The dangers in these areas were usually those of the natural world, which, admittedly, could be formidable. But at their worst, the Wastelands could be *terrifying*.

The Sparks that had fought each other in the chaos that came to be known as "The Long War" had unleashed upon each other a most astonishing range of creations—monstrosities born of madness and fury that had left whole towns—whole kingdoms abandoned. The Wastelands at their worst were full of hazards of all descriptions.

Agatha had heard stories of roving bands of half-human brigands, mysterious poisoned fogs, and a vast bestiary of Spark-created monsters.

There were always explorers chasing rumors of lost civilizations, hunting rare beasts, or searching for treasure. Many of the once-inhabited areas of the Wastelands were now desolate due to the actions of Sparks.

In larger cities, and in University towns like Beetleburg, there was a brisk market for Spark-made devices salvaged from such ruins. It was common for adventurous undergrads from the University to brave the abandoned laboratories and castles in search of the secrets of their past inhabitants. Agatha thought of all the times these teams of explorers didn't come back. Then, with a shudder, she thought of the other times, when they *did* come back. She remembered the bizarre stories they told, and the unspeakably strange specimens they often brought back with them. Perhaps some kind of weapon would be handy...

"There were some tools, I'll see what I can do." She lifted a brass tube, and then another, examining them with interest and making increasingly happy "hmm..." noises. Perhaps there *was* enough to work with here.

Now, Krosp was all business. "Right, then. You get to work. I'll get everything we can use and try to cover the wreckage a bit. No point in making it easy to spot from the air." He dived back into the wrecked gondola and retrieved a full pack, obviously left by one of the small airship's previous passengers. There was a woolen blanket attached to the pack with leather straps. Krosp unbuckled it and laid it out on a clear space near Agatha.

"You can use this as your work bench, and I'll stack what I find over here." He said. "Hey! Are you listening?"

Agatha nodded distractedly. She was humming now, and laying out parts from the weapons locker and the nearby engine of the airship in neat rows along the edge. She found the roll of tools she had used on the engine. As she waded back through the debris, she gathered armfuls of interesting-looking stray parts. Finally, she staggered back to the blanket and dropped the lot with a crash.

Opening the roll of tools, she extracted a medium sized hammer, a chisel and a trio of wrenches. She spent several minutes tearing select items off of the airship's now useless engine before once again carting an armload of interesting potential components back to her makeshift base.

Only then, surrounded by a satisfyingly varied amount of raw material, did Agatha begin to work.

About two hours later, she sat back and noticed a small stack of airship biscuits on a rock beside her. They were chewy and contained flavors Agatha had never encountered before, but she was so hungry that they tasted delicious.

Looking around, she saw that Krosp had been busy. All of the smaller boxes and items had been sorted and stacked around her. She vaguely remembered finding components readily to hand. She frowned. Sparks could be dangerously oblivious when they were deep within the grip of creation. She would have to try to keep this tendency under control, at least while they were out and exposed. The ability to construct a battle clank was of no use whatsoever if an enemy could simply walk up and brain you with a rock while you were busy tightening the screws.

The bulk of the wrecked ship had almost disappeared under a covering of stones and artistically arranged brush. A movement caught her eye. It was Krosp, climbing clumsily about in a tree, trying to detach the now deflated balloon. She hurried over and between the two of them, they managed to get it down and flat on the ground.

Krosp sat and surveyed it with annoyance. "How much of this do you think you can carry?"

Agatha lifted a corner of the treated silk and aero-canvas. "Depends how much else we have to haul, but it's pretty light stuff."

Krosp nodded. "Cut enough for a tent, and some more to keep you warm at night. We'll have to cover the rest. I don't want anything visible from the air." Involuntarily they both peered up into the sky.

She unfolded a standard airshipman's multiplex knife, and hacked free several square meters of fabric.

Aided by Krosp, she then folded the rest and stowed it out of sight beneath the closest stand of trees.

Then, she returned to her makeshift workbench, and returned with a strange device cradled in her arms. It was about sixty centimeters long and had obviously been constructed from parts of various weapons, as well as bits of the airship control panel, the ship's generator, and one of the emergency pack's can openers. It was held together with balloon sealant and wire. Krosp's shoulders sagged. "That's the best you could do?"

Agatha hugged the weapon possessively. "It's what I had to work with."

"Does it actually do anything?"

"Theoretically..." the rest of her statement wilted under Krosp's unnerving stare. "...I hope so," Agatha admitted. She swung the stock up to her shoulder, and found a chunk of the airship rudder that had escaped Krosp's clean-up. It was several meters up, wedged in a crack in the rocky hill. She sighted on it and squeezed the trigger.

There was a crackle of energy, a smell of burnt hair, and at least five square meters of rock vaporized in a ball of blue flame. Krosp stared aghast at the new crater in the hillside, which was already cooling with a series of pops and clinks. He turned to see Agatha gazing delightedly at the weapon. A thin wisp of smoke arose from the interior of the mechanism and spiraled gently into the morning sky. "Beautiful," she whispered.

"Very impressive," Krosp muttered. He shook himself. "Okay. We're done here. There's no way we can cover *that* up. Let's get going."

As Agatha turned, he noticed that a little brass trilobite, the traditional symbol of the House of Heterodyne[4], had been attached to one side. He pointed with one claw and gave Agatha a sidelong, questioning look. "Hmm?"

"I found it in one of the packs. I guess it was Lilith's. I... well, I figured if we're going to be wandering strangers, we should at least look like we're good guys. Lots of people wear them these days, you know. For good luck. They even sell them to tourists in Mechanicsburg, so nobody is going to see it and

---

[4] The town of Mechanicsburg, the traditional home of the Heterodyne family, sits upon a large fossil deposit. The most ubiquitous of these are indeed, trilobites. The trilobite appears in the city's coat-of-arms, is a popular and traditional shape for seasonal baked goods—most notably the gingerbread, and is usually the perfect size to slip into an old sock for use upon the odd, unsuspecting tourist.

think we're really connected with the actual family."

"Hmf." Krosp rolled his eyes. "Except, of course, that you *are*."

Agatha sighed. "True. But the point is, nobody would guess that just because I've got a trilobite badge. They'll just think: oh, look, another fan of the Heterodyne Boys."

She hefted the pack that held the small amount of useful supplies Krosp had been able to find in the wreckage. "I think we're going to need to find help soon. There really wasn't a lot here."

Krosp shook his head as he surveyed the site. "We've got the gun, some medical supplies and a little food."

Agatha frowned. "Not nearly enough. It won't last long." She remembered the exploding hillside. "And I don't think this gun is going to be of much use unless we're planning on hunting leviathan."

The cat waved his hand dismissively. "We'll eat what I catch, and save what's in the pack for an emergency."

Agatha looked at him critically. "I thought you'd never been off of Castle Wulfenbach[5]."

"Hey, cats are natural hunters. We're in tune with our environment wherever we go. Come on, we'll be better hidden in that tall grass."

Agatha peered ahead. "Those are trees."

Krosp shrugged. "Whatever."

---

[5] This is one of those instances where legends are surprisingly accurate. Castle Wulfenbach was a gigantic airship, close to a kilometer in length, that, at this time served as the de facto capitol of the Wulfenbach Empire—and the heart of the Pax Transylvania. Subsequent stories have tried to downsize this structure, but the evidence for its existence is incontrovertible. Thousands of personnel lived onboard, and many of them had not touched the ground in years.

* * *

Several hours later, night was beginning to fall. A delicious smell filled the clearing where Agatha leaned forward over a small fire and deftly rotated a set of sticks, each of which impaled a plump, sizzling sausage. Across from her sat Krosp, sullen, his fur matted and covered with bits of leaves and mould, glowering at the fire.

Finally, Agatha selected a sausage and nibbled at it tentatively. Satisfied that it was warmed through, she bit off the end and chewed, sighing with enjoyment. The hike had been challenging, but Agatha's foster-parents had always insisted that anyone who spent their days in a machine shop required a stout pair of steel-toed boots as a matter of course. Today, these had served her well.

She held out the stick invitingly. "Come on, have a sausage."

Krosp's glare intensified. "Obviously, I'm not hungry." A small growling sound from his midsection only caused his tail to lash a little faster.

Agatha did not help. "Hey, hunting out in the real world is different. You'll get something eventually."

"Of course I will. When I'm really hungry." Krosp's eyes were locked upon the sausage. Agatha amused herself by moving it gently from side to side and watching his eyes track it. Then she felt ashamed. She slid the sausage off the stick and onto a flat rock between the two of them, then resolutely ignored it.

"Maybe we can find a farm. We could—"

Krosp's eyes jerked away from the sausage and he glared at Agatha. "No! They'd ask too many questions, and even if they didn't, they'd *remember* us. People look after their own first.

When the Baron comes searching for us, we'd just be strangers that passed by. They'd owe us nothing."

"No, we'll try to get as far as possible while we can. When we run out of saus—uh—supplies, *then* we resort to asking for help."

Agatha nodded slowly. She pulled her glasses off and wiped them clean with her pocket handkerchief. "That's as well thought out a plan as we're going to get, I suppose. But at some point, we *will* have to talk to *someone*. If only to find out where we are." She carefully failed to notice that the sausage she'd laid out had vanished. She rolled herself up in the balloon fabric and lay down with her back to the fire. "Good night, O mighty hunter."

Krosp sat looking away through the trees in a preoccupied manner, his cheeks bulging. As she drifted into sleep, Agatha could hear him covertly chewing.

She was jolted awake at dawn by an exultant furry object landing hard on her stomach. She snapped her eyes open to see Krosp, his fur even messier, standing victoriously atop her blanket, waving a paw in which he clutched one medium-sized and terrified rat.

"Breakfast!" he sang out. "Breakfast caught by *me*! Mrowrr! Yowwrllll! Eat eat EAT!" He thrust the rat toward Agatha and grinned with manic pride.

Agatha stared at the rat in panic. The rat stared back. "I...." she thought quickly, "I thought you wanted us to get moving."

Krosp stared at her expectantly. "Yeah." He waggled the rat back and forth in front of her face. "So hurry up! Eat!"

Agatha closed her eyes. "I'll just eat some more stuff from the pack." She peeked.

Krosp's eyes were full of betrayal. "But... but I caught you food! Me! See? Here!" He bounced the rat around some more.

"I'm not eating this—" Agatha thought quickly, "um... I'm not eating this *raw*!"

Krosp considered this. "Mmm. You human types do kind of insist on that, don't you." He frowned. "I don't want to waste time cooking..."

Krosp moved aside as Agatha sat up. She tried to sound reasonable. "Look. Today I'll eat from the pack. Tonight, you can catch extra—" Again, she looked at the rat. She was deep in the Wastelands, with nothing to eat in her pack but six sausages, some cheese and an old apple. The rat was still, steadily returning her gaze. Agatha's heart sank. Well, she might have to eat them, but she would do her best to avoid saying it. "You can catch extra... erm... *things*, and I'll roast them overnight on the coals."

Krosp eyed the rat in his paw speculatively, then nodded grudgingly. Agatha reached out and scratched behind his left ear. "And I know you can do it, 'cause you're obviously an amaaazing hunting creature." Her voice became a soothing croon.

Krosp's eyes closed in bliss as Agatha's fingers scratched away. A small purr began to rise from his throat, then was cut short as the cat caught himself and snapped his eyes open. Suddenly, he looked serious. "Okay. Okay!" He pulled himself away from Agatha's hand and sat down hard on a nearby rock. He looked again at the rat and sighed regretfully, then, with a perfectly horrible crunch, bit off its head. The purr returned and grew louder as the cat chewed contentedly. "But you don't know what you're missing," he confided around a mouthful of rat. "The head is best raw."

Agatha froze at the sound of the crunch, stared in horror for several seconds, then slowly dropped the sausage she had been unwrapping back into its waxed paper wrapper. "Somehow," she whispered weakly, as she tucked it back into her pack, "I'll make do."

With the mountains behind them, they walked on through a rocky landscape, lightly wooded and crossed by the occasional stream. The countryside was beautiful in the early morning light, but neither Agatha nor Krosp was used to long marches, especially long marches that involved carrying full packs over rough ground. After the first hour, the conversation had flagged. The effort of moving as far away from the crash site as possible soon sapped their energy. The going was slow, and they stopped frequently to rest.

Soon, the light woods began to give way to thicker forest, and Agatha noticed Krosp glaring suspiciously into the increasingly thick undergrowth. She realized that she had been doing the same thing. The cat was probably as jumpy as she was, she thought. Hardly surprising. Neither of them had much experience with the outside world. Agatha had traveled a bit with her uncle when she was very young, but most of her life had been spent within the sheltering walls of the university town of Beetleburg. Krosp was a young cat, most likely born in a laboratory on Castle Wulfenbach. His life had been spent entirely on board the Castle.

Agatha smiled at the odd thought that this was the first time the cat had ever walked on the actual surface of the earth. Still, even her limited acquaintance with Krosp told her that he was no fool. They hadn't had time to discuss much beyond the best way to escape Castle Wulfenbach for good, but from various things Krosp had said, she understood that the cat had spent much of his time on Castle Wulfenbach reading books on military history, strategy and tactics, and studying maps of old battles. He had the mind of a furry little general, and was most likely imagining an enemy in every thicket—and planning what to do if it attacked.

As she marched, Agatha could feel the tension growing throughout her body. Her chest felt tight and the back of her neck and shoulders throbbed. She took a deep breath and pondered the situation.

The threat of aerial pursuit from Castle Wulfenbach made her fear the sky and the open spaces, so she was glad of the cover the forest provided. On the other hand, the sinister reputation of the Wastelands made her wary of the shadows under the trees and the crevices in the rocks. Although they saw no animal larger than a crow all morning, occasional cries and rustlings in the brush told of larger creatures nearby. These were, most likely, ordinary wild animals about their morning business—but the possibility of something more *unusual* made her imagination race.

To take her mind off the thought of phantom monsters lurking in the bushes, Agatha turned her mind to the more concrete danger that faced her. There would be pursuit from Castle Wulfenbach, she was sure. That the Baron would simply allow her to leave quietly was too much to hope for.

Agatha had just been rather dramatically revealed to be the daughter of the house of Heterodyne. Her father and uncle had been the near-messianic duo of heroic Sparks known as the Heterodyne Boys. Stories of their adventures and heroism had caught imaginations across the continent. Like it or not, Agatha's mere existence had the potential to shake the Baron's hold on Europa, and he knew it. No, Baron Wulfenbach would not leave her be.

Agatha remembered the stricken look that had crossed the man's face when he had realized who she was, and shuddered. And his reaction after that, his determination to keep her not only a prisoner, but sedated... the Baron clearly believed her to be extremely dangerous. The only mystery was why he didn't simply want her *dead*.

And then there was the Baron's son... he didn't seem likely to let her be, either... but that line of thought made her feel strange, and slightly pained, so she pushed it out of her mind—shaking her head hard to chase away the unwelcome thoughts.

She had been watching the ground as she hiked, now she looked up at the trees ahead of her. They had come through the thickest part of the forest, and were making their way along a gentle hill that ran down into a wide green valley. They spotted a river below, glinting behind the trees.

"We'll follow that downstream as long as we can." Agatha decided. "I know you don't want to be seen, but we can't live in the Wastelands forever. I need to get to Mechanicsburg, and I don't see how I can manage that if I don't even know where it is. With any luck, that river will lead to a town where we can get information without being too conspicuous."

Krosp harrumphed softly, and gave this some thought. "Hm. Yes, I suppose I *could* manage some reconnaissance in a town. That was part of my creator's reasoning when he designed me, actually."

Krosp was silent for a few more seconds, pondering, then

seemed to gain enthusiasm for the idea. "Yeah. This could be fun. Heh. I'll sneak around, find out where we are, steal us a map to Mechanicsburg, and catch us some wily sausages while I'm at it! Mrowr!"

Agatha was pleased to see that the thought cheered the cat considerably. As he marched, Krosp hummed softly with an occasional "Hmmm... yes..." and his tail twitched slightly as he plotted his cunning attack on some unsuspecting village. Agatha smiled. She was feeling a bit better, too. It was good to have a plan.

They were making their way through a sun-dappled stand of birch trees when a stifled sob brought both Agatha and Krosp up short.

"Did you hear that?" Agatha whispered. Krosp nodded. A rustling sound caused them both to look up into the branches over their heads. Perched in the crook of a tree was a small boy. He was about eight years old, dressed in a well-worn homespun outfit, complete with a dashing green cap. His feet were bare, but if the calluses were any indication, this was their normal state. Tears glistened at his eyes. When he realized that the two below had seen him, he froze into immobility.

Agatha waved up at him. "Hello! Don't worry, we're not going to hurt you." She looked around. There was no sign of human habitation near by. "Where are your parents?"

The boy slumped a bit. "I don't know. I was playing, and now I can't find my way back." By the end of this statement, his voice had begun to quaver.

Krosp looked at him speculatively, showing a small amount of tooth. "Really. Well, well. Our search for provisions might be over."

Ugh. Well, the cat *was* a monster created by a twisted mad scientist. Apparently he had learned all about military strategy, but still needed some lessons in manners. Agatha clouted him sharply on the head. "No!"

Krosp looked offended. "What?"

Agatha lowered her voice. "We're the *good guys,* remember? We do *not* eat children. We do not even *threaten* to eat children. He is not 'Provisions.'"

Krosp's ears flattened. "Whaaaat?! Why not? It's up in a tree! Maybe it's a bird!"

"He talks!"

"*Lots* of things talk! Maybe it's a parrot!"

"He's not a bird!"

Krosp looked back up at the now fascinated boy. "Squirrel?" he hazarded.

This caused the boy to burst out in a fit of giggles. The girl and cat looked up at him in surprise.

"I didn't know you were show people!"

Krosp looked at Agatha in confusion. "Show people? What's that? Can you eat them? Back on the Castle, Dr. Sanian had these little guys in jars, and they..." Agatha cut him off with another light cuff to the back of the head.

The boy nodded. "Whoo! Yeah! That's a great talking cat act! Hit him again!"

Agatha glared at Krosp. "I might."

"Hey!" Krosp stepped back and tripped over a log. He rolled over backward with his feet in the air, then leapt around in one twist and began licking a paw while glaring up at Agatha defensively.

At this the boy applauded and leapt from the tree. He hit the ground in a perfect tumbler's roll, turned another somersault and a cartwheel, then bounced to his feet in one fluid movement. At the end of this performance, he held his arms out wide and shouted: "Ta-dah!" He held the pose, grinning, as if waiting for applause.

Agatha nodded. "So your parents are show people—" She paused. "uh... too?"

The boy nodded. "Yup. Master Payne's Circus Of Adventure!"

Agatha was impressed. The way the boy said it, she could hear the capital letters. "So you don't actually live around here?"

"Nope. Just passing through! Like cheap beer! Ba-dum-bum!"

Agatha blinked. "I... I beg your pardon?"

The boy shrugged. "That's what my daddy always says. You can meet him when you take me home!"

Agatha looked helplessly at Krosp. "We'll try."

Krosp finished smoothing his fur, twitched his tail, and sighed. Then he effortlessly flowed up the tree. He closed his eyes and swiveled his head and ears while breathing deeply. Suddenly he froze and pointed. "I smell campfires and horses, and I can hear people calling from that direction." He opened his eyes. "Is your name Balthazar?"

The boy nodded. Krosp made little shooing motions in the direction he'd pointed. "Fantastic. Off you go. Good luck, kid."

Agatha hoisted up her gun and the two headed off. "All right, then. Let's get you back to your family."

"Huzzah!" the boy cried, throwing one fist into the air as he marched along.

Krosp stared after them and then, with a hiss, scrabbled back down the tree. He bounced directly into Agatha's path. "Hey! Whoa! No people, remember?"

Agatha stepped around him. "I'm not going to send him off by himself."

"Why not? He *got* here by himself!"

"And besides, he's already seen us, and we *do* need that information."

Krosp practically hopped up and down in frustration. "But I was going to be all *sneaky*!" he yowled.

The boy shook his head in admiration as he passed. "That is the greatest cat ever."

Krosp glared at him, then sighed and followed.

Soon, they broke through a surrounding border of blackberry brush and found themselves on the flood plain near the river. The well-preserved remnants of a Roman road wound past, and an ancient stone bridge arced gracefully over the water.

Encamped there was a collection of mismatched vehicles arranged in a rough circle. Most were normal circus caravan wagons, extravagantly carved, gaudily painted and adorned with all kinds of banners and odd decorations. Traveling shows of all kinds visited Beetleburg, and Agatha had always attended as many as her guardians had allowed, but even so she was impressed by the variety before her.

One of the wagons appeared to be constructed from parts of an ornate locomotive. Steam gently poured from its large smokestack. Another had no wheels at all, but rode below a small blimp, suspended by a network of ropes. Some of the wagons were constructed of odd materials, some were built in strange configurations, but all were brightly colored, proclaiming the wonders they carried and abilities of their owners. Even now, merely paused in the middle of a field, Agatha thought it one of the most impressive-looking shows she had ever seen.

A number of people were about, tending fires or eating. The boy whooped and pointed excitedly. There sat a wagon whose shafts were gripped by a squat, troll-like clank with a huge grin and a smokestack on its head. Agatha eyed it with interest. Even at rest, the clank looked powerful enough to substitute for a team of horses. "That one's *my* wagon!" He dashed forward, but was checked by a loud call to the right. "Balthazar!"

Without slowing, the boy veered about and ran straight into the arms of an obviously relieved young woman, who dropped an elaborate crutch and knelt to enfold him in her arms. "Mama!" He hugged her tightly. "I got lost!"

Agatha cleared her throat. "He's yours then. Good."

The woman looked up, surprised. She reached for her crutch with one hand, and thrust the boy behind her with the other. Agatha smiled awkwardly and tried to look harmless.

After a long moment, the woman relaxed and smiled back gingerly. "Yes, he is. Thank you." She hugged the squirming boy tightly, "I was so worried."

"We found him sitting in a tree. Um... I'm Agatha Clay."

"Trish Belloptrix."

Balthazar squirmed free. "She's nice, Mama! She's show people!"

Trish looked surprised. "Show people?"

Balthazar nodded vigorously, "Yeah! She's got a great talking cat act!"

Trish looked at Krosp, who was rolling his eyes and gnawing on a piece of grass. "Cat act."

Krosp waved a paw lazily. "Hey, howzit going?" he drawled.

Trish's face hardened, and she raised an eyebrow as she

reassessed Agatha. "That's your 'act' is it?"[6]

Agatha pointed at Balthazar. "*He* called it an act. Not me. We're not actually performers."

Krosp shuffled from one foot to another and waved his paws in the air over his head. "And I can dance, too! Voh-dodi-o-doh…"

Trish adjusted her crutch and pulled herself erect, leaning on it lightly. Agatha noted that although the woman had just one leg and obviously relied on the crutch, her movements were graceful and controlled, like a dancer's.

She was wearing a style dismissed in towns like Beetleburg as too rustic to be fashionable, but so elaborately embroidered that it looked more like an opera company's version of a peasant's dress, rather than the real thing. Still, Agatha could see that the clothing, while clean and well cared for, had been patched and mended numerous times. This was no costume, it was the everyday garb of a performer who lived her life in full view of her audience. It made sense. Most people found that traveling players were worth watching, even off stage. The general assumption was that, not being "from around here," they were exotic and slightly dangerous. You never knew what they might do next.

Trish smiled again. This time the smile was more genuine. She chuckled as Krosp continued to hop back and forth, humming to himself and waving the blade of grass above his head. "Ah.

---

[6] It was commonplace in Europa for professional entertainers to look down upon acts that displayed or utilized genuine artifacts of mad science without obfuscation. A talking cat act (for example) consisting of an actual cat—that actually spoke —would have been considered "cheating." On the other hand, a talking cat disguised and billed as a "talking dog" would be greatly admired. It's all about how you play the game.

The townies must love him." She gestured back to the wagons. "Why don't you come with me? We were just starting a late breakfast when I missed Balthazar. A meal is the least I can do."

Agatha hesitated, "Well... I don't want to be a bother... but..."

Krosp marched on ahead, grabbing the ragged end of Agatha's skirt as he passed and pulling her behind him. "Let's go. Food is always good."

Trish scanned the tree line where they'd emerged. "But... where are the rest of your people?"

Agatha shook her head. "Oh, It's just us."

Trish looked shocked. "You're walking around the Wastelands *alone*?"

Agatha nodded. "We were on an airship. It crashed."

Trish studied her. "Pretty lucky, then."

Agatha looked blank. "Lucky?"

Trish nodded. "That you found us. I doubt there's another human being within twenty kilometers of here. One that you'd want to meet, anyway."

Balthazar broke in, "And not just *anyone,* no! For here you will find the greatest dissemblance of heroes in all of Europa!"

Agatha and Krosp looked at him blankly. Trish patted him on the head. "That's 'assemblage,' dear." Balthazar smacked his head. "Right."

Krosp still looked blank. He looked at Agatha. "What? Heroes? What?"

But now that they had come closer, Agatha had been studying the signs on the wagons. The scenes and characters painted there told her everything she needed to know. "Ah—it's a traveling Heterodyne show!" she exclaimed.

Krosp looked blank. "These people are Heterodynes?"

Agatha sighed. "No, no. I told you earlier, remember? Not everyone with a Heterodyne badge is really connected... Um... Let's see... Do you know what theatre is? Acting?"

Krosp thought about this. There *was* a theatre on Castle Wulfenbach. It was used to make important announcements and presentations. And, due to one of the immutable laws of nature, because there was an underutilized stage, there was a Castle Wulfenbach Amateur Theatrical Society. Krosp had snuck in one evening and sat through three performances of "My Pardon, Sirrah, But Is That Your Piston?" a farce from Prague that had left him with several dozen questions about human relationships and a rather low opinion of theatre in general. "Sort of," he said.

"Well the Heterodynes were real people, who had real adventures, and people like hearing about them. So theatre troupes started doing plays about them, and it became really popular.[7] There are lots of Heterodyne Shows. I always tried to go see them when they came through... Er..."

Agatha faltered a bit as the weirdness of it all sank in. All those dashing stories of the Heterodyne Boys... they were about her father, a man she had never seen. Her uncle Barry—who had disappeared when she was small. These people did plays— usually rollicking adventures with lots of slapstick comedy—

[7] Heterodyne shows were a recent variation of the venerable tradition known as commedia dell'arte. Actors assumed various iconic roles, and while the plays themselves varied, the personalities of the main characters generally remained the same, and were well-known to the audience. Heterodyne stories were quite popular—so much so that many troupes came to specialize in them, and to bill themselves directly as "Heterodyne" shows. At the time that our story takes place, The Empire's Department of Entertainments, Circuses, Carnivals, Traveling Shows and Smugglers estimated that there were over a hundred and twenty such shows, though surely few were as elaborate as Master Payne's Circus of Adventure.

about her *family*. She caught her breath and blinked, seeing the circle of wagons in a strange new light.

"Not a bad way of putting it, miss." Agatha turned and discovered that they'd been joined by a young man with dark curly hair, a trim chin beard and another colorfully embroidered outfit. He had the air of a man with his mind constantly running over a hundred little details, all of which he was determined to see to before he allowed himself a much-needed drink.

Trish indicated the newcomers. "This is Miss Agatha Clay and her cat. The cat talks. Miss Clay, this is Abner de la Scalla, Master Payne's apprentice. Abner talks a *lot*. He also helps run things. Abner, Miss Clay and her cat found Balthazar in the woods and brought him back."

De la Scalla made a courteous bow. "Much thanks, miss." He turned to Balthazar. "Jump to it! Go tell everyone that you've been found. While you're at it, tell them that we're packing up and moving out as quickly as possible." Relieved that no punishment appeared to be looming, the boy gave a quick salute and dashed off.

Trish looked surprised. "Already? But we were going to—"

"Master Payne wants us out of this valley as soon as possible. There's something out there that's spooking the horses." He blinked. "Did you say the cat talks?"

Trish nodded. "He does."

Abner looked at Krosp speculatively. "Interesting."

Trish continued, "I promised them a meal, but we might ask Master Payne to let them join us, if only because she's traveling alone."

This fully engaged Abner's attention. "Alone? In the *Wastelands*?"

Agatha winced. "It really wasn't my idea. My airship crashed."

Abner studied her. "Aeronaut, weird-looking weapon, talking cat... You'll probably fit right in around here," he muttered. He then glanced uneasily back toward the woods. "You wouldn't know anything about whatever is out there, would you?"

Agatha shook her head. "We didn't see anything, and we slept out there all night."

"So—were you the only survivors?"

"Oh no, it was nothing like that, it was just us on board."

Krosp's head snapped sideways. "Whoa! I smell lunch!" He darted off.

Abner stared after him. "Did he...?" He focused more of his attention on Agatha now. "An airship, and you and... he... you were the only crew? That's small for a craft all the way out here. Where were you coming from?"

Agatha tried to look innocent. "Is it important?"

"Could be. I see a Wulfenbach sigil on your backpack there, and the watchman in the last town said he saw Castle Wulfenbach sail past the night before last, so I'm guessing that's where you came from. Do you work for the Baron?"

"No!" Agatha slumped. "I mean, I guess I did. For a while."

By this time, they had reached the central area of the camp. A few of the other performers eyed her speculatively, listening in. When they heard her last statement, they looked at each other.

Abner rubbed his neck. "But you don't work for him anymore, huh?" Agatha shook her head. "You're on the run then." She nodded. "Hoo, boy."

A wiry, grizzled man in an apron scratched his chin. When

he spoke, he had a slight Greek accent. "Wulfenbach, eh? He's trouble, that one."

Agatha whispered, "I didn't hurt anyone. I just... left."

The older man eyed her tattered clothing. "Looks like you 'just left' in a bit of a hurry."

Behind him, a girl asked pointedly, "And how did you escape?" She was tall and blonde, with striking good looks. Her dress was obviously new, and was a fashionable cut, but the gold thread and sequins that covered it made the girl look like a flashy theatrical parody of a stylish young lady.

Agatha didn't bother to object to the girl's choice of words. A great tiredness settled upon her. "My parents. They... they came to get me, but they..." A shudder ran down her spine. "It was horrible. There was an outbreak of Slaver Wasps, and a fight. I... I escaped in the confusion. But my parents... I still can't believe they're dead."

The mention of Slaver Wasps caused a murmur of dismay to flow through the crowd. Many people looked outright terrified. The stylish girl continued: "And you think they'll come looking for you. When was this?"

Agatha shook her head. "Yesterday. It was only yesterday."

Abner patted her shoulder. "You poor kid. I'm sure we could—" He didn't get a chance to finish. The girl gripped his shoulder and spun him about. She was icily furious now. "Don't you say another word!"

Abner looked surprised. "What?"

"This is important, and it's Master Payne's decision, not yours."

"I was just—"

"Just about to say something stupid!" the girl snapped. "Get

Master Payne!" The girl turned to Agatha, who was taken aback to see that her face was now as warm and friendly as any Agatha had ever seen. "You should wait here, my dear," she said sweetly.

Abner tried a final time. "We should—"

The friendliness vanished in an instant as she rounded on Abner. "If you say another word I will kick you in the fork and set your hair on fire," she hissed.

Abner opened his mouth. There was a pause. He closed his mouth. The two of them hurried off.

Agatha and the others watched them go. "I didn't mean to cause any trouble," she murmured.

There was a snort from behind her. "The only people who don't cause trouble are the dead."

The speaker was a lean, well-muscled girl. Her face should have been pretty, but her expression was sullen, and there was an odd look in her eye that Agatha found uncomfortable to meet.

Her skin was a warm, golden color that Agatha found beautiful, but very unusual. She was dressed in a hard-used set of blue leather pants and a vest. Her arms were bare, except for a set of dingy gold bands around her upper arms. Agatha noted with a small, embarrassed shock, that the girl wasn't even wearing a shirt.

Strapped across her front and around her shoulders was a sturdy leather and metal harness that held two sword scabbards on her back. The unusual handles of the swords they held bracketed her head. These at least, had been well cared for. They looked as if they had been recently polished and oiled. Her hair was twisted in a severe braid, tied in place with rags and bits of twine. For a sickening moment, Agatha thought that the girl's hair was so dirty that it had turned green. A closer look revealed that this was apparently its natural color.

Across her forehead ran a leather circlet—a small golden face mounted in the center. This was so cleverly-worked that Agatha momentarily thought it was moving.

The green-haired girl hooked a thumb at the departing pair. "Those two have been like that with each other ever since Pix— that's the girl in the tart dress—joined up. She's got a hard bite, but Abner, there, he keeps trying to talk to her. I guess he likes the abuse or something."

She was sitting on a log that had been dragged up to a fire pit, and now she moved sideways and waved Agatha over. A large iron cauldron hung from a chain and tripod arrangement. She snagged a wooden bowl from a stack and ladled in a huge helping of some sort of porridge, handing it to Agatha along with an elegantly hand-carved wooden spoon.

"She's a great actress though," the girl conceded. She reached down and produced a blue enameled metal pitcher. She leaned over and poured a dollop of thick cream into Agatha's bowl. "Here. Eat." She set the pitcher down. "I am Zeetha. Daughter of Chump."

Agatha's spoon stopped halfway to her mouth. The porridge smelled delicious, but—"Chump?"

Zeetha rolled her eyes. She looked like there was more she wanted to say, but all that came out was, "Just eat."

Agatha thought she should at least show willing. "I am Agatha Clay. Daughter of blacksmith."

Zeetha looked at her levelly and took a long slow breath through her nose. "No, really…" she said. "Just eat."

The porridge was delicious. It was thick, warm and filling.

Agatha thought about Krosp and his rat, closed her eyes, and sighed deeply, enjoying her breakfast's rich nutty scent and delightful lack of rodent.

Agatha saw that Abner had been serious about moving out. People were scurrying everywhere, carrying supplies and equipment. Looking closely, Agatha saw that the chaos was, in fact, not chaos at all. What outwardly appeared to be a disorganized swarm of people would descend upon a section of the camp, and begin sorting, organizing, packing and stowing everything upon one of the waiting wagons—all with a grace and breathtaking efficiency that made the whole thing seem like it was part of a performance. She mentioned this out to Zeetha, who nodded grudgingly.

"Right the first time. This was all choreographed by Gospodin Rasmussin over there." She pointed to a small, intense-looking man who was striding through the camp, rhythmically striking the ground with an ornately topped dance-master's cane. As he went past, Agatha could hear that he was counting under his breath in Russian.

Zeetha grinned. "We can get the whole camp packed and ready in less than six waltzes, or three polkas, if we're actually under attack."

Agatha finished her breakfast just as a crew swept in and began collecting the various cooking implements. She surrendered her bowl and watched as it skimmed through the air to land in a tub of similar bowls. Agatha had a sudden realization, and guiltily looked around. "Are we the only ones not doing anything?"

Zeetha leaned back and nodded. "You're a guest. I'm kept around to kill things, and at the moment," she said frankly,

"I'm keeping an eye on you in case I have to kill you." She saw Agatha's expression and shrugged. "You don't get out much, do you?"

Agatha had to admit that, up until recently, this had been the case.

Zeetha snorted. "You really escaped from Castle Wulfenbach?"

Agatha nodded. "Yes."

Zeetha eyed her speculatively. "You must be tougher than you look."

Agatha considered this statement. "I had help," she admitted.

Zeetha grinned. Agatha noticed that she had disquietingly large canines. "So? That's a mark in your favor. My people say that a good friend is like a strong sword."

"Your people?"

The momentary jocularity left Zeetha and she slumped a bit. For a moment, Agatha thought she wasn't going to say anything, then she sighed. "I'm from Skifander. Ever heard of it?"

Agatha blinked. She suddenly remembered a small cabin high in some heavily-forested mountains. It had snowed furiously earlier in the day, drifts piling up around the carved wooden walls. Agatha had been young, very young, and had returned from building an army of snow minions to find her Uncle Barry leaning against the cabin. Night was falling, and he was watching the stars emerge in the night sky. They had gazed at them together, and Agatha had said something about the night revealing her hidden jewels.

This turn of phrase had delighted her uncle, and that night, while they ate in front of the crackling fire, he had told her fabulous stories for half the night about—

"Skifander!" Agatha declared with a nostalgic smile. "The Warrior Queen's Hidden Jewel! Guardian of the Red Mountain! Oh, I remember that!"

The words had an electric effect. Zeetha's eyes widened and her jaw dropped. She stared at Agatha as if she had spontaneously grown a second nose.

Agatha was surprised. "I'm sorry," she stammered. "Did I get it wrong? It's been so long—"

Suddenly hands like iron gripped her arms. Zeetha's face was centimeters from her own. Her eyes were wild. "You know where Skifander is?"

Agatha blinked—"No! I—"

Zeetha shouted her down. "WHO DOES?"

"My uncle! He told me stories—"

"Where is he?" Zeetha was frantic.

"I don't know!" Agatha shouted. "He disappeared years ago!"

Zeetha staggered back, her eyes wide. "No!" she whispered. With a shimmer of steel, her swords appeared in her hands. "No, No, NO! NOOOO!" she screamed like an animal as the swords wove a glittering arc around them. Suddenly, Zeetha seemed to catch herself. Eyes still wild, she slammed her swords back into their scabbards and ran off, howling.

All around Agatha, objects began to fall apart. The people nearby slowly unfroze and turned to stare at Agatha.

The old man with the vest remarked, "Huh. She's never done that before."

A tall girl with a great mass of dark curly hair and an astonishing amount of exposed cleavage burst from the nearest caravan. "Smoke and the devil! What was that all about?"

An intense young woman in a grey leather uniform shrugged. "I have no idea. The two of them were just talking—and then Zeetha went nuts."

The tall girl turned to Agatha, who was still stunned. "What happened?" she demanded.

"I don't know!" Agatha wailed. "We were talking about Skifander and—"

The girl interrupted. "Wait—You've heard of Skifander? Really?"

Agatha looked at her. "Yes. Really." The look on the girl's face prompted her to ask, "Why is that so surprising?"

The tall girl slowly sat down. She studied Agatha intently for a minute and then nodded to herself. "Sorry. I'm one of the few friends Zeetha has." Agatha thought, rather uncharitably, that she was surprised Zeetha had any friends at all.

The girl introduced herself. "I'm Olga Žiga. Listen. Zeetha was—is—from this Skifander place. Apparently it's some ancient lost city in the jungle or a cavern or something."

Agatha nodded. She could believe it. "Lost" civilizations were surprisingly common, even outside of the Wastelands. Two years ago, a group of students had discovered one under old Rudolf's Delicatessen back in Beetleburg.

"Well a few years ago, this Skifander got itself 'discovered' by some Spark's expedition. When the explorers were ready to head back to civilization, the Queen decided to send one of her warriors out with them, an explorer of her own to go see what the rest of the world was getting up to. Zeetha was chosen. It was a big honor. She's actually a member of the Royal Family, though she doesn't go on about it.

"On the journey here, she got really sick. Feverish. She doesn't remember anything about the trip—except the hallucinations, and from her description, they were pretty awful. Floating around, furniture on the ceiling—wild stuff. Then, just as she was getting back on her feet, their airship was attacked by pirates."

"They killed everyone else on board, but decided to spare her. Personally, I think it was her hair. It's really naturally green, you know, and really pretty when she treats it well. They probably thought they could sell an exotic like her for a nice sum[8]. Plus, by then, she must've looked pretty helpless.

"Anyway, they took reasonably good care of her. That meant that by the time they got back to their fortress and let her out of her cell, she was nice and healthy. Oh, and in case I hadn't mentioned it before, Skifander is apparently some sort of city of warriors, and Zeetha had to earn her spot on the trip by beating everyone one else who wanted to go. So, as you might guess, she's a really good warrior.

"Well, she took them all on. All the pirates in the fortress. All of them. And she won. She killed them all. Again… All of them."

Olga paused, and Agatha thought she looked a little embarrassed. "Like I said, a good fighter, but… thinking really isn't her strong suit. So it wasn't until she'd finished them all off and burned down the fortress that she realized that she'd just killed anyone who might've had a clue about where she'd originally come from."

Olga sat back and sighed, smoothing her hair with a clash of bracelets. "Since then she's been wandering all over Europa

[8] While slavery was not tolerated within the Wulfenbach Empire, there were other lands, and other empires with no such rules. Also, it was a sad truth that certain unethical Sparks of the time paid quite handsomely for "laboratory volunteers" when they could get them…

looking for a way home. She joined up with us almost two years ago." She looked Agatha in the eye. "And you're the first person, anywhere, who's even heard of this Skifander."

Agatha puffed a lock of hair up out of her face. "I see. That explains her reaction." Agatha thought a moment. "I wish I knew more, but my uncle never said where Skifander was. He just told stories about it."

Olga stood. "But at least you've heard of it. Most of the others—" she glanced around. "Well, I think at least some of the others think she was just making it all up. And... Zeetha can tell. That really wears on her. You see how she is."

At this moment, Pix rounded the corner of a wagon. "Agatha!" she called out. "Master Payne is ready to see you!"

Olga stood. "Ah, I've got to pack. Nice meeting you." She took Agatha's hand. "I'm so glad you've heard of Skifander. It's been bothering her so much. Even if you don't know anything else...well... thank you for that." Olga turned with a wave and vanished back into her wagon.

Agatha turned to Pix, and the two set off together. Pix looked sideways at her curiously. "You've really heard about Zeetha's Skifander?"

"It was years ago," Agatha admitted, "But my uncle traveled all over. He talked about it like it was a real place."

Pix digested this. "And where are you heading?"

"Mechanicsburg." Agatha replied.

"Ah. The home of the Heterodynes. That's quite a way. You have family there?"

Agatha considered this. "That's what I'm going to find out."

Pix nodded. "Your best bet is to head west." She gestured over the trees. "Do you have a compass?" Agatha shook her head. "Oh, well, I'll bet we can find one for you to take with you easily enough. I'll ask around before you go."

Agatha nodded. A sinking feeling began to grow inside her chest. It didn't sound like they were going to let her stay.

A shrill mechanical squeal filled the air. Next to them, a wagon covered in garish gear designs rocked to a halt, wobbling slightly as it balanced upon a single, central wheel.

A diminutive woman with dark skin and a grimy leather mechanic's coverall swore and threw a large wrench to the ground. "What the hell is it *now*?" she screamed.

Agatha stepped up and cleared her throat. "Excuse me, but that noise means that your gyro gear needs repacking." The woman gave her long, blank, stare, but an older man, seated at the wagon's controls, slapped his thigh and laughed heartily. "Aha! See? It is as I *told* you!"

The woman frowned and turned away from Agatha in irritation. "Ah, what does *she* know?"

Agatha bristled. "I know that it's a Duchy of Blenshaf Gyro Wheel," she said frostily. "Your wobble plate is loose, and it also sounds like you've neglected to replace the sponge dampers. Probably because you can't find new ones. They're hard to get these days. You can make an acceptable replacement out of horse dung and straw. *And* from the way your wheel is spalling, it's obvious that that you don't have the correct formula for tread gunk."

The short woman turned back, all traces of annoyance gone. She regarded Agatha with interest. "You know Gyro Wheels," she stated.

Agatha nodded, slightly mollified. "My dad was a mechanic. We saw these all the time."

The man in the driver's seat was grinning. He had fair skin, bleached yellow hair, and a wide jaw. When he grinned, it covered a fair amount of his face. He also had a mechanical forearm and hand which he raised, pushing back his cap. He leaned forward. "Say, if you are going to being sticking around, would you want a working job?"

Agatha blinked. "What?" Behind her, Pix grimaced in exasperation and covered her eyes with one hand.

"I am Captain Kadiiski. Me and Rivet—" He indicated the woman, who gave her a friendly nod, "We have the dubious honor of being the poor, put-upon mechanics for this noisy collection of divas and geeks. But I must admit, with some small embarrassment, that the Lady Rivet and myself are what you would call piston-leg men. This miserable wheel has got us smoked."

Rivet nodded. "We could use another competent mechanic around here anyway."

Pix spoke up. "I don't think that's a good idea."

Reluctantly, Agatha agreed. "Yes, I've got to get to Mechanicsburg."

Rivet once again looked at her blankly. "So what's the problem? We'll be performing at Mechanicsburg in a month or two. Big cheese festival."

Agatha turned to look at Pix. "Really." Pix rolled her eyes.

Rivet continued, "Oh yeah. And in the meantime, you'll actually earn—"

"Rivet! Shut! Up!"

All three of them stared at Pix. Kadiiski frowned. "What is *your* problem of the sudden?"

"The problem," a voice boomed from behind them, "Is

that this Miss Clay cannot travel with us."

Agatha turned and stared. Before her stood one of the largest men she had ever seen, followed by several other members of the troupe. A quick reassessment and she realized that while he was tall, he wasn't exceptionally tall, and while he was heavy, he wasn't excessively fat, it was just that he... loomed large. This, she realized, was a man who filled the space he was in, whatever that space happened to be. He had a broad face framed by a mane of wild reddish brown hair, as well as a full beard and moustache. His eyes were magnified in a mesmerizing way by his small, thick spectacles.

He wore layer upon layer of waistcoats, each adorned with pockets, piping, buttons and chains, none of which matched. The whole ensemble was enveloped by a huge, elaborate coat covered with embroidered stars, moons and comets. At his throat was a family sigil badge, which, strikingly, was completely blank.

The man's voice matched the rest of him. It was solid and booming, and in this instance, grim. It was a voice which allowed no argument.

He addressed Agatha: "Miss Clay, I am Master Payne. I am sorry I must be so blunt. You did us a favor by returning young Balthazar, and we are grateful. But this is my circus, and I am responsible for the safety of the people in it. For that reason, our roads must diverge here."

Captain Kadiiski looked at Agatha, puzzled, then turned back to Master Payne. "What is wrong with her?" he asked.

The circus master made a chopping motion with his hand, signaling an end to any discussion. "She is on the run from Baron Wulfenbach. Her reasons are her own, and I do not wish to know them. But even ordinary townsfolk might be punished simply for aiding her." He fixed an eye on the mechanic, "And we have our own concerns, as you well know."

The Captain stepped back unhappily, and several of the other circus members glanced at each other nervously. Payne turned back to Agatha. His face was sympathetic, but his voice remained firm. "We don't want any trouble from The Baron, Miss Clay. We will forget that we ever saw you, but that, and wishing you luck, is the best that we can do."

They all looked at her. Agatha took a deep breath and squared her shoulders. "I do understand," she said quietly. "I'd better leave right away. Krosp?"

She looked around. The cat was not to be found. Suddenly, they heard a great yowling intermixed with swearing, and the intense young woman in grey leathers came around the corner, holding a thrashing Krosp by the scruff of his neck. She was furious.

"It *ate* them!" she screamed. "It ate my entire herd of mimmoths!" Every word was punctuated by a serious shake. "It took me a month just to get them to wear their little costumes! Mr. Honk had just learned to do the peanut trick! And this flea-riddled thing ATE them!"

"Sorry!" the beleaguered cat wailed.

The trainer froze. She stared at Krosp. "Did you just talk?"

The cat's eyes swiveled to Agatha and then back to his captor. "Yes?" he ventured.

She briefly considered this, and shook him again. "Not good enough!" She declared. "But when *I'm* done with you—"

Master Payne stepped in. "Professor Moonsock! Release the cat! They are leaving us."

The Professor glared at the large man, but she instantly let go. Krosp landed on his feet, then dashed behind Agatha's skirt. "We're leaving?" he asked.

Agatha nodded. "I... I'm sorry about your mimmoths, Professor. Um... Goodbye, Herr de la Scala. And, um," she looked back at the two mechanics, "thank you for the offer."

She then turned to Pix, who was looking away with her jaw set hard. The girl had been rude and unfriendly, and yet, Agatha felt an odd sense of disappointment. She found she didn't want to go without saying something. "Goodbye Pix. You... you really are a good actress."

She turned towards the woods and blinked hard. "Let's go, Krosp." Without a look back, she marched off into the surrounding forest, Krosp trailing behind.

The others watched them go. Guilt showed on many faces, but not Pix's. She stared at the ground woodenly as the pair departed.

Abner kicked a stone at his feet. "That was cold. The least you could've done was given her a kind word," he said to her back.

Pix whirled on him and Abner stepped back as he saw the tears flowing from her eyes. "Oh? Why?" she snarled, "She's doomed! Didn't you hear? She's in the Wastelands alone! I... I liked her! She seemed... I don't know, like someone I could have *talked* to! But I don't *care*! I don't want to get near Wulfenbach or anybody like him! No matter how nice, or smart, or, or *interesting* she is, she'd bring him and his monsters right down on our heads. You *know* she would! So she can't stay here and now she'll die. Well I've seen *lots* of people die and friendship and kindness never helped *them*."

Abner looked sick, "But that's so—couldn't we—"

Pix punched him in the chest. "You are such an *idiot*!" she screamed and stamped off.

Abner stared after her, holding his hand to his chest as he struggled to catch his breath. Despite his attempts at conversation, Pix had never said much about her life before the Circus. He had already suspected it hadn't been a happy one—Pix had been alone when she joined, with no friends or family to leave behind. Now, he wondered what had happened to her, that her reaction to Agatha had been so fearful, and so vehement.

Payne also watched her go. He patted his apprentice on the back. "The Countess will give me hell about this," he rumbled. "But Pix is right, if a bit overdramatic. Now, let's move out." When next he spoke, his voice boomed out over the entire camp. "And we move *On Stage*!"

All across the camp, people exchanged worried looks. Many glanced nervously at the sky. Traveling "On Stage" was *dangerous*.

Agatha realized that she had to stop moving, at least for a little while. She had come to the edge of the woods, and the ground ahead of her was a wide field of broken stone. She had marched over the previous hill on automatic-pilot, but this rough ground would require more attention than she currently felt capable of mustering. With a deep sigh, she sat on a boulder and contemplated the rocks ahead. They looked sharp.

Krosp gingerly settled next to her. Agatha realized that he'd been trying to talk to her, but she had been walking in a fog, and nothing had registered. He tried again. "Well. That could have gone better."

Agatha gazed blankly up at the sky and sighed again. "I know you said that people would look after their own, but I never thought we could harm people just by *talking* to them."

Krosp frowned. "They *did* seem a bit jumpy..." he waved it away. "But we were planning on avoiding people anyway."

Agatha nodded. "I know, but the way they were talking about the Wastelands... and they're people who actually know their way around out here... Krosp, I don't know if we can *do* this alone."

Krosp twisted in place to gaze back the way they had come. Even in the midday sun, the forest behind them looked dark. He slumped slightly. "I don't see that we have a lot of choice."

Agatha stood up. "No. No choice at all, really."

At that moment, a hellish noise rolled through the woods. Loud mechanical grinding and thumping sounds were mixed by the wild, thin shrieks of horses and the confused shouts of people.

Leaping to her feet, Agatha ran back through the woods. Krosp ran behind her, shouting at her to wait. They quickly arrived at the crest of the hill and stopped, brought up short by what they saw. Master Payne's circus was on the move at last, but it had definitely chosen the wrong direction.

A large, crab-like clank was breaking noisily through a last bit of forest and lumbering towards the wagons. Agatha had heard of such things—machines of war abandoned or lost in the Wastelands. This one had most likely been lying dormant for years. Its metal surface was rusted and pitted. Lichen and small bushes grew from cracks in its carapace. One of its mechanical fore-claws had been torn off some time in the past, but this did not stop the clank from wreaking havoc with the remaining stump of jagged metal. Exposed and damaged wiring crackled at the torn joint.

The wagon drivers had seen it approaching, and were attempting to disperse, but between the spring-swollen river and the walls of the valley, there simply wasn't enough space for them to turn easily en masse.

To make matters worse, the clank's rusty mechanism ground against itself painfully, producing ear-splitting grinding and shrieking noises. The noise was driving the horses into a frenzy. Drivers were yelling and swearing, cracking their whips furiously. Others risked being trampled as they hung onto bridles and tried to physically drag the horses about. Two wagons had already tipped over, and as Agatha watched, another went down, dragging its horses onto their sides, where they thrashed and screamed trying to break free.

As the old contraption cleared the trees, a great cracked lens, set into the face of the clank, began to glow. With a flare, a focused stream of green flame shot out and set a trapped horse aflame. The panic increased, and the wagons trying to escape rammed themselves into an impenetrable tangle.

The clank lurched toward the terrified people. "Wow." Observed Krosp. "That's not good." He frowned. "Wait. Don't they have any *defenses*? They're scattering like geese!"

Suddenly, a lone cart drove wildly away from the group, straight along the road toward the attacker. The clank, apparently attracted by whatever moving object was closest to it, paused as the cart swept past it and away down the road. It then swiveled about on its six legs, shot out a billow of smoke, and began to pursue the escaping wagon. Agatha realized that the road would lead both cart and clank directly beneath the ridge where she and Krosp stood.

"That must've been what was out in the woods." She said. "What'll we do?"

Krosp looked at Agatha like she'd lost her mind. "It's coming this way! What *we* do is run!"

Agatha gripped her gun. "No! I've got to help!" So saying, she leapt over the edge of the ridge and skidded down the rocky slope toward the valley floor. While the incline wasn't dangerously steep, she found that she was traveling faster than she had expected—and the weight of the gun she held in both hands made for some challenging problems in applied momentum.

When she reached the bottom, the wagon was hurtling towards her. Its canvas back had been charred by a close shot of the clank's green fire, and smoke poured from the remaining covering. In the back of the wagon, Agatha saw Olga, huddled down low, gripping a strut.

The wagon slowed as the horses reached a rise in the road. The clank raised its intact claw up high, then swept it down hard. At the same time, Agatha raised her newly-built gun to her shoulder and fired.

The claw smashed onto the back of the wagon, causing it to collapse and sending the rear wheels spinning off to either side. The passengers flew from the damaged vehicle, flailing in midair. An explosion erupted from the back of the clank and its rearmost right leg blew free. The giant machine rocked wildly for a moment, found its balance, and then spotted the wagon's driver on the ground. The man was groggily beginning to sit up when he turned to see the great clank looming over him. He screamed as it prepared to grab him with its rusty claw.

Agatha ran forward, trying to get between the man and the clank. If it followed the closest moving object, perhaps she could lure it away... but as she darted in front of the man, the clank took another step, and she was knocked to the ground. She looked up and realized that she had fallen directly beneath the device.

It was a terrifying moment. The great clank squealed above her and its heavy legs pounded the ground around her as it shifted its weight. Agatha swung her gun straight up and fired it directly into the clank's undercarriage. The resulting blast took her breath away and she gasped as she scrambled to her feet.

The clank wobbled and staggered to the side. Agatha barely avoided one of the huge legs as she reached the man on the ground and hauled him to his feet. He stared up at the smoking device that lurched drunkenly above them.

"It's still going!" he marveled.

Agatha yanked him out of the way of a falling bit of metal. "I hit the main engine." She could hear the increasing distress of the mechanism. "It's finished, it just doesn't know it yet."

Olga was still crumpled where the wreck of the wagon had thrown her. Agatha ran toward her with the man close behind. "You!" Agatha shouted as she ran. "Olga! Get up!" The crab clank, smoke pouring from its carapace, was slowly swiveling towards them. "Get up! Get—Ah!" The two runners jerked to a halt. As they came close they could see that Olga had landed head-first on a jagged patch of exposed rock. She was quite obviously dead. The man dropped to his knees. "Olga!" he moaned, "oh no!"

Suddenly a sound behind them made them turn. There was the clank, smoke and sparks now pouring from its joints, its gigantic metal claw descending towards them.

"LOOK OUT!" Agatha shouted. At the last second, she shoved the distraught man aside.

Agatha screamed as the claw closed, and the great lens flared. A green flash of energy lanced from the eye of the clank, igniting its captive's skirt, hair and flesh in a ball of greasy flame. It dropped its victim and began to turn—

But the repeated firing of the clank's heat weapon had been too much. The resilient, Spark-created energy source that had powered the damaged machine through its final rampage finally gave way, and the crab clank exploded. Flaming machine parts flew through the air, as the great metal legs slowly crashed to the ground like falling trees.

Krosp raced toward the wreckage, shouting for Agatha. At the same moment, a group from the circus wagons appeared, running up the road toward the man who was staring, horrified, at the charred figure at his feet.

TWO

Hark to the laughter of a Spark—
All Good Folk be home by dark.

—FOLK RHYME

His memories of that day were, for the most part, blurred. So much time had passed since then—and so many, many things had happened in that time. Still, that day's final scene would remain sharply etched in Klaus' memory forever. It was a scene he had replayed a thousand times in his head—the last time he had ever seen her.

Where had he made his mistake?

The room itself was an intimate chamber set high in a corner tower of a castle in the mountains—somewhere in the tangle of little kingdoms that sprawled north of Mechanicsburg. The view over the surrounding town was breathtaking, a panoramic sweep that carried the eye out across the wide valley and all the way to the encircling, snow capped mountains. Although it was late, countless lights twinkled below, echoes of music and laughter floating through the tower's leaded-glass windows.

The celebration had been going on all day. It would still, he was sure, be going strong when dawn came. The day before, the people of this town had been the terrified slaves of the Chatelaine of Red Glass, but that had all ended when Bill and Barry, the legendary Heterodyne Boys, accompanied by Klaus, Lucrezia Mongfish, and Zzxzm, the sentient magnet[9] accidentally crashed their airship into the ornamental fountain of Ruby Glass Castle. There, they discovered the hidden caverns beneath the town, and the terrible secrets they contained.

It was now forty-eight hours later. The Chatelaine's army of luminescent fungus men had been destroyed, every hapless captive freed.

The Chatelaine's death had been cause for rejoicing and celebration throughout the town, but it had cast a pall among the Heterodyne party. Bill and Barry always wanted to *reform* their enemies, not kill them. They would happily battle rampaging monsters with electrical grenade throwers or earthquake machines, but they were convinced that anyone, given a chance, could change their ways and work together to make Europa a better place. Whenever they failed, whenever a Spark was killed, they saw it as a personal failure. When the townspeople first realized they were free, the Heterodynes had silently tolerated the inevitable cheers and back-slapping; but

---

[9] Zzxzm was easily one of the Heterodyne Boys' odder companions. The result of a laboratory accident involving an experimental compass and an unattended lightning generator, he eventually retired to the North Pole.

when the music and beer had begun to flow, they had quietly slipped away. Klaus had tried to talk to them as they left, but Barry had pushed past him, growling: "I will accept that sometimes a villain has to die, but I'll be damned if I'll take free drinks for doing it."

It had taken hours for the rest of the Heterodynes' friends to escape the parties, and when they finally returned to the Castle, they had not been terribly surprised to find only a note waiting for them. Bill and Barry had gone on ahead, off to deal with a runaway knitting automaton in a neighboring town.

Klaus understood the Heterodynes' feelings, but he had seen the spore-chambers. And *smelled* them. Lucrezia had lured the Chatelaine inside with her shadow puppets, and he had unhesitatingly thrown the lever on the great glass furnace. Some things were best cleansed by fire.

It had all been followed by a long day of listening to boring speeches, and aiding in the selection of a new town council. Finally, Klaus and Lucrezia were alone with each other. It was the first time in over a week, but Klaus felt like it had been months.

The room itself was only small by the rather grand standards of the rest of the castle. It was entirely dominated by a colossal curtained bed. Layer upon layer of sumptuous hangings in a riot of velvet, satin and brocade were drawn back by ropes of gleaming tasseled silk, showing off yet more layers of gorgeousness. Exquisitely inlaid rosewood cabinets lined the walls. These were oiled and polished to a luxurious glow, which reflected the warm light from the lamps, and made it seem to hang in the air like a luxuriant golden mist.

When Klaus had first entered the room, he had wandered around a bit, opening cabinets. Idly, at first, but with more and more astonishment at each discovery, until he had finally given up and poured himself a calming drink from the magnificently stocked liquor cabinet. Apparently, the Chatelaine had truly been a connoisseur of decadent excess.

Lucrezia, of course, loved the place. She had watched his explorations with open amusement as she stood in front of one of the room's many ornate mirrors, slowly letting down her hair. When he had retreated to the bed, she had laughed and turned to face him.

Ah, *that* was a memory he knew would remain forever. Lucrezia standing, looking at him, slowly stalking him, her face taking on that hungry look she only showed when they were alone. She was dressed in a velvet bustier and a sheer pair of harem trousers—the ones he had purchased for her as a joke last time he was in Morocco. The joke was on him now. The trousers provided a tantalizing glimpse of her legs and clung to the lovely swell of her hips. She raised one arm above her head and posed, leaning on one of the bed posts. Then, still holding the post, she slowly bent forward, deliberately straining her overstuffed top. He knew how much she loved to tease him, but he didn't mind. It was a game they had played together for a long time now, and the outcome was always a win for both.

He allowed himself to run his eyes over her appreciatively, and was so caught up in what he saw that what she was saying didn't register for almost half a minute. When it did, it jolted Klaus out of his reverie cold.

"You *what*?"

Lucrezia smiled and exaggeratedly rolled her eyes before turning away. She gently swayed her hips as she selected a dusty cut glass ewer and slowly poured something cherry red into a small crystal goblet.

"There's no need to *shout*, darling," she sighed in that breathy tone of hers that always sent shivers down his spine. She turned about and posed again, with the drink in her hand. "I'm going to marry Bill Heterodyne. He asked me yesterday... *finally.*"

She raised the glass to her lips, but paused as Klaus interrupted.

That had been very well played.

"Lucrezia, are you out of your mind?"

She laughed delightedly and with a single, graceful move, moved onto the bed before him. Her hand slid delicately along his jaw. "Oh, you're so sweet," she said. She then sharply slapped him, and began to breathe a bit faster. "I *knew* you'd take it hard." She bit her lower lip and looked into his eyes.

She had amazing eyes. Green, deep and oh, so dangerous. "But I'm going to do it. I'm going to renounce my father's work and join up with the 'Good Guys.'"

Before Klaus could reply, she'd spun about and leaned back against his broad chest. This afforded him both the fragrance of her hair, an intoxicating blend of jasmine and carbolic acid, and a magnificent view of her cleavage. That was so like her. Lucrezia would never play only a deuce when she had a death ray as well.

Klaus closed his eyes. This didn't really help. "Oh, and *I* don't count?"

She shrugged against him. "Oh, Klaus. You may work with them—but you have far too much of a dark side of your own."

Klaus tried to analyze this. Thinking was always so... difficult with this woman around. "Oh?" he squeezed her shoulders gently. "So do you."

She laughed delightedly, spun about again and was kneeling in his lap, one hand gently tousling the back of his head. "Oh, I certainly *do*! But that's what you *like* about me, isn't it?"

His eyes flicked down momentarily. They both smiled. "One of the things," he conceded. His arms tightened around her.

She made a small movement with the hand holding the goblet. He loosened his grasp. She daintily placed the drink—

the still untouched drink—

on the bedside table, and then suddenly, she was on the other side of the mattress, just out of his reach, coyly looking at him over one exquisite shoulder. The light was perfect.

Had she planned that?

"Now Bill *knows* that I'm bad, but he thinks I can change." Klaus snorted. "He's wrong. They think that about *everybody*. I know you too well. You'll soon be bored out of your mind, and you'll *try* something." He had a sudden moment of realization. "In fact, this is probably all one of your schemes right now, isn't it?"

That had thrown her. Klaus knew he had been one of the very few people who could do that, which probably explained everything. Had it been too late, even then?

She looked at him seriously, no doubt for the only time that entire day.

"No, Klaus. This isn't a game. I am determined to change. I *do* love him. It should be enough." A brief look of frustration flickered across her face. "Besides, they *always win*. There must be *something* to their philosophy."

There. Then. That was when he should have gotten out of bed. Commandeered a coach, or an airship, or anything. Left town and gone back home. Locked himself in and got to work in his long-neglected laboratory on something... anything that didn't involve tearing across the countryside with bombastic heroes and their barking mad enemies and their enemies' beautiful daughters... instead, he'd been weak, fool that he was. Instead, he had simply leaned forward and fixed her with a stern look.

"This isn't about philosophy," he growled. It came out louder than he had intended. "Bill is my friend. I won't let you—"

She looked up at him and smiled. "Is that how you plan to change my mind?" she whispered, "By *shouting* at me?"

And then her mouth was under his lips, her body locked in his arms, and he in hers...

Much later, the lights of the village below still gleamed in the darkness as they collapsed for the final time. Klaus lay back, breathing deeply, the sweat drying from his skin. Lucrezia opened her eyes and languidly rolled atop him. Klaus's eyes opened wide in disbelief, but she merely began to gently tease her fingertips along the great scars that covered his chest.

Klaus relaxed and sighed in contentment, then reached out

and snagged the goblet that Lucrezia had oh-so-casually placed next to him. He gratefully drank it down. The liquor was sweet and crisp, with an unfamiliar tang.

Lucrezia watched him with heavy-lidded satisfaction, then a wistful smile spread across her face. "Oh Klaus," she whispered. "I *will* miss you. But I'm afraid I simply can't have you around *complicating* things." She ran her fingertip along his shoulder. "If *only* by being such a temptation." She sighed and snuggled against him. "I'm afraid you really *will* have to go," she said in a small, sad voice.

Klaus had smiled. "Hah!" he chuckled, "Anghowr d'jer thirg yg—"

He paused. That statement hadn't come out as he'd expected. He'd stared at the empty goblet in his hand. The goblet Lucrezia had filled *hours* ago. The goblet she hadn't drunk from. The goblet she'd—

"My *dring*," he enunciated as clearly as he could. "Hyu *pzind* by *dring*."

Her face swam into focus. She must've crawled right up to stare directly into his face—watching him with a charming scientific interest. "Not *poison*, silly," he heard her chiding him from a thousand kilometers away, "I'm one of the *Good* Guys now, remember?" She leaned in and chastely kissed his nose. "Goodbye, darling."

He reached for her as everything collapsed into blackness...

No, this was pointless indulgence. He had years ago realized that his grave mistake had not been made that night in the castle in the mountains. No, it had been made long before that, made when he had first known what Lucrezia was, and yet allowed himself to fall into a delicious, dangerous romance, instead of running for the hills as any sensible person would have done. Well, Sparks were not known for being sensible, but Klaus had liked to think he was above all that...

Baron Klaus Wulfenbach made an exasperated noise as he resurfaced from the memories that had held him captive. He shifted his weight trying to sit up, then grit his teeth in pain. At the foot of the bed, Doctor Merrliwee, a trim, serious-faced woman, glanced up from the machine she was adjusting and made a quick, no-nonsense gesture before returning her attention to her instruments.

The doctor's assistant bustled over and adjusted Klaus' pillows. "Please try not to move too much while the doctor is working, Herr Baron." Klaus ignored her and glared at the golden locket in his hand, the beautiful face of Lucrezia smiling back at him from the frame. Set facing her, in the other half of the locket, was a matching miniature of Bill Heterodyne—his old friend—so young—smiling happily. The painter had captured their likenesses with breathtaking skill.

Lucrezia had married Bill, as she said she would, and by all reports, been happy, for a time. He had been glad to hear that. But... what had happened to them? Where *were* they? Lucrezia had done such a good job of putting Klaus out of the way... it had taken him *years* to return home. And when he *had*...

* * *

He was no closer to knowing now than when he had fought his way home to find Europa in ruins. And now, after all this time, there was a girl. Lucrezia and Bill's daughter. Raised by Bill and Barry's old constructs, Punch and Judy, no less. And for some reason kept hidden away—a secret—apparently from *him*. Why? Hadn't he traveled with them? Fought by their sides through all kinds of adventures? Weren't they his old friends?

Klaus turned the locket over in his hand, and examined the back. It was a strange little device—and now that it was broken open—obviously much more than just a simple piece of jewelry. It had been taken from the soldier captured along with the Heterodyne girl back in Beetleburg, but it was obviously not the soldier's property. It even had the girl's name and address on the back. When questioned, the soldier, whose name was Moloch Von Zinzer, confessed to having first stolen the locket, then broken it by throwing it against a wall in a fit of rage. It was large and sturdy, the front decorated with the famous stylized trilobite of the Heterodynes. That, in itself, was not unusual. Throughout Europa, it was common for anyone with any kind of affiliation—to one of the Great Houses, old noble families, Universities, guilds or fraternal orders—to wear a sigil proclaiming their connection. A large pin at the throat was the most usual place for this little bit of heraldry. There were no official regulations about who was allowed to wear what—as long as one was willing to risk embarrassing misunderstandings, or even the possible wrath of legitimate members of the group in question—one could wear what one liked. The trilobite of the Heterodynes was worn everywhere, and simply marked the wearer as one of the vast group of people who loved stories of the Heterodyne Boys and their adventures. And yet... Klaus thought... for this girl—this new Spark who had slipped through his fingers, it had been the real thing—but how could he have *known*?

The locket opened on recessed hinges, revealing the portraits. Simple enough, to any casual observer. But the impact that had broken the mechanism had also caused the back of the case to pop off—to expose a small compartment behind Lucrezia's portrait. A similar compartment lay behind Bill's—Klaus had pried it open during his initial examination. The hidden mechanisms inside were now laid bare—strange watch-like movements that needed special lenses to see clearly. But this was clearly not a device for telling time. Deep within the framework of the tiny assemblage, Klaus could see fantastically coiled springs that powered tuning forks as delicate as human hairs.

Klaus had always had an artistic eye. This meant that, when dealing with Sparks, he was often able to identify the creator of a particular piece of technology through nothing more than their stylistic quirks—the type of gearing they preferred, for instance, or the type of stitching on a construct. Because of this knack, he was able to identify this locket and its mechanism as the work of Barry Heterodyne. And yet... it was more sophisticated, more... *intense* than anything he had ever before seen his friend create. Barry had always been a mechanical genius, it was true, but this little machine was a new high. It was clear to Klaus that his friend had poured everything he had ever learned into this little device. It would take time and careful study to understand its full potential.

Normally, Klaus would have found this exhilarating. An intellectual puzzle of this caliber came along all too rarely. Unfortunately, the appearance and escape of the girl, and all these implied, left him no time for such amusements. There was going to be trouble because of this, and it would require swift action.

Doctor Merrliwee straightened up and slipped a screwdriver into a loop at her belt. She then coughed discreetly. Klaus looked up. She had apparently finished tuning the speed-healing engine she had bolted around his leg, and was now about to activate it. She raised one eyebrow. "Are you ready, Herr Baron?"

Klaus took a deep breath and nodded. The Doctor nodded back, and flipped a series of switches. The machine chugged slowly to full power, lights began to flash, and a wave of hot, pulsing pain caused Klaus to clench his teeth so hard that stars swam across his vision. It would have to be endured. There was no time to allow himself the luxury of normal healing.

He lay back, closed his eyes, and ran through a complex series of mental exercises, shunting the pain to the back of his mind, where it could be locked away and ignored. After a minute or so, he breathed deeply, opened his eyes and turned his attention to the room beyond his bedside.

It was a large room, lined with tall windows, beyond which over a hundred assorted airships could be seen jockeying for position. These were some of the ships that danced attendance upon the behemoth airship, Castle Wulfenbach, but they were only a small part of the actual airship fleet of the Wulfenbach Empire.

The Castle's escort was in even more disarray than usual, due to the recent emergency. As Klaus watched, a fire-fighting tanker, its water bags shriveled, dropped before the window, on its way to replenish its supply from some lake or river below.

Little ships moved between the larger ones, searching for damage along the vast expanse of Castle Wulfenbach's hull. While escaping, Othar had bought himself an extra head start by causing havoc on board the Castle. He had triggered alarms, set fires, and released all manner of experimental subjects. Klaus made a mental note: he would have to think up some very solid defenses against this simple, yet surprisingly effective, strategy.

Klaus then paused and, with effort, reminded himself that he could *delegate* things like this now. With a tight smile, he scanned the crowd in the room and considered the abilities of each. Each member of his command staff was already overloaded with work—whose day should he make more interesting?

The people before him were a wildly varied lot, but they all shared the distinct look of People Who Got Things Done. Here were representatives from every corner of the Empire: Sparks, minions, mechanics and managers. Some were former enemies. Many were the results of experiments, given freedom, acceptance and purpose.

As they arrived, they clustered into small groups and conversed in hushed tones, waiting for the Doctor to finish her work. The mood was tense. Although quietly engaged with one another, everyone was keeping one eye upon their leader: the center of the Empire, the man who dictated the terms of the Pax Transylvania. With a final warning that he was under no circumstances to "fiddle with the controls," Doctor Merrliwee snapped her bag shut and stepped back. Klaus cleared his throat, fixing his assembled command staff with a serious gaze. Once they could see that their Baron was alive, alert and back on the job, a palpable wave of relief washed through the room. Everyone straightened up and prepared to deliver his or her reports.

Klaus had witnessed his people's extreme concern, as well as their obvious relief. Another stone settled onto the mountain of worries that weighed on his soul. The "Pax Transylvania" they called it—and also "The Baron's Peace." Everywhere the Wulfenbach Empire had influence, the fearsome battles that had once raged between warring Sparks were kept in check. The influence of the Pax Transylvania stretched from the Atlantic to Istanbul, and yet it was, for all the strength of the Empire, terribly fragile, resting as it did solely upon the shoulders of one man. Klaus had no illusions about the chaos that would ensue if he were to die, and he was still unsure of his son's ability to share the burden of the Empire.

Ah, but that was a worry for another day. A stream of functionaries filed past, bringing him up to speed on the aftermath of the day's disastrous events. Klaus listened carefully over the burbling and clucking of the healing engine on his leg, and did his best to project the demeanor of calm authoritarianism that his underlings found most reassuring.

The first report was from Doktor Øy, the minor Spark in charge of the laboratory decks. Øy was accompanied by a squat clank that scooted about upon a single small wheel, clutching a bundle of notes in its manipulators and blinking two large round lensed "eyes" that gave it an owlish look. "Some time between midnight and 2 A.M.," Øy began, "Someone activated the Hive Engine that my Baron discovered in the possession of the late Doctor Tarsus Beetle. It had been placed in the Large Dangerous Mechanical Lab. Doctor Vg was listed as working late in that lab. So far, we have yet to find Doctor Vg."

There was a burst of static, and the clank chimed in. "A Hive Engine is just one of the many nefarious devices constructed by The Other, the mysterious über-Spark who decimated the Great Houses of Europa a generation ago." Doktor Øy smacked the clank, and with a squeal, it subsided into silence.

Øy looked embarrassed. "Forgive me, Herr Baron, it has a bad habit of assuming that everyone around it is a child."

The tool doesn't fall far from the hand that built it, Klaus thought to himself. "Don't worry," Klaus assured him, "No one expects anything to work perfectly the first time."

Doktor Øy, who had rebuilt his "Moveable File Cabinet and Brain Stimulation Companion" seventeen times, grinned weakly and continued.

"A hive engine of that size is reported to release approximately one hundred warrior wasps. The clean-up crews have reported finding ninety-eight of them. They are still searching, but it appears that we have found them all."

Øy's clank once again buzzed to life. "The fight to free Europa from the scourge of The Other supposedly ended over a decade ago, but hive engines and other devices are occasionally still found. This is the first time on record that one has been purposefully activated." Doktor Øy was frantically slapping at a panel of buttons and switches on the clank's side, then gave up and pulled a spanner out of his pocket. He incapacitated the mechanism with a single, brutal blow. With an apologetic grin, he dragged it from the room.

Klaus frowned. Øy's clank had raised an important point. No sane person would have willingly activated a Hive Engine. He had to admit that there were plenty of non-sane personnel aboard Castle Wulfenbach, but there were limits. It was another puzzle, and the answer Klaus kept returning to was extremely troubling.

Also troubling was the ease with which the creatures had nearly overwhelmed Castle Wulfenbach's defenders. The next man to report was Colonel Chakraborty—the grizzled old veteran who was in charge of onboard security.

Stoically, Chakraborty recited evidence of the probable path the creatures had taken through conduits and service corridors—a route that had allowed them to move around the airship for quite some time before being detected. The fact that the creatures had spread as far and as quickly as they had was inexcusable. Alarms were in place that should have been activated immediately. Sentries that should have been present had somehow been reassigned. Controls had been sabotaged. At the end of his report, the Colonel silently handed the Baron his letter of resignation. Klaus considered it for a moment, and then eyed the Colonel.

"Before I accept this," he held up the letter, "you have twenty-four hours to explain to me what went wrong." The Colonel blinked, saluted crisply, and strode off, determined to make someone else's day very bad indeed.

Next to be called was a creature that closely resembled a gigantic green-furred gorilla. Thick metal bands, a complicated set of goggles that automatically adjusted themselves whenever it moved, and an enormously tall cap—complete with shako— were its only clothing. When the creature spoke, it revealed a mouthful of thick, sharp teeth. This was Sergeant Nak, one of the many constructs who, upon the death of the Spark who created him, had taken service with the Baron. Nak was in charge of the military forces aboard the great airship.

This was partly because of the brilliant mind that lay nestled behind those goggles, and partly because he was one of the few creatures that even the most unruly of the Empire's rag-tag military forces hesitated to fight.

As Nak approached the Baron, he extended a massive paw. Clutched within was a small bunch of flowers, tied with a festive blue bow. A cheerful tag exhorted the reader to "Get Well Soon!"

Klaus looked at this blankly and then forced himself to smile. Sergeant Nak was indeed a terrifying fighting machine, but he was also considerate to a fault. Klaus had noticed that for many people on Castle Wulfenbach, this only served to make Nak more worrying, and so he always made a point of encouraging the green-furred creature's kind impulses.

Nak's report was concise. The fighting had been intense, but in the end, the Baron's forces had prevailed. He gently unfolded a sheet of paper, and emotionlessly read off a list of those killed in the attack. He then read from another list, this time of units which could reasonably spare soldiers to replace those that had been lost.

The Baron pondered this for a moment, and made a few suggestions. Sergeant Nak saluted and shambled off.

Mister Rovainen, one of Klaus' army of laboratory assistants, had performed the examination of the dead Slaver Wasp Queen. He held his report in one of his perpetually bandage-wrapped hands, but never bothered to look at it.

"The device was constructed at least seventeen years ago, and was no doubt launched in one of the original attacks." Mr. Rovainen's voice was thick, and rasped with a buzz that made listeners want to clear their own throats.

This information piqued the Baron's interest. "How were you able to determine that?" Mr. Rovainen seemed to hunch deeper within his voluminous coat. "Doctor Vg. Before disappearing... Vg proposed a comparison test. Using brine crystallization rates. Vg..." Klaus could see that Rovainen was upset over the disappearance of his colleague. This was understandable, since the two had worked together for years. He took a deep phlegm-choked breath before continuing.

"I believe it was the age of the engine that resulted in a glitch in the Queen's development, causing it to delay the release of the direct slaver swarm."

A burst of static made everyone jump. Doktor Øy's owl-eyed clank lurched into the room. "Slavers come in two varieties. The familiar 'Warrior' class, and the far smaller 'slaver' class. These latter are the creatures that actually infect humans, using a combination of chemical and protean bonding, forcing their victims to become the shambling, mindless creatures colloquially known as Revenants. These revenants become the slaves of The Other. As yet there is no cure—" There was a sudden loud "pop" and the clank exploded into fragments.

Doktor Øy stepped into the room, wild-eyed and clutching a smoking gas gun. "I am so sorry about that, Herr Baron. It's back to the drawing board, apparently." He bowed and exited.

There was a stir at the doors, and the assembled staff made way for a newcomer who stood framed in the doorway. The Baron took a deep breath and nodded. His son Gilgamesh strode to his bedside. Klaus nearly smiled, but caught himself just in time. One of the few bright spots in the last twenty-four hours was the widespread recognition that it was Gil who had slain the Hive Engine's Queen. Unfortunately, just to make things more complicated, people had seen him being aided by the Heterodyne girl.

Klaus sighed. Another day, another crisis.

Almost as tall as his sire, Gil moved stiffly through the crowd. The young man was under a great deal of strain, but was doing a masterful job of hiding it. It would take someone who knew him well to see it. Klaus approved. A commander should not let his underlings see that he was under pressure.

Gil had a lot to be worried about, certainly, but could see that his father was in no mood to ease his mind. He stepped up and ran a critical eye over the healing engine.

Gil was a strong Spark, and his medical training had been excellent, but he could find no fault in the setup. He would have been astonished if he had. Dr. Merrliwee looked unassuming, but he knew that she was one of the finest medical minds of the Empire.

As always, his father's expression was one of barely-suppressed irritation. Gil was unsure just how angry his father was, so he took a neutral tone. "You wished to see me, father?"

"Idiot!" Klaus snapped back.

Gil winced mentally, but kept his face straight. Chastising him in front of the assembled command staff? His father must be very angry indeed.

The Baron continued: "How long have you known that the girl was a Spark?"

Gil sighed. His father had good cause to be annoyed. "I *suspected* it back in Beetleburg. I *knew* this morning."

Klaus' eyes narrowed. "And yet you let me continue to

believe that the Spark was Moloch von Zinzer, and that the girl was just his assistant. Wasting the valuable opportunity to study an apparently powerful Spark—a Heterodyne, no less—in the breakthrough stage! A once-in-a-lifetime opportunity like that, *gone*!"

Gil could see the shrewd sadness in his father's eyes. "Was it *that* important to you to catch me in an error?"

Gil felt like he'd been punched in the stomach. Had he been that obvious?

He had never known his father to be wrong, *never*.

He *had* always hoped, in a childish sort of way, that one day he would actually get to see his father make a mistake about something—anything.

Well he'd gotten his wish, and then some. He'd made a game of it, right from the moment he had noticed the grease under Agatha's nails. Helping Von Zinzer fake the Spark, taking Agatha to assist in his own lab—it was true that Gil had hoped to prove his father wrong, but there had been so much more to it.

Agatha had been something very new to him. He had wanted to keep her to himself, hidden away in his lab, for as long as he could before his father took her away. Watching her break through as a Spark had been miraculous. The delight that had played across her face when she had first laid eyes on the little pocket-watch clank and realized that *she* had built it—and that it actually worked—that alone had been worth all the trouble he could possibly be in now.

And there had been the fear, too. The fear of what would happen to her if his father were to study her, as he had so many other Sparks.

And then Gil had panicked. He'd moved too fast, said all the wrong things, and she had been angry, of course... and now he couldn't even apologize...

When Gil still said nothing, Klaus continued. "Did you know she was a *Heterodyne*?"

Gil shook his head. In that at least, he could honestly claim innocence. "No. I admit, that was a surprise. I didn't know about any of that until DuPree told me. She thinks the whole thing is hilarious." He winced again, visibly this time.

His father nodded briefly and he growled: "Well, now I know it too, as will the whole of Europa! And she's gone off with *Othar Tryggvassen* no less![10] For all we know, Othar might have killed her himself, once he discovered she was a Spark!"

Gil paled visibly at this. His body tensed, and he glanced toward the door. DuPree hadn't told him that Agatha had escaped with Othar. She'd been too busy laughing. If he went after her right now, would he be too late?

Klaus noticed the reaction and swore silently. Gil's obvious agitation confirmed several suspicions that he had hoped were unfounded. "I want you to leave immediately with Captain DuPree. The two of you will find this girl and bring her back."

---

[10] There are many who question why as tightly a regulated government as the Pax Transylvania allowed a wild card like Othar Tryggvassen the freedom to meddle as extensively as he did for as long as he did. The simple answer, gleaned from newly unearthed records, suggest that Klaus, who hated wasting resources, human or otherwise, made use of him. It is no secret that there were many Sparks who utilized their own people as experimental subjects. Sometimes with horrifying results. The problem was that legally, as long as a Spark did not attack anyone outside their own borders, the Empire could not interfere with a kingdom's internal affairs. Thus it now appears that Klaus' own agents steered Othar toward situations where he would be useful. The reason he was arrested was that he had begun to successfully eliminate some of the Empire's more useful Sparks. The arrest had to be made in secret, due to his popularity with the general public. Officially arresting Othar would have been a public relations disaster.

Gil nodded. He'd been expecting this, and was happy to go, but the addition of Bangladesh DuPree made things... difficult. "Father, I can't just grab her by force and drag her back here. She's a Spark, but she hasn't broken the peace." This was a rather fatuous argument, as Klaus had people dragged off all the time. These were usually people who *had* broken the peace, and spectacularly so, but the fact remained that the ruler of the Wulfenbach Empire certainly *could* arrest anyone he pleased, no matter what the reason. And so could his son.

Gil started as Klaus thumped his bed. "Don't be an idiot! She's not just a Spark—she is a *Heterodyne*!"

It was true. Agatha's very existence would be a threat to the Empire. The Heterodynes loomed large in the hearts of the people of Europa, and those who chafed under the Baron's rule, especially among the old ruling classes, would not hesitate to make use of their legend. A genuine Heterodyne heir would be the perfect nucleus around which a well-organized "popular" revolt could be made to crystallize. However Gil felt about Agatha, to his father, she could only be a powerful wild card that threatened his control over the all-consuming game he had been playing—and winning—for so many years. Gil knew his father well enough to know that the Baron would already be laying detailed plans in advance against the plots that would hatch, the uprisings, betrayals and power-grabs that would follow—if news of a new Heterodyne was allowed to spread. Gil also knew that, politically, having the Heterodyne heir firmly in the control of the Empire would be the most important of all those plans. But this was Agatha, not some hypothetical "Heterodyne Heir," and he found he didn't much like what "firmly in the control of the Empire" might mean for her.

Klaus continued: "Plus, she is the daughter of Lucrezia Mongfish. That alone warrants our attention—and our extreme caution."

This surprised Gil. He had heard rumors about his father and the wife of Bill Heterodyne, but they were rumors he had never paid much attention to. Scientifically speaking, he found the idea "icky." It seemed those rumors may have been true after all. Still, this was obviously neither the time nor the place to ask.

He tried a different tack. "Father, she's already angry with me. If I just go and arrest her—and with DuPree—" This argument slammed into the granite cliffside of Klaus' determination.

"You will bring her back here. As a prisoner. Is this understood?"

Gil tried one more time. "Father, of course I'll go after her. But if I can just *talk* to her, she might—"

"As a prisoner!" Klaus roared. "There will be no argument! You can save any romantic ideas you have for later." Gil's face went scarlet. Klaus paused, then continued, his voice slightly softer. "She must be contained as quickly as possible. There is no time for negotiations or compromises. Blame me, if you must. Let DuPree do the dirty work. Once she's here, you can talk all you want—although I would advise against it. Now go. DuPree is waiting on Dock Forty-Three."

With that, the Baron laid back and closed his eyes. With a touch of concern, Gil noted the evidence of strain on his father's face, and checked the actual settings on the speed healer. He blinked as he realized how much pain his father must be experiencing. Arguments at this time would be counter-productive. He would have to do what he could on his own. With a simple "Yes, Father," he turned to go.

Gil closed the great doors behind him, still feeling slightly ill. His thoughts were racing—he would have to move quickly. Suddenly, a plaintive cry of: "Hey! Wulfenbach! Over here!" caused him to look around.

Gil's eyes widened in dismay and surprise. Moloch von Zinzer sat uncomfortably in a steel cage, hung from a rolling framework and flanked by a pair of guard clanks. Gil could see that he had arrived too late. The hapless soldier's fate had been determined.

"I did what you wanted," Von Zinzer complained. "I pretended I was the Spark like you told me to. I didn't tell your father it was your idea." He shrugged. "Not like he was really listening to what I had to say, anyway. He was really angry." Gil could well imagine. Von Zinzer shifted in his cage. "Hey— you said you'd help me."

Gil stared at him helplessly. The man was an enemy soldier who had confessed to threatening Agatha's life at least twice, as well as, if you were going to be technical about it, assorted incidents of robbery, blackmail, threats of violence, assault, and burglary. Despite this, Gil found that he felt sorry for the fellow. He seemed to be a fairly ordinary sort of person—barely above a peasant—who had simply been unlucky enough to get caught up in the affairs of Sparks. From Gil's experience, this meant Von Zinzer had been doomed from the start. Behaving like a saint probably wouldn't have helped the man.

"Yes," Gil conceded. "I did say I'd help you." He reached into his waistcoat's inner pocket and withdrew a small black pill. "Here. Take this."

Moloch reached forward eagerly. "Great! Thanks! What is it?"

"Poison," Gil replied. "It'll kill you instantly." He glumly told himself that having such a thing to hand said all-too-much about his life.

Moloch slammed backwards against the rear of the cage, setting it to swinging. "What? Get away from me! You're crazy!"

Gil sighed. Of course, some people did have it worse than he did. He caught hold of Von Zinzer's leg and deftly tucked the pill into one of the soldier's pant cuffs.

"I am truly sorry, Herr Von Zinzer. I really am trying to help you." He eyed the destination tag affixed to the bottom of the cage. It read "Castle Heterodyne"[11]. "I know it isn't much, and I'm sorry. The way things are going, this might be more than I can do for Miss Clay."

He turned away. Von Zinzer called after him: "You madboys! You're all loony! If that's your idea of 'help,' no wonder you people are always killing each other! God help *anyone* who thinks you're his *friend*!" Gil froze, and then stiffly continued on his way.

A final burst of flame erupted over the delighted heads of the audience, and Master Payne bowed amidst a wave of cheering before continuing. "Before tonight's main show, we have a special treat for you! Our own Professors Moonsock and Therm will share a song that they learned on their last trip to the *Americas*!"

As Payne swept off, two ladies dressed in exotic (and

[11] Castle Heterodyne, located in Mechanicsburg, the home of the Heterodyne family, was, at this period, being used as a punishment detail for Sparks and other troublesome people that the Empire wanted to get rid of. In this, it did a superlative job. Further details will be revealed in future volumes. Honest.

rather daring) costumes strutted onto the stage, strumming what appeared to be tiny guitars. As they played, they circled each other in a jaunty, high-stepping dance, before facing the audience and launching into song.

Apparently, they were well aware that they had no bananas, but it couldn't be helped, perhaps the audience would care for something else? They quickly had the crowd merrily clapping in time and merrily joining in on the chorus.

Payne, observing from the wings, nodded in satisfaction, then continued backstage—through an open air labyrinth of canvas walls filled with puffing machinery and actors half in and half out of costume. People bustled to and fro, carrying props and lights.

Abner stood in the center of it all, a dozen people in varying stages of hysteria vying for his attention. Abner himself radiated icy calm. With a few succinct directions, instructions and threats, Abner sent them all on their separate ways. Payne smiled. The lad was getting pretty good.

As Payne stepped out of the shadows, Abner reached his hand around behind his back and handed the circus master a steaming mug of his favorite bitter apple tea. Payne frowned. "Save it for the paying customers, lad." He then smiled and took an appreciative sip. "How do things look?"

Abner shrugged. "A good crowd, sir. The whole town is here. It was market day, so I'd be surprised if there's anyone living between here and the river who isn't out front." Balthazar ran past carrying a red crate. Abner watched him go. "—and if that's what I think it is, it means we're almost out of 'Mimmoths On A Stick.'"

That was good news. Like most shows, the circus made most

of its profits from the sales of treats, remedies, charms, and small souvenirs.

"And the troupe?" Payne asked, although he already knew the answer.

"On edge. They're calming down now that the show's under way." A huge roar of laughter went up on the other side of the curtain wall. Payne eyed his apprentice. "And how are *you* doing?"

Abner took a moment to consider his answer. "It... it's like a storm brewing. I know *something* is going to happen. I just want to get it over with."

An odd breeze rippled the fabric of the walls. Payne cast his eyes upward. "Be careful what you wish for," he muttered.

Abner nodded. "But I think we have a chance. As long as whoever shows up is someone who will listen to us..." He shrugged. "And who knows? Maybe nothing will happen at all."

Payne looked at him askance. "Do you really believe that?"

Abner shook his head. "No, sir."

Payne again looked upwards in time to see the great black shape blotting out the stars. "Good. Because it's *show time*."

As always, the Circus Master's timing was impeccable. With a crash, huge rows of electric arclights snapped on overhead, blinding performers and audience alike. The Wulfenbach airship had silently drifted down over the crowd—unseen until it was less than ten meters overhead. Soldier clanks stood outlined in the cargo bay doors, and the great steam cannons slowly tracked about. A loudhailer crackled, easily carrying over the noise of the crowd below.

"ATTENTION! THIS IS THE WULFENBACH AIRSHIP *ISLAND QUEEN*. EVERYONE IS TO STAY WHERE THEY

ARE. PLEASE CO-OPERATE, AND NO ONE WILL BE HARMED."

In less then thirty seconds, the ship had settled low enough for a crew of airshipmen to leap to the ground. The ship fired its compressed air harpoon cannons, driving six great mooring stakes into the ground, thick lines trailing upward. On board, the great capstans rumbled to life, the hawsers thrummed taut, and the enormous ship began to sink down to earth.

On the ground, the airmen took up positions around the anchor lines, drew the swords at their belts, and assumed guard positions.

From the cargo bays, great metal ramps rolled out and slammed to the earth with a single resonant crash. The thunder of three dozen giant brass and steel soldier clanks marching down the ramps filled the air. In the center of the group strode Gilgamesh Wulfenbach and Captain Bangladesh DuPree[12], bickering like a couple who'd had a lot of practice.

"'No one will be harmed?'" she demanded. "How am I supposed to work here?" As DuPree considered success to be measured by the number of bodies she left behind, Gil thought any impediment to her efficiency was a thing to be encouraged.

"These people may know nothing," he pointed out.

Dupree rolled her eyes. "Oh don't start *that* again. I found the crash site, the place where she slept, and tracks of a caravan intercepting her. We followed those tracks and hey presto, a traveling show! She's here."

---

[12] Bangladesh DuPree was one of Klaus' more flamboyant employees. She was a former air pirate, a deposed princess, and a cheerful homicidal maniac. By any rights, she should have been jailed or executed. However, as has been said before, Klaus hated to waste potential resources, and whereas DuPree wasn't the most dangerous monster on his payroll, she was one of the most terrifying.

Gil didn't try to dispute this. DuPree was a phenomenal tracker. "Yes, yes, but this time we want the job done without incident. There's politics involved."

DuPree grimaced. Usually, when she heard the word "politics," it had something to do with Klaus yelling at her. "It's not my fault if I'm always sent to deal with unreasonable people."

Gil remembered that he had once tried to determine what kind of person DuPree considered "reasonable." Thanks to an experimental variant of self-induced shock therapy, he no longer remembered the details. "Just find her."

"Hmf." DuPree considered stabbing Gil in the eye, then rolled her eyes and told herself that it probably wouldn't shut him up anyway. "That's what I'm trying to do."

They stopped talking as they approached the crowd, attempting to present a united front[13]. The crowd had sorted itself into two distinct groups. The first was made up of the audience, who appeared to be trying to hide behind the local Burgermeister. The second was comprised the members of the circus, who were doing the same thing behind Master Payne. No one had been foolish enough to run. Of the two obvious leaders, the Circus Master was the most impressive looking, so it wasn't surprising that he was the one Captain DuPree chose to approach.

She stood for a moment studying his clothing and nodding in approval. It would be hard to slip a knife through all those layers. On the other hand, if she was going to kill the guy in charge, it would be to make a point. In which case, she'd want

[13] Both Bangladesh and Gilgamesh would have been distressed to read the field reports that assessed the two of them as being an excellent team. It had certainly kept the Baron from sleeping for several nights.

to be spectacularly flamboyant anyway, so politely slipping a knife between his ribs was already right out. She grinned at the thought. "You look like you think you're smart. Who's in charge here?"

Payne looked at Abner. Abner looked back. This appeared to be a trick question, and was most likely just an excuse to use harsher interrogation methods.

"Er... you are." Payne ventured.

DuPree beamed. "Wow! You're *so* smart—" her arm snapped out and snagged Abner by the collar, "I'll have to slap this guy around instead!" Abner rolled his eyes.

Gil cleared his throat. "DuPree—"

Annoyance flitted over the Captain's face. She tucked Abner's head into the crook of her arm. "I'm *working* here," she said in a tone of strained reason. "Do I come to your lab and tell you how to torture rats?"

Gil thought back to last week. "Frequently."

DuPree nodded. "Yeah! That's 'cause I know what I'm doing. Now stand back, and let me prove it." She roughly hauled Abner upright.

"But what do you *want*?" Payne shouted desperately.

DuPree paused. With Gil around, certain tiresome, bureaucratic hoops *did* have to be jumped through. Oh, well. "We're looking for a girl. Young. Sort of blondie-reddish hair. Healthy. Wears glasses. Caused a lot of trouble on Castle Wulfenbach a few days ago. The Baron wants her." Abner rolled his eyes imploringly at Master Payne, who shrugged. Bang continued. "Everybody here is going to line up, so we can look them over."

Payne tried to explain. "But she isn't here. Besides, I'm only in charge of the circus. The locals won't—"

"Too many details!" DuPree sang out. "Lesson time!"

She flexed the hand that held Abner and a powerful electrical jolt danced through him. When it cut off, he dropped to the dirt.

DuPree grinned and held up her hand. It was wrapped in a small machine that was still sparking slightly. She touched a dial and waggled her fingers. "This thing is great!" she remarked, grinning sideways at Gil. He angrily snagged her hand and examined it.

"That is a medical device! I made it for you to fix your hand! You aren't supposed to use it as a *weapon*!"

DuPree laughed and jerked her hand back. "So I *tweaked* it. I like it better this way." She glanced down at Abner, who was jerkily trying to sit up. "Trust me. If I'd just used my bare hands, he'd be in way worse shape."

Gil opened his mouth. DuPree cut him off. "Look—Is this the girl?"

"Of course not!"

"Is he dead?"

"I said no one would be *harmed*!"

"If they obey."

"Give them a *chance*!" Gil shouted.

Abner had shakily climbed to his feet. DuPree put a friendly arm around his shoulders. "Isn't this always the way?" she asked companionably, one world-weary subordinate to another. "Management thinking it knows what works in the field? This could take all night." She dropped her voice and spoke sotto voce, "Honest. If I was here alone, and you people were still just standing around, half of you would be dead. Then the rest of us could knock off early!"

"Everybody line up!" Payne roared. The crowd put their heads down and started shuffling into some sort of order when shouting erupted from the far end.

"Oy!"

"Hey!"

"There she goes!"

DuPree grinned. "A-ha! She tried to hide with the villagers and made a break for it!" A shriek filled the night. "—aaand a clank got her! Yeah!"

Conflicting emotions tumbled across Gil's face. Slowly his hand reached into his coat. "Amazing," he muttered. "I didn't believe—"

He froze as a stubby gun barrel pushed up into his jaw. DuPree grinned lazily. "Oh come on now, you're not going to try anything *stupid*, are you?" Gil's eyes swiveled downwards trying to identify the type of gun. She continued: "*Your* problem is you're still thinking 'fiancée,' when the word you want is 'prisoner.' She won't like it, but hey—she *obviously* didn't like 'fiancée' much either."

"Shut up!" Gil snarled as one of the clanks approached. A frantically struggling female figure was tucked under its arm. "Clank! Put her down—gently."

The mechanical soldier complied. "So what do you have to say about my methods now?" DuPree asked, smug. In the lights the girl stood, held in place by the clank's grasp. It was Pix.

Gil blinked. "It's not her," he said.

"What?" DuPree whipped around and stared at the captive actress in surprise.

Gil continued, enjoying the moment. "*Girl*, yes. *Red-blonde*, yes. Miss Clay? No."

"She could be in disguise!" But it was obvious that even DuPree didn't really believe that.

"It's not her." Gil repeated.

"But she ran!"

Gil nodded. "Yes, that *is* puzzling. You'd think we were crazy people with guns, battle clanks, and a great big looming airship. What could have *possibly* motivated her—" Gil stopped dead.

Bang looked at him closely. She could tell that he'd seen something. "Oh? What is it, bright boy?"

Gil was staring at Pix's feet. She was wearing a well-worn pair of sturdy shoes. Shoes he had seen before. "Those shoes belong to the person we're looking for." He looked Pix hard in the face. "Where is she?"

Pix stared at Gil. Then a light seemed to dawn and she visibly relaxed. "Oh! The madgirl! Jeez. I was afraid you was just out collectin' blondes!" She swept a hand through her hair and gave him an appraising sidelong look.

"Yeah, we met her on the road yesterday. She wanted to travel with us, but we knew she was some sort of criminal, 'cause she said she was running from the Baron! We didn't dare try to catch her, 'cause she had this whonkin' big gun, ya know?"

Pix dropped her voice conspiratorially. "Now we knew there was something out in the forest, ya know? Something big. So we sent her off that way." She narrowed her eyes. "Well, she went and *found* it all right, and she drove it right back at us! I guess she was mad 'cause we'd sent her away. But things didn't work out like she planned, 'cause it turned and grabbed her and completely fried her!" She saw the look on Gil's face and nodded in satisfaction. "Yeah, she was dead before she knew it, ya know? Like 'Whoosh!'"

Gil stared at the girl. His mind processed what he had just heard over and over again, trying to find a different meaning to the words. A red haze filled his vision. DuPree looked up at his face and her eyes widened. She stepped back for a better view, a shiver of anticipation running down her spine. This could be entertaining.

All at once, Gilgamesh was looming over Pix, her vacuous, imbecilic face the sole focus of his mounting fury. When he spoke, several people in the crowd jerked to attention. Anyone who had ever heard those harmonics in a madboy's voice never forgot the experience. "You say she drove a clank straight *at* you. That was a pretty rotten thing to do."

Pix nodded. If parts of her brain were screaming at her to shut up, the rest of it was apparently too stupid to listen. "Oh, yeah. Well, we're just lucky our plan worked so well. Who knows what she would have done if we'd let her stay, ya know? Just can't trust that kind, I always say." She seemed to realize that she was talking to "that kind" right now. A touch of worry crossed her face, but was quickly wiped away as a sly look took its place. "So... was there a reward?"

No one—not even DuPree, saw Gil's hand move, but suddenly there was a vicious-looking pistol jammed against Pix's face. It began to hum as a wheel on the side slowly gathered speed.

"A reward? For sending her to her death? And you're telling me that she *purposefully* set some kind of monster on a group of helpless people? You're lying! She would *never* have done that! Where is she?"

Pix looked up into Gil's face and saw death staring back. She dropped to her knees in fear, but couldn't bring herself to speak. The pupils of Gil's eyes almost vanished in his madness.

His thumb flicked a toggle on the gun and—

Abner grabbed Gil and tried to swing him about. It was like trying to move an iron statue, but it did have the desired effect of dragging Gil's attention away from Pix, and fixing it on himself. "Stop!" Abner yelled. "Listen to me! That isn't what happened!"

DuPree pouted. Things had just been getting interesting. "Hey!" She barked. "Who gave you permission to—"

"Shut up!" Abner didn't even look at her. He stood glaring at Gil. "Listen!" He insisted.

Without taking his eyes off Abner, Gil shot out his hand and plucked a knife from the air—just before it hit the man's back. In the same motion, he snapped the knife back at DuPree, where it buried itself in her hat.

"Talk." Gil's voice shook.

"These are the Wastelands!" Abner explained. "We have to be wary or we'd be dead! Yes, we met this girl, and yes, she wanted to travel with us, and yes, we sent her away. She scared the hell out of us! But the attack—that clank—it had nothing to do with her. She went off to the east. It came from the north. It just ripped into us, but she came back and stopped it with that damn big gun of hers. She died saving us. Pix here is trying to take credit for something that just happened, because she knows you're looking for this person and she's dumb and scared and hoping for a reward!"

DuPree sneered. "Pretty cold, after the girl saved you."

Abner shrugged. "Yeah? Well, so we're circus people," he said flatly. "Grifting is one of the ways we survive. But she did save us, and we buried her like she was one of our own."

Gil stared. His face was still terrible to look at, but the

madness had receded. Now, he was just terribly quiet, but his voice was still dangerous. "I don't want to believe either of you." He took a deep breath and studied Abner's face. "But your story—that—it's what she would have done. You will show me the place where you say this happened."

Abner looked worried. "But I... I can't. It's way back—" A large set of steel hands closed upon his arms and lifted him from the ground. Gil leaned into his terrified face.

"...and if you're playing me false, if you people *did* do something to her, I'll give you to Captain DuPree. Along with everyone else here."

A small gasp of wonder and delight came from Bangladesh. "Really?" she breathed, "Honest?"

Gil surveyed the crowd. "Every single one of them." He turned back to Abner. "Unless you tell me otherwise right now."

Abner looked like a man caught in a trap. "She's there," he whispered.

Gil nodded and turned around. At his signal, the clanks snapped to attention, and began to march back to the dirigible.

DuPree sighed and turned to Pix, who stood stupefied, gaping first at the retreating Gil, then at the captive Abner, then back again. She punched the girl's arm. "Well, you heard the cranky man, we gotta go. Don't worry, girlie, if your boyfriend here is telling the truth, he'll be back."

This seemed to shake Abner free of his shock. "Um... I'm not actually her—" he began.

"Abner!" Pix growled as she grabbed him by the lapels. "Shut up!" She kissed him fiercely before spinning away. She only took two steps before she spun about again. Tears were in her eyes, but her voice was steady. "You'd better come back in one piece," she threatened, "Or I'll find you, you idiot! Don't forget!"

Abner blinked in astonishment, but he shut up.

Less then two minutes later, the airship was moving off, its engines roaring. The audience members were vanishing fast—casting nervous glances at the circus and the sky as they went.

Payne grabbed the closest of the performers—a handsome, dark-haired young man in his mid-twenties. "Lars, pass the word—quietly. I want us packed and on the road in ten minutes."

Lars looked shocked. "But it's dark! And we're paid up here for the next two days!"

Others who had heard this exchange started to join in, but Payne cut them off. "I want us gone before the townies realize that we brought that airship here."

The implications of this sank in. Herr Rasmussin[14] nodded briskly, reached into his coat, and with a snap, unfolded his dance-master's cane. "Jig time!" he called out urgently. Everyone groaned.

The old campsite by the river was quiet now. The heaps of clank parts had cooled where they fell. The places where the earth had been torn showed raw, the grass still trampled. Where trees had snapped, the wounds were still bright yellow and oozing sap.

The main body of the crab clank was recognizable, but the

---

[14] By now, the keen student of Spark history will be asking, "Is this the same Count Leovanovitch Pieotre Rasmussin who was responsible for the destruction of the Royal Palace of St. Petersburg through the cunning use of excessive syncopated dancing , which caused a resonance disaster after the Tsar seduced his wife, Zolenka? The answer is, we don't know. But it wouldn't surprise us.

interior had been almost completely burned and fused. The legs of the clank had managed to fall in an almost artistic pattern, so the modest mound of the grave lay within an encircling corral of red enameled metal. A small sapling had been planted on the mound, and leaning against it was a strange-looking gun, obviously broken. Gil stood silently for several minutes, fingering one of the tree's bright green leaves.

Abner fretted. Finally, he could take it no longer. He had to say something. "That's… the tree is something… One of the girls… that's what they do in her village when someone dies. We didn't know what your… um, what she would have liked."

Gil nodded. "Dig it up."

Abner looked shocked. "What?"

Captain DuPree smiled evilly at him as the Wulfenbach clank that stood nearby reached around and unsnapped a long shovel from the rack on its back. "What's the matter, pal? Didn't think we'd do that, did you? Say, maybe I'll get to kill you after all!"

The clank dug quickly and efficiently, and it was only a few minutes before DuPree called a halt.

She hopped directly into the grave, and pulled aside the canvas winding sheet the clank had uncovered. A horrifically strong odor of burnt meat burst forth. Abner backed away, his hand over his lower face.

DuPree chortled and slipped the collar of her sweater over her nose and mouth. "Whoo! Damn! You can't beat home cooking!"

"Stop it!" Gil leaned over the edge of the grave. His voice was strained. He eyed the charred figure. "That… that could be anybody."

Captain DuPree slipped on a pair of leather gloves and exposed more of the body. There was a flash of green, as she pulled free a patch of burned clothing. Gil closed his eyes and looked ill.

After a few minutes, DuPree sat back and sorted through the objects before her. "Female. Young adult. Caucasian." She lifted a half melted twist of wire and glass. "Glasses." She flourished a swatch of the burned green tweed. "I remember this dress. No shoes. And no jewelry, except for this." The object in question was tossed up to Gil, who snatched it out of the air and examined it closely. It was a brass gas connector ring, stamped with the Wulfenbach sigil. He had last seen it as he had slipped it onto Agatha's finger. Even darkened by flame and coated in dirt from the grave, Gil recognized it. It wasn't even a real ring, just a worthless machine part, but it had a devastating effect on his heart.

He clenched it tightly and turned away. "Yes. It's hers. That's her."

DuPree stood up, stripped the gloves off her hands and tossed them into the pit. "O-kay! Clank! Get me a field coffin!"

Gil spun around. "What? What are you doing?"

DuPree climbed out of the hole. "Well, I'm not carrying her in my lap."

"Don't be ridiculous. There's no reason—"

She poked him in the chest with a finger. "Listen. Your father told me to bring her back. Here she is—back she comes. Argue with him."

Gil glared at her, then seemed to deflate. With a sigh, he turned away. "Why bother?"

DuPree stared at his back and frowned. This was worrying. Gil was always good for an argument.

Gil strode up to Abner, who stood nervously off to one side

of the airship ramp. "Herr de la Scalla, I have seen enough. I'm inclined to believe your story. We'll take you back once we're finished here."

Abner shuffled his feet. "Actually, sir, I'd rather just head back on my own."

Gil blinked in surprise. "What? Across the Wastelands? Don't be ridiculous."

Abner held up his hands placatingly. "This is a main road, I should be fine. It's relatively well-traveled—" he looked at Gil, "I don't want people thinking we're... you know... associated with the Baron." His eyes flicked toward where Bangladesh was supervising the clank and he dropped his voice. "And Captain DuPree there, I'm sorry, um... I'd really rather keep her away from my people."

Gil nodded woodenly. "That's very sensible of you. See the Quartermaster while we're finishing up here. He'll give you some travel supplies. And... ah, please convey my apologies to your young lady. I'm afraid I got rather... upset."

Abner stared. He hadn't expected *that*. "Um... I'm so sorry about this, sir." Gil looked at him blankly. "This girl—it's obvious she was very... very special to you, sir."

Gil nodded slowly and made an effort to pull his mind back from thoughts of Agatha—working intently on the flying machine—dancing with him to the music of the mechanical orchestra—fighting beside him during the Slaver Wasp attack—kissing him impulsively in the heady moment when they realized they had won and were not going to die after all. And finally, Agatha laughing at him, as he slipped the connector ring on her finger and completely botched what turned out to be his last chance to tell her what was in his heart.

"Special? Yes, she might have been. It might have been..." He trailed off, and a look of dark anger settled over his features. "But it isn't. Just *go*."

Abner went.

Gil stood alone for a long time, watching as the clank gently re-planted the sapling in the newly filled-in hole. He remained alone, looking at the tree, until the last of the clanks marched aboard the dirigible—and Captain DuPree shouted that if he didn't want to come aboard, she'd happily leave him behind.

The sun was sinking toward the tops of the trees when Master Payne signaled that the caravan could finally stop. The animals were lathered, and the people weren't much better. Payne had kept them moving through the night and all the next day, but there had been no complaints.

In this part of the Wastelands, the road was hard going—a pale shadow of its former glory. Everyone was exhausted from keeping watch for pursuing villagers, hostile forest denizens, or the return of the Wulfenbach airship.

When the front riders had returned to report that a lakeside glade with sufficient forage lay ahead, Payne had finally decided that they could risk making camp—if only because it would allow him the opportunity to get away from Pix, who had been fretting nonstop beside him throughout the entire trip.

It was charmingly obvious that Pix was worried about Abner. Unfortunately, her concern was vocally expressed in the form of an endlessly varied list of Abner's unforgivable faults, stupidities and errors. Really, the girl was making Payne seriously consider reviving the old Put-The-Annoying-Person-

In-A-Trunk-And-Drop-It-Into-A-Lake trick. But, he had to frequently remind himself, a good magician never performs the same trick twice.

"I can't believe Abner cut in on my scene so soon! I had a lot more material ready."

"Frankly, I thought the two of you worked very well together."

"Well, yes, but if he'd just let me keep going a little longer, they probably wouldn't have taken him. What was he *thinking*?"

Payne had already considered several scenarios where Pix had been allowed to continue to talk to the young man from the airship. In the latest one, it ended with him setting her on fire. He briefly allowed himself to savor this image, before dismissing it with a guilty start.

"I'd ask Abner when he gets back."

The girl stared ahead fiercely. "He'd *better* get back."

On another wagon sat Payne's wife, Countess Marie. She was a regal woman who came by her title honestly. As she had remarked several thousand times since, her life would have been quite different if she had not been attracted to a certain dashing magician who had the ability to pull the most astonishing things out of a lady's clothing, up to and including the lady herself. If pressed, she would smile and admit that "quite different" did not automatically mean "better."

The Countess set the wagon's brake, stretched, and slid down to the ground. She looked up at her companion, who had been sitting silently next to her. The girl was dressed in a billowy low-cut shirt and a tight, gaudy bodice which managed to leave something, if only a very little, to the imagination. Her face was overshadowed by a huge mass of thick, dark curls.

The Countess extended a hand. "Wake up, 'Madame Olga.'
It's time to rest."

Agatha blinked. She had been deep in thought. "Yes, I guess
so." She climbed to the ground stiffly, then looked around,
squinting her eyes. The Countess noticed and turned back to
the wagon. "Ah, yes. Here."

She fished a large pair of glasses out of a wooden box near
the seat and handed them to Agatha, who took them gratefully
and slid the looped wires behind her ears.

All around them, other wagons were stopping. People
preparing to make camp shouted to each other as they saw to
their animals. Agatha leaned against the wagon. "I still can't
believe that worked. Pix was amazing. A perfect, xenophobic
peasant." Agatha rubbed her forehead and breathed deeply.
"But the people they sent. They... it wasn't what I expected.
I'm sorry. I... I hope Abner will be all right."

The Countess began to unhitch the horses. Agatha
automatically began to help from her side. When the Countess
saw that Agatha knew what she was doing, she nodded in
approval. "Think nothing of it. Abner owes you. We all do.
That crab clank that killed Olga damaged several carts before
she and André led it off. I have no doubt that it would have
come back after it had finished them off."

She grabbed the horse bridles and tethered them to a nearby
tree. She tossed Agatha a curry comb as Balthazar bustled up
with two large leather buckets of water. The horses immediately
lowered their heads and began to drink.

The Countess continued as she began to rub her horse down.
"You saved our lives. And you tried to save Olga's, too, even
after we sent you away. We had to do this." She gave Agatha a

reassuring smile. "Anyway, Abner is no fool. He'll be fine. He's a fast talker—he's probably got them convinced you never even existed by now."

Agatha smiled back, then tentatively fingered the blouse she wore. "Hm. Still... dressing her in my things. Doctoring the body. And—um—especially taking her place. Even her name. It's not that I want to be caught, I know it's practical. It just feels so strange. Disrespectful." She looked contrite. "Sorry."

The Countess patted Agatha on the shoulder. "Olga was with us for over five years. She was a good friend, and I knew her very well. The life—traveling and performing—it was everything to her. She was never happier than when she'd pulled a really clever scam—convinced some rube that she was a runaway construct, or a grand duchess who had been swindled out of her fortune, or a lost explorer from the moon. She *loved* that sort of thing." She smiled at some private memory.

"And now? Now she gets to fool not just some gullible townie, but Baron Klaus Wulfenbach himself! If she weren't dead, she'd have killed herself to play this part."

Agatha digested this. "Show people are very strange."

She hadn't quite meant it as a compliment, but the Countess looked pleased. "You'll get used to it."

"That's what worries me."

The Countess laughed. Professor Moonsock strode up, a roustabout carrying a stack of horse blankets following along behind her. She shooed The Countess and Agatha away and began to examine their horses' feet.

The two women walked back to Professor Moonsock's wagon, where Agatha had been temporarily assigned a tiny fold-down bunk. The Countess patted a wheel. "I'm afraid you're stuck here again, but tomorrow we should have something more permanent sorted out."

"Really," Agatha protested, "You've already done so much—"

The Countess stopped her with an upraised hand. "Oh, have no fear, my dear. You'll *earn* your keep." She looked toward the center of the camp, where the old cook was busy shouting orders. Waving a long wooden spoon like a general's baton, he was directing a group of men who had already emerged from the surrounding forest with armloads of firewood. "If you feel up to it, I imagine Taki would appreciate some help once he's finished setting up."

Agatha was smart enough to know that her life with these people would be significantly easier if she was seen pitching in as eagerly as she could.

"Of course. It will be my pleasure."

The Countess nodded in approval and sailed off. Left alone, Agatha climbed onto the wagon bench and collapsed weakly.

She felt... hollow. She had expected to be hunted by the Empire, but she hadn't expected *him*. And yet, maybe she should have. Of course she should have. Hadn't he taken an interest in her right from the start? It had been Gilgamesh Wulfenbach who had questioned her so pointedly about the whereabouts of Adam and Lilith. Gil who had watched her carefully, brought her to work in his lab, and hidden the fact that she was a Spark from his father.

Krosp had warned her that Gilgamesh was up to something, and so he had been, but she still wasn't sure exactly *what*. Some kind of power play was going on in the Wulfenbach family, and Agatha had an uneasy feeling that she had narrowly escaped being made a pawn in a perilous game. Adam and Lilith had hidden her away from the Baron all her life—they had even *died* trying to protect her from him. And Lilith had said that Gil would only be the first of the powerful people who would try to control her—to use her for their own ends.

And yet, although she didn't—couldn't—trust him, she had liked him. Liked him very much indeed, if she was honest with herself, in spite of the fact that she had seen him do such terrible things… Liked him enough to briefly think it might be worth taking the chance…

All day, Agatha had struggled to forget the devastating pain on Gil's face when he believed she was dead. Had he really cared that much for her after all? Agatha shivered.

Krosp ambled around the corner of a wagon and leapt up to sit beside her. He nudged Agatha's arm with the top of his head, and she reached down absent-mindedly to scratch behind his ears. The cat tumbled over sideways into her lap and closed his eyes. "So that was 'acting' was it?" He growled. "I don't understand. How did that fool *anybody*? You smelled *exactly* the *same*."

The corner of Agatha's mouth twitched upward. "I don't think he noticed."

Krosp opened one eye at the pronoun. "Oh? Well *he's* obviously an idiot."

Agatha let this pass. "So what's Professor Moonsock going to do with you?"

Krosp opened both eyes and looked apprehensive. "Well, for starters, I promised to hunt her up some fresh mimmoths. She says: 'so you can talk, so what?' I told her I can swear, too, but she says she'll teach me to do something 'stage-worthy.'"

Agatha had yet to see Professor Moonsock's act, but earlier, she had noticed several large bats hanging out the Professor's laundry. Krosp's apprehension might be well-founded. "That sounds fun."

Krosp glared up at her. "Oh right. Like she can train *me*. What am I? Some moronic hound?"

"Oh, heaven forbid. So… you won't do it?"

"Of course I'll do it! She has *cream*!" The cat licked his chops. "I just don't want her to think it'll be *easy*."

Agatha nodded. Krosp curled into a giant ball and began to purr. Suddenly, he snapped his eyes open and stared up at Agatha inquisitively. "Say, you smell kind of sad. This isn't about that stupid Wulfenbach boy, is it?"

"No. Well, maybe…" Agatha paused, and then sighed. *If you can't be honest with your cat…* she thought to herself. Of course, most cats wouldn't include your secrets as amusing anecdotes in their memoirs, but still…

"Yes," she said, in a low voice. "Seeing him like that… I still feel like I've done something awful. I just wanted to run out and tell him that everything was all right, that I wasn't really dead. I almost…almost didn't care what happened at all after that."

Krosp rolled onto his back and watched her carefully—his head comically upside-down. "But you didn't," he said. "Why not?"

"Why do you think? Because it would have been *hugely* stupid."

The cat waited for Agatha to continue, but there didn't seem to be any more forthcoming. "That's it?"

Agatha nodded glumly. "Well, yes. Isn't that enough?"

Krosp's tail lashed a few times. "In my experience, that doesn't seem to stop most people."

"Ever since my locket was removed, I can think more clearly." She paused, trying to find the right words. "Krosp, you've read a lot of history. Have you ever read any Classical mythology?"

The cat flicked an ear dismissively. "A bit. I like history better."

"Then you should know what happens to mortals who get mixed up with the gods. It never ends well. The Wulfenbachs are like the Gods of Olympus, they've got the power of life and death over the entire *Empire*.

"Doctor Beetle was a Spark! A strong one! And he was so afraid of the Baron, he got himself *killed* rather than let the Baron take him away. Your creator, Doctor Vapnoople—I met him! The students on Castle Wulfenbach call him "Doctor Dim!" What did the Baron *do* to him?

"And who am *I*? I've got no power, no protection. Nothing. If I had gone with Gil, maybe... maybe he would have been happy that I wasn't dead, but what would happen after that? He would have taken me back to his father. The Baron killed Adam and Lilith! He gave orders that I was not just to be confined, I was to be kept sedated! And Gil..." Agatha took a deep breath and shook her head. "Even when he said he wanted to marry me, he made it into an order and tried to drag me off. And you saw how he acted with Pix..."

She hung her head. "...and even then, even *then*, it was still hard." She absently scratched Krosp's belly, and the cat stretched happily, closing his eyes and flexing his claws. "Even now, I feel kind of odd. He—they think I'm dead now. Even if I feel bad, I had to do it. It's all right, I'll get used to it. It's just... hard to believe it's over."

"Don't be a fool!" Zeetha snapped. She had appeared silently beside the wagon, as if she had dropped from the sky.

116

Krosp leaped up in shock, eyes wide, fur bristling.

Then, to Agatha's astonishment, Zeetha dropped to one knee and bowed her head. "Agatha Clay," she said quietly. "I never got a chance to thank you for trying to save Olga. Nor have I yet apologized for my earlier outburst."

This was certainly true. In the aftermath of the crab clank's attack, Zeetha had taken charge of Olga's body. She had changed the dead girl's clothing, and stood by protectively while various members of the circus had applied their arts—giving Olga the finishing touches for her last role as the burned corpse of Agatha Clay. All the while, Zeetha had chanted a beautiful, haunting dirge in a flowing tongue Agatha knew must be Skifandrian. When Olga had finally been lowered into the ground, Zeetha had made a small cut on her arm, and allowed six drops of blood to fall upon the winding sheet before the grave was filled in. Then she had turned on her heel and walked into the woods, alone. Agatha had not seen her since, and had begun to think that the green-haired girl had left the Circus entirely.

Agatha shrugged uncomfortably. "Everyone was so busy. Besides, to have lost your friend—I'm so sorry. I wish I could have done more."

Zeetha stood and nodded. "Olga *was* a good companion." She waved toward the camp. "These others are kind, but they were never convinced I was telling the truth. Olga believed me. She helped me when I really needed it. I will miss her. But I have known since childhood that Death is always waiting to cut in on the dance."

Then, to Agatha's surprise, Zeetha sat down next to her. She was...different from when Agatha had first met her. Where she had been rough, full of suppressed anger, she now seemed serene. Her eyes were no longer empty. When she looked at Agatha, her gaze was alert, with a hint of friendship. Agatha realized that the girl was younger than she had first thought.

Zeetha took a deep, contented breath and leaned back, slumping comfortably against the wagon door. Agatha hardly knew the girl, but this seemed so out-of-character that she couldn't help staring. Zeetha saw her surprise, and gave a rueful smile.

When she spoke next, her voice was soft. "Miss Clay, I have been wandering Europa for over three years now, searching for any news of my home. You are the first person who has ever even *heard* of Skifander." She took another deep breath and let it out slowly. "Can you understand? It was like I was asking after a fever dream. I... I was beginning to think that I had made it all up while I was sick. No one in any of the cities had heard of it, not even at the Universities. I was reduced to searching the Wastelands, interrogating every traveler I met. I thought I had gone mad."

She paused, and looked out at the encircling forest. "I was this close—" she held two fingers about a centimeter apart, "To picking a direction and just walking until I found either Skifander or death." She looked at Agatha again and grinned. "And I wouldn't have cared which I found first." She dropped her hand.

They sat silently together and watched the shadows darken under the trees.

Finally Zeetha continued. "But you—you have let me know that my home, my family, everything that made me what I am really *does* exist, and for that, I wish to thank you."

Agatha shrugged. "Oh, well, I—"

Zeetha leaned into her face and shouted: "By starting you on warrior training! Tomorrow morning!"

She leapt to her feet and glared down at Agatha, who sat, wide-eyed in shock. "It's '*over*.'" She snorted. "You speak like a child. The Baron's people will be back, or if not, there will be others like them. You must be ready!"

Agatha looked up at her angrily. "What makes you say that? It's a *perfect* plan. They think I'm dead!"

Zeetha cocked an eyebrow. "There is a serious flaw in this 'perfect plan' of yours. One that could undo everything at any time!"

Agatha puzzled over this, quickly running through everything they had done. She couldn't think of anything wrong...

When Agatha didn't answer, Zeetha gave a sardonic smile. "Just this: you're not really dead, now are you?"

Agatha and Krosp looked at each other.

Behind Zeetha, the cooking fires ignited with a dramatic roar, and, just for an instant, she stood before Agatha—a fearsome dark goddess rimmed by fire. She grinned again, revealing her sharp teeth. "Tomorrow morning."

THREE

The ladies pale go riding, riding—
On their spiders striding, striding.
stealing girls asleep in bed—
drinking all their blood so red—
...
When pretty maidens die of fright,
Their ghosts go riding through the night.

—TRADITIONAL WALPURGIS NIGHT SONG

The Baron stood in one of the vast hangar bays of Castle Wulfenbach, an all-too-familiar weariness settling upon his shoulders.

On the ground before him was an open field coffin. Within lay a charred corpse, clad in the remnants of a green tweed dress. He stared down at it silently. It had been a long time since he had so keenly felt the loss of his old friends—and his old life. The faces of the Heterodynes flashed through his mind, and for the thousandth time, he wondered what had happened to them. Where had they gone? Why was he alone left to keep the Sparks of Europa in line—when half the time it ended so damned badly?

A loud crunch made him look around. Bangladesh DuPree stood beside him, cheerfully munching on a pear.

"Ah. DuPree," he said carefully, his eyes returning to the body before him, "When I say the words 'alive and unharmed,' do any neurons actually fire in that brain of yours?"

The crunching stopped dead. Despite himself, Klaus counted under his breath until DuPree finally answered. "No, sir!"

He nodded. "I thought not."

Encouraged, Captain DuPree continued. "But I can't take credit for this one. Some old crab clank burned her down before we got to her. I saved you the sigil plate." She handed over a large enameled metal oval—cracked and blackened by fire. Sparks were notorious for "signing" their work, often decorating creations with heraldic colors or family sigils. The Baron encouraged this—it made it so much easier to assign blame.

In this case, the design was familiar. "Ah, yes, one of Von Bodé's[15] little toys." He tossed the plate aside. "Was my son... upset?"

Bangladesh snorted. "Oh, him? Sure was. Here he was all set to be a hero and rescue his girl, then he finds out he'd need fireplace tongs to get her undressed? Yeah—upset is one word for it."

---

[15] The Spark in question, one Hugo Von Bodé, had enjoyed sending his creations out on random voyages of chaos and destruction "Just to keep things from getting boring!" Klaus had taken some pains to ensure that his last minutes had been anything but.

Klaus rubbed his forehead. "Thank you, DuPree, for that... vivid imagery. You may go."

DuPree looked around, and then casually tossed her pear core into the coffin. "Let me know when you've got something else for me." She sauntered out of the room, calling after her: "And try to make it a fun one!"

Klaus leaned down and fished out the core. Allowing himself a rare display of temper, he fired it hard into a distant trash barrel, where it struck with a tremendous clang and sent the barrel toppling backwards. His secretary and second-in-command, Boris, was entering the hangar at that moment, and coolly caught it in two of his four arms, setting it back upright without ever taking his eyes off the paperwork he carried[16].

"Herr Baron?" he said quietly, "The Jäger Generals are here."

Klaus nodded. "Show them in." Boris walked back and called to someone just out of sight. There was a rumble of reply, and the Baron turned to greet the three creatures who entered—the largest bending his head to get through the tall doorway.

These were the oldest of the Jägermonsters, constructs created to ride with the mad Heterodynes who had plagued Europa generations before Bill and Barry's heroics had redeemed the family name. Long ago, these had been ordinary barbarian raiders, but through some process that Klaus had never been able to uncover, they were now nightmarish monsters—inhumanly strong, fast, and long-lived. All the Jägers were toothy, clawed

[16] Boris Vasily Konstantin Andrei Myshkin Dolokhov was one of the most fascinating of Baron Wulfenbach's inner circle. The Baron had rescued him from slavery and Boris repaid him with a lifetime of loyalty. Although he frequently assumed total control of the Empire when the Baron was injured or indisposed, he never seems to have been tempted to exploit this power for his own ends. He simply took joy in things functioning smoothly and efficiently. By all accounts, he was reckoned the most boring man in the Empire.

and hairy to some degree. Some even sported horns or tails. Still, these three oldest stood apart from their brethren as much as the younger Jägers did from the rest of Humanity. Klaus wondered if the Generals had been the prototypes, with the procedure then refined for the other Jägers, or if the physical changes the creatures experienced became more pronounced the older they got. If so, the three who approached him now were very old Jägers indeed.

When they reached him, the generals paused smartly "at attention" before the Baron. The three wore uniforms from completely different armies. This was another peculiarity of the Jägers, who loved the idea of uniforms, but never quite understood the concept behind making everyone wear the same one.

General Zog, the most traditional, wore mostly his own luxurious fur—shining white under a leather and brass warrior's harness that, although old, had been meticulously cared for. Zog was forever poised to sweep across Europa laying waste to all in his path—by himself, if necessary.

General Khrizhan was modern and cultured. He wore a bright red military uniform with huge epaulettes, all covered in shiny bullion, but no shoes. The general's clawed green feet were bare, and tough as old leather. Tusks curled upward from his great mouth. These were capped with gold that had been engraved to match the pattern of the rings in his pointed ears.

General Goomblast towered above the other two, a shaggy behemoth with a brass dome screwed directly onto his cranium. He wore soft clothing with an eastern look to it, and a huge pair of goggles over his eyes.

After holding their pose dramatically for thirty seconds,

the Generals seemed to feel that they had done their duty by military protocol. They relaxed, eyeing the Baron curiously.

"Generals." Klaus began. "I want to thank you for your recent efforts." The creatures acknowledged this compliment with serious nods. Without the Jägermonsters, the Slaver Wasps might actually have overwhelmed Castle Wulfenbach. Three of the monster soldiers had actually died, an extraordinarily high number.

General Khrizhan spoke up. "Yaz, Herr Baron. Ov course ve help vit de bogz, hey? Nasty tings. But… surely dere vos something else hyu vished to talk to us about?"

Khrizhan was the shrewdest of the old Generals—the one who remembered best what it had been to be human. It made him easier to talk to, but also more dangerous. This would be tricky, Klaus thought. Well, their reaction would be interesting…

"You have been enquiring after a…" The Baron pretended to think, "ah, yes, a Miss Clay?"

Zog blinked first. "Ah, vell, ve vas just—"

Khrizhan smoothly stepped on his foot. "Yas," he rumbled. "Ve did. Vy?"

The Baron moved back and indicated the coffin on the floor. "I am sorry, but she is dead. She ran afoul of an old clank while she was traveling in the Wastelands." The Jägers crowded in around the coffin and stared down at it.

Klaus paused. This was the dangerous part. The Jägers' loyalty to the House of Heterodyne was unshakeable. To have a genuine heir appear suddenly after all of these years, only to be killed… Anything could happen. He continued. "I am not happy about this… it… is not what I wanted."

The Jägers looked at him for a long moment. Even with their

distorted features, Klaus could see their confusion.

Zog glanced back at the burned corpse. "But…"

Goomblast shook his head. "Dis iz—"

Khrizhan pushed forward. "Uv course hyu deed not vish for diz poor gurlz death. Who vould vant soch a ting?"

The other two Generals looked at each other, but kept silent. Khrizhan continued, "She vos a very nize gurl. Ve… ve are very sad. Poor ting. Thenk hyu for letting us know, yah?"

Klaus nodded. This was going better than he had dared hoped. It was a bit odd, actually. "If you would like some kind of service held…ah, discreetly, of course?"

Khrizhan open his mouth and then froze. He stared at Klaus for several seconds. General Goomblast smoothly stepped into the conversational void. "We did not get a chance to… properly know de yong lady but Hy em sure dot de spirits uv her ancestors vould—"

"THE HETERODYNE IS DEAD!" Khrizhan's scream was no doubt heard through half of Castle Wulfenbach. The other two generals stared at him in astonishment. Then their heads snapped back towards the open coffin. Klaus could see the mental connections being made inside their ancient heads, they both then stared at him—

Klaus stepped back. This set the monsters off and with a great roaring and screaming, they proceeded to try to tear the hangar apart. In a blind rage, Zog came at the Baron with claws extended. It was a glorious fight, lasting almost half an hour, and afterwards, the Baron joined them in a bout of drinking that quite erased any doubts before they were even formed.

Ironically, it was the subsequent hangover that inspired Klaus to take the next step…

* * *

The bed was hard. It was really only a flat linen sack—stuffed with horsehair and laid out on a wooden shelf—but Agatha slept peacefully, Krosp curled snugly against her back.

Suddenly, a finger pressed lightly against her nose, and a soft voice whispered, "Beep!" Agatha snapped awake and saw Zeetha grinning at her in the predawn light. The green-haired girl set down a small pile of clothing, pointed at it with a significant look, and stepped out of the wagon, closing the door behind her.

A few minutes later, Agatha reluctantly crept out into the cold morning air. What Zeetha had left was a brown, toga-like shift. Agatha had spent several frantic minutes looking for the rest of the outfit. Her clothing from the day before was nowhere to be found. Scandalous stories she'd heard about actors began to sound worryingly plausible.

It looked like no one else was awake except for a couple of roustabouts, who were standing watch around the central fire. They perked up when they saw Agatha's costume, but a growl from Zeetha caused them to speedily avert their eyes.

Without a word, the green-haired girl took Agatha's hand and pulled her into the forest. She was carrying a stick about two meters long—its sharp, fresh smell proclaimed it a newly-trimmed sapling. Soon they stepped into a small glade, and Zeetha released her hand and turned to face her. The look she gave Agatha was serious.

Agatha crossed her arms against the morning chill. "Zeetha? What is going on? This outfit—?"

Zeetha smiled. "Remember? You start your warrior training

today. That is a close approximation of traditional Skifandrian novice garb."

Agatha shivered. "Skifander must be in the tropics, then." She rubbed her arms and looked at the sky. Birds began to call in the trees overhead. "Isn't it a bit early for this?"

Zeetha shook her head. "My concern is that I may be too late." She stepped closer. "Know, Agatha Clay, that the warrior tradition of the royal house of Skifander is old, proud, and jealously guarded.

"In this life, I am allowed to train one other besides my own daughters. I have chosen you. The bond between us will be stronger than that of friends. Of family. Of lovers. As of now, we are 'Kolee-dok-zumil.'"

Agatha looked hard at Zeetha and thought a moment. This sounded serious—what was she getting into? "What does that mean?" she asked.

Zeetha paused. "Ah—it's kind of hard to translate. Sort of like 'teacher and student.' Sort of like 'cause and effect.'" With a sudden, fluid movement, she brought the stick around and knocked Agatha to her knees. "Mostly like 'grindstone and knife.'"

Agatha was stunned. "What are you *doing*?"

Zeetha twirled the stick about her fingers. "Testing your reflexes. You're *supposed* to try to stop me. Try again!" She swung her stick.

About an hour later, Zeetha sighed deeply and sat on her heels next to Agatha, who had resorted to huddling on the ground with her hands over her head. "Pathetic," she pronounced. "No stamina. You can't dodge. You can't block. You allow anger to drive your attacks, and you can't even run away properly." She stood back up. "The good news is that you've got fast reflexes, and I'm greatly encouraged by the fact that I haven't been able to hit you exactly the same way twice."

Agatha stirred slightly. "So... this death thing that training is supposed to prevent... why is it bad?"

This earned her another smack across the rump. "*And* a poor attitude." Zeetha stretched her arms toward the sky, then squared her shoulders. "Lucky for you, I like a challenge!"

"This is lucky?" Agatha's voice was barely there.

"Sure! Nothing's broken, is it?" Zeetha turned to go. "That makes it a good first day. I'll get you some breakfast."

As Zeetha left, Krosp, who had been watching for some time, hopped from the wagon and sauntered up to Agatha. He gave her a sniff and then nudged her with his foot. "How'd it go?" he asked.

Agatha raised her face and her eyes were despairing. "Krosp," she wailed. "Help! She's going to *kill* me."

Krosp's whiskers twitched disapprovingly. "It *sounds* like she's going to toughen you up. Good! These are the Wastelands! You've got to be strong! You've got to be quick! If you want to stay alive, you've got to make *sacrifices*."

Agatha slowly pulled herself up into a sitting position. "Gosh. I—"

"And tomorrow, be a little more careful when you leave, okay? You almost woke me up."

Agatha told herself later that she *probably* wouldn't have *actually* hit him with it... she had just grabbed the rock without thinking. A good-sized rock, actually. It wasn't until she had raised it high over her head with a vengeful roar that Zeetha voice sounded behind her. "Hey! You're moving!" Zeetha set down a dish of oatmeal and looked pleased. "I'm really impressed!"

Agatha flinched, and dropped the rock onto her foot. As she clutched her foot in pain, Zeetha explained. "The point of the first day of training is to drive you to your absolute limit. To see just how far I can force you." She gestured to the rock. "You're not as weak as I thought."

The ramifications of what Zeetha was saying began to sink in. "No!" Agatha whimpered. "I *am* weak."

Zeetha laughed merrily, and swung the stick up with a flourish. "*And* you're sneaky! I admire that!" Down came the stick. "But you won't fool me again!"

Agatha, squealing, gamely tried to defend herself from the fresh volley of blows. Krosp looked on with detached interest as she staggered off—Zeetha trotting happily behind to deliver the occasional smack.

The cat stretched, then picked up Agatha's cereal. He ventured a taste, nodded in approval, and began to eat. "Mm! Delicious. She'll be sorry she missed this!"

Some time later, a large, shaggy raven crouched on the edge of Professor Moonsock's wagon, peering hopefully at the prone figure of Agatha on the grass below. She hadn't moved for a long time, which looked promising. Perhaps she was dead. The raven swooped down to land on her thigh. No reaction. Good. It took a peck at her. Still no reaction. Very good. Encouraged, the bird prepared to dig in—when a pebble whizzed out from under the nearest tree and caught it hard just above its tail. The raven gave an outraged "squark" as it flapped hastily into the air, circling around to settle back onto the roof of the cart. It could wait.

Countess Marie strode forward. She rolled her eyes at the comatose girl before her and shook her head. "Come along, Agatha. I know you're not dead."

A muffled voice escaped the moss. "You cannot prove that by any verifiable method."

Zeetha had let it be known that she had taken Agatha under her wing, and would be working her hard. There were no objections. In fact, this fit neatly with the order Master Payne had quietly given his troupe the night before. Grateful as the circus members were for Agatha's help, she was nevertheless a stranger. Until they bid her fare-thee-well at Mechanicsburg, she was to be kept busy and worked hard, hard enough that she would have neither time nor energy to get into trouble, or ask too many questions.

Marie was used to dealing with actors who had over-indulged the night before, and was infamous for her ability to get them on their feet and on stage without mercy. Agatha's condition, while not self-imposed, was familiar enough. She reached down with one hand, and effortlessly hauled the girl to her feet. "Let's get you moving."

Clean, dressed, and with a decent meal inside her, Agatha was soon willing to admit the possibility that life might be worth living.

Marie smiled. "We'll have you help out with a little of everything. That will give us a chance to see where you'll be the most use. To start with, I believe Embi could use an assistant."

Agatha swallowed the last of her oat bread and honey, then wiped her hands. "Who is Embi?" she asked.

The Countess smiled. "Ah! With all the excitement we've had the last few days, you haven't had a chance to meet everyone. Now, it's high time you experienced the true glamour and excitement of show business!"

Several minutes later, a man no taller than Balthazar—with skin so dark it was almost black—plopped a second huge basket of beets at her feet as he sang out "Aaaand this batch of glamour here!" He then sat down beside her and pulled a paring knife out of his astonishingly tall hat.

Agatha was all-too-familiar with the job before her[17]. She sighed, and set to work with a will. She was soon surprised to find the task more pleasant than usual, for Embi had a friendly air about him and the conversation flowed comfortably.

[17] Lilith, Agatha's foster mother, had been an exuberant proponent of the preserving, canning, drying and pickling of various fruits and vegetables. Agatha had once complained that this might make sense if the Clays managed a farm, but in fact, they lived in town, and all of the produce they processed was purchased from local green-grocers. Lilith had said nothing at the time, but one Whitsuntide night, Agatha had been awakened and discovered that, after midnight, her parents' forge served as a gathering place for constructs she had never seen before. These were twisted, bizarre creations. Things that could never feel comfortable out in public, despite the Baron's laws enforcing tolerance. They labored in the many unseen jobs offered by the University. Despite their often horrific appearance, Agatha found them to be intelligent, well-read, and urbane, in their own strange way. It was these creatures who received the bulk of the preserved food. The Clays always refused direct payment, but Agatha now understood the source of the many odd and useful things that appeared overnight upon the Clay's doorstep.

"That's a fine hat," Agatha said. "I've never really seen one like it. Is it from Paris[18]?"

"Ho! A common mistake!" Embi smiled. "But it is a style that was common in my youth, in a village in Africa that you'll never have heard of."

Agatha sat back and looked at the little man with surprise. "Then you really are a long way from home."

Embi sighed as he picked up another beet and stripped the peel off all in one long strip. "It is true. I am an explorer. I travel these savage lands in search of the rare and exotic." He saw the direction of Agatha's glance and hefted the beet in his hand defensively. "We don't have these back home."

Agatha laughed. "But then, why are you with the circus?"

"The same as yourself. It is an excellent way to travel through these inhospitable lands."

"Inhospitable?" Agatha glanced at the surrounding forest. "Well, the Wastelands, certainly... but I never thought of Europa as savage or exotic."

Embi raised an eyebrow. "You know, that's what *I* always said to visitors to *my* land."

Agatha considered this. "I see. What's your act?"

"Oh, some storytelling, exotic music, slight-of-hand..." Embi shrugged. "Mostly, I am short."

Embi was obviously an adult, but even for a short man, he seemed impossibly tiny. "Is everyone short where you come from?"

"Indeed!" Embi reached into the basket. "Why, when I left home, my newest nephew was the size of this beet." He held the

[18] Then, as now, Paris has always been a safe guess when outlandish or bizarre fashion is the topic.

vegetable a moment, and a far-away look came into his eyes. "He'll be a great-great-grandfather now, I trust." He sighed.

Agatha blinked as she ran the math in her head. "Wait a minute. You don't look—how old *are* you?"

The little man studiously began to peel his beet. He didn't look at Agatha. "I am... no longer sure," he said quietly. "But one hundred and thirty, at least."

Agatha sat back and considered this. "Is that *normal* for your people?"

"Ha!" Embi laughed, "No! When I was young and rash, I asked a boon of the Great Devil Goddess. In return, I took a sacred vow to see the wide world. I am to return to tell her all about it before I die." He slumped a bit and looked at Agatha with one eyebrow raised. "To be honest, I don't think either one of us knew just how wide the world *is*."

Agatha thought about this. "But what has that got to do with your long life?"

Embi fixed her with a stern glare, and Agatha suddenly felt like a naughty six year old. "Humph! One of the problems with people in these lands is that they do not take sacred vows at all seriously!"

From the shadows between two wagons, Master Payne and Countess Marie watched as Agatha laughed, chatted, and relieved beets of their skins. After a few minutes of eavesdropping, they drew back farther behind the wagons, and the circus master turned to his wife.

"And so, my dear, what do you think?"

Marie bit lightly on a knuckle and frowned. "It's too soon

to tell. She seems very nice. Brave and good-hearted, but then that's not the question, is it?" She studied Payne. "You're worried about something."

Payne gave a snort of annoyance. Among his players, he had a certain reputation for imperturbability, which he took pains to cultivate. His wife, on the other hand, was never fooled. He felt like he was onstage, attempting a conjuring trick that he hadn't quite mastered. "Moxana has started a new game," he said.

Marie exclaimed in surprise. "Started over? This far into the season? For Agatha? Why didn't she just add her, like she has for everyone else?"

Payne shook his head. "I don't know."

Marie was intrigued. "But which piece—"

Payne interrupted her. "Not just a new piece. Not just started over—this is a completely new game. A different game, with different rules." He shook his head. "I'm still working it out, but this Miss Clay is the center of the whole thing."

Marie's eyes widened. "What is she?" she whispered. "What have we done?"

Payne looked at her and gave a single, mirthless bark of laughter. "We did what we had to do. You said it yourself. We couldn't leave her. That may have been... truer than you'd meant."

"But we couldn't... ah." Marie absorbed this. "I find Determinism a very lazy philosophical viewpoint," she groused, "But... a new game..."

Payne gently slid his hand around her shoulders. "If we hurry, we'll be in Mechanicsburg in a little over two months. She plans to leave us there. With luck, and a bit of care on our part, she may never notice anything."

Marie nodded, but her voice was skeptical. "Two months. With this lot?" The couple shared a significant look and shrugged in unison.

From the peaked roof of one of the wagons, Krosp watched them walk off, arm-in-arm. *Well, that was interesting,* he thought.

As Agatha finished peeling her basket of beets, a stout, bipedal clank carrying an enormous load of logs emerged from the forest and strutted toward them. Perched atop the large domed head was Balthazar, who waved excitedly when he saw them. "I brought wood!" he sang out. "Where do you want it, Herr Embi?"

The little man nodded approvingly and pointed to the beginnings of a fire circle that lay nearby. "One more load and you're done for the day, lad." He looked at Agatha's basket and smiled. "And it looks like you are done as well, Miss Clay. Good job! There'll be borscht tonight!"

Agatha needed no more prompting. She darted off after the clank. There was something about it that had seemed odd, and she wanted a better look at it.

The device moved slowly, and she easily caught up to it. Agatha examined it as she walked alongside. Balthazar smiled down at her from his perch. "Pretty neat clank, hey?" he said with pride.

Agatha nodded. "Indeed it is. Where did your family get it?"

"He." Balthazar corrected her. "This is Smilin' Stev. My dad used to be a smith for the Porcelain Count of Niktalten. He's the guy who used to take down airships with his clockwork falcons. When the Baron beat him, Dad took Stev here as his back pay." The boy affectionately patted the clank on the head. "He's nothing fancy, so none of the bad people we run into think he's worth stealing. He just pulls our cart and fetches wood and water."

A light dawned. "Ah—That's what confused me."

Balthazar suddenly looked wary. "What?"

Agatha pointed at the mechanical troll's limbs as they pistoned along. "Has your father ever opened Stev up? These joints are really complicated. And look at the way these plates overlap. I think this clank may be a bit more sophisticated than you think."

"Dad says Stev is slow and stupid, just like Mama likes 'em."

This pronouncement effectively broke Agatha's chain of thought. "Wait... *what*?"

Balthazar smiled at her innocently. "Dad plays Punch in the Heterodyne plays[19]."

"But—"

Suddenly, Agatha realized that while she had been intent on the clank, she had been flanked by Rivet the mechanic, and André, the troupe's music master. Rivet was assuring André that Agatha was a decent mechanic—or at least talked like one. She turned and smiled cheerfully. "Hello, Agatha!" she chirped. "Feeling bored?"

Agatha saw that escape was impossible. "This doesn't involve root vegetables, does it?"

Rivet considered this. "No."

"Or hitting me with sticks?"

[19] Historically, the construct, Punch, had been one of the Heterodyne Boys' constant companions, along with his wife, Judy. In the Heterodyne plays, Punch was portrayed as an oafish, freakishly strong clown. This greatly annoyed Agatha's foster-father, Adam, who had in fact, *been* Punch, before he changed his name.

André frowned. "Hardly. If I remember correctly, you told Master Payne that you could play anything with a keyboard?"

Agatha perked up. "Yes! He was asking me if I had any performance experience[20]. Lilith gave me lessons—ballroom dancing and piano, mostly. Sometimes, I got to play the big organ at Transylvania Polygnostic, too. And there was that accordion Doctor Vogel had hidden in his lab. He didn't know we knew about it, but one time…"

André interrupted her. "And you're a mechanic! It's too perfect!"

They led her to the baggage wagons. "You'll like this— we have a repair job for you! When that clank attacked, it completely smashed our calliope." André untied a rope holding down a canvas cover and whipped it aside with a showman's flourish. "Behold! The Silverodeon! Once the finest steam-powered music machine this side of the Carpathians."

Revealed was a carved and painted cart that held an accumulation of scrap metal and twisted piping. Agatha could tell that this was the wreckage of some sort of musical instrument, but the damage looked like it had been caused as much by sheer neglect as by the clank attack.

"But… really?" Agatha stepped up to the wagon and took a closer look. "I wouldn't think it's been played in years."

[20] Professional traveling entertainers were expected to be able to sing, dance, juggle, tell jokes, and play several musical instruments. In addition, they were supposed to have some secondary side-show skill, such as knife throwing, fire eating, acrobatics, or being short. At any given time they had to be able to memorize enough material that the circus could perform two full shows, in excess of two hours, every day, for two weeks without repeating anything. Proficiency with weapons was also considered a plus. To join a quality show such as Master Payne's, one would also need some non-entertainment skill that would be useful to the troupe, such as brewing, mycology, or picking pockets. But hey, it beat working.

André shrugged. "Ah, it just looks like that. We've discovered that if something appears too shiny and new, we run the risk of losing it to some damned princeling out for a new toy."

Balthazar had said something similar. Agatha ran an eye over the circus wagons ranged before her. It explained a lot.

"But how can I fix this? That is, if I had the right tools, I think I could do it, but it'll take more than basic cart repair tools for a job like this…"

Rivet grinned. "Ho! Tools I've got! Come on over here."

Agatha turned to André. "I'm surprised you can't fix it."

He dismissed this with an elegant shrug. "Ah, while I know keyboards, I am, alas, no mechanic. Rivet here, while a fine mechanic, does not play. At the very least, I'm hoping you can get the basics sorted out before you leave us at Mechanicsburg."

Agatha grimaced. "Well, I'll try, but without a shop, without proper tools—"

They stopped beside Rivet's wagon. It was covered in elaborate panels, which upon closer examination, Agatha noticed were actually cabinet doors. Rivet pulled out a ring of keys and began unlocking them and throwing them open one after the other, giving a proud little "Ta-dah!" with each reveal. Agatha watched this performance with growing astonishment. Within the cunningly-wrought cabinets were rack upon rack of gleaming tools, lovingly placed. Once all the doors were open, Rivet began fiddling with additional latches, unfolding and extending displays to reveal new wonders.

And wonders they were. Even some of the obscure tools she had only seen used in the most specialized labs at Transylvania Polygnostic were represented—often with a left-handed variant, and in a variety of sizes.

Delicate watch-making tools crafted from gold wire and ivory were a single rack away from a collection of monkey-wrenches that could have been used to uncouple the main fuel lines aboard Castle Wulfenbach. Tools constructed of everything from wood to what appeared to be tempered glass were artfully laid out around objects that even Agatha, with all her University experience, was having trouble identifying. Below the tools were what must have been hundreds of built-in drawers that contained nails, screws, bolts, and fasteners in a bewildering variety of shapes and sizes, with each compartment neatly labeled.

Agatha stood back and took in this immense collection of ironmongery. She now understood why Rivet's wagon had to be pulled by a team of six draft horses.

"Sweet lightning," she whispered. "This is an amazing collection. I don't think the University has some of these!" She reverently picked up a locking wrench. "They're beautifully made." Craftsmen often constructed their own tools as an important part of their apprenticeship, but this collection ran across dozens of different trades.

Rivet nodded. "I find them out here in the Wastelands. Abandoned towns, crashed airships—you can find all *kinds* of stuff if you know where to look. I keep the best, rebuild and refurbish the rest. They're good sale and trade items no matter where we go."

Agatha picked up a curious piece that looked vaguely like a screwdriver. She depressed a small switch and the device began to vibrate in her hand with a high-pitched ululation. Nearby, a brass padlock sparked and fell open.

Rivet looked surprised. "Is that what that does? I'd wondered."

Agatha carefully put the device back. "You'll let me use these? With tools like these, I should be able to fix anything— anything at all." Her voice was thick with admiration.

André grinned. "Wonderful! I will get you some paper, I'm sure you'll want to draw up plans. Oh, and you'll want to talk to Otto. He can configure his wagon engine so that it can run a lathe, mill or saw, anything you need."

Agatha nodded, but she was only half listening. Her mind was already tackling the problem. Deep in thought, she wandered back to the old calliope.

Rivet watched her go, sighed, and began shutting up her wagon. It was a rather time-consuming operation. When she spoke, it was in a low whisper. "André, I just don't understand what Master Payne is thinking. There're plenty of *real* repair jobs I could use her on." She glared at the music master. "Finest music machine east of my ass. That stupid old thing is just a wreck that Lars found. I was planning on stripping it for scrap."

André sniffed. "Don't be crude, it suits you all too well. You want her to help with repairs? Then by all means ask her. Master Payne said to keep her so busy she doesn't have time to think." He waved a hand to indicate Agatha, who was now atop the calliope wagon, resolutely tugging at a twisted pipe, "Voilà! It is done!"

Rivet hesitated, than sulked a bit. "But she's going to mess with my tools."

"Better to share your tools, than lose your neck."

All Rivet had to say to that was a resigned "Harumph" and the conversation was over. Krosp, lurking behind a wheel, found this extremely frustrating.

* * *

At lunchtime, Agatha asked Zeetha: "How will Abner find us again? Haven't we traveled an awfully long way since he's been gone?"

Zeetha reassured her. "We're in the same river valley, and we're keeping to the old road. The caravan always moves pretty slow, and Abner's a good woodsman when he has to be. I won't start to worry about him for another week, at least."

Even so, it wasn't long after lunch that Agatha saw Zeetha walk off along the wooded road in the direction they'd come— and when, later that afternoon, Abner emerged from the woods atop a sleek chestnut stallion, Zeetha was trotting along beside him, grinning.

Gunter, the big man who was Balthazar's father, saw them first and roared out a welcome that also served to alert the rest of the camp. Everyone dropped what they were doing and converged on the returning pair.

A dark-haired young man reached them ahead of the others, and grinned up at Abner. "Hey! You're alive! And back quick, too!"

Abner laughed. "Sorry, Lars! You can't rent out my half of the wagon just yet." He patted his mount, who was eyeing the gathering crowd nervously. "For which you can thank this fine horse."

Lars examined it critically, and nodded in admiration. "Wulfenbach's people give him to you?"

Abner snorted at the thought. "Ha. I don't talk *that* fast. I found him wandering loose near a campsite that had... well, it had been attacked by something."

Instantly Lars went tense. "Attacked by *something*? By *what*?"

"I don't know. It was something nasty. The place was wrecked pretty bad." He dismounted. "Believe me, I was glad to find this guy. I wanted out of there fast. Some of the remains I found... well...whatever got them mauled them pretty bad before it ate them." He saw the look on Lars' face and shook his head. "Hey, give me *some* credit. I made sure I wasn't followed. I rode down the river for close to two kilometers."

Lars thought about this and nodded reluctantly. "Yeah, that sounds good. Sorry, Ab, worrying is part of my job." He faced the rest of the crowd. "But that's still close enough that I want everyone to be on the alert!"

While Abner and Lars talked, Professor Moonsock and Dame Ædith were examining the horse. "Looks mighty famished to me," Ædith said.

Professor Moonsock ran a hand over the horse's ribs and frowned. "Certainly feels boney," she admitted. She tried to grab the animal's head. "He'll definitely need fattening up before we can have him working. Come on, old fellow, let me see those teeth." At this the horse snapped his head back and reared. Ædith caught the smaller woman before she hit the ground. "Closemouthed beast."

The professor dusted herself off. "He just needs to be fed a bit. Get to know us. Apparently we don't all have Herr de la Scalla's winning personality."

Abner shrugged modestly, then froze as a voice behind him called his name. He closed his eyes and took a deep breath before turning.

"Pix," he said simply.

They stood less than a meter apart. Everyone else tried hard to look like they were interested in something else—and failed dismally. Pix spoke first. "Are you all right?"

Abner nodded. "I am."

"Well... well good." Pix desperately cast about, trying to think of something to say. This confused her—she usually had plenty to say and didn't hesitate to say it. But now she realized that there were thousands of things she wanted to say to Abner, and that she was terribly afraid of saying the wrong thing. Suddenly, she was annoyed. This actually helped—*now* she could talk. "So what was the idea of horning in on my act, hey?"

This was not quite what Abner had expected. "What? But... I *had* to!" He protested. "I thought he was going to *kill* you!"

Pix considered this. "It was a close thing, wasn't it?" she admitted, "But I don't think he was the kind to shoot an unarmed girl. He was making too much noise. I had him pretty rattled, after all."

Pix turned to Agatha. "But it would have helped if you'd told us you were running from a *lover*. We all thought they were looking for you because you'd *stolen* something." Everyone looked at Krosp.

The cat drew himself up haughtily. "Wrowr! As if I'd go and let myself get *stolen*! I rescued *her*!"

Agatha sputtered, "He... he is hardly my lover! And I am not..."

Pix patted her shoulder sympathetically. "No, no, don't worry. We've all had experiences we'd like to forget. I expect he took *shocking* liberties."

Dame Ædith bit her lower lip, her eyes glowing with interest. "Oh yes, *that* kind always does! I expect he did terrible, vile things—"

Professor Moonsock perked up. "Oooh—really? You poor girl, you *must* tell us all about it!" She looked at the others. "Purely for therapeutic reasons, of course." The others nodded solemnly, and then looked expectantly at Agatha.

Agatha's outraged protest was cut off when Zeetha stepped forward. "All right, ladies. Enough." Agatha looked at the green-haired girl gratefully. "Anyway, whatever he did couldn't have been *too* horrible, she almost ran right out to him. I thought I was going to have to hold her *back* for a minute there."

Agatha blushed. "That... that's because I thought he was going to shoot *Pix*!" she insisted.

Zeetha nodded sagely. "Of course. Well, in any case, don't worry. I have something that'll take your mind off of him." She flourished the training staff. "More training! Now *run*!"

Everyone watched until the two girls were out of sight— some with sympathy, but most with amusement. Then, with pleasure borne of the knowledge that no one was likely to chase *them* with sticks, they smiled and returned to their work. Abner and Pix were left standing awkwardly alone.

Abner took a deep breath. "So Pix, I seem to remember this kiss."

Pix went red. She glared at Abner, "Oh, you *seem* to, do you?"

Gently he took hold of her shoulders. "Perhaps I *should* have said that I'll never forget it."

Pix went redder. "Oh."

Abner waited for a moment, but that seemed to be all she was going to say. Gingerly, he slid his arm around her shoulders. Pix looked up at him. She was beautiful. He'd known that, of course, but never before had he quite noticed *how* beautiful. Perhaps he should tell her this. "Let's talk," he said.

Pix nodded. "Yes."

Some time later, Lars lifted the lid of a barrel. Agatha was huddling inside. "Ah. There you are." He laughed.

She looked up at him with pleading eyes. "Have pity on me, whoever you are."

The young man grinned. "Yeah, I guess we haven't met. I'm Lars. I'm one of the show's advance men."

Agatha looked up at him. He was very handsome, with dark hair and well muscled arms that showed under his short sleeves. "Is that some technical term for a leading man?"

He laughed again, and effortlessly lifted her from the barrel. His hands were large and steady. "No, although I *do* play Bill Heterodyne a lot. No, an advance man travels ahead of the circus. We scout the terrain ahead. It's our job to keep the show from riding into a nest of monsters or wasting time going down a road that ends up being washed out—things like that.

"When we get to a town, we make sure it's not full of cannibals or blood frogs. If it seems okay, then we have to find a place for the show to set up, figure out who we have to bribe, collect local information that might be good to include in the show, and try to get a good deal on any supplies we need."

"That sounds pretty dangerous." Agatha said, then thought a little about Zeetha, and Zeetha's stick. "Hey, the next time you go, take me with you!"

That got yet another laugh. Agatha liked the sound of it. "Ah, are you one of my fans, already?" Lars chuckled, "I know I have a magnetic personality, but..."

"No!" Agatha was blushing a lot, today. "I mean, I just thought it would be a good way to escape—"

"Interesting. Usually we get farm girls who want to *join* the show to escape."

"Oh? Escape from what?"

Lars grew serious. She had asked the question lightly, but suddenly Agatha wondered what he'd seen. "The tedium of farming. A family that thinks of her as nothing but a servant, or worse. The dull lad she's doomed to marry. A town that remembers every one of her mistakes..."

"What do you do with them?" Agatha asked.

Lars immediately brightened. "Why, we *take* them, of course!"

Agatha looked surprised. "You do?"

They had been walking away from camp as they spoke, following a path that led across a shallow brook. Lars gallantly held out a hand to help her hop across on the flat stones that served as a bridge.

He nodded. "Sure. Some panic their first night away from home, and most of them, having succeeded in escaping their old life, leave us at the next town. But some—ah, *some* people set foot on the stage and never step off."

Agatha gave him a shrewd look. "Like yourself."

"Ha! Caught!" He struck a dramatic pose and his voice boomed forth. "You see before you a former cheesemaker's apprentice, who foolishly stopped to see a traveling Heterodyne show when he was *supposed* to be delivering a wheel of Hungarian Kashkaval!" Lars threw his arms wide and looked impressive for a brief moment, but he had chosen his stage poorly. His boots slipped on the wet rocks and he toppled, plunging ankle-deep into the water. Agatha laughed and helped him up.

On the bank, Lars continued. "It was *The Heterodyne Boys and Their Anthracite Burning Earth Orbiter*." He sighed happily at the memory. "That was over ten years ago and I've never regretted it."

Agatha smiled. "My favorite was always *Race to the West Pole*."

Lars clapped his hands. "Oh, yeah. That's a good one. We haven't done it in a while, though."

"Why not?"

He shrugged. "Different shows work better with different actors. It's not like it's a problem, there's so many of them, you know? It just hasn't come around in the rotation." He eyed Agatha speculatively. "It's about due, actually. Hmm... but there are some tough scenes in *West Pole*. Remember the scene on the burning submersible?" His voice suddenly shifted timbre, becoming lower and more intense.

"Renounce your father, lest his evil corrupt you!"

Lars paused, and looked at Agatha encouragingly. Agatha shivered. His voice, as he'd said the line, had sent an electric tingle down her spine. She thought back to the last time she'd seen the play.

It had been years ago, in Beetleburg, during one of the annual Lightning Festivals. Booths and revelers had crowded the streets. It had been easy to slip away from Lilith, who had been busy dickering over a set of exotic canning jars—and who, Agatha knew, would not have approved of her foster-daughter's enthusiasm for the show playing on the makeshift stage in the market square. It had been a rare forbidden pleasure, and Agatha had watched intently. Later, she would replay the wonderful story over and over in her head.

Lars had begun the scene where Bill Heterodyne and the villainous Lucrezia Mongfish were trapped together aboard the slowly combusting submarine. It was one of her favorite scenes, and she knew how it went:

"One cannot be corrupted by Science! And Science alone is my master!"

Lars nodded approvingly and moved closer. "Then your master is mad! As mad as you have driven me!"

"Is it madness to see clearly? You only confuse me!"

Lars swept her into his arms. "Allow me to elucidate."

Agatha tilted her head back and looked him in the eyes. "… It could be an interesting experiment, if I but dared…"

"Don't tell me you fear the experiment?"

"I fear the result! But the experiment itself—why, that is but *Science*!"

"For Science, then!"

"For Science!"

On the stage, it was an intense scene, romantic and passionate—and it was meant to end with a torrid kiss. Agatha and Lars blinked at each other. He held her tightly in his arms, pulled close so that their faces were only centimeters apart. She, gazing up into his face, was clutching at his shirt and pulling him down toward her in a most unseemly way.

They broke apart and Agatha fanned herself with her hand. The weather seemed to have turned unseasonably warm, and her heart was pounding.

Lars took a deep breath and grinned. "Say! You're pretty good!"

Agatha licked her lips. "Really? I never… ah… so that's acting? I… I wonder if…" A strained wheeze stopped her, and she glanced sideways at Lars. He was staring fixedly up over her head. "Lars?"

He gripped her arm tightly. "Shhh! Geisterdamen," he whispered.

Agatha slowly turned to look, then froze in shock. Before them were a pair of gigantic, blue-white furred spiders. Eight long legs hoisted each creature's body easily six meters up into the air. They wore harnesses and saddles, with packs, gear and weapons strapped behind. Astride each of these monsters was a tall, slender young woman. Moving only her eyes, Agatha glanced back and forth between the two and realized that they were identical. Both had extremely pale skin, long flowing white hair, and the same peculiar outfit of folded and draped fabric. Chillingly, both also had the same wide, pupil-less eyes.

The women were regarding Agatha with interest. Their spiders leaned down until the riders scrutinized her from less than two meters away.

"Twerlik?" The far one was apparently asking a question[21].

The closer one raised a staff and casually pointed it at Agatha. "Su fig?" She responded. She leaned back. "Klibber meeenak seg ni plostok vedik kliz moc twerlik?"

The second rider frowned. "Zo—zo flooda vedik."

"Botcha hey za vedik moc nodok."

"Za nedik eve za gwoon."

[21] The language of the Geisterdamen, developing as it did without any Indo-European influences, has always been a thing of unfamiliar cadences and bizarre word structure. To recreate the sense of confusion and unfamiliarity that the linguistically cosmopolitan Lady Heterodyne must have experienced the first time she heard it, we have helpfully rendered all of the Geisterdamen's dialogue as gibberish.

"Hic mok?"

The second rider shrugged and indicated the circus' camp. "Zo—voco cheeb? Kloopa. Obongs. Set ve?" She crossed her arms. "Za 'actors.'"

This startled the first rider almost as much as it did Lars and Agatha. "*Actors*!"

The second rider made a clicking noise and her spider straightened up and began striding off. The first rider followed suit. Agatha could hear her asking plaintively, "Woge-ze fleepin *bo* 'actors,' bin?"

This was answered with a derisive, "Yan, do hip za *cheeb*."

"Hif ni!"

And with that final exchange, the strange women and their giant mounts were swallowed up among the trees.

Lars abruptly sat down on the ground. He looked ill. "I didn't even hear them coming," he moaned.

"Who were they?" Agatha asked.

"People call them Geisterdamen. Weißdamen. Spider Riders... all *kinds* of things. They've been around for a long time now. They're always on the move. Nobody knows anything about them, really." Lars paused before continuing:

"Except—you don't want to fight them. They're really dangerous when you do that. Farmers say that they cause revenants, steal children, blight crops..." He took a deep breath and then bounced to his feet and grinned. "Of course, they say the same things about traveling shows, so..."

Agatha was still staring at the opening in the trees where the giant spiders had disappeared. "I've never even *heard* of them."

Lars shrugged. "There're lots of things hiding in the Wastelands that you townies never hear about." He looked at Agatha appraisingly. "Want us to drop you off at the next town?"

Agatha looked steadily back at him. "No thanks."

Several of the other circus members burst into the clearing. "You two okay?" Abner asked.

Lars shook his head. "I swear, Ab, I didn't even hear them coming!" A thought struck him. "Is Balthazar—?"

Abner waved his hands. "He's safe."

Captain Kadiiski, who had insisted that Agatha call him Otto ("As you are obviously a civilian"), took his hat off and wiped a sheen of sweat from his brow. "I hates me those creepy girls," he confided to Agatha. "You should come with me," he continued. "A wagon we have now prepared for you."

This was welcome news. Agatha appreciated Professor Moonsock's hospitality, but the animal trainer had clearly grown oblivious to the smells of her performers, and seemed to find nothing off-putting about mimmoths nesting in the bread-box.

As she followed Captain Kadiiski away, Abner turned to Lars and asked, "So—Just before the White-eyes turned up— did I hear part of *West Pole*?"

Lars nodded. "Indeed you did. I think we should roll it out for the next town."

Abner sighed the sigh of a manager who has to deal with persnickety talent. "Put it on the list. There's a *bunch* I'd like to do, but it's got a lot of Lucrezia in it, and our *Prima Donna* hates playing Lucrezia."

Lars nodded, and his head turned toward the receding Agatha. "This may no longer be a problem."

Abner blinked. "Oh, really? You think she's that good?" He appraised Agatha's retreating form with new eyes. "Now

I wonder how Pix will react to that?" His evil chuckle was cut off when he realized it would be *his* job to tell her.

Lars punched his shoulder in sympathy. "Go get her, Arlecchino."

Otto led Agatha through the camp and stopped with an arm grandly outstretched toward a wagon that stood slightly apart from the rest. "So sorry, Agatha, but as you are the new kid, you got to take the old Baba Yaga."

Agatha, however, was delighted. The contraption before her had a standard wagon body, approximately three meters wide and six long. It was shaped like a miniature Russian dacha, with the addition of a small onion dome jauntily perched atop the curved, peaked roof. The whole exterior was beautifully carved and then meticulously painted in several dozen garish colors. In this at least, it matched the rest of the circus wagons. What set this wagon apart was that, instead of wheels, it stood high above the ground on an enormous set of beautifully detailed mechanical chicken feet.

Agatha had admired it from afar. Until she had joined the circus, she had never seen anything like it, which, considering Adam's "love of a good challenge," was a pretty high bar to beat. She had wanted to get a better look at it, but had been too busy—and now it would be hers?

Wonderingly, she reached out and ran her hand over one of the enormous drumsticks. It was covered in individual, gilded metal feathers. Rivet's head popped out from behind the mechanical claw. She grinned at Agatha. "Oh you're going to love this."

Agatha already did[22], but her spirits began to droop as Otto and Rivet continued:

"Driving her is the bear," Otto grunted. "She is a double-clutch Belgian overgear snap-piston system. They never really caught on. Smart girl like you should get it in a month or so. Or you will die in embarrassing stick-shift accident." Agatha surveyed the tangle of open-gear operating levers. This was an all-too-possible scenario.

"There's no gyros or shock absorbers to speak of," Rivet contributed. "She steers like an ox." She led Agatha toward the back. "She moves well on rough terrain, which means you'll pull ahead of the rest of the troupe. This is good—" She pointed to a small wood stove set atop the rear bumper, "because you'll have to stop every twenty minutes to refuel the boiler. If you're not careful, this will also make you an honorary point rider, which means you've got a good possibility of flushing out any beasties that might be lying in wait on the road ahead. So be careful and try not to get too far ahead of the group."

Otto nodded. "Plus, the roof, she leaks." He thought for a moment. "Oh yes, and if you do not park her correctly, the left leg piston will start to lose pressure, and she will fall over sometime in the night." He clapped his hands together. "Boom," he said glumly.

Agatha looked at him from under lowered brows. "Anything else?"

Otto waved his hand dismissively. "No. I personally am not

[22] It is true that most madboy devices are built for purely utilitarian purposes: I want to go faster; How can one person stack all of these starfish; I will gain the respect of my peers if I can turn this entire town into ham, and so on. But there are some things that burst forth from their creator's brain simply because they want to make the world more aesthetically pleasing. So what if it doesn't help one conquer the world? It looks awesome. It's Art.

one of those who believe that it is haunted. That is nonsense, no matter what everyone says."

Rivet tried to lighten the mood. "The *good* news is that you get to bunk solo."

Agatha glared at them. "If all that is true, then this thing is a walking disaster area! Why do you even bother to keep it running?"

Rivet opened a hatch. A double row of jeweled ovals, each meticulously etched with swirling patterns and encrusted with glittering jewels were revealed. She shrugged. "We need the eggs."

At dinner, Agatha was again dragooned into helping serve. When she finally had time to eat, the food was filling and delicious. In addition to the promised borscht, there were succulent roast hares and fresh loaves of poppy-seed bread. Taki, the cook, had kept Agatha busy all afternoon, basting the hares with a spicy yogurt mixture. For dessert, the cook opened a large stone crock and dished out a creamy sweet cheese, which everyone eagerly slathered upon the remaining crusts of bread.

Thinking of Lilith and her warnings on the subject of strong drink, Agatha contented herself with several cups of the Countess' specially-brewed sweet tea.

During the meal, members of the troupe took turns entertaining the rest with music, sleight-of-hand, and assorted soliloquies. Some of these last were touching, some amusing, and one made absolutely no sense to Agatha, although Zeetha had found it hilarious, especially the part about the mad doctor and the impossibly tiny man who played the piano.

One of the more outré performers, a tall Asiatic fellow who appeared to be covered in luxuriant golden fur, and who introduced himself as Yeti, successfully juggled various fruits and vegetables even as Zeetha sliced them into smaller and smaller bits.

As Agatha helped clear the plates and bowls away, the party split into two groups, one playing musical instruments, the other dancing merrily. Everyone was relaxed and happy, and the conversations were fascinating, but the second time Agatha nodded off, and then jerked awake, she gave up. She said good night to her companions and headed for bed.

Exhausted, Agatha climbed aboard the Baba Yaga and gently shut the door behind her. She pulled herself up a short ladder to the sleeping compartment, which ran the entire length of the vehicle. The wagon bed was tilted slightly forward, thus Agatha had to pull herself upslope just to reach the back wall. There she managed to fold down the bunk platform. As she was adjusting the heavy support chains so that the bed would lie level, Krosp leapt up from below. He found one of the small windows, and curled up on the deep sill. His tail lashed jerkily.

"What's with you?" Agatha asked. She found a built-in cedar chest and exclaimed over the luxurious eiderdown-filled mattress she found inside.

Krosp peered out the window. Outside, the music continued, along with the occasional burst of laughter and appreciative whistling. He turned away. "There's something these people aren't telling us."

Agatha opened another chest and pulled out a patchwork quilt that looked as if it had been made from old costumes. She arranged it on the bed. "That's not surprising," she said, after a deep yawn. "We're certainly not telling them everything about *us*."

Krosp waved a paw dismissively. "That's *their* problem."

Agatha finished tucking in the quilt. "What *exactly* is bothering you?"

"These people have no weapons. Well, no weapons worth anything, anyway. There are smells… that make me think they've got something, somewhere, but I've been looking around—and there's *nothing*!"

Agatha frowned. "Those pointy things most of the guys are wearing are called 'swords.' The blunt ones are called 'guns.'"

Krosp hissed and began to pace the length of the compartment. "Please. I mean *real* weapons. When that crab clank attacked, they scattered and ran!"

Agatha frowned. "Well, of course they did. So? Their guns are just guns. The Baron doesn't let people have anything too Sparky. So they wouldn't do much against a clank like that."

"That's just it! I read some of Wulfenbach's reports about the Wastelands. That clank was *nothing* compared to some of the stuff that's supposed to be out here—and yet we're supposed to believe that these people have been traveling around out here for years—essentially unarmed?" He sat and glared out the window. "They should all be dead!" Agatha climbed aboard the bed and began to undress. Krosp continued musing. "No. They must have *something*."

Agatha frowned. "But then why didn't they use it against that crab clank?"

Krosp looked at Agatha. "The only thing that makes sense is that they were hiding it from you."

Agatha frowned. "From me?"

The cat nodded. "That clank attacked right after we left. They couldn't be sure we'd gone far enough."

"But why?"

Krosp slumped. "I... don't know. Maybe it's just that you're a stranger?" he said unconvincingly.

Agatha shook her head. "Krosp, that thing picked up Olga and *fried* her. What could I *possibly* do that would be worse than *that*?"

Krosp pounded his little paw against his forehead. "I don't *know*! I'm *missing* something!"

He turned and came face-to-face with a little clank that looked like a pocket-watch. It had legs, arms, and a single mechanical eye that peered at him curiously. It waved at him and chimed.

The cat shot underneath Agatha's skirt. "Where did *that* come from?" he yowled, peeking out from underneath the hem.

Agatha smiled. "It's one of mine. I found it hiding on the airship." She paused, "Well, I suppose 'hiding' is the wrong word, its spring had run down."

Krosp glared at the device. "I don't like it."

Agatha used a foot to push him out from under her skirt. "*You* don't have to. Anyway, it's harmless, I have to wind it every day or it'll stop."

Krosp looked unconvinced. He jumped onto the bed and licked his paw, then settled down in the exact center. "Pity it's so useless. Now, that gun you built—*that* we should have kept."

Agatha finished getting undressed—leaving her camisole and long pantalettes to serve in place of a nightgown. "We've been over that. Leaving it on the grave was supposed to look like a mark of respect for the stranger who saved them from the crab-clank. To make Wulfenbach think I was the one in there, right? Anyway, like I said, the Baron's people would *never* have let us keep it."

Krosp, still in the center of the bed, kneaded the quilt up into a tidy little nest around him. "Yes, yes..." he muttered, laying his head on his paws and preparing to sleep.

"Besides," said Agatha casually, "We don't really need it." She reached into her travel bag and pulled out a device made of wood, glass, and what looked like decorative brass tubes pulled off the calliope. "I've already built a better one."

Krosp jerked upright. "You're worried too."

Agatha nodded as she scooped up the cat and deposited him at the foot of the bed. "Not *worried*, exactly..." she said, as she slid beneath the quilt, "I just have this... *odd* feeling. And it's been getting stronger all day."

Several hours later, the last of the musicians yawned and declared themselves too tired to play another note. As the troupe headed off toward the wagons, Master Payne tucked his petite-gaffophone under his arm and frowned. "A bit of a late night for you, isn't it Lars?"

Lars waved reassuringly. "I can stand the occasional late night. Besides—" He glanced over at the wagon that he shared with Abner, "Ab's talking to Pix about *Race to the West Pole*." The Countess and Master Payne grimaced. Pix was known for her temper, and she had been the troupe's unrivaled leading lady ever since she joined. Even if she didn't like playing Lucrezia, no one was quite sure how she would react to another actress taking what she would see as "her" role. Still, they hadn't heard any actual shouting...

Lars continued, "Anyway I figure they're into the 'kiss and make up' part by now, and if I'm any judge, that'll go on for a while. I thought I'd just take the first watch. I'll still be good to go in the morning, never fear. Augie and I will be waiting for you slow coaches in the next town."

Payne nodded, "Fare thee well then," and with his arm tucked around the sleepy Countess, he took his leave.

Lars stood up, stretched, and tossed a few more logs onto the fire. Around him, the circus settled in for the night. The murmur of the last few conversations dwindled away. Otto's stentorian snoring could faintly be heard, despite the excessive amount of soundproofing André and Rivet had designed for his wagon. Soon the only sounds were the popping and crackling of the fire. Despite his assurances to Master Payne, Lars felt his eyelids drooping.

A sudden clatter brought him up to a crouch, his hand on his sword hilt. It sounded like it had come from the makeshift paddock. Slowly a shape materialized against the darkness. Lars stood still, and then blew out a sigh of relief. It was the new horse—the one Abner had ridden back to camp. The animal had somehow broken its tether and was wandering loose.

Lars held out his hand and slowly moved toward the horse. It watched him for a moment, like a pet pony expecting a carrot. Then it opened its mouth, revealing several rows of sharp, glittering teeth. Lars froze in astonishment. The monster snarled, reared up on its hind legs and *leapt* at him, easily covering the intervening six meters.

His reflexes taking over, Lars dropped and rolled toward the creature, yelling as loudly as he could as it landed directly above him. He scrambled for footing as the monster twisted about, feet stamping furiously as it tried to crush him.

With his feet under him, Lars launched himself sideways and landed near the fire, grabbing a protruding branch as he tumbled past. He heard the creature's scream of rage as it leapt after him, and, ignoring the pain in his hand, he thrust the burning wood up into the monster's face. The beast snarled as it lunged forward, jaws snapping over the flames. Lars was showered with burning embers as the branch shattered. He desperately scrabbled backward, staring in horror as the beast swallowed the burning stick. The monster was preparing to lunge, when a voice shouted—"*Eyes!*"

The monster whipped its head toward the sound, but Lars slapped his hand over his eyes.

FOOM! A blue actinic glare lit the entire area. Lars could sense it, even from behind his shielding hand. The horse-creature screamed in rage and pain as it staggered back.

The next instant, a fusillade of shots struck its side. The firing continued for almost a full minute. The force of the shots knocked the beast to the ground, until finally, Otto lowered his mechanical arm and dug into his pocket for more bullets. "I hit it directly!" he yelled. "Is dead, yes?"

Trish, next to Otto, lowered her crutch. It could now be seen that this was an automated rifle of exotic design. She bent it open with a "crack!" and snapped in a fresh drum of ammunition. "I'm not sure—" she began, closing the weapon with one jerk of her arm. She raised it to her shoulder as the beast lurched back to its feet. It glared at them and showed its teeth, as dozens of spines erupted from its head and body. It screamed again and stalked toward them purposefully.

"—But I think we got it mad," Trish cried.

"Stev!" Guntar shouted, "Destroy!"

With a rumble, the squat automaton strode forward. As he moved, he shuddered and shrugged, unfolding his joints and growing as he advanced. Smilin' Stev suddenly looked a lot more dangerous. The enormous grin plastered across his face widened—and a buzz saw slid out of his mouth, shrieking as it gained speed.

The monster saw the approaching clank and paused. As Stev came within reach, the creature wheeled about and delivered a punishing kick with its rear legs, punching two enormous dents into the machine's hide and sending him flying backwards. Stev hit the ground rolling. When he stopped, he was on his back, limbs waving feebly.

By this time the rest of the circus performers had appeared, most of them carrying strange bits of equipment. A high-pitched squealing filled the air, causing everyone's teeth to vibrate painfully. "Cover your ears!" André yelled, "I'm using the sonic cannon!"

Dame Ædith appeared atop one of the wagons. She opened a huge prayer book to reveal a hand-held machine cannon, and began firing wooden stakes at the creature. "Aut vincere aut *mori*!" she screamed.

Yeti lumbered forward. He took a string of huge beads from around his neck and wrapped it around his hand. The light around him began to bend slightly as he advanced. "Stay back," he called out, "I am contemplating the gravity equations!"

Professor Moonsock rushed up, wearing nothing but a leather waistcoat and bloomers. She gleefully pulled the stopper from a large canister covered with warning symbols. " Fools! None of that will work!" she announced joyfully, "I am releasing my poisonous skywurms!"

At this announcement, the entire company turned *away* from the spiny horse-monster and screamed "No!" But it was far too late. A horde of glowing purple insects boiled forth from the canister. They spun about in the air, and then, at a signal from their delighted mistress, dived en masse toward the bemused horse beast.

As the wurms neared their target, the monster reared up and spat out a stream of foul-smelling flames that engulfed the entire swarm.

Guntar blinked in astonishment. "It breathes *fire?*"

Professor Moonsock stomped in fury. "Cheating! Cheating! That is *so* unfair!"

At that moment, Yeti clapped his huge hands together and boomed forth a low "Ooooommmmm..." The horse gasped, and its knees buckled.

From the darkness, Zeetha leapt onto the horse-creature's back, her swords crossed before her. As she landed, she swept her arms forward, and the blades effortlessly sliced through the creature's neck.

The head flew off with a surprised expression frozen upon its features. The body shuddered, but before anyone could react, the creature's chest split wide open, revealing a gaping, fang-filled mouth that gibbered and squealed. Zeetha, astonished, had recovered quickly and was repeatedly sinking her swords into the creature's back, but long tentacles burst out of the open maw, and plucked her into the air. Helpless, she roared in fury as she was pulled toward the creature's huge mouth.

Suddenly, the thing exploded in a spatter of brilliant blue

light. Zeetha was thrown sideways, and crashed against a cart, followed by tiny pattering scraps of monster.

The circus players stood transfixed. The only sound was an ominous "vreeeeeee—" as the weapon Agatha held under her arm recharged. She stood in the firelight, studying the performers and the assorted devices they held. She looked around at the damage those devices had caused to the surrounding area. Finally she nodded and lowered the gun.

"Well," she said to Krosp, "There's your answer." She turned to Master Payne. "I think I understand now. You're *all* Sparks. Aren't you?"

Everyone looked at Master Payne. He opened his mouth to answer—and was cut off when Lars let out an unearthly shriek.

Oddly, at the sound of Lars' scream, the circus players seemed to relax, as if this were the signal that all was clear. Trish bent over him as he sat on the ground near the fire. "It's okay!" she said soothingly, "Take a deep breath."

This didn't help. "HORSE!" he screamed. "HORSEHORSE HORSEHORSE!"

Agatha stared. "What in the World is the matter with him?"

The Countess shook her head. "Panic attack. He gets them after things like this."

Agatha looked surprised. "Oh. But... that's kind of unusual for a Spark, isn't it? Doesn't he wind up doing it all the time, then?"

"He's not a Spark."

"What? But—"

Marie spread her hands. "Many of us, yes, but not *all* of us."

Taki bustled up with an anticipatory grin upon his face. He was carrying a beautiful, large, golden-brown pie. "Panic attack, eh? Finally! Thought I'd never get a chance to try my newest Calming Pie!"

Before anyone could stop him, the cook strode straight over and slapped the pie directly into Lars' face. Lars froze. Everyone held his or her breath... and then from around a face full of pie could be heard a strangled, "horrrff!"

Agatha looked at Marie with suspicion. "That was supposed to calm him down?"

The Countess rolled her eyes. "Those of us who *are* Sparks aren't always that *good* at it. There's a reason we get called 'mad' you know."

The cook shrugged irritably. "All the calm must've leaked out. I'll bake a fresh one."

Yeti had retrieved Zeetha, and now held her carefully in his arms. Master Payne examined her foot, which looked bruised. He gingerly wiggled it, causing her to gasp in sudden pain.

The Circus Master clucked his tongue. "You've sprained that ankle. One of Professor Moonsock's self-tightening bandages should have it fixed up in a few days, but you'll want to stay off of it."

One of the other performers bustled up. "No! Wait! This is the perfect opportunity to test out my 'relativistic pain theory'! Let me get my hammer!"

One of the puppeteers snorted derisively. "Bosh! We should amputate! We can try out my new steam-powered feet!"

Zeetha snarled at them both and brandished a sword. "Come near me, and I will kill you!"

With the ease of long practice, both Sparks turned away. "Fine. Suffer then," the hammer man said.

The puppeteer was obviously more disappointed and turned

to eye the still babbling Lars. A speculative gleam grew in her eyes. "You know," she said hopefully, "I'll bet Lars wouldn't panic if his feet could run at two hundred kilometers an hour!"

The hammer man looked at her scornfully. "Absurd. The stress would tear his legs apart."

The puppeteer grinned and rubbed her hands together. "Ah—Old fashioned *flesh* legs, yes, but—"

"Enough!" Marie shouted, giving them a stern look. Around them, several equally-alarming conversations came to a halt. "All Lars needs is a lie-down and some *quiet*!"

The crowd shuffled its feet sheepishly, looked disappointed, and began to disperse. The Countess nodded in satisfaction and then turned to her husband with a thoughtful expression. "And...and perhaps a *soothing tonic*?" she said—a small, manic grin spreading across her.

Payne nodded amiably and gently pushed his wife along. "That's a *wonderful* idea, my dear. Why don't you go brew one up?" The Countess gave a slightly mad chuckle of triumph and darted off.

Master Payne gusted out an enormous sigh and turned back. The circle of firelight was now empty except for Agatha, looking perplexed, and Lars, still babbling about horses and pies.

Payne addressed Agatha warily. "And you, Miss Clay—do *you* have any ideas for calming Lars down?"

"Me? Heavens, no!"

Payne grinned in relief. "Excellent! You may stay. Help me get him up, won't you?"

Soon enough, they had Lars sluiced off and installed in his own bed. Abner had been dispatched to look in on everyone as they settled in. After the night's excitement, Payne wanted to be sure that no one was out building anything "helpful."

Lars had calmed down a bit. He was no longer babbling, and lay quietly, burrowed deep under his bedding. Only his face showed over the quilt, staring out at the world with wide eyes.

Agatha placed a damp cloth on his head and turned to Master Payne, who sat slumped wearily in a chair, watching her. "So?" she asked.

Payne nodded wearily. "So the point is, *everyone* knows what a Spark is, right? Just ask the people who come to our shows. A Spark is the madman in the castle on the hill, cackling away while he builds monsters. Sparks are Flamboyant! Fearless! *Powerful! No one can stop them!* When you say 'Spark,' that is the sort of fantastical creature a person thinks about."

Payne's voice had risen to a dramatic height, but now he sighed and wiped a hand across his face. When he spoke next, his voice was tired.

"*You'd* probably think of the Heterodyne Boys, or The Master of Paris." He shook his head. "But most people remember the bad ones. Petrus Teufel. Lucifer Mongfish. The Polar Ice Lords. If only because they make for better stories. That's what Sparks are like.

"But the Spark, like any other talent, comes in varying degrees. Think about it. How do you know when someone is a Spark?

"The answer is when they create something too mad too ignore. That's all it takes, really. But what about someone who's brilliant, has the Spark burning brightly within him, no doubt about it, but is born to an impoverished village cobbler? Without any education or resources, what can *they* do? Build a dangerous boot?

"The worst off are those with just enough of the Spark that those around them can identify them, but not enough that they can defend themselves."

Payne gestured out at the circus. "Most of us, here, are Sparks without power. We are not rich, and, my Countess excepted, we have no rank. We have no castle walls to hide behind, and our talents are not strong enough to fend off the world. We are easy prey for those who would have use for us. So, we play madboys on the stage and openly perform our mundane miracles using easily spotted smoke and mirrors. The audience sees simply players in a show, and we are able to hide in plain sight. Even from the Baron."

Realization dawned in Agatha's mind. "You thought the Baron had sent that crab clank. That's why you didn't fight back."

Payne nodded. "The Baron or someone like him. When we think the wrong people are watching, we travel 'on stage.' Remember that term, please. There are many who have a use for Sparks, weak or strong, and they have any number of tricks for hunting us."

Agatha was silent. She had seen enough at the University, and later on Castle Wulfenbach, to know that Payne's words were true. The thought made her feel heavy, and tired.

"I understand. Well, it's late. I guess I'd better go—"

"NO!" Lars frantically pushed himself up and grabbed Agatha's arm so hard that a small shock of pain went through her. "I want her to stay here!"

Payne looked surprised. "Miss Clay? Why?"

"Because she's got a great big monster-killing gun!" he exclaimed. "And I want it, and her, right here!"

Krosp shrugged. "Can't really argue with that logic."

"Don't worry." Agatha smiled at Lars as she pried his hand from her arm. She turned to face Master Payne. "I'll stay. I don't know if I could sleep now, anyway."

Payne sat back and nodded. "Thank you, Miss Clay, I appreciate it."

A quiet snore surprised them. Lars, eyes closed, was already deep in slumber.

"Strike a light!" Master Payne declared. "That was quick."

Agatha smiled. "Well! No one has had that much faith in me since—" Suddenly, she thought of Gil, his image so clear in her mind that her breath caught and her eyes began to sting. She turned away.

Payne looked quizzical, "—since?"

"Nothing important." Her voice was husky, "Never mind."

Master Payne looked thoughtful. "I see." He stood up, and said in a hearty voice: "Good night then!" Agatha simply waved a weak goodbye. She was lost in unhappy thought.

When Payne stepped down from the wagon, he found Abner waiting for him. The young man was slightly disheveled, and hastily tucked in his shirt as he asked: "Is Lars all right, sir?"

Payne nodded. "Oh, yes. Miss Clay is going stay with him."

Abner shook his head. "Well, we've got our proof. She's a Spark, and a strong one, I'd bet."

"That's a sucker bet and no mistake." Payne shook his head. "And she's on the run from Wulfenbach. Aspects of Moxana's new game are starting to make some sense."

"And yet you don't look happy," Abner observed. He lowered his voice. "We... could *lose* her. At the next town."

Payne stretched and rolled his shoulders. "No, Ab, I don't think we *could*." The two men started to walk. "Nothing good would come of it. I can almost guarantee it." He shook his head. "She wants us to get her to Mechanicsburg? Let's just do it as quickly as possible, and get it over with."

The body of the horse-monster needed to be disposed of. Several men had been hauling wood and building a pyre a small distance downwind of the camp. As Payne and Abner arrived, Rivet and Otto were just lowering the carcass onto the pyre with a device that resembled an inside-out forklift. The cook used a tiny hatchet to broach a small cask, and everyone stepped back as he soaked everything with a colorless liquid. He took extreme care not to get any on himself, and when he finished, he sprang back—tossing the empty cask on the pyre as if it were already on fire. Everyone looked expectantly at Payne. The Circus Master stepped up and with a flourish, shot a thin jet of green fire from his fingers. Wood and monster exploded into flame.

Payne nodded in satisfaction and turned to Abner, who was settling himself against a log. "Use all the wood and fuel you need, but I want that thing reduced to ash before morning. That's when we're moving out."

Abner gave a lazy salute. "If anything happens, I'll give the signal. You know, the one where I scream like a diva."

"Good man." Before Payne went back to his own wagon, he took a last turn through the camp, making sure to assign extra watch duties to everyone unwary enough to cross his path. Just before he climbed the steps to his own wagon, he saw Pix heading toward the roaring fire. She was loaded down with an enormous counterpane and a picnic basket. Payne grinned, and closed the wagon door behind him.

* * *

Back in Lars' wagon, Agatha had lit the lamps, and made herself comfortable at the wagon's tiny fold-down table. Krosp was blithely rummaging through the cupboards. Agatha considered telling him to stop, then decided that she was too tired to bother. She would scold him later.

"Hide the Spark," she mused. "I've heard of people *trying* to do it, but they never seem to succeed."

Krosp sniffed at an empty china bowl. "It's easier for these guys. They have less to hide."

Agatha thought about some of the devices she had glimpsed before she had blasted the monster horse apart. "I don't know about *that*. But even if that is the case, I can still learn a lot from them."

Krosp had opened a door and removed a covered plate. He lifted the lid and discovered a wheel of buttery yellow cheese. He sniffed approvingly, and bit off a sizeable chunk. Agatha swatted the back of his head in disgust as she scolded him. "Krosp! Manners!" The cat blinked resentfully, but carefully took a knife and cut a thick wedge off of the unbroken side of the cheese. He passed it to Agatha and went back to gnawing away at the rest. "The problem is that because they're trying so hard to appear harmless, they're vulnerable."

Agatha was thoughtful. "Yes, they can't carry around anything unusually powerful without giving themselves away. Hiding really big stuff would be hard." She paused for a moment as an idea percolated in her mind. "Hmmm... I'll bet I could do it."

Krosp's ears flattened with alarm. Agatha didn't notice. "Yesssss—" her voice intensified, "With the tools and materials available, why, I could build defenses that would keep them safe from *anyone*!"

Krosp waved his paws. "Whoa, whoa! Without being obvious? The whole idea is to look innocuous, remember? Anyway, they probably won't want to let you mess around with their stuff!"

Agatha was excited now. "Plans!" she declared. "I'll draw up plans and they can *see* what I can do."

Krosp considered this and nodded grudgingly. "That should give them some *warning*, anyway. Hold on…" He opened an upper cupboard and returned with a stack of paper and some pencils.

Agatha snatched them from his paws and began sketching furiously. "When I'm done," she declared, "we'll be the most normal-looking circus on the face of the earth!"

Krosp rolled his eyes. "Very reassuring."

Hours later, the first subtle hints of dawn began to appear. Krosp was curled up inside an earthenware bowl that a few hours ago had contained a black pudding. Now, the pudding was contained within Krosp. Agatha was still hunched over the table. Beside her, the lamp guttered, and with a final puff, went out. She blinked and sat back, her back popping faintly. She stretched mightily, and looked slightly astonished at the blizzard of paper strewn about the little room.

With a sigh, she began collecting the papers, pausing to examine each one as she picked it up. Hearing her chuckle, Krosp came awake with a grunt, stretching all four legs upward in a huge yawn. "Done?" he asked.

Agatha nodded proudly. "Uh-huh. Want to see?" She held up a page covered with intricate drawings.

Krosp's brow furrowed. "What is this? A nutcracker?" He tilted the page slightly sideways, and realized that the "nuts" in the picture actually had tiny screaming faces. "AAAAHHH!" He shrieked and flung the paper away.

Agatha looked surprised. "What?"

Gingerly, Krosp picked up another page and examined it. He frowned and waved the page at Agatha accusingly. "A merry-go-round that can level a small town seems a bit... overboard for 'self defense.'"

Agatha examined the plans. She didn't remember drawing that one—it *was* pretty horrible. Still, she was rather pleased at how she'd drawn the fleeing townspeople.

"Well..." she hazarded, "It could be a really *evil* town..." She saw Krosp glaring at her. "Okay, okay." She shuffled all the papers together with a touch of regret. "I doubt I'd need anything this extreme anyway." A colossal yawn caught her by surprise. She looked out the window and, for the first time, noticed the predawn light. She glanced at Lars—he had slept soundly all through the night.

"I believe I am now ready to get some sleep," she confessed. She turned in her seat and pain exploded throughout her frame. She froze—suddenly remembering the grueling workout Zeetha had put her through the day before. "Acetylsalicylic acid!" she gasped.

The cat looked around. "Where? *I* don't see the acid."

Agatha would have glared at him, but even her eyeballs ached. "No," she said patiently, as she carefully hobbled forward, "I have to *find* some." The wagon door swung open and there stood Zeetha, leaning on a sturdy crutch. She grinned when she saw Agatha.

"You're awake! Eager for training, eh? Well, I'd *heard* Sparks were tough."

Agatha realized that there was only one door to the wagon, and thus, no escape. "No," she whispered.

Zeetha laughed and dragged her into the clear morning air. "No more mollycoddling!"

The wagon door shut. Krosp stared at it for a moment. Unfamiliar feelings surged through his tiny, feline heart. "Why, this must be pity," he thought in wonder.

A snort from behind announced Lars' return to consciousness. "Is someone here?"

Krosp leapt onto the bed and stood on Lars' chest. "That would be me." Lars looked up at him owlishly. "This is when you offer to feed me," Krosp suggested helpfully.

Lars nodded fuzzily and pushed Krosp aside. He climbed out of bed, freshened up at a washbowl, and began looking through the cupboards. A frown crept across his features as he peered into one empty container after another. "Where'd Agatha go?" He asked as he upended an empty pitcher. "Off to bed? I'll bet she was pretty beat."

A faraway bleat of pain caused Krosp's ears to twitch. "She will be."

To Krosp's horror, Lars then noticed the stack of paper on the table. "Wow. *She* was busy." He picked up the top sheet and frowned. "Is this some sort of cherry pitter?" He tilted the page slightly sideways—

"Hey! I smell food!" Krosp yowled, grabbing at Lars' pants. "Open the door! Let me out! Hey! Hey! Open the door! Hey!"

Lars paused. A tantalizing aroma was indeed coming from somewhere outside. He tossed the paper back onto the table and opened the door.

"Is that breakfast I smell?" Lars called out cheerfully as he marched through the tall grass outside the camp. Abner looked up from beside the embers of the fire. A few glowing bones poked out of the pile of ash.

Lars stopped dead and looked sick. "Er—I sure hope not." he muttered.

Abner grinned. He was enveloped by a huge quilt, the remains of a leisurely picnic strewn at his feet. Still asleep, but cuddled close up against him, was Pix.

"Mornin', Lars," Abner said softly. He nodded in the direction of the pyre. "Doesn't look so scary now, does it?"

Lars looked askance at the fire. "That depends. What's for breakfast?"

"Oatmeal—"

Lars looked relieved.

"À la monster!" Abner crowed.

"Half-wit." Lars growled.

His friend shrugged modestly. "It's a gift."

Lars agreed that indeed it was. Pix made a small contented sound in her sleep and snuggled in closer to Abner.

Lars raised an eyebrow. "Pix sure looks happy."

Abner smiled at her tenderly. "We sat up all night watching this thing burn."

Lars looked impressed. "Wow. And I thought *I* knew how to show a girl a good time."

Abner shrugged. "Well, we had a good long talk."

Lars looked stern. "Just talked?" He asked skeptically.

"Just talked."

"Hmph. You look pretty happy for a couple who 'just talked.'"

Abner grinned again in a way that had Lars rolling his eyes. "Guess we liked what we heard."

Master Payne strolled up. "Good morning, all. Ready to go, Lars?"

Lars gave a small bow. "I can eat in the saddle, so all I have to do is find some breakfast and my partner in crime, and we can set out."

Payne nodded. "Excellent. Augie has been ready to go for the last half hour. He's waiting for you near my cart, looking over maps and calling you several interesting and creative names. He's got your horse all saddled, *and* he's got your breakfast—so get going. The sooner we're away from here, the better, and I daresay the ladies in the towns ahead are waiting." Lars trotted off obediently.

When Lars had gone, Payne selected one of the iron cooking spits and poked at the remaining bones, peering curiously into the ashes. "So," he asked. "I don't suppose there was anything *interesting* hidden within our monster here? Jeweled heart? Enchanted princess?"

Abner shook his head. "I'm afraid not, sir. For what it's worth, it smelled like horse."

"Pity. Well, we'll just have to come up with something interesting ourselves. We'll make a good story out of it[23]."

Zeetha came toward them, leaning heavily on her crutch. She carried Agatha slung over her shoulder. When she saw the

---

[23] This sort of historical revisionism is quite common amongst entertainers. If something amazing or terrible happens to them out in the wilderness, then by golly, when it gets told to the paying customers, it's going to have a satisfying conclusion. It's analogous to writing a business loss off on one's taxes.

two showmen she rolled her eyes and grumbled: "Bah! Novices today! Ask them to move some rocks and they just collapse."

"I think she was up all night, watching Lars," Master Payne remarked.

Zeetha looked surprised, and then delivered a sharp smack to Agatha's backside. "Idiot! You have to *tell* me these things!" When this got no response, Zeetha looked worried.

"Lars is getting ready to ride out, put her in his bed." Master Payne ordered. "He won't mind, and I'll have Rivet drive the Baba Yaga today."

"Yeah, okay. That'll be good." Zeetha agreed. "That chicken thing moves like a drunk." She carried Agatha off toward the wagons.

Everyone was eager to be on the move as soon as possible, and the camp was a flurry of activity. Horses were being hitched, fuel added to boilers, and belongings stowed.

Lars and Augie were already mounted, Lars on a long-legged black stallion and Augie on a stout Serbian Clicking-Horse. They were nearly ready to head out, but first they joined the point riders, who were still busy making a thorough check of their equipment and mounts.

These three would escort the caravan, keeping watch for any trouble as they rode. Pushed up onto their foreheads were strangely-designed goggles that could give them spectacular views of the surrounding landscape as they rode. The five men took a few minutes to discuss the route ahead and compare maps. When they were done, they drew their swords and formally saluted each other. Then, Lars and Augie galloped away down the road. The point riders set out at a more sedate pace.

This was the signal for Abner to blow the "ten minute" whistle. Everyone was now putting out the remaining fires, tightening straps and climbing aboard wagons.

The Circus Master's wagon was the first to set out, its brilliant black and orange roof tiles gleaming in the morning sun. It was pulled by a towering, snow-white draft horse and a sleek black mule with a long twisting horn rising between its fuzzy ears.

As the next wagon began to roll, Payne stood upon the footboard and called out: "A fair road to us all, my friends! And now—a little traveling music, if you please!"

At this, Balthazar, sitting on the roof of his family's wagon, struck up a jaunty melody on his horn. André had found the bizarrely twisted, multi-belled instrument in an abandoned pawnshop, and then had never been able to get a note out of it. Balthazar, however, *could* get notes out of it, lots of them, and of great variety. And, as the horn was big, shiny, and terrifically loud, the boy had become extremely attached to it. He practiced with it constantly, knew lots of songs, and now played well enough that the rest of the troupe's "joking" attempts to hide the instrument had all but stopped.

To the curious music of the horn, alternately blasting like an elephant and twittering like a flock of tiny birds, the wagons pulled one-by-one onto the road and rumbled along toward their next show.

The ancient road that originally stretched from Imperial Rome to the Thracian province of Dacia was still the preferred route for anyone who traveled through the region. Although there were places damaged by time and weather, it was mostly in good repair—more so as one approached a town or castle. Travel became easier as the circus left the wilder parts of the Wastelands behind them, and traffic in both directions increased.

Still, as the wagons bumped along the weathered paving stones, Master Payne sat with his eyes turned skyward. Every time the wagon jolted through a hole where a stone had gone missing, the idea of retiring the venerable caravan wagons and outfitting a set of circus dirigibles sounded better and better.

This was not a new thought. It was an idea often raised after the troupe had escaped some monster, dodged bandits, or fought off a horde of cannibalistic mole-people. In other words, the subject was on the Circus Master's mind a lot.

He was intrigued by, and not a little envious of, the new wagon belonging to Herr Helios, the aerialist. It was little more than a traditional wagon suspended from a small blimp. It had no engines, so the strange little aerial cart had to be towed along whenever the show traveled, but it gave the Circus a nice touch of the exotic and looked good when they paraded into town. Once, though, the tow rope had broken, and only luck and the quick action of Professor Moonsock and her trained albatross had prevented Herr Helios from drifting away to parts unknown.

But Payne considered Helios' craft to be an intriguing "first draft." He took a clinical pleasure in each new design flaw Herr Helios encountered. Imagining how he would prevent similar problems with his own, at-this-point-theoretical, airship was an amusing way to pass the long hours of travel.

Marie, who was driving, easily recognized the dreamy look in her husband's eyes. She glanced at the sky and pulled a face, but left him to his thoughts. Although she had qualms about abandoning the traditional wagons, she suspected that most of them boiled down to an irrational fear of rolling out of her bed and falling five hundred meters to the ground.

She'd told herself that if Payne ever did get hold of an airship, she'd just have to brew up something that would keep her afloat. This line of thought had produced some intriguing speculations.

And thus, dreaming their respective dreams, the circus rolled on.

Several hours later, Agatha awoke. She was so warm and comfortable that she was slow to emerge from her heavy fog of sleep. Finally, with a start of recognition, she realized that the bed she was curled up in belonged to Lars. Last she remembered, Lars had been the one asleep here.

She remembered a vague nightmare involving large stones and Zeetha, but she couldn't remember falling asleep. She relaxed and stretched. Well, she had been up all night, and the bed really was soft, and had a delightful masculine smell about it. This traitorous thought brought her sharply awake, and in one great leap she burst from beneath the warm covers.

A set of unfamiliar clothes had been laid out. The outfit was covered in the colorful folk embroidery worn by the rest of the performers. Agatha felt happy as she pulled them on—the skirt and bodice were a perfect fit[24]. It was a little thing, but

---

[24] The troupe's dressmaker, Organza Fifield, had once won a bet by visually deducing the correct clothing sizes of an unfamiliar group of men who had, at the time, been dressed respectively, as an armored knight, a monk, a construct with three arms, and a pantomime horse.

it seemed symbolic, as though she had been accepted into the troupe for real now.

She glanced at the table. There were no papers to be seen—the drawings she had worked on all night were gone. She rummaged through the cupboards and lifted the mattress on the bed. Nothing. A small twinge of panic snapped at the back of her skull. She didn't want her new friends to get the wrong idea... even Krosp had been unusually horrified by some of the designs. Then, she realized that Krosp had most likely been the one who took them. Still, Agatha felt a bit piqued. She'd worked hard on those plans.

She pushed open the door and stopped in surprise. "We've moved!"

The circus had pulled off the road, and was camped in a wide field dotted with pine trees. Agatha took a deep breath. The smell made her think of the Christmas holidays[25]. Nearby, a fast-flowing river burbled down a rocky slope.

Guntar and Otto looked up from the dismantled husk of Smilin' Stev. Guntar waved a wrench in greeting. "Good afternoon! You've been asleep most of the day!" Several sawhorse tables surrounded them, covered with carefully laid out parts and tools.

Otto chimed in: "Is true. We hit a stretch of the good road, found this spot and camped early while we still have much bright light for working!"

[25] In the Transylvanian region, Saint Nikkolaus is known as a benevolent Spark who has learned how to bend time and space in such a way that he can deliver presents to good children everywhere in one night. His companion, Blank Peter, is a construct, who does all the heavy lifting. So onerous is this job, that Blank Peter actually wears out from the strain (cookies depicting him are a holiday favorite, and small children take a sadistic joy in "nibbling Blank Peter Down."). Jolly old St. Nikkolaus then selects several "Bad Children," takes them back home to Spain and uses them to create a *new* Blank Peter. Thus the Christmas season continues to be a time of both joy and terror, as it should be.

Guntar nodded. "We'll have ol' Stev here good as new in no time. He broke down three times today, and I don't like holding everyone up."

Balthazar was sitting on a nearby boulder, balancing a gear on a stick. "But it was kind of weird, that old Baba Yaga didn't break down once."

From inside Stev's shell, Rivet's voice echoed. "It was *damn* weird. No breakdowns, no jamming, and I swear the gearage improved *while* I was driving it." She popped up from the depths and gave Agatha a piercing look. "What the heck did you do to it?"

Agatha looked back blankly. "But... I haven't done *anything*. Not yet..." Rivet looked at her with raised eyebrows. "I mean, I looked it over, and I made some sketches, but everyone's been keeping me so busy that I just haven't had the time."

Rivet's eyebrows were now drawn down in a scowl. "No." She shook her head. "No. I refuse to believe that you're some kind of magical Spark who can fix something just by 'making a few sketches.'"

Agatha held up her hands. "Well it wasn't me!"

Rivet thought a moment, and looked like she was running through the events of the previous day in her head. "Yeah... you *were* busy all day yesterday. Huh. That's really weird. But..."

Rivet did not like mysteries. She disappeared back into the damaged clank, grumbling: "*Somebody's* been messing with that furschlugginer chicken house, and *I* want to find out *who*!"

Under the eaves of a nearby wagon, three miniscule clanks paused, cables dangling from their delicate mechanical hands. The cables were already partially strung, winding behind woodwork, through reworked cabinetry, and along newly redesigned axles.

The clanks looked at their leader in silent appeal. The little golden pocket-watch clank looked up from the sheaf of drawings it was studying and waved them back to work.

A short distance away a scene of shocking animal cruelty was unfolding. Unusually, the expected roles were reversed, but none of those involved appeared to appreciate the irony.

Krosp stood atop an upended barrel, enthusiastically pumping away at a concertina. He was also making a game attempt at singing and dancing. His song ranged from unearthly high-pitched yowls down to disturbing rumbling growls, all delivered with the vocal energy of an opera singer in a bar fight.

The troupe members who formed the small audience sat stunned by the spectacle before them.

"It's... it's just such a waste," Abner said over the cacophony. "A cat who sings! Dances!"

Marie sighed. "But... not very well."

Professor Moonsock had her hands over her ears. "He's *terrible*!"

The Countess tried to find a positive side. "But he is a real cat who really sings and dances." Krosp's concertina playing was so awful that Marie couldn't even try to find a good side to it.

Payne nodded slowly. "That's the problem, I think. He's unmistakably real." Krosp came to the end of the song and finished with a shrill musical flourish that cracked one of the lenses in Professor Moonsock's glasses. "It might be best if we kept him off the stage entirely. We don't want to lose him, after all..."

"Lose him!" Professor Moonsock snorted. "Are you kidding?

If anyone tries to steal him, we'll just have him sing for them!"

Krosp flattened his ears. "Ridiculous! I know I'm not yet ready for the Paris Opera—" André gasped and sat down, looking pale. "But this is hardly Paris! You can't *all* have tin ears! This show *needs* my talent!"

Payne nodded judiciously. "I quite agree! Not using someone as unique as you would be quite a waste."

Abner perked up. "Background wow?"

Payne nodded. "Background wow."

"Background what?" Agatha asked Krosp as they trudged across the field.

"The idea," Krosp said, "is to have a few 'fabulous monsters' in the background. Doing everyday, normal things."

"Like how they have Yeti running the concession stand[26]?"

"Yeah, he's the example they gave me. He's big and looks great, but apparently he gets a nosebleed and faints if he goes onstage. But he's strong as an ox, so he helps set up the tents; he's got a good voice, so he does announcements; and he's great at making change, so he sells snacks. The rubes are supposed to see him and say: 'Golly-gee, if *that's* what they have selling crunch muffins and cider, let's go see what kind of *amazing* things are in the *actual show*!'"

Agatha was impressed. "That's pretty clever."

"Classic misdirection," it was a term Krosp had just learned,

[26] Yeti claimed that he came from an enlightened, five-thousand-year-old utopia, the last remnant of a lost civilization that had deliberately hidden itself away from the eyes of mankind high in the Himalayan Mountains near Tibet. He further claimed that everyone there was as tall, as furry, and as Sparky as himself. Nobody believed this, of course, since Yeti's accent sounded exactly like the ones found in the Chinese neighborhoods in Istanbul, but they agreed that it was a great story.

but he used it with grudging approval.

Agatha tried to project cheer. "Well, don't look so down. It's an important part of the show! And you can still practice with the other stuff, um, well, outside of camp somewhere, probably... and, and until then, you really do *look* wonderful!"

Even though Krosp's ears were flattened against his skull, Agatha could tell that he agreed. The cat now wore a brilliantly red, military-style, high-collared greatcoat with elegantly fringed epaulets. It was encrusted with almost a kilogram of shiny gold trim, frogging and stamped buttons, and it was a perfect fit. Against Krosp's white fur, the effect was stunning.

"It was very nice of them to say you could keep it," Agatha continued.

Krosp shrugged as they came to the wagon that held tack and animal feed. The horses and other creatures that pulled the circus wagons were clustered nearby. "They don't need it any more, Balthazar outgrew it."

Agatha tried again. "...and it really does bring out your natural leadership qualities."

Krosp eyed her dangerously as he selected a flat shovel. "No kidding."

"Really. And... and don't forget that you're making a valuable contribution—"

Krosp tossed a shovelful of horse dung into a bucket. "Just *drop* it," he snarled.

At that moment, Balthazar trotted up, a large wooden bowl of what looked like mechanical flowers balanced on his head. "Hey, Agatha! They want you at Master Payne's wagon!"

With guilty relief, Agatha left Krosp behind. "What's going on?" Agatha asked the boy as he danced ahead of her.

"We'll be hitting the town of Zumzum in a day or two, so they're assigning parts for the show."

Everyone was clustered around a big fire pit that had been built in the center of camp. Abner and Master Payne sat together, between two great ornate chests that stood open. A thick, leather-bound ledger lay in Payne's lap.

"Master Payne is checking what we did in Zumzum the last time we came through two years ago." Balthazar explained. "That way we give them a fresh show."

Payne made a notation in his book. "—and we'll finish up with some of Dame Ædith's knife throwing."

"Glorious!" she declared.

"And this time—" Abner warned, "Do *not* ask if there are any vampires in the audience."

"By my faith! How was *I* to know that fool was *joking*?" she groused, "What sane man would joke about *vampyres*?"

"One less now, I suspect," Abner replied. Ædith folded her arms and sat back down with a huff.

Payne clapped his hands. "This brings us to the main performance, and the show we will be performing."

There was a sudden uproar, as many of the troupe members called out suggestions.

"Ooh! Ooh! *Clockwork Sundial*!"

"How about *The Fog Merchants*? There's some ladder business I want to try in scene two."

"Could we *please* do something with some music? Might I suggest *The Racing Snails of Dr. Zagreb*?"

Abner waved his hands for quiet. "It's already been decided.

We're doing *The Heterodyne Boys and the Race to the West Pole.*" He paused and let this sink in. Frowns turned to smiles and nods of appreciation.

"A welcome change of pace, that one," Dame Ædith conceded. She darted a look at Pix. "But I thought our Pix did not like playing the Lady Lucrezia."

Pix nodded. "Indeed I don't. But *West Pole* has some of the best scenes ever written for the High Priestess, and I'm *finally* going to get to play them. *Agatha* can play Lucrezia, and she's welcome to her."

Agatha felt her jaw drop. "What? But I've never *done* any acting!"

Pix smiled at her. "Don't worry. She's the ingénue—the most boring part in all of theater. All you really have to do is rant around and look pretty. The rest of us will make sure it goes smoothly."

The other players looked startled. Lucrezia was the lead female role in most of the Heterodyne plays. Admiring looks were directed at Abner, who was studiously examining the binding on one of the scripts. He looked up. "Don't look at me, people. I was ready to wrestle the axe out of her hands if I had to, but she really means it."

Pix grinned mischievously. "Oh, dear, surely you all didn't think I would throw a tantrum? Tsk. I don't want the frilly, pretty roles, I want the *good* ones! *I* am an *actress,* and don't you forget it!"

Abner stood up. "It'll be fine," he announced. "I expect everyone to help her out. Lars says she's already pretty good, and I've learned to judge his instincts." He stepped up to Agatha and handed her a small, leather-bound booklet. "Besides, he plays Bill, and he's really good at onstage coaching. Trust him."

Agatha held the booklet as if it might explode. "But what if I can't do it?"

Abner shrugged. "Well, if it comes to that, we've found that none of the Heterodyne plays really *suffer* if Punch and Judy start throwing pies."

There was a pause as Agatha digested this. "I'm going to go study my lines," she announced.

As she scampered off, Taki puffed out his chest and grinned. "Another demonstrable success for my *Unified Pie Theory*!"

Abner sat back down. "Yeah, yeah. So publish already." He handed the cook a booklet. "You're Klaus."

"Of course!"

Hours later, Agatha was back in the Baba Yaga. She lay on her bunk, legs halfway up the wall and head hanging over the edge[27]. "Do not tempt me," she recited. "Your brother approaches, and I must go!"

Krosp flipped the final page of the script. "Um—blah, blah, exploding bananas—blah, blah, pole of my heart..." He closed the booklet. "That was your last line." He looked up. "Good job. I'm impressed. You read it through twice and you've already memorized it."

Agatha waved a hand dismissively. Before Doctor Beetle had passed down the order that she was to be allowed to sit in on any class she pleased, Agatha had often been chased out of the lecture halls at Transylvania Polygnostic University. She had got

[27] Science has proven that this position actually improves memorization. One of the reasons older people have difficulty remembering things is that they refuse to sit like this because they feel foolish doing so. More fool they.

to the point where she could usually remember the contents of a chalkboard after just a glance. Lately, this talent for memory seemed to be getting even stronger. "I thought about it a lot," her voice trailed off and her face took on an odd look.

Krosp frowned. "Something wrong?"

Agatha rolled onto her front. "This all feels so strange... I mean, if I really *am* the daughter of Bill and Lucrezia Heterodyne—"

Krosp frantically waved one paw for silence even as he leapt across the room and slammed the little window shut. Agatha lowered her voice.

"Well if I *am*—then these stories—*all* the Heterodyne stories—are about my family. My *parents*." She sat up. "This part: Lucrezia. I'm playing my own mother. And Lars is playing my father."

Krosp scratched his chin with a rear foot. "So?"

Agatha hugged her pillow uncomfortably. "So... there's kissing and stuff. It feels weird."

Krosp nodded sagely. "Okay, so when you kiss him, don't think of him as Bill Heterodyne. Think of him as Gilgamesh Wulfenbach. You liked *him*."

The pillow slammed into the cat so fast he didn't have time to dodge.

"I don't want to be reminded of that," Agatha growled. She *had* kissed Gil once, on impulse, after the terrifying fight with the Hive Queen. But that had been a quick, one-sided victory kiss, and she hadn't even seen his reaction. She still cringed at the thought of it.

"I will *not* be kissing Gilgamesh Wulfenbach. Now, or ever again." she declared—trying to push his face from her mind.

Krosp peeped out from under the pillow. "I know that! You're kissing that what's-his-name. Lars."

Agatha paused. "What?"

"Well he's the one who plays Bill Heterodyne, right?"

Agatha remembered her surprise at the easy strength with which Lars had lifted her free of the barrel. The friendly look in his eyes as he laughed with her. The little tingle she had felt when his voice shifted as he had dropped into character. That had been... interesting.

Thoughtfully Agatha retrieved her pillow and settled down to sleep.

Lars. He wasn't even a Spark. Kissing him should be safe enough.

FOUR

When Jägermonsters hunt for you
Remember what you mustn't do:
Don't jump in a butt of wine,
 They'll find you hiding there just fine.
 Don't hide with the grain or meat,
  You'll be the first thing that they eat.
 Don't hide with the dung or offal,
  They'll just spread you on a waffle.
 Don't hide in among the dead,
  They'll eat you up with jam and bread.
 But hide in water, soap and lye,
  and far away from you they'll fly!

—CHILDREN'S SONG

It was a beautiful morning in the town of Zumzum, and the shops lining the square were doing brisk business. The square itself was a large open area covering a full hectare. Part of it was paved in dark blue stone, but a good half of it was still greensward, occupied by a small flock of sheep and a few cows, idly grazing. A bored-looking child with a stick sat watching the animals, lounging back against the base of a squat tower that stood to one side. The tower, with its limp windsock hanging from a pole, hinted at occasional airship traffic. Zumzum was right on the edge of the Wastelands, but it wasn't yet completely the middle of nowhere.

A covered market bordered the paved side of the square. It was just a slate-shingled roof atop sturdy wooden posts, but it kept the sun and rain off. Five small boys with brooms were inside the empty structure industriously sweeping at cross-purposes. Tomorrow would be the weekly market-day, when farmers from all over the area would make their way to town to buy and sell, drink, and exchange gossip. Tomorrow, the square would be a noisy, bustling place, full of excitement. Tomorrow would be fun. Today, however, was boring. Miserably, miserably boring.

Three pairs of eyes stared out at the scene glumly. Their owners were watching the movement of the shadows across the green, counting down the hours until market day, when they would have something to look at besides grazing livestock.

"She's gunna *keel* uz hyu know," muttered the one on the right, for easily the hundredth time.

The one in the middle rolled his eyes. "Hy know, Hy *know*."

The left one snorted. "Ho! Ve should get off so easy."

The one on the right tried to nod, but that didn't work very well. He gave up. "Hyu gots dot right, brodder."

The middle one considered this solemnly. "Hy vill admit dot she ken be unreasonable, bot in dis caze, Hy tink mebbe she gots some cause."

The right one scowled. "Iz dot supposed to make me feel better? Iz not vorkink."

The one on the left brightened. "Hey! *Vait* a minute! Mebbe ve gets lucky! *Mebbe* ve be *dead* by der time she gets here!"

The three considered this. "I hadn't thought uf dot," the middle one admitted.

The right one sighed. "Iz hyu crazy? Den ve'd really be in trouble." Suddenly, his attention was caught by the group of people in showy clothing walking toward them across the grass. He brightened. "Hoy! Brodders! Company!"

Master Payne and Lars stared up at the three Jägermonsters hanging by their necks from the gallows. They were a strange-looking trio—all the Jägermonsters had presumably once been human, or at least, that was the rumor, but whatever change had been worked on them long ago had given them strange, monstrous features that set each of them apart, even from his fellow Jägers.

The first of the three, in addition to the pointed ears and claws common to most of his kind, had long flowing hair and skin of a purplish hue that looked as if it had been that color even before its owner had been strung up. His face was finely boned and handsome, with sharp teeth that jutted over his lips from his lower jaw. The second sported a large ram's horn—

curling out from one side of a mop of dirty blonde hair. His feet were huge and unshod, with two great toes that looked like fat bird claws. The third had skin so olive it was actually green, and dark, untidy hair that ran down the sides of his wide face into a little pointed beard. He, of the three, was the only one who still wore a hat—a green billed cap that matched his skin topped by a pair of worn goggles. A long plume like a horse's tail sprang from a small carved skull in the top center, to cascade down his back. The creatures swung slowly in an almost nonexistent breeze, hands tightly tied behind their backs.

"Are you *insane*?" Payne turned to Lars. "We can't perform here!"

Lars cast a glance at the watchman, a grizzled old soldier wearing armor emblazoned with the town seal. The man stood back deferentially, but he was observing them closely. His face was carefully blank.

"I know, sir." Lars rolled his eyes. "Believe me, I tried. But all entertainments have to be performed in the town square. As it was, I had enough trouble convincing them to let us camp on the meadow. I actually had to pay out some coin for that."

Payne frowned, but he knew Lars was good at his job. If money had to be spent, it wasn't because Lars was a fool. Even so, this was a bit much. "Performing next to corpses is disrespectful! *And* unhygienic!"

Now Lars really looked uncomfortable. "Ah, well, if *that's* your only qualm…"

The green Jäger grinned down at them apologetically—flashing an alarming collection of large, pointed teeth. "Sorry for der problemz," he called out in a friendly, slightly strangled, voice.

A man of Master Payne's dignity rarely leapt into the air in surprise. Lars grinned in spite of the situation. He felt privileged to have been a witness to it. "They're still *alive*?" Payne was incredulous.

"They've been up there for two days, sir." Lars said, "Apparently, they just aren't dying."

Payne stared at the watchman in confusion. "But... after a hanging... they're supposed to be cut down after twenty-four hours. The Baron's rules of conduct and hygiene..."

"That's a bit of a grey area, sir," the watchman answered stoically. "According to our Mayor, that's twenty-four hours after they're dead and all."

Payne glanced at Lars, who nodded. "The Mayor's got a betting pool going over how long they'll last."

Payne's lip curled. "Lovely."

"Oh, he is that." Lars agreed.

"Well..." Payne looked at the town. Its charm had soured in his eyes. "Fine. One night. We re-supply essentials only, charge double and leave at dawn."

Lars was surprised. "But I've paid for three days. Tomorrow's a market day—" Payne gave him a look that stopped him cold. "One night. Yessir."

As they moved off the Jägers grinned at each other. "Did hyu hear dot?"

"Yah! Ve gets to see a show. For free!"

It was going to be an interesting day after all.

* * *

Tonight would be Agatha's first show as a real part of the troupe. Agatha had expected Zeetha to forego the usual morning training—but that had proved wishful thinking. She had been awakened—before sunrise, as always—by the now-familiar beep on her nose.

Zeetha's foot had healed quickly, and she had celebrated the removal of her bandages by singing a boisterous song in Skifandrian as she trotted behind Agatha on her morning run. Before the run, she had presented Agatha with two heavy buckets full of water, and whenever her pupil had spilled any, or showed signs of slowing down, Zeetha had cheerfully kept time by swatting her across the backside with the freshly-cut switch she carried for just that purpose.

As a result, it had taken some effort for Agatha to stand up straight, wave and smile as the circus caravan rumbled through the cheering crowd at the town gates.

As Zeetha was fond of reminding her, Agatha was still in hiding. To the world outside Master Payne's Circus of Adventure, she was still Madame Olga: the teller of fortunes. In the odd corners of her days, when Agatha was not peeling vegetables, repairing bits of machinery or running from Zeetha's stick, she practiced the essential skills she would need for her new identity: observation and lying. The troupe's sharpshooter, Thundering Engine Woman, was quite a good fortune teller herself, and she had been coaching Agatha in the tricks of the trade. As the circus rolled into the town of ZumZum, she stood at Agatha's side waving, smiling, and muttering last minute advice. "Remember—eye contact, knowing smile, then look away mysteriously. And for goodness sake, show a little more ankle!"

* * *

An hour later, the square had been transformed. The cows and sheep had been moved aside, and now the wagons were arranged in a tight circle on the green. Sideshow booths had been set up, and, even though they would leave the next day, the circus roustabouts were assembling the largest and most elaborate of the Circus' stages.

The preparations were all of great interest to the three Jägers. Having nothing better to do, they held a long, lazy discussion of past Heterodyne shows they had seen, comparing them to the real people and events on which they were supposedly based. When they got tired of that, they made a game of guessing what each performer's act might be. Through it all, they cheerfully called out helpful suggestions and friendly remarks to the female members of the troupe, who grimly ignored them.

Suddenly, the wind shifted. The green Jäger stiffened in surprise. The other two were in the middle of a drawn-out argument over the best way to dip a cat in caramel, when he growled at them. "Hey! Shot op! *Shot op!*"

The other two looked sideways at him with mild astonishment. "Use hyu *noses*!" he ordered.

They paused. Then, as best they could, they drew in great breaths of air, slowly savoring the mélange of odors that filled the square.

Suddenly, the middle Jäger opened his eyes wide. The one on the end sniffed a moment longer, then his eyes also bugged. The three monsters darted their eyes about, intensely examining each person in the square until, finally, they all found their target. They glanced at each other, excitement showing plainly in their eyes.

It was going to be a very interesting day indeed.

When Thundering Engine Woman caught sight of the gallows with its dangling Jägers, she stopped dead. "Okay. Right here will be perfect." She dropped the handle of the small cart she had been hauling behind her and glanced at the ground, mentally measuring an open space to one side of the posts.

Agatha looked up and blanched. "Here? Are you kidding?"

The other girl shook her head. "Nope. When people see something like that, they start to wonder what's going to happen to *them*. They'll flock right in, and anything *you* tell them will seem a lot better in comparison. You'll make a fortune." She dragged the cart to a good spot and began to remove the canvas wrapping.

"That seems kind of... callous."

The girl nodded as she tugged the last of the cover away. She folded it and set it on the grass, well away from the cart—now revealed as a complex crate made of polished wooden and brass slats. "Probably, but I shoot things for a living. If you want sensitivity, go talk to André. Now, watch carefully. You'll have to do this yourself, next time."

Agatha continued to stare at the Jägers. "But what did they do?"

Thundering Engine Woman snorted. "Be Jägermonsters and get captured. Doesn't take a whole lot more than that around here." She took hold of a pair of handles and pulled.

Jointed poles unfolded and silk billowed.

Agatha bit her lip. "But—won't the Baron be upset?"

At this, the old watchman, who had been leaning against a nearby wall, came toward them. "The Baron don't care about *them*, Miss."

The two women looked at him in surprise. Agatha would have sworn the man had been drowsing in the late-morning sun. "Sergeant Zulli, at your service, ladies," he said, touching his polished helmet. His smile was indulgent, as though he were addressing children. "We're too small and out of the way here." He waved a hand at the tattered windsock. "It's a rare event when we even see the Baron's patrol ships overhead."

"But still, if someone comes looking for them—"

"No need to fret about that, Miss. These fine fellows aren't part of the Baron's forces. What we've got here is a genuine pack of *wild Jägers*!"

Agatha stared at the three in surprise. They grinned down at her silently.

Zulli continued, "And to them with long memories, them what remembers the old Heterodynes, that makes these critters fair game." He paused for a moment to look up at the captives. From the expression that settled on his face, Agatha guessed that the old guardsman's memory was very long indeed.

"But Bill and Barry—"

Zulli snapped out of his reverie and smiled again. "Bless you, Miss. Of course they were the good ones." He ran an appraising eye over her so frankly that Agatha blushed. "Young thing like you, they're probably the only Heterodynes you know." His eyes again looked into the distance, watching scenes that had happened long ago.

"But before them there were the old Heterodynes—The Masters of Mechanicsburg. Murdering devils, every one of them. The Jägers rode with *them,* back then, in a great howling horde. They'd come riding down, swarms of them, killing for sport, pillaging and looting, laying waste to whatever they couldn't carry off. They made a point of hitting our town for tribute every four years or so, sure as the moonrise."

As the old sergeant spoke, the Jägers, too, seemed to be looking into the past. Agatha watched them closely now, feeling a bit less sympathy than before.

"*That's* what the old folks remember," Zulli concluded. He pulled an obscenely carved pipe from his pocket and struck a match on the purple Jäger's boot, then puffed in satisfaction as he looked up at the three subdued creatures. "For them folks, living and dead, this is just an example of the wheels of justice grinding slow but fine." The old man's jovial mood seemed to have soured, and his face had set in hard lines. "Good day, ladies. Looking forward to your show." He gave them an abrupt half-salute and strolled off.

Agatha continued to study the Jägers, who stared back at her solemnly. She felt an odd sense of betrayal. The Jägers back on Castle Wulfenbach had been... she paused in her thoughts, confused.

Well, she couldn't really say they'd been especially kind, or terribly smart, or even particularly *helpful*... but she realized that she had liked them—been drawn to them. *Trusted* them. Trusted them to do what, exactly, she couldn't say, but the fact was that she had felt comfortable around them. Now that she knew about her family, that made sense, but...

"I hadn't ever really thought about the old Heterodynes,"

she admitted. "I mean, I knew they were... *bad*, but nobody ever really talks about it."

Thundering Engine Woman tacked up some loose bunting. "Yeah, well, Bill and Barry really redeemed the Heterodyne name. I think their family history is probably the reason they were always trying to do so much good." She stepped back and examined the booth with a nod of satisfaction. "But people still scare their kids with stories about the Jägermonsters. *They* were—" she paused, and stared upward as if something had just caught her attention. "Actually, damn creepy is what they are."

Agatha followed her gaze. "What do you mean?"

"They've been staring at you non-stop." Agatha realized that this was true. They hadn't taken their eyes off her through the whole conversation with Sergeant Zulli. They were still watching her, silently, their expressions unreadable.

Agatha shivered. "Maybe we should set up somewhere else?"

"Too late." The fortune-teller's tent was completely unfolded now. Silken walls fluttered in the breeze, striped with deep blue and purple sprinkled with golden stars. Yeti had strolled up with a stack of signs under his massive arm, and was standing with his head tipped back, examining the setup. He selected a wooden board, and hung it on a pair of hooks outside the tent:

WHAT IS YOUR FATE?

MADAME OLGA

MISTRESS OF

THE SCIENCE OF

TELLURICOMNIVISUALIZATION

SEES ALL!

KNOWS ALL!

Thundering Engine Woman rubbed her hands together and grinned. "And look! Your first customer!"

It was true. Already standing in front of the booth was a shy-looking young woman in drab clothing, obviously trying to work up the courage to go in.

Agatha dithered, "But I'm not ready! I haven't looked over my notes! I've only got part of my costume on!"

Thundering Engine Woman snorted. "You can put the finishing touches on later. Look, if they'll believe *I'm* a real American, they'll believe *you're* a real fortuneteller."

"You're not a real American?" Agatha blinked in surprise. Thundering Engine Woman had long black braids, and was dressed in flashy beaded buckskins.

"Whoo. You *are* nervous. The real Thundering Engine Woman traveled with the Heterodyne Boys! How old do you think she'd be by now? I'm just an actress from Italy—but I tell them I'm from America and the crowds eat it up. They'll swallow your act, too. Just remember they mostly want a sympathetic ear and validation of decisions they've already made." She gently pushed Agatha forward. "Oh yeah, and lie a lot."

"Okay, okay, I can—" Agatha stumbled with the push, and found herself face to face with the young woman, who stared at her blankly. Agatha straightened up and thought quickly. She really wished she had had time to put on her fancy headdress. Oh, well. She placed her hand upon her brow theatrically and intoned: "I sense that you have... questions."

The customer's eyes widened. "Wow! How do you *do* that?"

Agatha was thrown for a moment, but she quickly regained her composure. "Enter my tent, child. The power of SCIENCE shall reveal all!" With a flourish, she held open the tent and gestured the girl inside. Perhaps fortunetelling would be easier than she'd thought.

Yeti and Thundering Engine Woman watched this performance with amusement. When the tent flap was closed and murmuring voices could be heard from inside, Yeti smiled. "Not bad," he conceded.

Suddenly, Agatha's astonished squeal arose from within the tent. "YOU DID *WHAT*?"

"I'd say she needs work," Thundering Engine Woman sighed.

A minute later, Agatha held aside the tent flap with a shaking hand. The quiet young woman stepped out, eyes demurely cast toward the ground. Agatha's voice had an odd pitch to it as she gave her final pronouncement: "Have no fear, my child, the data indicate that all will be well." She stood in the doorway with a grin frozen on her face until the girl was out of sight.

Yeti stepped up. "Something wrong?"

Agatha blushed. "People around here are... very strange."

Yeti tried hard to keep his face blank, but his black eyes shone with amusement. "Well, you have to keep an open mind," he said, fighting back a smile. "People in different places do different things. It doesn't necessarily make them *bad*, it just makes them *different*. That's one of the fun things about travel."

Agatha looked at him. Yeti should know. Zeetha had told her that he came from a land high on a distant mountain, and that he had traveled through all kinds of exotic places for years before joining up with the Circus. "It isn't that. It's just... how can I give people advice when I don't understand the problem? Maybe everything that girl was telling me is perfectly *normal* here. For all *I* know, she was only worried because she'd used the wrong *spoon*."

Yeti's curiosity was definitely piqued. "Well, you can go pretty far using common sense, logic and—"

"Whooo! I hear you got a *spicy one*!" Zeetha bounded out of nowhere and draped an arm across Agatha's shoulders. "Gimme the details!"

Yeti shrugged. "And when necessary, ask an expert."

"You're an expert in…?" Agatha blushed, "erm… weird stuff?"

Zeetha raised her eyebrows and gave her a long, mock serious look. "Oh, yes indeed. Skifander's patron goddess is Ashtara—she who, among other things, watches over luuurve!" She threw her arms into the air and flowed into a sinuous, undulating dance that caused Yeti to fan himself appreciatively. "*Our* holy days are *fun*! Cha cha cha!"

Agatha relaxed enough to laugh. "Well, I think I just found you a new bishop."

Zeetha snorted in derision and punched Agatha's arm. "Ha! You're just getting started. Talk to me in a week!"

After that, Agatha was busy for hours. The fancy headdress she had planned to wear as Madame Olga sat untouched in its hatbox, since so many people had come to have their fortunes told. Finally, Dame Ædith's knife throwing exhibition had drawn off the crowd, and from the "oohs," "aahs," and occasional "Aiee!" it was apparent that she had their attention.

As Agatha was about to open the hatbox at last, Balthazar rolled up, balancing atop a barrel. It was time to prepare for the main show, and he had been sent to fetch her. A small cold lump formed in her chest.

Feeling light-headed, Agatha closed up the fortuneteller's tent and made her way to the now-familiar canvas labyrinth that had sprouted behind the main stage.

As soon as she arrived, someone gave a shout, and the backstage staff pounced. She was unceremoniously stripped down and buttoned into a costume—someone barked: "Close your eyes!" and began smearing makeup across her face and neck, and someone else began to tug at her hair, pinning it up in what felt like a very odd style.

Agatha told herself that, as an actress, she would eventually get used to swarms of people rushing past while she was undressed. She closed her eyes and tried to imagine that she was simply a subject in one of the bizarre sociology experiments back at Transylvania Polygnostic University that had occasionally scandalized the town. Agatha herself had never taken part in one—the waiting lists were enormous.

Marie poked her head through the doorway. "Ten minutes," she sang out. "Nervous?"

Agatha grimaced. "Only because people keep asking me that."

Guntar stood in the corner, getting an elaborate set of construct stitching applied to the exposed parts of his body. He laughed. "Relax! If you mess up, we'll cover for you."

Balthazar trotted up, a wobbling rack of pies as tall as himself balanced on his head. "Here's the rest of the pies, daddy!"

Agatha eyed the tower of pastry. "Okay, *now* I'm nervous."

Marie startled her by clapping her hands together with a sharp pop. "No, no, no! You're not nervous, you're *Lucrezia Mongfish*! You're mad! You're bad! You're *dangerous*!"

Agatha nodded. "Yes! Yes! 'I think too much—therefore I

am mad!' Grrr!" She tried to smile like a Jäger, and succeeded well enough that Marie took a step backwards in alarm.

"That's...that's very good."

Abner appeared, clutching a sheaf of paper, and snapping his fingers. Agatha heard a line of dialogue coming through the curtain that separated her from the stage: "I pray the mistress is in a good mood—" The line sounded familiar...

Marie took Agatha's arm and firmly steered her towards the stage. "That's your cue! Go!"

Agatha found herself directly behind center stage, her nose nearly brushing the curtain edges. She took a deep breath, grabbed one in each hand, and threw them back, roaring: "Of course I am! For it is a *glorious* day—"

"FOR *SCIENCE*!!" the audience thundered back.

Agatha took a deep breath and froze in horror. There, looming at least a head above the rest of the audience, was the unmistakable figure of Othar Tryggvassen.

Panic welled up inside her. Othar! Othar had tried to kill her, just for being a Spark! She had barely managed to save herself by pushing the self-proclaimed hero over the side of the airship as they had escaped from Castle Wulfenbach.

Yet here he was, alive, larger than life, and evidently having a wonderful time. Well why not? He had just discovered an entire troupe of Sparks. He could fill his quota for the month without even having to open his eyes.

It was "Bumbling Minion Number Three" who saved the day. The actor had been warned that he might have to deal with a case of "first night nerves," and he was ready. As Agatha turned to flee, he clung tightly to her hand, cleared his throat, and shouted: "Has the trap been set, Mistress?"

The gears of Agatha's mind finally engaged. That was her cue. The response she had practiced so many times burst from her mouth before she realized what she was doing: "Yes! And soon, *all* of the Heterodyne secrets will be *mine*!"

And so the show went on. She'd just have to warn everyone when she got off stage, if Othar let her live that long. From the way he was cheering along with the crowd, he would at least let her finish the play.

She managed to remain Lucrezia Mongfish all throughout the first act, but as the curtain closed, she felt her hands beginning to shake. Before she could find a place to sit or collapse, she was grabbed from behind. The fastenings down the back of her dress were being released in quick sequence. She would have to be back on stage in only a few minutes, and required a complete costume change. "That was a great first act," Marie said.

Agatha allowed herself to relax slightly. Othar still hadn't attacked...

Trish nodded as she threw a new costume across Agatha's shoulders and began to tighten a series of cleverly strung laces. "Very edgy! It was like you expected someone to shoot you or something."

The idea made Agatha go tense again. She took a deep breath. "I think I saw Othar Tryggvassen out there! The big blond guy with the weird visor glasses?"

Trish grinned. "Oh, you saw him? Yeah, he loves our shows!"

Agatha blinked. "He's—you've all met him before?"

The Countess whipped a huge bunch of false curls out of a hatbox and began to fasten it to the back of Agatha's head. It felt like she was using nails. "He gets around a lot. We've seen him five—"

"Six," Trish corrected her.

The Countess nodded. "Correct. Six times in the past year. He buys a lot of popcorn."

"And he hasn't shot anybody?"

Trish gave her an odd look. "Of course not. It's good popcorn. He gets free refills."

Then, Agatha remembered that the Sparks of Master Payne's Circus of Adventure took pains to hide their true talents. Othar most likely saw nothing here but ordinary actors and sideshow wonders. The Spark *could* be hidden.

Finally, Marie stepped back and gestured meaningfully—it was nearly time for her next entrance.

Relief had lifted Agatha's spirits, but the nervous energy that terror had lent her remained. When Lucrezia Mongfish strode into her laboratory in a towering rage and demanded of her three cringing minions: "Who has deactivated my beautiful frogs?" the audience pointed as one to Bill Heterodyne, who lay stripped to the waist and shackled to a huge wooden laboratory table. "*He* did!" they screamed.

All in all, it was a tremendous success.

The rest of the show passed in a kaleidoscopic whirl, and then...suddenly... Lars was kissing her.

They had carefully pecked at each other during rehearsals, but for the real show, Abner had ordered them to hold the kiss as long as the audience cheered them on.

The audience cheered them on for approximately six and a half years. When it was over, Agatha tottered dizzily backward, her face burning. She stuttered through her last lines and fled the stage with as much grace as she could manage.

The Countess caught Agatha as she entered the wings. She

adjusted her hairpiece and tucked her disheveled costume back into place just as the final curtain fell. Then she spun Agatha about and gave her costume one last expert tweak, exposing shoulders and an alarming amount of decolletage in one quick tug before propelling her back onto the stage. She landed hard against Lars, who caught her expertly in the crook of his arm.

At her entrance, the applause doubled in volume. Cheers and whistles filled the air.

Agatha had never received such overwhelming approval as she was getting now—nearly everything she had done at the University had either been ignored or had gotten her into trouble. She drank in the adulation, astonished at how satisfying—how *right* it felt. She ventured a peek at the audience to see how Othar was reacting, and was surprised to see that he was gone.

Lars beamed as he waved to the crowd. He leaned down and whispered in Agatha's ear: "I knew you'd be great!" He took her arm and led her toward the edge of the stage. "Now we head on down and mingle."

Agatha nodded. Othar was much less likely to try to kill her in the center of the crowd—he might hit an innocent bystander—and she didn't think that would fit with his delusions of heroism. She donned her glasses, pulled her costume back onto her shoulders, shook out her skirts, and straightened up to follow Lars—only to walk directly into Othar. He was standing patiently off to one side of the stage, obviously waiting for her. Agatha gave a little shriek of surprise.

Othar laughed genially. "So! Madame Olga!" he boomed, "You are, I'm told, a sayer of sooths and a teller of fortunes, yes?"

Agatha was taken aback. He couldn't possibly have forgotten

her already, could he? Lars leaned in and answered for her. "Indeed she is, sir!"

"Excellent!" Othar looped a muscular arm around her shoulders and began to walk her away. "I would like my fortune told! Now, if you please!"

Agatha was so stunned that she allowed him to gently steer her toward her tent. Less than a minute later, Othar was dropping onto a cushioned chair—leaning his elbows on the ornate little table that stood before Madame Olga's skull-draped throne. Agatha took her time at lighting the vast collection of candles and lanterns that hung around the tent, trying to collect her thoughts.

"A fine performance!" Othar said as he leaned forward, peering at the dials and meters set into the huge brass-bound crystal orb that rested on the table.

"Thank you." Agatha was confused. Othar's body language conveyed no sense of menace whatsoever. Somehow, this only made the tall, jolly man even more frightening.

Othar idly scratched his beard. "You seem a bit on edge."

Agatha spun about to face him directly. "The last time I saw you, you tried to *kill* me!"

"Oh, that." Othar waved a hand in dismissal. "That was before I knew that you were a Heterodyne."

Agatha started. "How could you possibly know that?"

"Why, not long after we—" he coughed politely into his fist, "—parted ways, I ran into a young man who I believe to be your cousin: a Master Theopholous DuMedd?

"You didn't do anything horrible to him, did you?"

Othar paused, and a frown flitted across his features. "Ah, I see. No, I was unaware that he was a Spark." He sighed.

"What a pity. At any rate, he was traveling with a small group of the Baron's hostages who had snatched the opportunity presented by my rather dramatic departure to affect their own escape from Castle Wulfenbach. All very nice young people, and all fans of mine, as it happens!

Young DuMedd told me everything. He was very glad to hear that you were in good hands as my spunky girl assistant!"

Agatha glowered. "I am *not* your assistant. You tried to *kill* me."

Othar waggled an admonitory finger at her. "See? That's why friends shouldn't keep secrets from one another."

"I don't keep secrets! Not from my real friends." Agatha was digging through a small chest to one side of her throne. Who knows what the previous Madame Olga had kept in it? Maybe she could poison his tea.

Othar sat back and folded his arms. "Ah. So these traveling players know who you really are?"

This brought her up short. "No," she admitted, after a deep breath. "No, they don't."

Sergeant Zulli stood atop the city wall, watching the moon rise from behind the eastern mountains. He had just spent a half-hour instructing one of the new recruits in the correct use of the town's prized night scope—and was hoping the boy would prove himself a fast learner. The instrument was huge, an ornate, cumbersome affair full of mirrors, lenses and strange, colored filters, bristling with switches, knobs and gauges all up and down the sides. It had been a gift to the town long ago, built by the local lord—a Spark who occasionally had trouble containing his monsters. Even Zulli had to admit he had no idea how it actually worked, but work it did, and very well, too. A competent operator could view all three roads leading up to the town as clear as day, even on a moonless night[28].

Tonight, Zulli could hear the crowd below—roaring with laughter at the circus' antics. Things were going smoothly, and he was beginning to think he would soon be able to join the fun, when the boy suddenly started back from the scope's eyepiece with a yell of alarm, nearly falling from his perch.

Zulli was at his elbow instantly, steadying him with one hand. "Anybody you know?"

"No sir! There's something coming up the East Road."

Zulli frowned. "Some *thing*—"

"I don't know what it is, but it's big and it's fast."

"That's never a good combination." Zulli removed his helmet and fitted his eye to the scope.

"It should be coming up on the five lengths mark," the boy said.

Zulli spun an engraved wheel and pointed the instrument at a distant road sign—the large white V newly repainted and shining in the dark. He brought the sign into focus just in time to see a blur rush past. He snapped upright, eyes wide. "That's *damn* fast!" The old guard took off at a run, shouting back over his shoulder: "Ring the bell—and get some archers to the East Gate! That's an order!"

Zulli dashed along darkening streets, lit by only the

---

[28] Admittedly, attacks these days were few and far between, but Zumzum had a fair number of young people who maintained a fine old tradition of nighttime assignations. This assured that the scope was manned almost constantly. Sergeant Zulli always glumly predicted that when the town *was* attacked, it would be on a cold and rainy night.

occasional lantern. Now, he could hear the alarm bell tolling from the central watchtower. He cast his eyes about frantically for someone—anyone—he could commandeer to help spread the word, but the streets were empty, the shops dark and locked tight. *Everyone in town must be at the damn circus,* he realized. He hoped that his fellow guards would hear the bell and respond, but the music of the circus and the noise of the crowd drowned out everything else. They might not hear the bell, or they might be too drunk to care.

He skidded around the final corner and swore in dismay. There before him was the East Gate, portcullis up, the great oak and iron doors still wide open. This staggering bit of incompetence was explained by one look at the men on duty. It was Smek and Bodine, a pair of the Mayor's otherwise unemployable relatives. Zulli promised himself he'd break whoever had assigned them to the same shift.

"Red fire!" he shouted as he ran up, "Are you Sparksons *deaf*? Close the damn gate!"

The two guards gaped at him. Bodine was in a state of flustered confusion, but managed to squeak: "But... but Assia Velichou and Pavel Dakar are still outside!"

"They're hunting mushrooms," Smek drawled helpfully.

Zulli delivered a resounding smack to both of their helmets as he tore past them. "You cretins! They've got thirty seconds to get dressed and back inside before we close the gate! Do you hear me out there?" he addressed the darkness beyond the gate in a voice like thunder: "Something's coming! We're closing the gate! Get in here NOW!"

Smek was the smarter of the two. He dashed off and began tugging at the great iron hook that locked the left gate open.

Zulli tugged at the right, while counting under his breath.

Bodine dithered beside him. "We can't just leave them out there—it's dark!"

"Thirty seconds!" Zulli roared as he pulled the hook free.

Smek was already tugging his half of the gate closed. "What's coming?" he gasped.

"I don't know," Zulli admitted, "but you'd better hope it kills you, or Assia's father *will*!"

"S-s-sir!" Bodine whispered. His voice was strangled, terrified.

Another voice spoke. "Hy vish to enter dis town."

The tones were rich and sweet, but the accent froze Sergeant Zulli fast. *We should have killed those Jägers*, he thought.

There was a gust of warm air behind him. He turned slowly, and found himself face to face with the largest brown bear he had ever seen. Deep brown eyes watched him steadily. Avoiding the bear's gaze, he found himself staring at the huge pair of gold rings in its left ear, then at the matching pair in its right. A delicate cough dragged his attention upward. The bear's rider was a Jägermonster, that much was obvious. Its deep blue cloak hung aside slightly, revealing an oddly distorted breastplate. Startled, Zulli realized that the rider was female. Old military man that he was, Zulli had of course heard rumors, jokes, and all kinds of lascivious stories, but he had only half believed them. He had never seen a female Jägermonster before. Now, with one gazing down at him from atop her gigantic bear, the light of the huge gate lanterns throwing vast shadows behind them, the sergeant felt a small flicker of curiosity through his pall of terror.

Her long hair was a fine silvery grey, and her skin—what

little could be seen of it—was a deep olive green. The lower half of her face was muffled under a soft scarf, and her wide-brimmed hat was pulled low over her face. The eyes that showed between were large and expressive. She gazed at him calmly—she wasn't angry... yet.

Zulli opened his mouth and found it had gone dry. He swallowed with difficulty and tried again. "The... the town is closed. Until dawn."

The Jäger sat back and made a pretense of examining the gate. "But de gate iz not yet closed. Hy merely seek—"

A "tung" sounding from the wall overhead was Zulli's only hint that his fellow guards had finally arrived. The rider had already noticed them, of course, and moved her hand before the sound even came, calmly plucking a crossbow bolt out of the air. She examined it briefly, and then casually snapped the shaft in half with her thumb.

"Hy forgiff." She announced to the air. "Vunce." She leaned down towards the shivering watchmen. "Hy em lookink for my boyz."

Thank the Blessed Zenobia they're still alive, Zulli thought. He was just beginning to form a polite answer, when Smek, unable to contain his terror any longer, proved just how stupid he really was by screaming: "FIRE!"

Agatha sank into the fortuneteller's throne and leaned forward with one arm on the little table—positioning herself to fling the telluricomnivisualization ball at Othar's head if he made any sudden moves. "Look" she said. "I'm only going to explain this once. The Baron thinks I'm dead. Gil... thinks I'm dead. That's *good*. That's what I want. I don't want to be a Heterodyne. I don't even want to be a Spark. Not if people like you are going to show up trying to kill me. So I won't. I'll stay here. I'm done with all of that. Finished. And I am certainly not going to go off hero-ing with *you*. Understand?"

Othar leaned back so far that his chair rested on only its two back legs. He crossed his arms behind his head and his mouth twitched upwards in a small, infuriating smile. "Really?" It was more a statement than a question.

At that moment, a great roar erupted outside the tent, followed by screams and a clash of weapons.

Agatha leapt to her feet, knocking over the table and sending the scrying ball whizzing past Othar's ear. The lightning gun that she had been quietly holding under the table was now in full view, but she didn't care about secrecy any more. Ignoring Othar, who had fallen backward off his chair, she swept aside the curtains and took in the scene outside.

Through the blaze of the circus lanterns she could see an enormous bear, towering high as it reared back and gave another tremendous roar. A dozen members of the town watch, and easily twice as many townsmen, were swarming around its feet in desperate battle. Things were not going well for them.

The bear lashed out, its wide paws knocking men about with terrible ease. Astride the creature rode a woman swathed in a midnight-blue cloak, silver hair flying. She deflected arrows and sliced the tops off pikes with a sword that was easily two meters long. It wasn't so much a battle as it was a rout.

"Hy em rapidly loozink my patience," the woman shouted. Agatha paused as she realized that the rider was a Jäger and, as far as Agatha could tell, hadn't actually killed anyone.

Just then, the rider noticed Agatha. She took one look at the lightning gun in Agatha's hands and snarled in fury. Turning her great bear, she faced Agatha directly, and charged.

Agatha desperately pointed the gun and fired. A sharp crack rang out as a burst of dazzling blue light filled the square. When her eyes cleared, Agatha saw that one of the wagons was burning, but the bear and its rider were nowhere to be seen. It was only when the bear crashed back to earth that Agatha realized it must have leapt straight up to avoid the blast. *I didn't know they could do that*, she thought in a daze, just before the bear's rider slammed into her.

The Jäger dashed the weapon from Agatha's hand and stomped it with a booted heel, smashing the center flat with a crackle of blue sparks.

She grabbed Agatha's wrist and leaned in close. "Und now," she hissed, "Ve see vat happens to clever leedle fingers vat play vit nasty leedle toyz—" As the Jäger spoke, she pushed Agatha's index finger backward toward her wrist.

Agatha thrashed backward and screamed in pain. Suddenly, Othar swung in, delivering a solid boot to the side of the Jäger's head, so that she went spinning away from Agatha.

"That's *my* Spunky Girl Sidekick, I'll have you know!" He boomed cheerfully.

Agatha scrambled to her feet. "I am not—"

"Agatha! RUN!" screamed Krosp, who had followed her out of the fortuneteller's tent. Agatha turned, only to find herself staring into the gaping jaws of the bear—its hot breath on her face. Krosp was already in mid-leap, claws extended. As he landed, he buried them in the bear's sensitive nose. The huge animal shrieked in agony and flinched backward, furiously swiping at its face with its paws as the cat ran up its back and launched himself up and away.

Agatha spun about and ran. She passed Sergeant Zulli clutching his limp and bloody arm. He was kicking at the prone watchmen and yelling. "—*Guns*, damn you! Get up! Open the armory and get the *guns*! Shoot all *four* of them!"

Without thinking, she changed her direction until she found herself standing in front of the gallows, and its three Jägers. In the flickering light the three grinning faces took on a demonic quality that sent a shiver down her spine.

The green one spoke. "Problems... Mistress?"

Agatha took a deep breath. "Someone—another Jäger—is attacking the town. The guards are going to shoot you. All of you. I'll cut you down, and you'll get her out of here when you escape."

The purple one nodded. "Oh, yes?"

She paused, "And you'll leave the townspeople alone."

The horned one smiled lazily. "Oh, uv cawze."

Agatha grit her teeth and glowered up at them. "Swear. Swear that's all you'll do. Swear... on your loyalty to the House of Heterodyne!"

Their eyes went wide at this, and this time their grins were honest ones.

"Good vun!"

"Schmot gurl!"

"Ve all so svear, Mistress!"

Agatha dashed away and returned with the smaller chair from Madame Olga's tent. She climbed up next to the closest Jäger, and began hacking at the rope with the folding knife she kept in her boot. It wasn't the best tool for the job, but it was sharp. "I'd better be right about you," she panted.

The rope parted, and the green Jäger landed heavily on his feet. He scraped the ropes binding his wrists against a stone wall—so brutally that they parted. Hands free, he grinned up at her. "Too late to vorry about dot *now,* sveethot!" he called as he bounded away.

The Jäger woman held Othar aloft by his hair as she prepared to slice his head off. "Hyu fights pretty goot," she panted, "But hyu iz too demmed annoyink to be any fun." She raised her sword.

"Schtop! Hyu horr'ble monster-y ting uf evil!" The voice was loud and strong, and a hush fell over the square.

The Jäger blinked in surprise and lowered her sword. "Vot?"

Ranged before her, striking theatrically heroic poses, were the three Jägers from the gallows. They had found weapons, and, inexplicably, hats.

The green Jäger stepped forward and brandished a fist full of gleaming throwing knives held in a very professional-looking grip. "Ve iz Jägerkin," he announced in a ringing voice. "Charged by de ancient contract, vit der job uv savin' all dese pipple!"

The watching crowd of townspeople looked at each other. This was news to them.

The purple one flourished a sword that shone red in the firelight. "Yah, and ve gets to do it by gettin' hyu *outta* here!"

The horned one twirled an immense three-bladed halberd with an effortless twitch of his fingers. "Now—iz hyu gunna run, or iz hyu gunna *die?*"

The female Jäger stared at them for a moment, snorted in amusement, and then, with one flowing move of her arm, tossed Othar high into the air. "Ha-ho! *Dis* vill slow hyu down!" She shouted, and then turned with a swirl of her long blue cape and dashed away. Othar described an elegant parabola high into the air and then crashed to the ground. The Jäger woman stopped, turned, and stared in surprise at the crumpled hero.

The three other Jägers looked at each other uncertainly.

"Sorry," the horned one called. "Vas ve supposed to ketch him?"

The purple one shrugged and grumbled: "Dunno vhy, *Hy* dun like hm."

The green Jäger leapt forward. "Vhatever! Come *on*, brodders! Ve gots a monster hunt!"

At this, the other two brightened up. With a shout of "Ve HUNT!" the three brandished their weapons in one last showman-like flourish, and raced off after the bear and rider— through the streets and out into the dark night beyond the town gates.

The amazed crowd stared after them, wondering whether to applaud. It was only when Master Payne bellowed, "Fire!" that the spell was broken and a crew assembled to douse the burning circus wagon.

With the fire out, the monsters gone, and the gates firmly bolted shut, it was time for a party. The tavernmaster whose house bordered the square had stood everyone a large mug of cider, and the townspeople, as a whole, were feeling extremely accomplished. A pack of monsters run off, a fire put out, and a rather good stage show, all in one night! Why, Zumzum would be the next Paris[29]!

Only the Mayor did not share the festive mood. He huffed up to Sergeant Zulli, his face red and angry. Thanks to the sling on his arm, the old soldier was accepting his latest free drink with his left hand.

The Mayor clutched a severed rope in one fist, and shook it in Zulli's face. "Look! See? This rope was *cut*! That's how those Jägerscum got free! One of those *show* people, I'll be bound!"

Zulli sipped his drink. "A good thing, eh?" He flicked his eyes around the crowded taproom, then gazed back at the Mayor with a significant look.

The Mayor frowned as he surveyed the happy crowd. A large number of the men were sporting bruises, but nothing more serious than that, and the worst bit of property damage had happened to out-of-towners, who hardly counted at all. He could see that everyone was in a surprisingly good mood, and his political sense told him that now was the time to make himself visible, be jolly and congratulatory, and take as much credit as possible. But he wasn't quite ready to let go of his disappointment. He puffed out his moustache. "But now no one will win the bet," he muttered petulantly.

Zulli nodded again. "*Also* a good thing, I think."

The Mayor snorted and tossed the rope to the ground. "Bah!" He looked over at Master Payne. "It was them all right." He glowered at Zulli. "I assume you know what to do?"

Sergeant Zulli actually smiled. "Already done, sir."

* * *

[29] It wasn't.

Later, Master Payne and Abner were examining the burned circus wagon when Rivet strolled up. "Get this—the Sergeant there said we can fix our wagon in town for free!"

Payne was astonished. "Really?" He glanced around the town as if seeing it for the first time. "Well, well," he murmured. "We might have to stay a few days after all."

Abner rubbed his hands together. "Wonderful! I've just been talking to a Frau Velichou who wants us to perform at a *wedding*!" This was also good news. A wedding was a plum job, with lots of tips and free drinks. Payne almost smiled.

Agatha and Othar stood apart, watching the celebrations. Othar was bruised from all his tumbling about, but was surprisingly undamaged. Agatha was beginning to think the man was made of rubber. She shook her head. "*You're* the one who caught them? By playing a game of *hangman*?"

Othar was visibly pleased with himself. "The Jägermonsters love to play games, but they're fuzzy when it comes to rules. That's something you should remember as you set out to fight evil."

Agatha cocked an eyebrow at him. "I told you, I'm not *doing* that. Going out looking for trouble to 'fight evil.' It's ridiculous. You can't make me."

Othar threw his head back and burst out laughing. Agatha stared at him. "*Make* you?" He took off his visor and wiped his eyes. "You ran straight at the danger without even thinking. That is who and what you are." Suddenly, the big man's voice was grave, his manner serious. "You say you want a normal life." He sighed deeply, "We all say that at one time or another. You certainly deserve your chance at it." He stepped back and looked her up and down.

"I'll find you in about three months," he told her. "And we'll see how 'normal' your life is." Then he leaned down, and to Agatha's astonishment, gave her a soft peck on the cheek. His blue eyes were bright and warm.

He grinned and replaced his visor. "But sincerely—Good luck." And with that, he walked back to the tavern, and the admiring crowd that was waiting to hear his tales of adventure and buy him drinks.

Agatha watched him go, her hand gently touching the spot where he'd kissed her.

Krosp materialized at her elbow. "How can someone so stupid be so smart?" he groused.

Agatha dropped her hand and turned away. "He only sees what he wants to see," she growled. "Which is why he's completely wrong about *me*."

Krosp's eyes narrowed as he stared at her. His whiskers twitched. "Ah. Right." He sighed, "Of course."

From the trees of the forest outside town, the Jäger woman listened to the celebratory noise spilling out into the night. As she turned her back to the lights of the town, a huge black shape detached itself from the shadows and lumbered toward her. Even in the darkness, she instinctively found the great bear's moist nose leather and gave it a fond pat. "Ah, Füst. Who iz a goot bear?"

Füst snorted happily and nuzzled her hand. Without turning, she addressed the air. "Hokay—Hy know hyu eediots iz dere. Come on out."

From the deep gloom under the trees, the other three Jägers

appeared—smug grins on their faces. The Jäger woman looked them over. "Maxim, Ognian und Dimo. Vot vas dot all about? Iz hyu seriously telling me—"

"Dot ve found a Heterodyne? Ho, yaz!" Maxim's purple eyes shone in the darkness.

Ognian's toothy grin seemed to reach to both ears. "It'z a gurl. But de schmell, de voice..." He thumped his halberd on the ground—"She iz uf de bloodline!" he declared.

Dimo nodded quietly, but with certainty. "Dere iz no mistake, Jenka," he agreed.

"A gurl?" The others nodded. Jenka abruptly sat down. The three stepped forward in concern, but she waved a hand in reassurance. "Dot iz... sooprizink." She sat still a moment, and then, with a single graceful bound, leapt astride her bear. She pointed at the other three. "Hyu three vill stay vit her."

Dimo was surprised. "Iz dot all?"

Jenka took a deep breath. "Our task vas to find a Heterodyne. This ve haff done." She sat back. "Now de qvestion iz—vot iz to be *done* vit her?"

The three looked at each other in surprise. "Hyu gots to ask?" Maxim was puzzled.

Jenka consulted the stars and began steering her bear between the trees. "It haz been too long. Hy vant... instructions." She waved a hand at them. "Until den, just keep her alive."

And with that, bear and rider vanished into the night.

FIVE

PASSHOLDT FRIED CRÈME "TINGS"

Preparation Time: 35 minutes

Cooking Time: 30 minutes

INGREDIENTS

80 g (3/8 cup) sugar

80 g (2/3 cup) unbleached flour

4 eggs

500 ml (1 pint) fresh whole milk,

brought to a boil and allowed to cool

The zest of half a lemon, in strips

1 Tablespoon mild fruit liqueur

Salt

Unsalted butter, for frying

A piece of stick cinnamon

Breadcrumbs

PREPARATION

In a bowl, beat two whole eggs and two yolks (reserve the whites) with 4 tablespoons of cold milk, the sugar, and the flour.

In the meantime, put the remaining milk in a pot with the lemon zest, cinnamon, and a pinch of salt, and bring it to a boil. Remove it from the fire and slowly add it, in a thin stream, to the flour mixture, beating the mixture steadily with a small whisk to keep lumps from forming.

When you have finished adding the milk, pour everything back into the pot in which you boiled the milk, return the pot to the fire, and cook over a gentle flame, stirring constantly and gently, until the cream thickens. Though an occasional bubble is all right, you do not want it to boil hard, or it will curdle. Continue cooking and stirring for 5 minutes, and then remove the pot from the fire. Remove and discard the zest and cinnamon, and stir in the liqueur.

Turn the cream out into an ample, fairly deep dish, spread it to a thickness of about 2 cm (3/4 of an inch), and let it cool completely.

Cut the cream into diamonds. Lightly beat the remaining egg whites, dredge the rhombs of cream in them, and then in breadcrumbs, and fry them in butter until golden. Drain them on absorbent paper and serve at once.

—STREET FOOD RECIPE FROM
THE TOWN OF PASSHOLDT

The circus wagons had been parked for hours, and the players were growing bored. People were strolling about, although none ventured very far, peering over the edge of the chasm, sitting atop their wagons reading, playing games, or watching the sunset.

It was a breathtaking chasm, surrounded as it was by magnificent mountains, which were washed purple and orange by the light of the setting sun. A fierce river could be heard roaring by somewhere in the shadows below, the sound booming upwards from between the sheer rock walls.

A poet would have taken one look at it all and dashed off something about the stark grandeur of nature, the quality of the light, the glory of all things, and still had time for dinner.

Luckily, around fifteen hundred years ago, a Roman engineer had taken a look at it and decided that it would be a good spot for a bridge. He had been a good engineer, and the bridge was still there.

A few of the circus members were stationed strategically, keeping a wary eye out on the surrounding countryside. They were the ones who first saw the two small figures rounding the turn of the road they had come up, and trotting (unsteadily in one case) up the slope towards them. But as things were pretty boring, the two were soon the center of attention.

When they reached the near end of the bridge, they stopped. Zeetha clapped her hands once in dismissal, and Agatha slid to her knees, panting.

Pix strolled over. "So, you two finally caught up."

Agatha glared up at her. "You left without us!"

Pix raised her eyebrows. "Zeetha said you'd catch up."

Zeetha laughed and tousled Agatha's hair. "That's right! Nothing spurs a good run like fear!"

Pix's mouth quirked upwards. "You're really enjoying this, aren't you?"

Zeetha grinned. "Oh yeah."

Agatha climbed to her feet and vainly attempted to pull the

hem of her small outfit further down her thighs. "Humf. If you thought you'd been abandoned in the Wastelands in this thing, you'd know what fear is." She looked around for the first time and frowned. "Why are we all stopped? You weren't waiting for us, were you?"

Pix shook her head as she led them to the cook wagon. A small, fat cauldron sat strapped in place in a sand-lined cooking box. Pix lifted the lid and a savory aroma wafted out. It was a pork goulash, thick with wild garlic, onions and spicy paprika. She handed Agatha two bowls and with an enormous iron ladle, scooped out a pair of generous servings. Zeetha reappeared with a loaf of dark bread, which she twisted in half, releasing a puff of steam into the chilling air. She handed Agatha one of the half loaves, and the two dug in.

Agatha swallowed and sighed happily. "I was so tired and hungry I forgot to ask. Why is everyone stopped here?"

Pix stole a chunk of Agatha's bread and nibbled on it daintily. She waved her hand to indicate the far side of the bridge. "The next town is Passholdt."

Zeetha interrupted. "Hey! That's the town that makes those fried cream things[30]!"

Pix nodded. "That's right. They're also the earliest open pass through the mountains." Pix looked troubled as she absent-mindedly wiped down the pot and ladle. "We should have been there by now." She looked at the now rapidly setting sun and frowned. "But Master Payne stopped us here, and he won't

---

[30] While mercantile trade was common within the Empire, there were certain local specialties that simply didn't travel well. For the best Viennese pastries, for example, you had to go to Vienna. Every town had a local beer, seasonal fruit, wine, fried dough recipe or scam for cheating tourists that the locals were proud of.

cross the bridge until Lars and Augie come back. I don't know why he's being even more cautious than usual, but I'm sure he knows what he's doing." Her face made it plain that she wasn't sure at all.

On the bridge itself stood Master Payne and his apprentice. Master Payne was on the roadway. He'd strode over almost every centimeter of the bridge at least twice, minutely examined every block and seam, and finally deciphered and translated every ancient line of chiseled graffiti with an ill-concealed temper. Abner, on the other hand, had stood motionless atop one of the wide stone railings for up to an hour at a time, a quietly ticking copper and brass telescope trained upon the far road.

Payne strode over to where the younger man stood and sternly addressed his feet. "As master of this circus and your employer, I demand that you give me the telescope."

"Of course, sir. You just climb up here to this superior vantage point and I will tender it to you immediately," Abner replied without moving.

Master Payne glared up at Abner, glared at the meter high railing, considered his dignity and muttered vile implications about Abner's family in Estonian. Abner ignored him. This tirade was cut off by one of Payne's pocket watches beginning to chime the hour.

"It's getting late," Abner said quietly. "They should have been back hours ago. I know it's still a bit early in the year, but at the very least we should have seen *somebody*." He stamped his foot. "This is the only bridge for fifty kilometers, but we haven't seen anybody coming from this direction."

Payne grimaced. "Yes. This is looking worse and worse." He breathed deeply. "There's something odd in the air." Abner took a deep sniff. Payne waved his hand impatiently. "I've been watching Moxana's game. I don't like what I'm seeing. Something is going to happen."

Abner continued his slow pan of the countryside. There were signs of civilization. Stacks of wood, a small shrine by the side of the road, but it all had an air of neglect to it. "Here in Passholdt?"

Payne shrugged. "Soon enough that I want to know the status of the town before we cross this bridge."

"A sensible precaution," Krosp remarked casually. Both Master Payne and Abner started violently, which almost resulted in the younger man pitching over the edge of the railing. Despite his new bright red and gold coat, Krosp had proved annoyingly good at sneaking up on people. "I thought I'd met everyone in the circus by now," he continued. "So who is this Moxana?"

Payne and Abner stared at each other, and then simultaneously broke into chuckles. The younger man returned to his watching. "Heavens, it must sound odd."

Payne grinned. "Oh my, yes. We'll have to introduce you to Moxana as soon as possible."

Krosp studied them. There was something strange here. "Yes. I'd like that."

Suddenly Abner froze. "Whoa," he exclaimed. "Is that them?" Through the telescope, he now saw two figures had emerged from the tree line and were riding furiously towards the bridge. The horses were galloping full out. As they came into sight, one of the figures reared back in its saddle, took the reins in his teeth, and began waving his hands furiously.

"What the devil is Lars doing?" Abner muttered, "The damn fool's going to fall off his horse."

"Can you see any pursuit?"

Abner swung the telescope across the horizon. The ticking sped up as the focus mechanisms desperately tried to adjust. "I don't see anything. But they're riding so hard—" Abner lowered the scope. "We'd better pull the wagons back."

Payne turned and almost tripped over Krosp, who was staring fixedly, not across the bridge, but back at the wagons.

"Don't try to move all the wagons out," he snapped. "You won't have time. Get all the women and children into the wagons furthest down the road. *Quickly!*"

Payne gestured to the distant riders. "But we have time—"

Krosp leapt up onto the bridge rail, grabbed hold of a lock of Master Payne's beard and jerked it back towards the circus. "Look at the horses!"

Abner gasped. "They're going crazy!" Indeed they were. All of the horses in the circus were rearing and bucking in harness. Several of the wagons were already rammed against each other in a carter's nightmare of locked wheels and tangled reins.

Krosp took a deep sniff and the fur on his tail bristled alarmingly. "They smell what I smell. Whatever it is, it's bad, and it's closer than Lars and Augie."

Payne and Abner glanced at each other, then Payne was running faster than anyone who didn't know him would have thought possible. Abner cupped his hands and began to shout, in his best showman's voice—"To arms! To arms!"

Agatha was in the main room of the Baba Yaga, just buckling her skirt when she heard the call. She slammed her hand against a ceiling panel, which popped open and her latest weapon dropped into her waiting arms. It was a round metal tube topped with a series of glass and copper spheres. As she dashed outside, she spun a small crank on the side. Small red lights began to wink on.

Outside, she found the circus rapidly separating into two groups. Children and the non-fighters were being hauled out of their wagons and sent back down the road to the last three wagons, which were already in the delicate process of being turned around.

The other group was much larger, and weapons and other devices were being charged and brandished about. A subset of this group was grimly trying to calm the horses. Professor Moonsock appeared with an armful of hoods, which when pulled over the horse's heads began to calm them down.

Krosp leapt to the top of the nearest bridge pillar and howled out orders. There was a significant pause as everyone stared at him, and then, as one, they turned to Master Payne, who, breathing deeply, arrived at the foot of the bridge. He had heard the last few orders Krosp had issued and made an instant decision. He pointed to Krosp and ordered the crowd, "Do as he says!"

Krosp nodded once, and again began issuing orders. Agatha took all this in from her vantage point atop a small boulder. "I don't see anything," she said to Zeetha.

"Don't say that like it's a good thing," the green-haired girl replied.

Everyone could see the approaching riders now. Dame Ædith scowled. "I... see no pursuit, yet they ride as if pursued by the hounds of Hell."

Abner swung the telescope up again. "They've pulled their weapons out," he reported.

One of the roustabouts hefted a long pike. He twisted the

handle and the blade began to turn, slowly gaining speed. "What are we looking for, Herr Cat?"

Krosp had closed his eyes, and was sniffing deeply in different directions. "I don't know. Something we don't expect."

"Oh, that's helpful."

Embi spoke up. "Augie and Lars. They're trying to signal us about something. Something we should know. What do they see from there that we don't?"

Everyone looked around.

"The wagons?"

"The hillside?"

"Us?"

"What can they see that we *can't*?" asked Agatha.

Krosp froze. Then he leapt down and grabbing Agatha's skirt, dragged her to one side of the bridge. "That gun of yours puts out a big flash of light!"

"Well... yes... but that's just a result of the electro-voltaic discharge—"

"That's the boom part, right?"

Agatha rolled her eyes. "Yes," she conceded.

"Perfect!" He dragged her to the edge of the chasm and pointed. "There! Shoot down there, underneath the far side of the bridge." The area in question was lost in blackness, so Agatha simply aimed under the end of the bridge and snapped the switch.

A blue lance of energy sizzled into the rock wall, blasting away chunks of stone, along with a number of the creatures that were pouring out of an opening under the bridge, clinging effortlessly to the bridge's underside, and clambering across the chasm.

Realizing that further secrecy was pointless, they shrieked

in unison, and began to pull themselves up and over the bridge walls, as well as the cliff in front of the defenders, where they had obviously been hiding.

It was possible that they'd been human, once. If so, they'd been impossibly stretched out. Their arms and legs, fingers and toes, were long and thin, and they moved with a snapping sound that filled the air. Their faces were stretched as well, their lips pulled back in a rictus of rage by their chisel-like teeth. Their eyes glowed red as they swarmed towards the startled performers. There were hundreds of them.

The deepening twilight was shattered by the sounds of two dozen weapons going off in unison. The first wave of creatures collapsed, exploded, or were blown backwards into the chasm. Instantly they were replaced by a fresh wave.

Thundering Engine Woman swore as she snapped a fresh set of rounds into her massive twelve shooters. "There's too many of them and they're coming too fast."

Zeetha leapt forward and skimmed across the cliff edge, slicing as she ran, tumbling another dozen of their attackers off. "Perhaps we die. But we fight to give the wagons time to escape."

Raucous laughter filled the night. Stopping circus performer and monster alike. "Ho ho ho! Now vot's de fun in *dot*?"

Atop one of the circus wagons stood the three Jägermonsters from Zumzum. The one in the middle continued, "*Ve* fights to keel!"

And with a howl, they leapt, transforming in midair into a whirling blur of teeth, claws and sharp metal that mowed down monsters wherever it touched. "Come on, hyu keeds," the purple skinned cavalier sang out, "Hyu gots to fight like hyu means it!"

The wielder of the great pole axe added cheerfully, "Dere's lots uv monsters for efferyvun! Woo hoo!"

Master Payne blinked, and then his voice roared over the battlefield, "DON'T SHOOT THE JÄGERS!"

The green Jäger tore the throat out of a creature, turned to Payne and elegantly tipped his hat in thanks, before whirling back into the fray.

Along with the Jägers, Zeetha carved a swath of destruction that earned her a constant stream of admiring comments from the monster soldiers. The four of them gave the other performers time to reload and recharge their weapons before unleashing another pyrotechnic volley.

"These damned creatures go down blessedly easy," Dame Ædith remarked as she fired another sharpened stake into a creature's eye.

Abner glanced under the bridge. By the dying glow of the molten rock where Agatha's weapon had struck, he could see that the flow of monsters from the tunnel under the bridge was unabated. "Yes, but how many of these things *are* there?"

Krosp had also been watching the rhythm of the battle and did not like what he was seeing. Despite their best efforts, the circus was retreating. Step-by-step they were receding from the edge of the chasm, which allowed the monsters more room. A small part of his brain noted and filed the fact that although they leapt and swirled throughout the battlefield, there was always at least one Jäger within two meters of Agatha.

This was good, as after the first blast, her gun had begun to smoke, and she was pressed up against one of the circus wagons, a multi-tool in her hand, frantically poking about inside it.

A groan next to her caused her to look up. Professor Moonsock was preparing to ignite a fresh whip, but she had paused, a sick look on her face. "They didn't make it," she said dully. "Augie and Lars are cut off." Agatha saw that this was all too true.

The two had reached the center of the bridge, but the sound of the horses' shoes had no doubt alerted the creatures underneath, and they had swarmed up and over the sides in numbers impossible to push through. The two men were now hemmed in. Their horses were rearing and wheeling, dealing terrible damage with their iron shod feet, while Lars swung a large sword with deadly efficiency.

Augie fired a last shot from a large rifle, and then started using it as a club. The sight caused Agatha to gasp, "Lars!"

One of the Jägers followed her gaze and then grinned at her. "Ho! Hyu vant heem?" He bellowed out a roar, which was answered by the other two Jägers, who immediately started cutting a swath in their direction. He continued to Agatha, "Ve go get heem!" To the other two he commanded, "To de bridge!" With a howl they chopped their way through the advancing hoard.

A movement in the distance caught Abner's eye. He grabbed the telescope, swung it up to his eye, and cursed.

Krosp leapt over an outstretched monster's claws and landed next to him. "What?"

Abner pointed to the distant road. "More of them. A *lot* more of them are coming out of the woods and are heading straight towards us."

Krosp hissed and jumped to a higher vantage point. He cupped his paws before his face and shouted. "We need to take out the bridge! Destroy the bridge!"

Payne ignited another monster and stepped back. "Timmonious," he roared. "The explosives in Red Wagon!"

"Insufficient," a small man in a large leather apron replied. He paused to squirt a stream of liquid at a set of attackers who screamed as they began to smoke furiously and threw themselves over the precipice. "It's a very well constructed bridge! Look at the care they took placing the—" His analysis was terminated by a monstrous claw closing over his head.

"I think I can do something about it," Agatha shouted. Her work within the depths of the gun had new purpose. "But I want to wait until Lars and Augie are safe."

On the bridge, one of the horses had been pulled down from under Augie. The other was still holding its own against a ring of monsters, but was obviously tiring. The two men were trying to stay close enough to the remaining horse that they were protected by its desperately flailing hooves without being struck by them themselves. It was a nerve-wracking position.

They were surrounded by a ring of monsters, clustered thickly enough that they continually got in each other's way. Lars chopped and slashed with his sword, while Augie had replaced his now shattered rifle with a pair of large, ornate hammers.

For a lack of anything better to talk about, the two were arguing. "These are Monrovian dueling hammers," Augie explained patiently.

"They look ridiculous," Lars retorted. "I'm going to be embarrassed to be found dead within three meters of them. Someone might think *I* was using them."

This was ended by one of the Jägers appearing between the two startled men. "Ho ho! Hyu iz wery fonny guyz. Hyu gots to poots dot in hyu show!"

"Don't encourage him," Lars replied hotly.

Abner squinted through the telescope. "Are... are they *chatting*?"

"I'm surprised they're not *dancing*!" Agatha slammed the cover down on the gun, which had started vibrating as more and more lights began to come on along its length. "CLEAR THE BRIDGE!" she yelled.

"Hoy! Time to go!" Effortlessly, the Jäger scooped up Lars and Augie and tucked them under his arms. The other two Jägers had swept the immediate area free of monsters, and although more continued to pour over the side of the bridge, the structure was clear enough that they were able to head back at a trot.

"A gurl like dot," the Jager explained, "Ven she sez 'moof'—" The remaining two Jägers answered in cheerful chorus, "Hyu *MOOF*!"

The circus performers concentrated their fire on the remaining creatures on the bridge, allowing the retreating party to move relatively unhindered. As soon as they touched the road, Agatha wound up and slung the now sparking gun with all her might. It arced towards the center of the bridge. Just before it would have landed, it detonated with a blue-white explosion that knocked everyone to the ground.

When the lights faded from her eyes, Agatha could see that the bridge was gone. There was nothing left but some stone rubble growing out of the ancient chasm walls.

Around her, everyone else began to climb to his or her feet. The creatures were up first, but instead of attacking, they stared at the remnants of the bridge and shrieked in despair. The nearest one to Agatha unfroze and swiveled towards her just as Master Payne stepped up behind it and ran it through with a cutlass. The creature coughed wetly as the sword pushed out through its chest, and it bonelessly collapsed when it was withdrawn. Looking around, Agatha saw that the remaining creatures were going down with similar ease.

On the opposite side of the chasm, a growing crowd of monsters could be seen. They screamed and shook their fists at the circus, a few of them getting so excited that they fell, shrieking, into the depths.

Once the monsters around them were dispatched, some of the performers began to turn their weapons on these observers. After the first few fell, the rest retreated and loped back up the road.

The circus milled around. Lars began to shake. "We... we did it! We got out!" His voice began to rise.

Abner swore and pushed towards him. "Oh no, not now..."

The Jäger nearest Agatha, the wielder of the great pole-axe, raised his eyebrows questioningly and jerked a large clawed thumb towards Lars. "Vot's hiz problem?"

"Lars gets hysterical after a fight," Agatha explained. "It's hard to calm him down."

The Jäger walked over to Lars and rabbit punched the back of his head. With a sigh, Lars collapsed onto the roadway. The Jäger turned back to Agatha and smiled proudly. "No it ain't."

Agatha looked at Lars. "Oh dear. I'm sure that's wrong," she looked over at Zeetha. "Although I can't think why."

Abner turned to Augie, who was staring at the nearest Jäger in horrified fascination. "How are *you* feeling?"

"Wonderful!" Augie proclaimed loudly, "Never better! Calm and collected!"

The green Jäger nodded. "Hokay."

Master Payne had been examining one of the dead monsters. With a grunt, he climbed to his feet. "All right, Augie. What's the story?"

The older man sighed and leaned against the nearest wagon. "We didn't get much past the bridge when Lars began to get twitchy. It took us awhile to figure out why. There weren't any other riders. There wasn't any sign that there had been any riders from the town for quite awhile. Lars insisted we leave the road and he looked around. That's when we noticed that there weren't any animals. Not even birds. This is spring, they should be all over the place. But we couldn't find any active burrows. No fresh nests. No fresh tracks. No droppings. No bodies. No bones. Nothing."

Agatha looked troubled. "But you kept going."

Taki handed Augie a bottle of brandy. He gratefully took a pull from the bottle and wiped his mouth. "Passholdt isn't just any old town we can swing around, Miss Clay. There're only a few passes open this early in the year. It was a hard winter."

Abner spoke up. "We've seen dead towns before. They're creepy, but we can pass through them if we must. Plus, it's always possible that while the surrounding area might be affected, the town itself might have held out and is still secure." He looked at Augie questioningly.

The advance man wearily shook his head. "No such luck. We stayed off the road and in the woods as long as we could. The farms around the town were deserted. A few were burned out, but the rest were just abandoned. All the livestock is gone. So was the stored grain and seed stock. The silage lofts were mostly full. Whatever happened, happened last fall or over the winter.

"We finally got within sight of the town. The fields were

empty. Haven't even been turned. The city walls are still intact. We didn't see any smoke, or sentries, but Lars still took over an hour sneaking up to a tree tall enough that he could look over the wall."

Augie took another deep drink. "Inside the walls, he said that most of the buildings looked intact, but there were smashed carts and wagons and bones. Bones *everywhere*. Apparently people kept coming to Passholdt for quite awhile." Another drink.

"And crawling over everything were those... things. There weren't any people or animals. Just them. They were sprawled on the roofs, shambling through the buildings, picking through the bones. Hundreds of them. Thousands, probably. Lars said that as he was climbing down, he snapped a dry branch. Just one as big around as your finger," Augie held up an index finger to demonstrate. It was shaking slightly.

"He said that the ones nearest to him whipped their heads around towards him and started shrieking. That spread through the whole town and they all started running towards us. Well, he dropped five meters straight down to the ground and we grabbed the horses and started running." He looked at the remnants of the bridge and a shudder went through him. "And they still beat us here," he whispered. "We were damned lucky they started from inside the town."

Master Payne turned away and looked at the bridge. "Well, no one will get caught by them from this direction. Unfortunately, this leaves us in a bit of a predicament."

"Us?" Agatha gestured over the chasm. "What about the townspeople?"

Augie looked at her. "For all we know those *were* the townspeople."

"You don't know?"

"How the devil would I know?"

Agatha nodded. "Losing the bridge will certainly make it more challenging, but it does mean that they won't be expecting anyone to come from this direction. That's good."

Master Payne looked at her blankly. "Good for what?"

"Our attack on Passholdt."

Abner blinked. "Our *what*?"

Agatha shrugged. "Attack might be the wrong word," she conceded. "But we have to do something to try to save the people of Passholdt. I guess the first step will be to analyze one of these corpses and see if these creatures were once human. Perhaps we can—"

The concentrated glares from her assembled listeners finally registered, and Agatha's monologue stumbled to a halt. "No?" she asked.

Master Payne sighed and removed his spectacles. "Many newcomer Sparks make the same mistake, Miss Clay. But I confess that I'd thought you more... grounded[31]."

Agatha was confused. "I don't understand."

Payne nodded. "We are *actors*, Miss Clay. We only *pretend* to be heroes." He spread his hands and his spectacles hovered in midair. "We are fakes. These are tricks. Our lives, the lives I am responsible for, are dangerous enough without questing for adventure. We are Sparks, yes, but pitifully weak ones, and we *know* this. It is this knowledge, the knowledge of just how weak we *are*, that keeps us alive."

Agatha interrupted, "But the town—"

[31] Grounded was the term used when a Spark was sane enough to function on a day-to-day basis. It says a lot that many people, including Sparks, are unfamiliar with the term.

Payne snatched the floating spectacles from the air and slammed his great fist down upon a wagon yoke. "At our next stop we will inform the Baron's people. These are his lands? *He* can keep them clean!"

Agatha tried one last time. "But—"

"BUT *NOTHING*!" Payne roared. "For all we know, those things are... are some new form of *revenant*, and the only thing that can be done for them is to *kill* them!" He wheeled about and looked Agatha in the eye. "Could you burn down people? Women and children? Even if you knew—you *knew*, that they had irrevocably become monsters?"

Agatha tried to step back, and found her way blocked by the side of a wagon. She swallowed. "I... no..." She looked down. "I don't know," she whispered.

Payne stepped closer. "The *Baron* can. The Baron *has*. I *respect* him for that, but I do not want to *be* him. No sane man would." He grasped Agatha's chin in his hand and dragged her eyes back up to face his own. "Now you drop any ideas you have about being another Othar Tryggvassen, unless you want to leave my show and manage your heroics on our own. Do you understand?"

"Yes!" Agatha wrenched her head from his hand. "Yes, I understand!" Tears filled her eyes, "But I don't have to like it." She turned to go and found Zeetha blocking her way.

Zeetha reached out and grasped Agatha's shoulders. "Remember this," she hissed. "Remember this union of understanding and rage. This is the balance that will keep you fighting. And to make sure you remember this occasion—" Agatha's eyes widened in fear—until Zeetha slung a comforting arm across her shoulder. "A drink."

As a relieved Agatha was led away, Payne turned back to the rest of the circus, who were busy not meeting his eyes, until he clapped his great hands together. "I don't like it either," he announced quietly. "But I like dying even less. Move out."

At this, a collective sigh went up from the group. They dispersed and soon the wagons began rumbling down the hill. Payne stood apart looking out at the ruined bridge until Abner came up and coughed discreetly.

Payne nodded without turning. "Is the warning sign posted[32]?"

"Yessir. Of course, we'll want to post another at the turn off."

Payne nodded again. Now that the bridge was out, there was no reason for anyone to climb the two-kilometer slope. He hoped the Baron would take care of this soon, but it was quite possible that he would abandon the road, and simply increase the amount of air traffic to the area. Payne had seen it happen before. He gave a final pat to the ancient stonework before he turned away. It had been a very good bridge.

Abner continued. "I told Dr. Kleeporg to preserve one of the monsters. I thought the Baron might want it[33]."

Payne again nodded. "Good. Now let's get moving. I want us as far as we can get by morning. Anything else?"

---

[32] Regular travelers throughout the Empire were issued warning signs by the Empire and required to post them, as well as report on problems they'd encountered. The penalties for anyone except the Baron's troops removing a warning sign usually involved becoming a warning sign yourself.

[33] In addition to rewarding travelers who posted warning signs, the Baron's agents were known to pay well for unusual specimens. Initially, there had been a number of people who had decided to "put one over" on the Baron by constructing and selling him fake madboy tech and handmade chimeras. The Baron bought them all, and the counterfeiters had a good laugh—until these same fakes appeared at various museums and auction houses, where they made the Empire significantly more money than it had paid out.

A voice rumbled from above his head. "Vell, now dot hyu mentions it…"

The two men spun in surprise. The green Jäger was squatting on the roof of the cart, a huge grin smeared over his face. "Hello dere."

Payne visibly pulled himself together. He had found himself facing far worse while traveling in the Wastelands. "My humble thanks," he said sincerely. "You really helped us here."

The monster soldier looked pleased, and graciously inclined his head. "Eet vas only fair. Vun of hyuor pipples help us, so ve tink ve shood help hyu beck, jah?"

The Jäger with the triple bladed pole arm unfolded himself from under the wagon. Both Payne and Abner would have sworn there was nothing there.

He looked smug. "*End* ve did eet mitowt killink ennybody hyu know! Pretty sveet, hey?" The grin he gave the two men was so alarming that they involuntarily took a step back, directly into the arms of the purple Jäger who had materialized behind them. He slapped an affable hand upon each of their shoulders. This elicited a small scream from Abner.

Payne rallied and grinned back. The Jägers mentally gave him an "A" for effort. "Pretty sweet indeed. As a token of our esteem, if you need any supplies—"

The purple Jäger interrupted. "Dere iz sumting dot ve vant."

Payne nodded. "Excellent! We can certainly—"

The green Jäger spread his hands. "Ve vants to join de circus."

"*WHAT?*"

The Jäger with the pole-axe nodded in agreement. "Jah. Ve vant to be circus guyz."

Payne and Abner looked at each other in amazement. Payne

scratched his shaggy head. "But...but what can you *do*? What could we do *with* you?"

Abner shook his head. "The audience—"

The green Jäger waved his hands dismissively. "Jah, jah, dey hate us. But dots joost ven vees valkin' around being us. Pipple *expect* to see strange tings in a show like dis."

The purple Jäger puffed his chest up proudly. "End dey dun get much stranger den us," he declared.

An odd look came into Master Payne's eyes. "But what *could* we do with them," he murmured.

The younger man looked at him askance. "You can't *seriously* be considering this. Them? Onstage?"

The purple Jäger swept a hand through his long luxurious hair. "Ve vould be perfect. Hy em Maxim," so saying he gave a sketchy, but serviceable, cavalier's salute. "Hy tink Hy iz de leadink man type."

Payne and Abner stared at him blankly.

The pole axe wielding Jäger leaned in. "Vot's 'leadink man' mean?" he asked sotto voce.

Maxim waggled his eyebrows. "Hit mean hyu gets to kees de gurl," he explained.

"Hoy!" The horned Jäger turned to Abner and grinned engagingly. "Hy vants to be a leadink man too!" Abner's eyes were staring to glaze. The Jäger stuck out a clawed hand. "I'm Ognian." Reflexively, Abner gingerly took Ognian's hand and was given a quick, seismic rattle.

Maxim smacked the back of Ognian's head. "Eediot! Hyu kent be a leadink man."

Ognian pouted. An alarming sight on a person with a mouthful of sharp teeth. "Vy not?"

Maxim shrugged. "Dere's only vun leadink man."

"Sez who?"

"Iz hobvious! Eef hyu gots two, deys gunna lead in different directions."

Ognian thought about this. "So vy hyu?"

"I tink ov hit first."

"But dere vas two Heterodyne Boyz."

Maxim's eyebrows shot up. "Say—hyu iz right!"

Ognian grinned. "But dot's hokay! Dis vay ve *both* gets a gurl!"

A flicker of worry passed over Maxim's face. "Hy dunno. Some uf the gurls de Heterodynes keesed vos pretty scary."

"Bot dot's de best part," exclaimed Ognian gleefully, "Ve'd be keesink *actresses*!" He smirked, "End hyu *know* vot dey say about *actresses*!"

Maxim looked at him expectantly. "Um... No Hy dun't."

Ognian shrugged. "Hy dun neither." He grinned again. "Bot Hy bet ve's gunna find out!!"

The third Jägermonster smacked Ognian on the back of the head. "Qviet, hyu eediots! Eef deys find out how irresistible ve iz to de vemmins, dey neffer gunna let us join." The other two realized the sensibility of this advice and arranged their faces into a semblance of innocence before facing the two men again.

"Zo," the green Jäger said. "I'm Dimo. Vat doz hyu tink?"

Abner and Payne stared at the three and then looked at each other and nodded. "Clowns."

Dimo, Maxim and Ognian grinned. Perfect.

* * *

Lars blinked. The familiar, early morning sounds of the circus drifted through an open window. The clink and rattle of cookware. The unnerving clucking of Professor Moonsock's syncopated chickens. The gasping and panting of Agatha as she ran past his window, pursued by Zeetha.

He snuffled back into the comforting goose down mattress, as his mind idly went over yesterday's events—

Which brought him bolt upright, every muscle poised for flight. Gasping, he looked around, and realized that he was safely in his own wagon, and not in fact, being eaten by monsters. He slumped in relief, and then a new memory surfaced. Hadn't there been... Jägers?

"Goot mornink, sveethot."

The cheerful voice from right behind him sent Lars bolting from his bed. When he landed with his hunting knife clenched in his fist, he was astonished to see one of the Jägers sitting at his table with his feet up, gnawing on a dried sausage. He was appreciatively flipping through Lars' supposedly well-hidden collection of British "artistic" postcards.

After a long frozen moment when nothing happened, Lars gestured with the knife. "Put those down! And what are you doing here?"

The Jäger glanced at him and then deliberately picked up the next card. He whistled appreciatively. The girl pictured was riding some sort of velocipede. Ognian thought she looked a bit chilly.

Lars began to feel rather ridiculous. He waved his knife around a bit more in a half-hearted manner.

"Oh, schtop dot befaw hyu hurts hyuself." Ognian looked at the next card. This girl was obviously a soldier. She had a rifle and everything. In the Jäger's opinion, she was wearing a mighty fine looking hat. He casually tucked the card into his coat pocket. "Hy'm supposed to make shure hyu vos okay after hyu voke up." He looked at Lars directly. "So how iz hyu?"

Lars lowered the knife. "Wait... Did I pass out? I've never done that before." He then realized that the back of his head throbbed with a dull ache.

The Jäger looked away furtively. "Oh, dot. Hyu gots smecked by a piece ov der bridge." He handed a chunk of stone over to Lars. "See?"

Lars examined it. It was indeed a piece of the bridge. He turned it over. Scratched into the stone was the message: I HITT MR LARZ. (SYNED) A BRIK.

Lars stared at it for a moment and then slowly put it down on the table. "I see."

The Jäger let out a gust of breath and gave him a sharp toothed grin. "Hyu gots to vatch owt for dem leedle devils," he confided.

Lars nodded slowly. "Right. So..." He briefly considered a plethora of questions and settled for, "How long are you staying?"

Ognian grinned again. "Forever! Ve joined hyu circus!"

Thousands of negotiations with suspicious, armed, or downright insane townspeople kept Lars from doing anything other than raising his eyebrows. "No kidding?"

The Jäger looked at him with a quick flash of approval. "No keedink. Dey pracktically insisted after we's gets hyu off dot bridge."

Lars reviewed that particular memory and then unhesitatingly stuck out a hand. "Thank you for that."

Ognian gave it a quick shake. "Dun tank us. Tank dot gurl vat told us to go get chu. *Ve* thought hyu vas haffing fun."

Lars paused. "Which girl?"

"Dot Agatha Clay? She vas vorried about hyu. Go figure."

"You do what she says?"

The Jäger shrugged. "Vouldn't hyu?"

Before Lars could answer, a liquid sound drew his gaze out the window. There stood Agatha, a smiling Zeetha handing her a second bucket. The first had been tipped over her head, and the abbreviated training outfit clung to her like a second skin. The second bucketful only served to enhance the effect. Lars' breath caught, and he swallowed. Casually he turned back to the Jäger and shrugged. "...Maybe," he conceded.

The door opened and Abner stuck his head in. "Knocking," he called out cheerfully. "Is he awake?"

Lars waved. "Hey, Bunkie."

Ognian clapped Lars on the shoulder proudly. "See he's avake and talking and no more schtupid den he vas before!"

Abner nodded. "So I see."

Lars let this pass without comment. The Jäger scooped a few more postcards into his coat pocket, carefully placed his fez upon his head and swiped another string of sausages. "Hokay," he announced. "Hy iz gunna go look for breakfast!" So saying, he casually slouched through the doorway, eliciting several small screams from passing circus members.

Lars slumped onto his bunk. "Payne is really letting them stay?"

Abner nodded thoughtfully. "Yeah. He didn't even try to argue with them too much. I dunno how everyone else will like it..."

Lars laced his hands behind his head and relaxed. "Well, they saved my bacon, so I've got no—" A frown crossed his face. "What the heck—?" He felt under the coverlet and pulled out a pair of lacy pink undergarments.

He stared at them in surprise, and then a slow grin spread across his features. "Well, *well*! I wonder whom *these* belong to? Guess I'd better bring them to lost and found—"

A red-faced de la Scalla snatched them from his fingers. "Shut up!"

Lars looked at him slyly. "Must be mighty *convenient*, sharing a cart with someone who's gone so often."

Lars hadn't thought it was possible for his friend's face to get any redder. He was wrong. "...Maybe," Abner admitted.

Lars leapt up and grabbed Abner's shoulders and gave him a good shake. "Ahh! Finally! My little pal is all grown up!"

Abner swung at him, but Lars easily avoided it. "Relax, I have no doubt you surrendered your honor only after putting up every resistance. Did she at least promise to make an honest man out of you?" A business-like throwing knife smacked into the shelf next to Lars' head. He ignored it. A thought struck him and he looked serious. "Am I going to have to move out?"

Abner paused, and thoughtfully tucked a second knife back within his vest. He shrugged. "Naw. Well... yeah... maybe."

Lars nodded. "Thanks, that about covers it."

"Well, it's a big step."

"It sure is. All my stuff is here."

Abner smiled. "But you know? It feels right."

Lars smiled back conspiratorially. "With Pix? I'll bet it does."

Abner blushed yet again. Lars was impressed that he hadn't passed out. "Hey—I'm trying to be serious here."

Lars swept in and got the smaller man in a headlock. "I know! That is why you need me more than ever, you poor, doomed fool!"

"All right! All right!" Abner broke away and grinned. "I can't wait until it happens to you."

Lars laughed and grabbed two glasses and a wine bottle. To his surprise, it was empty, as were the remaining six. He remembered the Jäger and shrugged. "A sentiment expressed by the enraged fathers of a thousand towns!"

Abner smirked. "You laugh. But one day someone will ask you, 'Who's your girl?' and a face will flash through your mind and it's going to sandbag you completely."

Lars was indeed caught by surprise, as the image of Agatha, smiling at him, filled his head. He felt his heart skip a beat and a sick realization filled him, even as Abner was saying, "It's going to be hilarious to watch." It would have been. It was a pity he missed it.

A gentle knock at the door, along with a melodic "Morning," interrupted him. Abner turned to find Pix on the stoop. The two exchanged a relatively chaste kiss. "So how is Lars?"

"He seems okay."

A shaky voice from within the wagon called out, "Actually I think I want to lie down."

Pix nodded. "Have you eaten yet?" Abner shook his head.

"Good. We're staying here for the day while Master Payne figures out what to do. So I found us a nice spot in the woods. Here's a blanket—" She handed Abner a thick rolled pad, "that we can spread out, and a lovely meal we can eat together—" she hefted a large wicker basket. Then she stepped close and whispered softly into Abner's ear, "...eventually."

The two moved off through the camp, followed by amused and knowing glances. Pix looked thoughtful. "So with Passholdt gone..."

Abner nodded. "I'm afraid we'll have to go through Balan's Gap this year. Master Payne says we'll discuss it tonight, but I don't see any alternative."

"Doesn't Moxana—" Abner silenced her with a finger to her lips. Swiftly he reached into a nearby barrel and pulled out a squirming and spitting Krosp.

"I *thought* so," Abner declared. "Can I help you with something? Before—" he glanced at Pix, "I go eat?"

"Moxana!" The cat squalled. "You said that you'd introduce me to Moxana!"

The showman hesitated and then sighing, lowered Krosp to the ground. "So I did. Let's go."

Krosp looked surprised. "Really?"

Pix looked annoyed. "NOW?"

Abner answered them both. "It won't take long."

They left Pix with the food and made their way to one of the baggage wagons. This one was richly adorned with an astronomical motif. Stars and comets swirled along the sides, interspaced with astrological signs and sigils. A small cupola sprouted from the roof.

Krosp frowned. "I didn't think anyone lived in these."

Abner smiled. "No one does." He selected a large ornate key from the ring at his waist and operated the lock. The door swung open with a groan and Abner waved the cat inside. "Krosp, meet Moxana."

The inside of the wagon was stuffed with various props and stage mechanisms. In a cleared space in the center was a small, fancifully carved and decorated wheeled throne. A closer examination revealed the seated figure of a women, dressed in an exotic outfit and adorned with extravagant golden jewelry from several different cultures.

The cabinet before her was richly ornamented with various inlaid woods and gilded finials. Within easy reach of the seated figure were brightly painted wooden boxes held shut by intricate golden clasps. Directly before her was a game board, almost a meter square.

However, the nature of the game itself was not easy to discern. Looked at one way, it was a chess board. A slight shift in perception, and it could be for the East Indian game, Pachisi.

At this point, an astute observer would realize that there were easily a dozen different possibilities, depending upon the pieces employed. At the moment, the board was littered with pieces from a half a dozen different games haphazardly arranged in an unrecognizable pattern.

Krosp stared and then turned to Abner. "Moxana is a clank?"

Abner smiled. "Of a sort." He reached over and released a set of clasps upon the front of the cart. The front lowered upon hinges, revealing a large empty section, except for the axle of the cart, and an intricate arrangement of rods and wires connected to various spots on the underside of the game board. "She's actually a puppet. Run from down here."

Krosp peered at the area and frowned. "Seems a bit small."

Abner swung the panel closed and refastened the clasps. He then twisted a few bits of decoration, and the clasps were hidden from casual observation. "Indeed it is. That's why we don't put her out these days. Originally, she was run from the inside by a dwarf named Kurtz. He was killed three years ago by some bad clams."

Krosp looked surprised. "Bad clams?"

Abner nodded, "Yes, they had axes. Anyway, no one else could fit inside."

Krosp looked at the cart again. "Embi. Or Balthazar."

Abner pulled a rag off a nearby chest and ran it over the figure as he talked. "Yes, I have high hopes for Balthazar, but at the moment his endgame is terrible."

Krosp blinked. "Endgame?"

Abner nodded. "Moxana is supposed to be a clank that can play chess."

Krosp studied the top of the board with a skeptical eye. "This doesn't look like any chess set-up *I've* ever seen."

Abner shrugged. "Chess is what *we* used her for. But yeah, Master Payne says that the board can be used for almost twenty different games that he's familiar with, and probably a bunch more that he isn't. But in these parts, if you want to impress someone, you play them at chess." He sighed. "I've taught Embi the basics, but chess just isn't his game. Can't really wrap his head around it. The man's a demon at Omweso, though. That's a game he brought with him from Africa. There's this board, with a bunch of little indentations—"

Krosp interrupted. "But I've heard people talk about her— it—like it was alive!" He leapt up to the board and gingerly poked at the seated figure. It remained motionless. He noticed that although it had fully articulated eyelids with long full eyelashes, which were closed, as well as a small perfectly sculpted nose and ears, the figure had no mouth. He batted at it again.

Abner looked embarrassed. "Well we all tend to talk like she is. Kurtz was a really good puppeteer. Before you knew it, you'd ignore him and be talking to the puppet. The audience always loved it, so we did it a lot. Got into the habit of telling her our problems, asking advice, you know..."

Krosp folded his arms. "No, not really. She's got no mouth. How did she offer this advice?"

Abner looked at Krosp and frowned. When he spoke, it was carefully. "She... can do more than play games. When we thought the populace wouldn't get too spooked by it, she did oracular readings. Tarot cards, pendulum divination, there's this 'Ching' thing from the orient that uses sticks—Kurtz was pretty good at the woo-woo stuff, but—" Abner looked like he'd said too much.

"But—" Krosp prompted.

The man sighed. "It was Kurtz who started it. He said that sometimes... Moxana made her own moves, and that they always...meant something. Something more than he could see."

Krosp studied the figure again. "And you buy this?"

Abner shook his head. "I don't know. I was a lot greener in those days, and Kurtz always loved to spin a good story, but...these days, whenever things get a little strange, we say 'Moxana's rearranging her board.'" He blew out a breath and grinned. "I guess that's pretty silly, eh? Kurtz loved messing with people."

Krosp looked at Abner for a moment, took a deep sniff and then studied the mechanical figure again. He noted that although most of the figure had a fine coating of dust, the game board was sparkling clean.

He turned back to Abner. "Interesting." He paused, "You

know, I play chess. I could run her for you."

Abner looked startled. He quickly looked at Moxana and then back to Krosp. "But—"

Krosp continued smoothly, "You *would* like to have her on display again, yes?"

Abner stammered, "Well... yes... of course... but—"

Krosp nodded as if it was settled. "We'll have a few games later. You can see how good *my* endgame is."

Abner acquiesced weakly. "Of course. Later..."

Krosp grabbed his hand and gave it a few hearty pumps. "Good! It'll be more use than my shoveling dung, I'm sure!" Abner was aware of claws pricking his fingers. He saw the hunter's gleam in the cat's eyes. Krosp pulled his paw back, gave it a quick lick and rubbed it over his head. "And now, I'd better go find Agatha. She's helpless without me, you know."

With that he hopped down and strolled out the door. Abner stared after him and frowned. Behind him there was a faint whirr and several quick, quiet clicks.

Turning he saw several chess pieces set up upon the board. He made a quick analysis and blew his lips out in a puff of self-disgust. "Check." He eyed the silent mechanical figure and turned to leave. "Yes, thank you. I got that."

Several weeks passed. The circus worked its way through a series of small kingdoms that actually bothered to maintain the roads.

As a result, they made good time, and occasionally were able to play two shows a day in two different towns.

True to his word, Krosp proved to be a surprisingly good chess player. Easily beating everyone in the troupe except for

Master Payne, who confided in the cat that "People hate to play against a magician, they're never sure if they lost because I beat them or because I was able to pull a queen out my nose when they weren't looking."

Krosp nodded sympathetically, then lashed out with lightning speed and batted at the sleeve that Payne *wasn't* gesticulating with, knocking free the rook of Krosp's that he'd hidden there. The cat snagged it in midair and placed it back on the board. "Yes," he agreed, "I can see how other people would find that frustrating."

Payne harrumphed and sat back, which is the only reason he saw the tip of Krosp's tail nudging one of the cat's pawns forward.

The two played every day thereafter[34].

Zeetha continued Agatha's training. This was in two parts. In the morning Agatha was run around, and in the evening, after dinner, she watched while Zeetha went through her own exercises.

While she leapt and swirled, she gave a running commentary about what she was doing, technical terms and the history of the swords themselves.

They were called *Quata'aras*, and instead of a pommel that was an extension of the blade of the sword, they had a perpendicular handle, which put the blade in a line with the wielder's forearm. Agatha considered that, from an engineering perspective, this would give the weapons a lot more power. Zeetha moved with such grace that she easily masked this power, until she made a delicate move and cut down a nearby tree. Agatha very much wanted to be able to move like that, and itched to try her hand with the weapons themselves.

---

[34] Krosp did indeed try to run Moxana. The experiment was abandoned after he got his whiskers caught in the mechanisms for the second time.

One morning, after an exciting, impromptu performance the previous evening, when Zeetha had deftly bisected an attacking swarm of overly large yellow jackets on the wing, Agatha was awakened by the now-familiar nose beep and found that she was expected to run around the camp while lugging a small blacksmith's anvil.

Agatha balked. "When do I get to learn to use a sword?"

Zeetha paused. "You're not ready to even touch a Quata'ara yet." Agatha opened her mouth, but her memory flashed back to the time on Castle Wulfenbach, when one of the Baron's students, Zulenna, had demonstrated just how much she had to learn about Europa-style fencing, which was the sword-style Agatha had known about all her life.

With a sigh, Agatha bent her knees and lifted the anvil off the ground. She turned to see Zeetha looking at her, her lower lip pushed out in a moue of disappointment.

"Oh wait," Agatha said, "let me guess. This was where I was supposed to insist you let me wield a Quata'ara, even though you, my Kolee, have told me I'm not ready. Possibly I'm supposed to harbor some day-dream that I have a magical affinity for these swords, which will allow me to side-step all this tedious training.

"No doubt this would have led to some hilarious, but painful lesson reaffirming that I am, in fact, not yet ready to touch the swords. I'll skip that, if I may."

She was about to say more, but the flush working its way up Zeetha's face stopped her cold. Without another word, she hugged the anvil to her chest and fled. With a roar, Zeetha followed.

That night, a bruised and nearly comatose Agatha lay face

down on her bunk, attempting to formulate a philosophical worldview that would make the pain more bearable. This was proving quite difficult, possibly because it hurt to think.

Agatha tried to review the day, but beyond a certain point, her memories faded into a red fog. All she could remember was finally being allowed to drink what felt like liters of water and being too exhausted to eat. Oh, and the Jägers. She remembered them.

Even though Master Payne had announced that they were joining the circus, they'd hardly been in evidence. They were seen, lurking about on the fringes of the camp. They occasionally came in for something to eat, or an awkward conversation, but no one knew where they slept.

It was obvious that they were not used to dealing with people they weren't trying to kill, and were still trying to figure it out. They never appeared in a town, and sometimes they weren't seen from one day to the next, especially when other travelers joined the circus at an overnight camp, or were traveling in the same direction.

But they'd been there today. Their usual lazy, insouciant grins replaced by a grim watchfulness. It seemed like every time Agatha had come around a corner, one or the other of them had been somewhere nearby. There had even been one time when she'd been staggering along, the anvil now strapped to her back, and she had stumbled. From nowhere, a pair of strong green hands had caught her and gently set her back onto her feet.

It was shortly after that that Zeetha had released her for the day.

As if summoned by her thoughts, Zeetha's head popped up

through the ladder well. Agatha twitched, but otherwise did nothing.

Zeetha prodded her with a finger, possibly to see if she was still alive. She looked guilty. "How are you doing? I—ah... I was told I might've worked you a bit more than I should've today."

Agatha shrugged. It hurt. "I'm sorry I was disrespectful, Kolee," she whispered.

Zeetha grimaced and proceeded to light several candles and lanterns. She then unbuckled her harness, slipped off her swords and hung them from a peg. The small cloth bag she carried proved to contain several ceramic jars. She opened them one after the other and laid them out in a row on a nearby shelf. Strong herbal scents began to fill the room.

Without a word, she stripped Agatha of her clothes, moving her gently, but pitilessly. When she was done, small stars were lazily pinwheeling past Agatha's vision.

Zeetha selected a jar, scooped out a handful of creamy paste and rubbed it into her hands. The smell of paprika grew stronger.

She knelt beside Agatha and began vigorously kneading the paste into her shoulders. Agatha's eyes bugged out and a small "eeee" escaped her lips. The ointment started out soothing, but proceeded to get warmer and warmer until by the time Zeetha was kneading it into her lower back, her shoulders and arms felt like they were on fire. Zeetha ignored Agatha's squeaks of pain and methodically worked her way down Agatha's back.

Suddenly, she spoke. "When *I* asked my Kolee for the sword, she told me I wasn't ready. But when I asked again, she gave it to me.

"It was so heavy, I was convinced she'd slipped me one

made of lead." She shifted slightly and started working down Agatha's left leg.

She spoke slower now. "I was younger than you are now, of course. I needed two hands to hold it, and within thirty seconds I had chopped down my aunt's favorite fruit tree, broken two floor tiles and my toe."

She switched to Agatha's right leg and worked her way back up. "Everybody does that at least once. Challenges their Kolee. Tries to prove that they're Ashtara's Chosen One." She was silent as she selected another jar and started from the beginning.

Agatha's teeth snapped together in shock. This time the contents of the jar felt like ice, and she imagined great scalding clouds of steam erupting from her tortured skin. It took her a few seconds to realize that the pain was fading as well, as if it too were being boiled away. She gave a small groan of relief.

Zeetha gave a small smile. "Like I said, we all do it. The stories are always trotted out at family get-togethers, and everybody always has a good laugh. My teacher's teacher always said—" and here Zeetha's voice took on a reedy quality, "There's no better way to keep a warrior from getting killed than to have her almost do it to herself."

She paused halfway up Agatha's right leg. She was silent long enough that Agatha looked over her shoulder to see what was wrong. Zeetha knelt there, tears flowing down her face. She looked at Agatha and sniffed.

"Except of course, when they *do* manage to kill themselves. My cousin, Zoniax, she was so much faster than I'll *ever* be. But they gave her... they let her..." She broke down sobbing. Before she knew what she was doing, Agatha found herself cradling the crying girl in her arms.

"It was such a waste," Zeetha sobbed. She took a deep breath and pushed herself away from Agatha's arms and looked her in the eye.

"What you did today was smart. When a warrior is being forged, they don't train her to be smart. Being smart makes you ask questions, and no War Queen wants an army full of fighters asking questions." She smiled at the thought. Then she got serious again.

"Now you—you're never going to be a warrior. But if you ask enough smart questions, *you* might live long enough to be a War Queen."

Then she gave Agatha a fierce hug and a kiss on the forehead. Without another word she finished the massage, covered Agatha up and extinguished the lights. A second later, Agatha heard the wagon door click shut.

Agatha lay there for a moment digesting this. Then quickly dropped off to sleep.

The next morning, as she stood shivering, Zeetha casually handed her a pair of padded sticks, complete with handles. Agatha hefted them. They seemed heavy. Zeetha drew her own swords, they gleamed in the faint light.

She spoke gently. "Do not think of it as 'holding a sword.' You must learn to think of the Quata'aras as extensions of your own arms. Soon enough, you will learn not to think about them at all..."

The last shreds of spring melted away and summer arrived. The days lengthened. The traffic on the roads increased. Peddlers, tinkers and other travelers increased. Once another traveling show arrived at a large town where the circus was already setting up. What could have been an awkward situation instead turned into a "Battle of the Entertainers," which lasted for two days, pulled in three times as many customers as usual, sold six times as much refreshments, and ended in a draw.

Agatha continued to play Lucrezia in the Heterodyne shows. She found it to be fun. The only problem was that she seemed to be having an increasing awkwardness with Lars, especially during their big romantic scenes. More than once, Abner was waiting for him in the wings, an annoyed look upon his face.

Meanwhile, Pix had relearned a basic truth about the *commedia dell' arte* style of play, which is that the romantic leads tend to be the least interesting characters onstage.

Now this tradition was ameliorated a bit by the fact that both Bill and Lucrezia were full blown Sparks and either one of them was just as likely as the other to pull a doomsday device out of his or her back pocket, but this merely "raised the bar" for the ancillary characters, which helped to explain why the romantic leads proceeded through to their pre-ordained union relatively calmly, valiantly trying to ignore the various clanks, minions, constructs and Sparks that colorfully swirled around them, occasionally throwing pies.

Pix demonstrated that she was actually a very versatile actress indeed. In addition to the enigmatic High Priestess[35], she impressed everyone by breathing new life into hoary old characters such as The Clever Construct, The Oafish Minion, The Wise Witch of the Wood, The Saucy Courtesan, The First

---

[35] The High Priestess was a favorite stock character in the Heterodyne Plays. She represented all of the exotic Sparks who ruled mysterious, far-off lands and lost, barbaric civilizations who started out as antagonists, but invariably fell in love with Barry Heterodyne.

Victim, The Clueless Public Official, The Lost American, and The Tragic Abomination of Science.

Furthermore, in the time since Pix and Abner had started keeping company, Pix had mellowed quite a bit. She was a lot more friendly and personable, and actually willing to do some of the thousand and one tedious little jobs that the circus required, and she did them with a rather dopey look on her face while humming happily. It was driving everyone crazy. Astonishingly, she even managed to talk about something other than herself for minutes at a time.

Opinion was divided as to whether this change could be credited to her opening up on stage, or to Herr de la Scalla.

Master Payne and Abner had consulted their maps and sighed. A little more time would be spent on this side of the mountains, but that just meant that they'd spend a little less time on the other side. Towns might be visited a year or two early, or skipped altogether, but life on the road taught one to be flexible.

Travel was certainly smoother this year. Even in the wilderness between towns, the circus had yet to encounter any highwaymen. Nor had it been attacked by rogue monsters, clanks, or wild animals. The odd thing was that other travelers reported the usual number of these impediments, usually in great detail. This particular mystery was resolved to Payne's satisfaction one day when the circus drove past a small clearing. Within it was a cheerful fire, which was roasting the remains of what appeared to be a shark with six legs and a mouth at either end. The three Jägers were to be seen lazing around it, and they waved happily as the wagons trundled on by.

Everything was going smoother. The Baba Yaga was the

most dramatic example, but it wasn't the only device that mysteriously improved. Throughout the troupe, people began to notice that fuel efficiency was increasing. Gear systems became more intuitive. Mechanical break-downs almost disappeared. Windows stopped sticking. Doors stopped creaking.

No one could explain it. Everyone *knew* that Agatha had something to do with it, even though they never saw her doing anything.

In retrospect, many people have asked why no one ever just came out and confronted her about it. To understand this lapse, one must consider the culture of the troupe. First and foremost, everything that happened was an improvement. No one wanted to be the one to "kill the golden goose," as it were. Perhaps more importantly, this was a culture that appreciated a good trick, and they wanted to figure out how she did it without having to be told.

As a result, they fixated upon the superficialities, and never saw the larger changes even as they were happening around them. A most excellent trick indeed.

One afternoon, after the troupe had stopped for the day. Agatha was chatting with the Countess as she was sorting old gears and selecting which ones to set to soak in a bath of kerosene. Balthazar raced up "Hey Miss Agatha," he called. "I was out collecting wood, and I found you another wreck!"

Agatha smiled. "Wonderful! You keep finding me parts and I'll get that organ finished yet!"

The boy beamed. "This one is a really big old clank! It should have lots of parts!"

Agatha wiped her hands on her trousers and stood up. She grabbed a bulky workbelt and buckled it around her waist.

"Well then, let's see if we can find you a sweet cake, and then I'll collect my tools and we can check this clank out."

This last exchange took place within earshot of Lars and Yeti, who were inventorying the chemical wagon. Lars looked worried. "Hey. She's going off into the woods to mess around with an old clank?"

Yeti raised a shaggy eyebrow in surprise. "Yes. Just like she's been doing for a while now."

"But... by herself?"

"Balthazar is going with her."

"But he's just a kid."

Yeti scratched his chin. "I'm sure they both know to stay within shouting distance."

Lars grabbed Yeti's arm and attempted to drag him along. This had the same effect as trying to pull an oak tree. "Come on! It could be dangerous!"

"And you want to follow them?" Yeti frowned. "Lars, are you feeling all right?"

Lars tried pulling him again. "Stop fooling around and let's go!"

With the dispassionate sangfroid of the very large, Yeti shrugged and rose to his feet, allowing himself to be pulled along. This promised to be interesting.

Several minutes later, Agatha and Balthazar stepped into a forest clearing and Agatha felt her breath catch in wonder. The space was like a green cathedral. Shafts of light pierced the darkness, which was filled with dancing motes of light. Slumped to the ground, nestled amongst a mass of broken moss and fungi encrusted logs, was an aged colossus of a clank. Agatha did a quick calculation and whistled softly to herself. When it stood erect, the clank must have been over ten meters tall. She looked at the damage caused when it had fallen, the rust and corrosion that covered every surface, except where moss and lichen had taken hold. By her estimate, this clank had been abandoned for close to twenty years. Whatever empire it had served had no doubt fallen long ago. Agatha looked around. For all she knew, this section of forest had once been part of a thriving town. The Wastelands were full of places where civilization had succumbed to outside forces. Agatha shivered.

She turned to Balthazar. "There's going to be a lot more here than we can carry. Do you think Smilin' Stev could get a wagon in here?"

Balthazar considered the uneven path they'd recently trod. "Maybe not. But he can still carry stuff out himself. He won't care how many trips it takes."

Agatha nodded. "Please ask your father if I can use him then." Balthazar gave her a crisp salute and bounded back towards the camp.

Alone, Agatha picked her way to the foot of the colossus. She examined the surface of the great clank, and scowled at the condition of the metal. She pulled a small pry bar from a loop on her belt, and with a quick jab and snap, pulled up a section of plate. She examined the mechanisms underneath, and what she saw pleased her quite a bit. She began to hum to herself. From a pouch, she pulled a small monocular, and scrutinized the front of the clank. She found what she wanted up near the head. She gave a satisfied smile and put the viewing device back in its pouch.

She then pulled out a fat metal disc and attached a long, silken rope to it. Still humming, she whirled it around her head several times and threw it towards the top of the clank. With a

"THUNK" the disc stuck to the clank, revealing itself to be a magnet. As it turned out, a very strong magnet, as Agatha used the attached rope to haul herself upwards along the face of the recumbent giant.

Once she reached where she wanted to go, she looped the rope around her seat and clipped it to an attached "D" ring. She examined the surface before her and then scraped away a thick layer of moss. A small service panel was revealed. She perfunctorily examined the lock and then took a large hammer from her belt and smacked it squarely. The surrounding metal crumbled into a spray of rust, while the steel lock briefly hung in place, and then tumbled to the ground. Again the pry bar came out and with a tooth gritting squeal, the panel swung open.

Agatha took a cloth and wiped several glass surfaces. To her surprise, a dim light flickered behind one or two of them. She grasped a large control lever, and with some difficulty, spun the dial to "AKTIV."

A shudder ran through the giant figure. Sparks erupted from various joints and extremities. The single great eye in its head flared red, and with a terrible slowness, swiveled down and observed the small girl hanging from its chest.

The great arms jerked, ripping loose from a cluster of small trees and slowly swung towards her.

At this, the hidden watchers broke from cover and ran towards the giant. "Hang on, Agatha," Lars yelled, "We'll distract it!"

Surprised at their appearance, Agatha held up a hand and shouted back over the roaring and squealing of the awakening clank. "What? Just a minute."

She then pushed away from the control panel, and as she

swung back, lashed out with the heel of her boot, shattering the control lever housing. The lights flicked and died, and great figure shuddered once, then collapsed back onto its bed of smashed trees.

Agatha calmly unhooked herself and then slid down to the base of the now motionless figure. "Now what was that?"

Yeti and Lars stared at her. After a second Lars stepped forward. "Are you all right?"

Agatha looked back at the supine clank. "What? This? Sure! I helped my father with old stuff like this all the time. People were always finding dead clanks in the woods." She patted a metal leg. "It's always best to disable them permanently before you start trying to take them apart."

Yeti looked at Lars. "That sounds safe enough."

Agatha looked confused. "Well, of course. Didn't Balthazar send you to help?"

Lars nodded. "Oh, yeah—"

Yeti interrupted. "No. Lars was worried about you poking about in the woods all alone."

Agatha looked at Lars, who gave an embarrassed shrug. Agatha smiled. "Well you don't know how much it means to me to have the two of you here."

When Balthazar arrived with Smilin' Stev, he was surprised to find Lars and Yeti straining to hold up one of the great clank's arms, as Agatha squatted underneath and pulled out various components. Sweat was pouring down Lars face, and his face was set in a determined scowl.

Yeti looked over at him and smiled. "You *did* say it might be dangerous." He shifted his feet. "Happy?"

Lars rolled his eyes and grunted. "Shut... up!"

* * *

Several hours later, after the useable parts of the great clank had been stripped and transported back to the circus, Lars gratefully sipped a beer and watched the Sparks sort through the scavenged material. Since Balthazar had discovered it, and Agatha had harvested it, they were the people to bargain with, and the trading of parts and future favors was in full swing.

Agatha's foster-mother had tried for years to teach her how to dicker in the marketplace. Sadly, Agatha had never had the knack. But now that the locket that had suppressed her mind was off, lessons and techniques that had been patiently drummed into her head long ago were resurfacing. Admittedly, she was bargaining against actors, mountebanks and thieves who had no scruples about using their skills against each other (it was how one stayed sharp, after all), but she was holding her own, and Lars, who was an interested observer to the whole proceeding, realized that her skills were improving from one transaction to the next.

He frowned. He was feeling unusually conflicted when it came to Agatha. He tried to analyze this. Physically, there was no question. Agatha was ripe and round in all the right places. The final onstage kiss should have been something he looked forward to.

He had certainly planned on getting to know her better, but every time he saw an opportunity, he found himself holding back. There was something that was keeping him from pursuing the girl, and it was starting to bother him. He was beginning to fret that he was actually falling in love with her.

The very thought made him twitch.

When the haggling was done, and people were sorting through their prizes, Agatha came up to Lars, and knelt next to him.

She looked nervous. "This is for you," she said. She handed Lars a small device. "I noticed you still used a tinderbox."

Lars examined the device. He twisted the knob and a small flame puffed into being. He twisted it back and it disappeared.

"It's to thank you for helping me move stuff back to camp." Agatha said quickly. Lars noted that her face was quite red.

"Thank you, Agatha. That's mighty nice of you." Lars sighed to himself. He'd been given numerous devices such as this by helpful circus members over the years. He continued to use the more primitive methods because some of the towns he scouted looked suspiciously at anyone who wielded a device more complicated than a knife.

But with the eye of a man whose hobby was women, Lars could see that Agatha was... interested in him. This made his hesitation even more inexplicable.

He made a show of putting the firestarter into his belt pouch. Agatha smiled. "So," Lars said, "while I have you here, may I ask an impertinent question?"

Agatha looked wary. "I suppose..." she said uncertainly.

Lars leaned in and talked quietly. "Do you have a *boyfriend* waiting for you in Mechanicsburg?"

This had clearly not been on the mental list of questions that Agatha had been anticipating. "Oh, no," she replied. "I was told that I have family there."

Lars nodded. "Any boyfriends *anywhere*?"

Agatha looked away. "No, I... No. Not anywhere. Not ever," she whispered.

Lars leaned back. "Really. Because, that madboy from the airship that came to get you? He seemed *awfully* upset when we told him that you were dead." Lars looked away, but continued to watch her from the corner of his eyes. "And *I'd* heard—"

"I don't care what you *heard*—" Agatha snapped, "But we weren't... we weren't *anything*!" She looked away. "He was probably just disappointed that he wouldn't be able to drag me back to the Baron in chains." She glared at Lars. He noted that her eyes glistened. "And what business is it of *yours*, anyway?"

Lars crossed his arms and gave her a leering grin. "Well, when I'm up on stage *kissing* you—" He was pleased to see a flush of color bloom upon her face, "It'll be good to know that I don't have to keep one eye out for some jealous guy jumping up onstage and causing trouble—and yes, it *has* happened." He smiled at a memory. "Now *that* was one heck of an onstage pie fight."

Agatha looked contrite. "I see." She shook her head and smiled. "No, you won't have to worry about *that*."

Lars clapped his hands together and stood up. "Great! Then I can start *acting* less, and enjoy myself more!" And with that, he strode off towards his wagon.

Later that night, in her wagon, Agatha sat hugging a large pillow, as Zeetha slowly brushed out her long golden hair. For what, by Zeetha's estimate, was the thousandth time, Agatha asked her, "But what did he *mean* by that?"

Zeetha rolled her eyes and grinned "I haven't the foggiest idea," she lied.

SIX

LUCREZIA: You, sir, should remove your pants.

STRANGER: Indeed?

JUDY: Indeed, it's time. We have all laid aside modesty but you.

STRANGER: I... wear no pants.

LUCREZIA: (Terrified, aside to Judy.) No pants? No pants!

—THE HETERODYNE BOYS AND THE SOCKET WENCH
OF PRAGUE (ACT 1. SCENE 2D)

What it meant was that the Heterodyne shows became a lot more... interesting. There was a tension between Lars and Agatha now that was quite evident to the audience, and the final onstage kiss usually produced a cathartic eruption of applause and cheering that could last for minutes.

Agatha's nights were full of peculiar dreams, and she actually found herself welcoming Zeetha's morning exercises.

The frustrating thing was that off stage, her relationship with Lars seemed like it was being directed by two different people. One day he would be friendly and attentive, and the next, strangely distant.

Agatha kept trying to figure out if she was doing something wrong, but was unable to discern any pattern to Lars' behavior.

Finally, in desperation, she mentioned her predicament to Zeetha. The green-haired girl pondered for a moment and then nodded. "An excellent choice. He's experienced enough that he'll be able to show you a good time, nice enough that he'll be gentle, and independent enough that there should be no hard feelings when you move on."

Agatha, red-faced, seized upon the one part of this analysis that seemed conversationally safe. "What do you mean 'Move on?' Why should I—"

Zeetha interrupted. "*You're* the one who said that you were only with us until Mechanicsburg. That's just a little over a month from now."

Agatha opened her mouth in surprise. "But... but I thought..." She paused. What *was* she thinking?

Zeetha had been polishing her swords. She stopped now and leaned in, putting a firm hand on Agatha's shoulder. "Hey. This—" she gestured vaguely at the surrounding circus—"This is not where you belong."

Agatha frowned. "What do you mean?"

Zeetha looked troubled. "Explaining things other than fighting isn't really what I'm good at. But I'm your Kolee. I know you." She waved away any potential objection. "Not story stuff, like your favorite color or how you shaved the cat when you were six years old or... or crap like that. But I *know* you, Agatha Clay... if that's your real name—" Agatha started. Zeetha made a calming motion with her hand.

"No, no. That stuff isn't important. See, I know what *kind* of a person you are. Better than anyone here." She paused, "Except maybe for the Countess and Master Payne. They're even sharper than they look.

"But you, you're not like these people. Sure, they're Sparks, but you... you're a whole different level. You just haven't had a reason to show it yet." She sat back and cocked her head to the side. "When you do, you won't fit here anymore."

"But..." Agatha looked around. "But they like me here. I like acting. I like traveling. I..." she looked down shyly. "I am honored to be your zumil."

Zeetha leaned in and gently beeped her nose. "You will always be my zumil, silly girl." She stood up and stretched. "But a warrior must learn that nothing ever stays the same, which is why the things we want in life must be grabbed before they slip away. In this case, the thing you want to grab is Lars."

"But I'm not really sure that I want to grab his—" Agatha realized what she was saying, and put her head in her hands, profoundly grateful that Zeetha was the only one listening.

Zeetha laughed and tousled Agatha's hair. "Relax, no one's expecting you to marry him." She frowned slightly. "But he *is* acting uncharacteristically shy."

Things got odder. Onstage, Lars took every opportunity to get close to her. To touch her arm, to run his hand along her jaw. His eyes smoldered, and their climactic kiss was beginning to dominate Agatha's dreams, as well as some of her daytime musings.

But off stage, Lars remained formally polite, when he could be found at all. Increasingly, he took every opportunity to leave the troupe, for any number of perfectly plausible reasons. It was evident that he was utilizing the tricks he'd learned to avoid confrontations in a half a hundred towns. It was only obvious because he was using them all for the same audience.

Agatha tried to dismiss her feelings and distract herself by working. After all, aside from this irrational infatuation, she enjoyed her day-to-day life quite a bit, and there was always something to keep her busy.

Great strides were made on the Silverodeon. One quiet, foggy morning, Agatha actually managed to produce a tortured set of hoots and squeals from the pipes, which caused everyone to run out, weapons in hand. But this, along with the work the various troupe members piled upon her, was not enough, and the Sparks around her began to feel the result.

Almost all of the Sparks in the show found themselves being questioned by Agatha about their work. These sometimes turned into marathon sessions that left them feeling, as Augie put it later, "As if she turned me upside down, poured all my theories out onto the ground, examined them, kept the good stuff, and pointed out the rubbish."

Indeed, there was a bit of a Renaissance amongst the lesser Sparks, as a number of theories and concepts were aired out and scrutinized. There were also, it has to be said, some hard feelings, as a few cherished ideas were thoroughly disproved, sometimes in embarrassing detail[36].

[36] Indeed, one Herr Doktor Flatmo actually left the circus in disgrace when Agatha's mathematics revealed that his so-called "perpetual motion engine" actually required a slight push every ten and a half years in order to keep running. Oh, everyone was very nice about it in public, of course, but still...

The result was a quietly rising tide of chaos and small disruptions. Small, but to those who knew to watch for such things, quite noticeable.

And thus it was that one evening, in a small village with an insatiable appetite for candied mimmoths, after the show had ended and the troupe had bedded down for the evening, Lars found himself strongly invited to have a drink with Master Payne and The Countess.

The inside of their wagon was done in a tasteful blend of dark inlaid woods, rich fabrics and stained glass. Within the compact space, souvenirs and trophies gleaned from decades of travel caught the eye, and everywhere, there were cards.

Playing cards from throughout history and hundreds of cultures were carefully mounted upon every flat space large enough to accommodate it. Elegant cards made from starched silk, impossibly thin slices of wood, decorated with gilt and crushed gems, alongside a thousand different varieties of paper and parchment adorned with everything from crudely drawn symbols to excruciatingly detailed miniature oil paintings.

As they made small talk and settled into place, Payne nonchalantly pulled a series of cords and levers. It quickly became evident that the wagon was a marvel of compact engineering. It seemed that almost every surface swiveled, unfolded or slid out to become or to reveal something else. By the time the old magician was done, a table, complete with tablecloth and settings, had appeared, as had several plates of snacks, along with a bottle of wine and three glasses. As Payne leaned back and adjusted his cuffs, a small arm swung down and a tiny music-box-like mechanism played a jolly tune as it deftly removed the cork from the bottle before swinging back up and out of sight.

The Countess offered Lars a savory egg-cream tart as Payne carefully poured him a glass of deep red wine. "A little something the Countess put up a year or two ago. Do let me know what you think."

Lars sipped. He was suddenly reminded of a Spring Festival. The air was cool and fresh, the sun—clear, but not too bright. The music, the laughter, the first kiss of a shy girl—

He shook himself, and examined the drink in his hand. He slowly nodded in appreciation. "That's mighty good stuff, m'lady." Marie looked pleased.

Payne steepled his fingers together. "So Lars, perhaps you've noticed that things around here have been a bit..." He looked at his wife.

"Higglety-pigglety," she said promptly.

Payne frowned. "...Chaotic," he suggested.

Lars shifted uneasily. "I have, sir. But that doesn't have anything to do with me..." He looked at the two of them. "Does it?"

"The *direct* cause appears to be Miss Clay." Lars looked to the side. Marie continued. "She seems to be..." She looked at Payne.

"Agitated?" He said.

"Frustrated," she corrected. The two of them swung their gazes upon Lars. "You wouldn't know anything about that, would you?"

"I didn't touch her," Lars said defensively.

Again the two glanced at each other. Payne harrumphed awkwardly, and tried to assume his best man-of-the-world demeanor. He opened his mouth—

"Why in Heaven's name not?" Marie asked. Payne rolled his eyes.

Lars saw that the Countess was looking at him expectantly. This was when he fully realized just how difficult it would be to extract himself from the encircling furniture. He blew out a breath, took a deep drink, and sat back.

"It... It's not that I don't want to," he found that this discussion was easier if he kept his eyes focused on the wineglass in his hand. "I'd... kind of planned on it. But... do you remember Doktor Spün and his Cylinder of Touch[37]?"

Payne nodded. Hiring Doktor Spün had been one of his rare personnel mistakes. His firing had been cathartic however, even if it had taken awhile to put out.

"That damned thing was beautiful. You wanted to touch it. To feel it. *I* wanted to. But I knew—I *knew* that it was a bad idea. I had that walking into a bad town feeling. I *told* you at the time, remember?"

He took another sip of wine, and finally raised his eyes to Payne's. "I... I get the same feeling from Agatha. I want to touch her. Red fire, I want to... but, then I get the feeling that if I get too close, there's going to be trouble."

Payne slowly sat back, and thoughtfully poured the young man another glass of wine. He then turned to the Countess. "I've seen Moxana's game. I can't argue with that."

Marie regarded Lars and slowly tapped her chin. "You've never...dallied with a girl possessed of the Spark, have you?"

Lars looked surprised. "No, m'lady. All the town girls I..."

---

[37] The Cylinder of Touch was a breathtaking creation of colored glass and wire. Its creator, Herr Doktor Potrzebie Spün, invited customers to place their hands on it to "Feel something extraordinary!" It evidently had been *quite* extraordinary, considering how much they screamed.

he paused, "—talk to, are regular folk. There's never been any available ma—uh—*gifted* ladies with the show." He thought about this. "You think that's it?"

Payne shrugged. "Only an idiot would think about knowingly involving himself with a woman with the Spark, — *if* he planned to take advantage of her."

"I wasn't—!"

Payne held up a hand. "Neither one of us thinks you're *that* foolish, my boy. But wooing even a normal lady is not something a fellow should do lightly. You have a finely tuned sense of danger. I think it only natural that this would be a situation that would cause it to sit up and start screaming."

Lars thoughtfully took a drink. "I think I see what you mean, sir."

Payne nodded. "Now, both the Countess and I think you an honorable person." Marie cleared her throat. Payne continued smoothly "—In your own way. Which is why, at the very least, you should stop giving her these mixed signals. It's not fair to Agatha. Settle it one way or the other before she gets so wound up that she dismantles half my circus."

Lars sat back, and slowly sipped his wine. What he was afraid of was the unknown. The mysterious thing that reached out from behind your back and grabbed you.

When he knew what a particular danger *was*, Lars was surprisingly good at dealing with it. There was the screaming afterwards, of course, but no one is perfect.

Another thing Lars was good at was talking to women. Now in this case, he was dealing with an infatuated, naïve, and inexperienced woman who could literally warp the laws of nature and probably turn him into a carrot if he did her wrong.

But when he thought of it that way, it began to seem like an interesting challenge…

There had been a thunderstorm the night before, leaving the air cool and crisp, and putting a sparkle on the leaves of all the trees.

The circus was currently parked next to the map dot that was known to the locals as the village of Borlax. The local solstice stock fair was winding up, tonight would be the last show and tomorrow the circus would be back on the road. Today, however, the locals were engaged in a final frenzy of deal making that involved more histrionics and high drama than the actors dished out in a month. Thus, the troupe was enjoying a little extra free time.

Many were critiquing the locals' use of hyperbole and invective. Rivet and Captain Kadiiski were replacing a broken wheel on one of the caravan wagons. Agatha was examining a small device she had discovered hidden in the back of her wagon. It was a complicated little hand-cranked thing of gears and spheres within spheres. It looked like it should produce music of some kind, but she couldn't figure out how it worked.

Suddenly she released a catch, there was a small click, and a gear slid into place. She gave a satisfied grin and blew a lock of hair out of her eyes.

At that moment, Dame Ædith strolled over. "Good day to you, Miss Clay. If I may take a moment of your time?"

Agatha nodded. "Is everything satisfactory?" The vampyre hunter had asked Agatha to do some minor repairs upon her wagon.

The older woman paused, and marveled at the small device

in Agatha's hand. Agatha graciously passed it over and wiped her hands on a square of rag. "Ah, that is the thing," Ædith continued. "It rides right smoothly, and the brakes are now most effective..." Absent-mindedly, she spun the crank on the device and gave a small delighted smile as a number of spheres spun and twisted about each other, accompanied by a barely heard high-pitched twittering.

"...But?" Agatha interjected.

Dame Ædith kept spinning the crank, but frowned. "But now the accursed thing doth make this most vexatious *clicking* noise."

Agatha looked surprised. "Clicking noise?"

"Aye, and a right loud one too. I thought—" What she thought was never to be revealed, as at that moment a large brown bat cannoned into her hat, and with a great deal of flapping and squeaking, tried to climb under it. Dame Ædith shrieked and batted ineffectually at the creature, in the process throwing the device into the air. Agatha caught it before it crashed to the ground. As she did so, she saw that there was a faded paper label stuck to the bottom, which she had neglected to examine. It read "Bat Summoning Engine." Under this, in a crabbed hand, someone had added the notation; "excessively effective."

She looked up. The bat was clinging to Dame Ædith's hat, even though the woman was now waving it about frantically trying to dislodge the creature. Agatha surreptitiously slipped the device into a tool bag and said brightly, "I'll just go take a look, shall I?"

Dame Ædith's wagon was as garishly decorated as any of the others, but when you got close enough, it became evident that the décor consisted of holy symbols. Hundreds of them, fitted together chock-a-block, forming an intricate pattern that drew spiritual comfort from hundreds of different faiths and belief systems, in no evident order of precedence.

The roof bristled with totems, icons, spirit flags and ætheric antennae constructed of everything from precious metals to bones and seashells. Signs covered the sides, promising cures for anemia, sleepwalking and a "fear of garlic." Agatha had noted that the exact nature of the "cure" was never specified.

Whenever the wagon moved, an ingenious gear system automatically rotated a plethora of prayer wheels and played simple melodies upon several gongs and chimes. There was also a fat copper chain that dragged along behind, because, Agatha had been informed, Dame Ædith's cart was struck by lightning on an average of once a month. A fact the vampyre hunter found "statistically inconvenient." Privately, Agatha attributed this to the excessive amount of metal used in the decorations.

Whenever the cart moved, even over the sound of the gongs and chimes, there was an excessively loud clacking sound. Agatha frowned.

Dame Ædith stomped over as Agatha was finishing a test run of the wagon. The bat clung to her hat and appeared to have fallen asleep. It was apparent that she had given up trying to dislodge it, and was now determined to ignore it.

"That's it," Dame Ædith said triumphantly. "Ever since thou worked upon it, it hath been doing that, and 'tis beginning to drive me unto the brink of madness."

Agatha nodded sympathetically. "I think I can fix this."

Dame Ædith looked relieved. "Praise be!"

"—But," Agatha continued, "I'll need a screw-down ripple

wrench. I think Rivet has one. Could you get that for me while I get started?"

Ædith nodded and ambled off. Agatha started knocking on various wheels with her knuckles, until Ædith was out of sight. She then dropped to the ground, and crawled under the wagon until she reached the front axle. Even the undersides of the wagons were painted and decorated, and the axle was encased inside a garishly decorated box frame. Agatha felt around the back until she found the set of small fasteners.

"Look," she muttered softly as she worked, "I know you're just trying to help, and I know this cart was noisy before. But you're overdoing the noise." She undid the last fastener and swung up the front of the axle box.

This revealed a complicated system of gears that had been added to the axle. Their purpose was obviously to power a set of small automatic winding keys for the row of small clanks that were hooked up to them. When they saw Agatha, they waved at her.

"If something is too loud, people will pay attention to it, and we want you to stay hidden, right?" The clanks all began clicking. This was obviously the sound that the cart had been producing. By trial and error, they lowered the volume until the clicking was barely audible. Agatha nodded in satisfaction.

"I have found thy ripple wrench." Dame Ædith's voice caught Agatha by surprise, causing her to bang her head on the underside of the wagon.

She slammed the cover down, snapped closed the fasteners and crawled out. She stood up and brushed off her knees. "I think I fixed it without needing it. Sorry I sent you off for nothing."

Dame Ædith looked pleased. "No apology is needed for excessive competence." She climbed onto the wagon bench, clucked her tongue and the wagon moved off. The familiar cacophony of various gongs and windmills filled the air, but of the clicking, there was no trace. Dame Ædith looked pleased at first, but as she continued to circle the wagon, a small frown creased her features. She called out. "Thou will think me inconsistent, but now it's..." she looked embarrassed, "It is *too* quiet. I keep thinking my wheels are fain to fall off."

Agatha nodded and gave the front wheel a swift kick. Instantly a soft clicking started up.

"That should do it," she stated confidently.

Dame Ædith looked pleased. "Aye." She looked at Agatha. "But how didst thou—?"

Agatha waved a hand dismissively. "Science."

A faint snort of amusement from behind her caused her to turn. There was Lars, several script books in hand, shaking his head at her.

"Science? That's the best you can do?"

Agatha was at a loss for words. "I don't—"

Lars looked serious. "Look, some of the towns we roll through? If you do something unexpectedly smart, they'll start screaming 'Madgirl' before you've taken two steps."

He waved the scripts. "You've got to have a story. You have to make a joke. You have to distract them. Confuse them. Entertain them. Don't give them time or reason to think about what you've done."

Agatha looked lost. "But... I don't know how to do that."

"I've noticed." Lars again hefted the scripts. "So I thought I'd run you through some situations."

Agatha felt an inexplicable wave of happiness bubble up through her. "Really?"

Lars nodded. "Sure. You're smart enough that it shouldn't take long before you get the idea."

He turned away slightly, and offered Agatha the crook of his arm. She stared at it in surprise. She'd longingly seen couples walking arm-in-arm, but no one had ever wanted to do so with her.

Correctly interpreting the cause of her hesitancy, Lars gently took her hand and deftly wove it into place.

As they strolled off, Dame Ædith leaned back on her wagon seat and gently rubbed her chin.

In her opinion, as a student of humanity, there would either be a September wedding or massive destruction. She slid down onto the padded floorboard and turned her eyes skyward.

Due to tricky problems with calibration, Dame Ædith had yet to be able to quantify the efficacy of prayer, but as always, she remained convinced that it was better than doing nothing.

Taki tossed another log onto the fire. He lifted the lid of a gently bubbling cauldron of goo and took a sniff. He stirred it with a large iron ladle, and nodded in satisfaction. Guntar, who had been watching the proceedings in respectful silence, handed him a mug of cider and continued the conversation that had been suspended.

"—Then, after I crawl out of the dungheap—that's when I get hit with the pie!"

Taki frowned at him in disgust. "No, no! It's too much! You shouldn't play Punch like a complete idiot!"

Guntar waved a hand dismissively. "This from the man who plays Klaus[38]."

Taki specialized in playing Klaus, a role many performers considered too dangerous to touch, for obvious reasons. He nodded seriously. "Yes, but Klaus keeps his dignity. Or tries to. He tries to be a hero, and occasionally does some good. *That's* what makes him funny. You've got to have balance."

Guntar waved a hand dismissively, "I know that. But I've researched this character—"

"All of your research is biased, third-hand anecdotal hearsay."

"So what's my alternative?"

"Chow!" This cry was from Ognian who, along with Maxim, gave every indication of being pulled towards the cauldron by their noses. They peered over the lip of the pot and took a deep appreciative sniff.

Taki looked worried, "Um... actually, that's glue. We're repairing—" Ognian waved aside his objections and, with a flourish, drew forth a bowl from a deep pocket in his coat. He scooped out a large dollop, and slurped it down. He smacked his lips and scooped up another bowlful. "Hoo! Dot's goot!" He ladled out a helping for Maxim and the two began to down bowls of steaming glue almost as fast as they could scoop them up.

Guntar smiled jovially. "So, you're part of the show now.

---

[38] On the surface, this was a legitimate observation. In his carefree youth, Klaus Wulfenbach had been a frequent companion-in-arms to Bill and Barry. But in subsequent years, as he had become more prominent, the Muse of Comedy had not been kind to him. In the Heterodyne plays, young Klaus was usually portrayed as an excitable coward. The first to turn tail, the first to gloat when he had the upper hand, the first to beg piteously for his life when captured, and after the inevitable victory, the first to claim the credit. Klaus was perfectly aware of these portrayals, yet allowed them to continue. The reason was simple: he found them hilarious.

We should work out some routines."

Maxim paused in his eating and cocked an eyebrow. Guntar explained. "I usually play Punch in the Heterodyne show."

At this Maxim's face lit up. "Oh jah! Ve see dot in town!"

Guntar nodded. "Yup. Big, slow and stupid, that's—"

Maxim interrupted, "Hyu iz so lucky ve iz here!"

Guntar blinked. "Lucky?"

Maxim nodded. "Oh jah, hyu gots heem all wronk! Ve kin help hyu dere, ve *knew* heem!"

Taki, who had been watching the level of the cauldron drop with some trepidation, now grinned. "You don't say!"

Maxim nodded again. "Meester Ponch vas amazink. Strong as an ox!"

Ognian chimed in. "But lots schmarter!"

"Shoo! Very goot at making de plans."

"He save my life vunce!"

"Oh jah, he vas kind to all sorts uf dumb enimals."

"End he vas soch a gentlemen!"

"Ho yez! No matter vot happened, alvays mit de dignity!" Maxim scowled. "Hit makes me so mad ven pipple tink he vas schtupid! Just becawze he vas so beeg and couldn't talk."

Ognian finished his eighth bowl with a lick and stowed it back into his coat. "Dot vould haff hurt him de most, Hy tink, he vas alvays very concerned about pipple tinking all constructs iz schtupid or evil."

Guntar looked like he had suffered several body blows. He gave a sickly grin. "But... surely... ah... didn't he have a... a lighter side?"

Maxim pondered this, and smiled. "Oh, uv cawrze! He vould build these amazink toyz for de orphan cheeldrens!"

Taki tried to laugh, but had decided to taste the glue and now discovered that his mouth was sealed shut.

Master Payne and his wife observed this all from a distance. As the Jägers started pulling on the cook's jaws, they turned away. Marie had that little line between her eyebrows that Payne had come to dread.

"Payne," she said. "I've seen you convince bandits to contribute to the Actor's Retirement Fund."

Payne smiled at the memory, but remained wary. "Your point, my dear?"

"There's a reason there are no Jägermonsters in the Heterodyne shows. People really hate them."

Payne shrugged. "Well it's not like they're insisting on performing. We hardly see them."

Marie eyed him closely and continued slowly. "You could have gotten rid of them if you'd wanted to, but you haven't even tried." A unnerving "crack," a groan of pain, and a "Hoy!" of victory caused her to glance back. "In fact, you feed them."

Payne opened his mouth, looked at his wife and closed it again. "Ergo," she continued, "You are Up To Something. You have *got* a reason, but you did not tell *me*."

A few beads of sweat appeared upon Payne's brow. Marie clasped her hands together and looked vulnerable. Payne flinched. "The only time you don't tell me something is when you think it's dangerous, because being a fragile, sheltered noblewoman, I might faint at the thought of experiencing physical harm like a common person."

She sighed, and seemingly from nowhere, produced an enormous cast-iron frying pan easily one hundred centimeters in diameter. "And then," she said sadly, "I have to damage one of the *good* pans by smacking it against your thick, common skull until you *tell* me—"

"BALAN'S GAP!" Payne screamed, cowering. "We have to go through Balan's Gap!"

Marie paused, and then lowered the pan. "Oh, dear. You're expecting more trouble from the Prince." She thoughtfully tapped a finger against her pursed lips. "And you think having them along might help discourage him from…"

Payne looked out from between his fingers. "Yes?"

Marie cocked her head. "That's very clever for a commoner."

Payne drew himself up and preened. "Why, thank you, my dear." The two of them smiled at each other, and then leaned in for a delicate kiss. Just before their lips met, they were startled by a snuffling sound from overhead. They froze, and swiveled their eyes upwards to see Dimo crouching on the roof of the wagon beside them. A large tear dripped from his bulbous nose.

"It iz zo nize, ven married pipple tok to each odder." He leapt to the ground and slumped back against the wagon and grinned. "Und now, Hy tink hyu should tok to me." He smiled at the Countess. "But mitout de pan."

Several minutes later, the three were walking a short way away from the circus. Dimo was silent. Finally the Countess asked, "Will you help us?"

Dimo looked at her and grinned in a way that made her squirm. "Eet soundz like fun. Bot—" He held up a clawed finger, "Hy gots to discuss hit vit Maxim and Oggie."

"Do you think they'll agree?"

Dimo laughed and deftly slid his arm around the Countess' waist and drew her close. "For a nize doll like hyu, ve do all kindz uf tings!"

Marie stiffened. "Do you mind?"

Dimo looked surprised, and then darted a look at Payne, standing next to him. A light dawned. "Ho! Yaz!" He dropped his voice to what he no doubt thought a whisper. "Ve gots to be sobtle in front uv you's haitch... oh... zee... bee..." A worried look crossed his face, and he gave up. He jerked a thumb in Payne's direction. "Hyu know, heem." Payne rolled his eyes.

At that moment, they heard a sound drifting through the air. Marie stopped dead. "What in the world is that?"

Dimo smirked. "Ho! Hy knows dot vun. My family vos musical. Dot—" he pronounced, "Iz music!"

The two humans regarded him blankly for a moment. Then Payne spun about. "No!" A look of shock crossed his face. "No, it can't *be*!" He took off at a run and the other two followed.

To Payne's amazement, the source of the sound was indeed the Silverodeon.

The original instrument had been a simple steam calliope that had been fitted with some organ pipes salvaged from an old church. For the next twenty years it had been hauled around to various harvest festivals and occasionally used to scare bats out of barns.

The circus had discovered it after it had been smashed by a particularly large and grumpy bat, who had gone on to take down several airships before one of the Empire's warships had blown it apart.

That rusty collection of cheap iron and old brass bore no resemblance to the glittering contraption that was still unfolding from the wagon bed as the magician approached.

Clusters of pipes and tubes sprouted upwards from the back of the instrument, resembling some sort of art nouveau hedgehog. Along the side, valves and pistons rippled, catching the eye and drawing it to the cockpit, where at least four keyboards, as well as what appeared to be the controls from an ancient locomotive, were being played by Agatha[39].

Sweat poured from her as she played, great sweeping arpeggios and surging waves of melody that sent shivers down the spines of her listeners. This was the first time that Agatha had played—really played, since the shackles had been removed from her mind. She found the music triggering feelings and emotions within her that she strove to express, a creative cycle that went on and on and on.

The listeners never were able to determine just how long they stood there, enraptured by the music, but when it ended, when Agatha finally brought her hands down in a final gentle chord and slumped forward, many of them found themselves weeping and cheering simultaneously. Agatha jerked up, amazed that everyone was suddenly there. A sudden pain in her fingers caused her to grimace, and then smile ruefully. She was out of practice.

Rivet awoke to find herself next to André, who was standing stock still, as if he was afraid that when he moved, he would forget everything he had just heard. "But it was *junked*," she said to him. "You said it was just to keep her *busy*."

---

[39] As has been mentioned, Agatha's foster-mother, the construct Lilith (AKA Judy, the famous construct companion to the Heterodyne Boys), not only played the piano, but gave lessons in Beetleburg. According to anecdotal evidence, while young Agatha had trouble concentrating on tasks that involved engineering or math, music apparently came easier. At Lilith's insistence, Dr. Beetle arranged for her to receive advanced training from some of the music masters at Transylvania Polygnostic University. An assessment from when Agatha was fourteen reads; "Subject has a refreshing appreciation of music. Superior mechanical aptitude. However it is my considered opinion that she lacks the fire and raw emotion required of a great player." (from The Heterodyne Collection/ Transylvania Polygnostic Library, Beetleburg)

André smiled at her. "Never have I been so glad to be wrong."

Payne plowed his way through the crowd and stopped next to the cockpit. "Miss Clay, I'm…" he gave up. "I'm speechless."

Agatha blinked. "Is that good?"

The Countess smiled, "It's practically unheard of." This earned her a snort from Payne.

Agatha winced apologetically. "Please don't think it's done, I just wanted to test the keyboards." Payne stared at her. Agatha nervously buffed a bit of brass trim, "I'm almost finished with the latest mechanism. That'll let me add more instruments. Maybe even some little singing automata." Payne's eyes had begun to glaze. *Oh dear,* Agatha thought. *I'm boring him.*

"I was also thinking, maybe a kind of… a kind of ball, all covered in little mirrors and…"

This particular revolution in popular entertainment was brought to a halt by the sudden ringing of a bell. Agatha looked around in confusion. She knew the signal bells that the actors used for meals, attacks, meetings, and excessive drinking, but this one was unfamiliar. She realized it was coming from a small cupola atop one of the prop wagons. The circus people were looking between the bell and Agatha nervously.

Krosp dropped down next to her. "It's coming from Moxana's wagon."

Payne's eyebrows rose. "She must have heard the Silverodeon." He turned to Agatha. "I suspect she wants to meet you, Miss Clay."

Abner stepped up. "I'm sure Krosp told you about her."

Agatha nodded. "He told me enough to pique my curiosity, certainly. Unless I miss my guess she's some sort of autonomous clank construct, apparently with some attribute that resembles prognostication, which no one in the circus can understand, but is doubtless simply utilizing some heretofore undiscovered branch of science, which would explain why you try to keep her out of sight."

Master Payne looked at her, obviously considered saying something, but in the end, just waved her into the wagon.

It took a bit of maneuvering for all of them to fit into the tight space, so it was Krosp who first noticed—"Hey! The chessboard is gone."

Suddenly, the seated figure moved. Her eyes snapped open with a soft click. They were a vivid, electric blue. Her gleaming white porcelain arms came up and swept out over the board, which was now a pad of brushed green baize, embroidered with an intersecting set of lines and circles with a shining silver thread. Her movements were smooth, and gracefully stylized.

She slid her palms together and a deck of large, ornate cards appeared between them.

Payne grunted in surprise. "I haven't seen her use her cards in ages," he muttered.

Moxana placed the stack face down and with the tip of a finger, swirled the deck into an elaborate spiral. She then selected the card that lay in the center and flipped it up, exposing the face.

They all craned forward to examine it. Agatha had never seen a card like this before. Adam had occasionally had friends over for a late night game of cards in the back room of the forge. Agatha had been pressed into service bringing them beer and snacks. But this card was not embellished with any of the familiar four suits.

It was a colored picture of a globe hanging in the night sky, part of a mechanism of great brass and crystal gears. A large turn-key was inserted into the heart of Africa. At the top, along the margin was the Roman numeral "XXI" and at the bottom, written in a fine Carolingian miniscule hand, were the words—

"*The Device*." Payne adjusted his spectacles. "That's the card Moxana uses to indicate herself[40]."

Moxana nodded, took the card back and unhesitatingly tore it into small bits. As the others gasped in surprise, one of her hands snapped out and clasped Agatha's right hand and pulled it towards her. Agatha allowed her hand to be turned palm upwards. Moxana then dropped the shredded card into her open hand, reached out to take her other hand and placed it palm down upon the first. She then released both hands, brought both of her arms back to her sides and went still.

Everyone looked at each other, but nothing else happened. Agatha raised her hand. There, upon her upturned palm, was the card, restored and whole.

Agatha stared at this for several seconds, and then looked at Moxana. "You're broken," she hazarded, "And you want me to repair you."

Payne and Abner stared at each other in astonishment. "Could you do that?" Abner asked.

Agatha shrugged. "Depends on what's wrong. May I take a look?"

---

[40] From this description, as well as the others in this chapter, we can be fairly certain that Moxana was using the legendary Queen's Tarot Deck. This deck was commissioned by Albia of England, and illustrated by the Polish alchemist Cagliostro. Albia supposedly designed many of the cards herself, in the process renaming most of the Major Arcana. Today, only three complete decks are known to survive. One is in the British Museum, one is in the Restricted Collection of the Louvre, and one is in The Hermitage in St. Petersburg. The implication that Moxana possessed a deck, while intriguing, has yet to be actually confirmed. The Queen's Tarot is of particular interest to scholars, because according to anecdotal evidence, everyone who used it either went mad or spontaneously combusted.

Moxana nodded with a click. As Abner unlatched the front, Agatha reached into a pocket and pulled out her pocket-watch clank. A tap on the back, and the central eye clicked on, sending a bright beam of light across the wagon's dim interior. She slid to her knees and crawled into the depths of the cabinet. A faint humming could be heard as she poked around. This was cut off suddenly as Agatha's body jerked in surprise. She pulled herself out again with an amazed look on her face. She turned to the two men.

"Did you *know* that this is a Van Rijn?" she whispered.

Master Payne gave her an appraising look. "I did. I'm impressed that *you* do[41]."

Agatha reached out and gently took one of the clank's arms. She peered closely at the mechanisms in the finger joints. "My old Master used to talk about Van Rijn and his work endlessly. They were one of his passions." She put the hand down. "Beautiful," she murmured. "You'd never know she was over two hundred years old. There are *still* things we just don't know how to duplicate…"

She turned to face Master Payne. "I'd rather not just go poking around inside her. I didn't see anything obviously wrong. What's the problem?"

---

[41] Andronicus Valois, the Storm King, that charismatic historical figure who united Europa against the Heterodynes, pioneered the practice of absorbing a conquered enemy's forces. A strategy that Klaus Wulfenbach later adopted with great success. The greatest of the King's Sparks, was one R. van Rijn. Details about the man are frustratingly vague. We know that he claimed to be from one of the old Dutch Kingdoms and that he was always afraid that he would be assassinated, though he would never explain why. Contemporary writings suggest that he went to great lengths to obscure information about himself from becoming common knowledge, to the point where he even refused to sit for a portrait by the King's artist-in-residence. Some have suggested that he was a fictional creation, and that his work was actually made by Andronicus Valois himself. The Muses themselves vehemently deny this.

Payne shrugged. "I'm not sure—"

With a ping, Moxana snapped into action. Her hands swept up the cards, except for two, that spun about upon their corners before flopping down together, face up. In addition to *The Device*, there was a card that showed a spinning top balanced upon an upright wheel that was rolling off the edge of a cliff. It had the number "XV" at the top, and the label at the bottom simply read: *Movement*.

When Payne saw this, his face sagged and he closed his eyes. "Of course," he sighed. "Tinka."

To Agatha's unspoken question, he explained. "We used to have another clank we displayed along with Moxana. This one was a dancer. Her name was Tinka." He paused, and then continued. "Both Moxana and Tinka were originally part of a set of nine clanks constructed by the artificer Van Rijn for The Storm King." He again paused.

"The Muses," Agatha supplied. Then realization of what she had said penetrated and her eyes went wide. "The Muses? *The* Muses? *Moxana* is one of the Storm King's *Muses?*"

Payne nodded. "The same[42]."

Agatha was overwhelmed, and understandably so.

---

[42] The Storm King's Muses were unquestionably Van Rijn's greatest accomplishment. They were a set of nine clanks designed to embody various attributes that Van Rijn considered important for a ruler to know. They would guide, teach and instruct the Storm King in the various disciplines that would enable him to not just win a war, but wisely govern afterward. While there is no question that Andronicus was a superb administrator and manipulator, his journals reveal that the scope of the Empire was beginning to tax even his capabilities. As far as The Muses themselves, much has been claimed about their abilities, and many of these claims seem outlandish. However Van Rijn, in one of his few surviving letters ("Letter to 'D'." Currently held in the Non-Animate Library of Munich), confessed that with the Muses, he had produced something that he himself did not fully understand. —"But they have most kindly told me not to worry about it."

"But they were lost!"

"They lost themselves. If they had not done so, they were convinced they would have been dismantled by Sparks seeking to understand and duplicate Van Rijn's work. And so, they hid."

Agatha looked at Moxana. "But—As part of a traveling show?"

Payne spread his hands. "Actually it was a very perspicacious move. Before shows such as ours became Heterodyne shows, they were usually just traveling wonder shows, with a large collection of freaks and oddities. Some of the most popular items displayed were fake Muses. They were famous, after all."

He reached out and ran a hand gently over the back of Moxana's throne. "Moxana and Tinka had stayed together, and disguised as fakes, they survived, and traveled across Europa for over a hundred and fifty years, doing what they were designed to do. Instructing, inspiring and waiting."

"Waiting for what?"

Payne sighed. "For a new Storm King."

Krosp's brow furrowed. "But—"

Payne forestalled his objection with an upraised hand. "Don't even start. They were built to serve The Storm King. Until there's a new Storm King, they wait. If there never *is* a new Storm King, then they will wait *forever*. They are machines. Rational argument will only go so far."

Agatha nodded. She'd seen her share of otherwise brilliant mechanisms determined to walk through walls or wash pots until they'd been scrubbed into metal foil.

Payne continued. "But travel, especially in the Wastelands, is dangerous, and if you do it long enough, then the odds will turn against you." He shrugged. "I found Tinka and Moxana in a wrecked wagon amongst the ruins of another show. Whatever attacked didn't consider them valuable.

"They were happy enough to join my show, and I was able to protect them for almost twenty years."

Payne stopped and his shoulders slumped. Moxana reached up and gently patted his hand. Payne smiled at her and continued. "And then, three years ago, we were doing our spring traverse of the mountains, just as we're doing now. In those days, we preferred to go through Balan's Gap."

Krosp perked up. "I've heard of that. It's where the coalition of forces under The Storm King actually managed to stop Bludtharst Heterodyne's armies." He turned to Agatha. "Very famous battle, that. Until then, it looked like the Heterodynes would sweep all the way to the Danube, but instead, they were forced to overextend themselves and—"

Agatha put a large bucket over the cat. "You get him going on military history and he's good for several hours. You were saying?"

For some reason, Payne had to reassemble his thoughts. "Balan's Gap, yes. Big town. Lots of traffic. Lots of loose coin. The local ruling family is the House of Sturmvarous, currently headed by Prince Aaronev the fourth. A strong Spark. He used to be a major player, but when Wulfenbach rolled through, he submitted quietly enough, and he's been a good little vassal ever since.

"Of course, being the ruler, it's still within his power to confiscate...well... anything he wants, really. And out of the blue, what he wanted was Tinka, and there was nothing we could do." Payne removed his spectacles and fastidiously cleaned the spotless lenses. Obviously, the memory still angered him.

"There was still snow on the ground that year. Which is why Moxana had been left in her wagon. I'm guessing that's why they didn't take her as well." He looked at the clank and shook his head. "Perhaps it would have been better for her if they had."

Payne turned to Agatha. "The Muses were renowned as beautiful, miraculous machines. The common folk always ascribe emotions and actual self awareness to them, a fallacy that more educated people know better than to fall into." He hesitated. "But, I think… in this particular case… the common folk might be correct."

Agatha said nothing, but her mouth twitched. Payne waved his hand. "Yes, yes, I know. Anthropomorphism is a danger whenever you deal with any sufficiently sophisticated mechanism. It would certainly be easier to create a mechanism that merely *simulates* emotion.

"However there is no denying that in the last three years, Moxana has become less and less responsive. Even when she is active, she remains absorbed in her own private games. Recently she has begun shutting down for days at a time. Just before we found you, she'd been quiescent for almost a solid week. Even if her grief is artificial, I think it's destroying her.

"And that is why we are crossing the mountains as early as we are, this year. I want to get her to Transylvania Polygnostic University."

Agatha blinked in surprise. "In Beetleburg? But that's where I came from."

Payne looked interested. "That could prove useful. We should get there a few weeks after we go through Mechanicsburg. I want to get her to Dr. Tarsus Beetle, the master of the University.

No one knows more about The Muses than he does. We've corresponded in the past, but he doesn't know I possess an actual Muse." Payne shrugged wearily. "He's not someone I actually trust, but I've run out of ideas."

Agatha sighed. "Doctor Beetle is dead."

Everyone looked startled at this. "What?"

Agatha carefully picked her words. "I'm sorry, but it's true. I was his student before I was on Castle Wulfenbach[43]. He can't help you."

"Damn." Payne looked distraught. He looked at Moxana and he looked even worse. "Damn!" He pounded his fist against a nearby chest, denting it with the force of his blow. "We're committed to Sturmhalten now. We've lost too much of the year. And now I see it was for *nothing*!" He focused back on Agatha. "But you were his student?"

Agatha nodded.

"Well you're certainly a stronger Spark than any of us. Hopefully he taught you well."

Agatha looked wary. "Why?"

Payne patted Moxana's chassis. "I think... maybe... what Moxana needs, is a new sister. I'd like you to try to build one for her."

Agatha was already shaking her head. "Ridiculous. How could I possibly hope to duplicate the work of one of history's greatest Sparks? Work that no one else has been able to equal in the last two hundred years?"

---

[43] Dr. Beetle, the Tyrant of Beetleburg and master of the University, had been a friend of Barry Heterodyne, and one of the few people who had known the truth of Agatha's lineage, as well as the secret of her locket. He had kept her as close as possible by making her one of his lab assistants. The Lady Heterodyne has acknowledged that he was responsible for teaching her much about laboratory methodology, small town management, and advanced ranting.

Payne shrugged. "I have no idea. But you would have an actual functioning Muse to study. And—" He paused and looked at Moxana expectantly. With a faint sound, the seated figure nodded slowly and then placed her hands flat upon the board. There was a soft "click" and the board swung upwards, revealing a shallow, hidden compartment. Nestled within was a large book. It was bound in brown leather that had cracked with age. The pages within were thick hand cut sheets of vellum, with dozens of ribbons, scraps of papers, leaves and other objects serving as impromptu bookmarks. Upon the cover, embossed in gold that still gleamed against the dark leather, was a simple "R.v.R."

"More importantly, you'd have Van Rijn's notes."

Hours later, the opened book before her, reams of scribbled notations littering her wagon, Agatha had one of her little clanks in her hand. Its eye rolled in alarm as she selected a sharp bladed screwdriver. Agatha's eyes glittered with excitement. "Hold still," she commanded. "I've got six ideas for how to improve things already, and that's just from chapter one!" The clank squirmed and looked at her beseechingly. "Relax. You should be incapable of feeling pain."

A sound made her look up. Arrayed next to her door were the three Jägers. They stood quietly, obviously nervous, but there none the less. A part of Agatha's mind took note of the fact that she had not even heard them enter. "Yes?" she ventured.

The green Jäger, the one called Dimo, stepped forward. "Ve must tok," he said seriously.

Agatha looked at them and then carefully put down the

screwdriver along with the relieved clank. Instead of distracting her, the presence of the monster soldiers seemed to cause her brain to work harder.

"You've been avoiding me ever since you joined up with the circus, but now we must talk? Why? What's happened?"

Maxim grinned and swept his hair back in a theatrical gesture. He leaned in towards Agatha past Dimo, who looked alarmed. "Oh, vell, hyu know, who *vouldn't* vants to tok mit a pretty leetle gurl like hyu?" He leered.

Dimo grasped his sleeve. "Maxim! No!" He looked at Agatha's face, which had frozen in a mask of cold fury. "She iz schtill in de madness place! She could—"

With a deft movement, Agatha knocked off Maxim's hat. The mask of sophistication shattered and the purple Jaeger snarled, "Dot vas my *hat*!"

Agatha stepped closer to him. "What do you want?"

Maxim stared at her, saw the icy calmness that radiated off of her, and with a grin, gracefully dropped to one knee and bowed his head while placing a hand over his heart. "Forgiff me, mistress," he whispered.

Agatha made a moue of displeasure. "And that is quite enough of *that*," she stated. "Get up. These people don't know who I am."

Maxim nodded and stood back up. "Ve underschtand, lady."

Agatha looked at him skeptically. "I doubt it."

Maxim grinned. "Ve find tings out. Hyu iz escaped from Baron Wulfenbach. He tinks hyu iz dead. Now hyu iz goink to Mechanicsburg."

Dimo spoke up. "Iz dangerous to travel through der Vastelands mitout protection, so hyu join der circus. Efferbody vants a nize borink jouney. Ve agrees, so ve has helped out a bit mit dot already. Eet giffs us schomting to do at night, jah?"

Ognian stuck a clawed finger deep within an ear and wiggled it about. "Dot Master Payne, he vants a nice qviet trip too. Ezpecially sinze he's got dot fency magic doll he vants to keep hid from der medboy in Balan'z Gap."

Maxim nodded. "Yah. Dot family alvays had der sticky fingers and efferyvun iz afraid dot she gets stolen like her seester. She iz a clenk, bot if she gets dismantled, it chust der same as dyink, jah? Herr Payne tink dot since old Sturmvarous got vun nize toy from dis circus, he gun come sniffink around to see vhat else dey gots since den."

Dimo shrugged. "But dot Payne, he's a schmot guy. He gots a goot plan."

Ognian pulled a large insect out from the depths of his ear and regarded it with satisfaction. "He vants us to help. But hyu iz our mistress. Hyu gots to say it is hokay." With a flourish, he popped the insect into his mouth and chewed.

Agatha goggled at the three for a minute. Dimo elbowed Ognian, who looked guilty and stuck his finger back in his ear. "Sorry bout dot. Do hyu vant vun? Hy should have asked."

Agatha shuddered. "No, thank you." She paused. "You all seem...remarkably on top of all this." She regarded the three creatures before her. "Are you *really* Jägers?"

Maxim and Ognian looked surprised and glanced at each other. Maxim slid a small mirror out of his tunic and worriedly checked himself.

Dimo chuckled and slowly rubbed his jaw, which produced a sound analogous to stroking a stiff hairbrush. "Dot... iz a goot qvestion. Sometimes Hy vunder." Maxim and Ognian looked at him questioningly. "Haff all dose guys mit der Baron gone soft offer der years? Or haff ve become... sharper because ve leaf der group und haff to learn how to *tink* better?" He spread his hands. "Hy tink mebbee both."

Agatha narrowed her eyes. "The group... You mean the other Jägermonsters that work for the Baron?" Dimo nodded. "Why did you leave them?"

Dimo looked at her seriously. "For hyu."

Maxim nodded. "Ven der Baron offered the Jägerkin employment, ve knew ve had to take it. He said dot he needed us, but not as much as ve needed him. Ve served der House of Heterodyne. For der last twenty years or so, dot vas all to der goot, but der Jägers haff served der Heterodynes for hundreds uf years, und dot vas vat people remembered. Vitout der Heterodynes, ve needed somevun like der Baron to protect us.

"But if dere vas even a possibility dot anodder Heterodyne existed, ve could not, in goot conscience sign on mit der Baron. So ve agreed to serve him, mit the condition dot if a Heterodyne *vas* effer found, ve would be released from der Empire's service.

"Now, der Baron agreed to help us search, but it vas suspected dot searchink vould not be a high priority. So der Generals asked for a sqvad of *volunteers*."

Dimo picked up the narrative. "Ve were to leave the group. Go forth into der vorld, und not return until ve had found an acceptable Heterodyne heir, no matter how lonk it took. Ve knew it vas...suicide mission. Ve had kept track uf der family tree. Ve *knew* dot der Heterodynes vere gone. Ve vould neffer be able to go beck."

He stopped, overcome with emotion. Ognian gently

punched him on the shoulder and continued. "But because uf us, der Jägerkin could hold der heads up und say dot ve had not abandoned our masters. Dey vas free to join der House uf Wulfenbach. Der Baron protected dem, and dey fought for der Empire."

The Jäger grinned. "Und now hyu show op und spoil all our plenz!" A tear formed in his eye. "Because now ve... ve gets to go beck. And I neffer—" he gulped, "I neffer thought—" Suddenly he folded up at Agatha's feet and to her intense embarrassment clasped at her knees. "Ve haff missed you," he choked out. "Please, *please* be real!"

Agatha stooped and gave the distraught monster a hug. She looked up into the faces of the other two Jägers, who were displaying mixed emotions at the scene before them. "I *am* real," she assured them. "I really am."

She pulled an embarrassed Ognian to his feet and then sat back down. "Now tell me about Master Payne's plan."

Several days later, the circus cleared a last patch of forest and rolled onto a very well-maintained road running parallel to the bank of a fast-flowing river. According to Master Payne, this meant that they had officially exited the Wastelands.

This was cause for a small celebration. Bottles were passed about and musical instruments made their appearance. Thus it was a jolly troupe indeed that pulled up before the stout, reinforced gates of a small fortress that barred the road over the river.

Although small, the garrison bustled with activity. Farmers were delivering hay, a squad of new recruits loaded with large packs lumbered past, harried by a bellowing Sergeant. Stacks of stores were being moved by sweating troopers, who were stripped to the waist. Several nearby airship gantries stood empty, but showed signs of recent use.

Everywhere in evidence was a sigil depicting a sword thrust down through the spokes of a gear, which was adorned with a pair of heraldic wings. This was the Sturmvarous family crest. They had arrived at the border of Balan's Gap.

Questions were asked. A desultory examination of the wagons was made, a small discreet payment, as well as several bottles, exchanged hands, and the wagons rumbled through the fortress and over the well-maintained stone bridge. More than one circus member noted the carrier pigeons that left the fortress shortly thereafter and flew on before them.

The lowlands on this side of the river consisted mostly of rich-looking farmland, with fields of freshly sown dark earth, dotted with small settlements.

Almost immediately, however, the road swung upwards, and they began to climb the foothills leading up to the actual pass over the mountains.

The superior quality of the road was a pleasant change after weeks in the Wastelands, and once all of the spare horses were hitched up, the climb was slow, but uneventful.

Quickly enough, the trees began to change from deciduous to conifer. By the time the circus pulled into the small alpine village where they'd spend the night, there was a bit of a chill to the air. There were also dark, gathering clouds. The troupe's part-time meteorologist assured Payne that there would unquestionably be a heavy rainstorm in the next few hours, as well as the always-present danger of meteors.

There was no show that night. With the threat of rain, Payne had refused to set up the outdoor stage. With his permission, many of the performers headed over to the inn, a large, grandiose building that was beginning to show signs of neglect. It had been built in the days before airship travel had begun to steal the wealthy road traffic.

There would be no Heterodyne show this evening. The proprietor of the inn had agreed to split the evening's profits if the troupe performed in the tavern, and while there wasn't enough space for a proper stage show, it was a perfect venue for individual musicians, buskers and jugglers to try out new routines.

Agatha and Zeetha were heading there themselves, when they came upon Lars tending a small fire.

Lars had been a lot more attentive of late. Agatha found this flattering, but she had discovered that while Lars was undoubtedly what people in books referred to as a "boon companion," he had certain deficiencies that she, personally, found troubling.

As Lars would have been the first to point out, he wasn't particularly intellectual, had no inclination towards mechanics or chemistry, and frankly admitted that he wasn't even much of a reader.

On the plus side, he was tall and muscular, displayed a great deal of interest in Agatha, and when he spoke in his onstage "Madboy" voice, her heart began thumping in a most distracting manner.

She had shared these observations with Zeetha, who had shrugged. "So he's not much for intellectual discussion?"

Agatha shook her head.

"Good kisser though, eh?"

Agatha had blushed and nodded. Even though all they had done was kiss once a night onstage, these kisses *had* been getting better and better.

"So kiss him enough that he doesn't have a chance to mess things up by talking."

Agatha frowned. "That seems like an extremely poor blueprint for a long-term relationship."

Zeetha rolled her eyes. "Start with kissing him twice in one night. Then decide if you *want* to work your way up."

This suggestion certainly had a lot to recommend it, so when they reached Lars, Agatha stopped, and casually said, "You go on ahead. I'll be there eventually."

Zeetha just grinned, and trotted off.

Lars unrolled a horse blanket upon the ground, and patted the empty space beside him invitingly.

"Not going to the inn?" Agatha asked.

Lars shook his head. "I had a bellyful of that lot yesterday. They water the beer and underpay the tavern maids. Besides, someone's got to watch the wagons." He pulled a small silver timepiece out from an inside pocket and consulted it. "My watch'll be over soon anyway." He looked up at the low-lying clouds. "Before it starts to rain, if I'm lucky. You?"

Agatha stepped over and, feeling quite daring, sat down beside him. "I don't like taverns much. I don't like the smells." She leaned back a bit and looked at the dark clouds overhead. "I think that's what I like best about living on the road. It always smells so nice."

"You got *that* right," Lars agreed. He reached behind him and pulled out a dark green bottle. He flipped open his knife and set about removing the wax sealing the cork. "Of course,

I spent five years apprenticed to a cheese-maker, so just about *anywhere* smells better than that." He pulled the cork with a pop, buffed the lip in a gentlemanly way with his sleeve, and offered her the bottle.

Agatha took a sip. It was sweeter than she expected. She passed the bottle back. "I don't know about that. I was a lab assistant. For stick-to-your-clothes stink, I doubt you can beat your exotic coal-tar derivatives."

Lars took a drink. He started to speak, and then began laughing.

"What?"

Lars shook his head. "Here I am thinking I'm going to impress a pretty girl by talking about the terrible smells of various loathsome cheeses." He took another drink and handed Agatha the bottle. "Mighty suave, huh?"

Agatha cocked an eyebrow. "Well I *am* impressed at how smoothly you slipped the 'pretty girl' line in."

Lars stared at her for a moment, and then sheepishly looked at his boots. "Well, it's not like I was lying." He glanced at her again. "If you're going to cynically analyze everything I say, then I might as well start talking about cheese again."

Agatha rolled her eyes. "If that's my choice, I think I'd prefer it if you stopped talking."

Lars turned towards her. "All right."

He reached out, gently pulled her towards him and kissed her. It was a slow, relaxed kiss, and yet Agatha felt her heart racing. When they stopped, she took a deep breath. "That wasn't *exactly* what I meant."

Lars raised his eyebrows. "Oh. Is that a problem?"

Agatha opened her mouth and he kissed her again. This time

the kiss was harder, and when they broke apart, Agatha could feel that her face was flushed.

"Wait," she gasped.

Lars smiled. "I have been. This is what I was waiting for." He leaned in again, and then checked himself. "You don't like it?"

Agatha did like it. A lot. But there was something that was... not right—she tried to convince herself... "It... it could be an interesting experiment," she whispered.

Lars paused, and then dropped into his madboy voice. "Don't tell me you fear the experiment?"

With a small growl, Agatha mashed her lips to his. This caught Lars by surprise and he tried to pull back, but found himself held fast by Agatha gripping his vest. The kiss intensified and she pulled him even closer. Lars felt a small burst of panic and wrenched his face back, breaking the kiss.

Agatha looked at him. Her eyes flashed in heavy-lidded irritation. She pulled him back towards her—

"Stop!" Lars gasped out.

Agatha blinked in astonishment, realized that she was holding him fast, and released him so suddenly that he fell backwards.

Lars felt his heart racing like he had just escaped from some sort of trap. He looked up at Agatha, slightly disheveled, breathing quickly, with a bit of a wild look in her eye, and wondered if he had.

For her part, Agatha was analyzing what had just happened. She looked at Lars and realized that while he wasn't that interesting intellectually, if he talked to her in his onstage voice, he could recite a bread recipe and she would do whatever he wanted. This disturbed her. On the other hand, it had been an exceptional kiss.

Suddenly, there was the sound of amused throat-clearing,

and they turned to find Captain Kadiiski standing on the other side of the dying fire, seemingly fascinated with the cloud-obscured night sky.

He glanced their way, and seeing that he had their attention, bowed. "Good evening! Am sorry to be breaking up no doubt fascinating discussion of various intellectual subjects, but it is my turn to stand the watching." He paused, "So when did someone steal Master Payne's wagon?"

Agatha and Lars whipped about, and seeing that all was well, glared at the grinning mechanic.

"Very funny," Lars said sourly as he offered Agatha a hand up.

Kadiiski nodded. "It is that." He tipped his hat to Agatha. "So! Are you offering stimulating conversation to all of us lonely watching men?"

Agatha blushed. "I... ah..."

Kadiiski guffawed and made shooing motions. "Off with you both before I am made dead from the cuteness."

They did. From the inn, a song about the Storm King, accompanied by much table pounding, boomed out from the open doors. A local staggered out and was exuberantly sick.

Wordlessly, they turned back towards the wagons.

All too soon, they found themselves at the foot of the Baba Yaga's ladder. Tentatively, they kissed. It went on for some time.

Finally, Lars took a deep breath. "Okay. I gotta... I gotta go grab some shut-eye."

Agatha nodded, and with some difficulty, removed her hands from Lars' vest. "Right. Say good night to Herr de la Scalla for me."

"Oh I won't see him, I'll be bunking under one of the wagons."

"What? Why?"

Lars grinned. "Well, Pix has kind of moved in. I'll be getting a new wagon soon enough, but it's no big deal since I'm so used to sleeping outside anyway." He paused, "Although, if you can think of a place I could stay…"

Agatha looked up at Lars and her breath caught. For a moment, the lights from the inn illuminated his profile in such a way that she was reminded of Gilgamesh Wulfenbach.

But it wasn't Gilgamesh, and it never would be. She had run from him and made sure that he never came back. Ever.

No, it wasn't Gilgamesh. It was Lars. A man who liked her. Who…who wanted her, even though he knew what she was. She looked around. This was her world now, and Lars was one of the people in it. A good person. Maybe good enough…

All of this flashed through her head in a split second.

"I don't know," she whispered. "It sounds tempting. Really tempting. But…"

Lars knew when to push and when to fade. Sometimes you wanted a girl to be thrown a bit off balance. He gently ran a hand down her cheek and smiled. "—But that's a big step. No problem."

Agatha had been expecting a little more pressure. "Really? You'll be okay?"

Lars dramatically put a hand to his heart and strove to look excessively noble. "I assure you that none will be disturbed by my weeping." Agatha's eyes narrowed, and Lars chuckled, lightening the mood. "No, seriously, I'll be fine outside—"

A boom of thunder rattled loose objects as it rolled across the sky and a wall of rain crashed down upon them.

Seconds later, they were inside the wagon, clothes dripping. Agatha fetched a towel from the small cabinet under the washbowl and silently began dabbing it at Lars' face.

"Or, I could stay here," he conceded. Without taking his eyes off of hers, Lars nodded. "That bench seat should be comfortable enough."

Agatha opened her mouth and he kissed her again. This was a forceful kiss, intense, but quickly ended. He pulled back slightly and waited to see how Agatha would react.

She tipped her head back—

A frantic hammering began upon the door, causing them both to jump. Agatha pulled it open to reveal a soaked and bedraggled Krosp. He marched in and stoically allowed Agatha to remove his dripping coat and towel him down.

"I feel most put upon," he announced when she was done. "I am going to bed." With that, he scrambled up the ladder.

Agatha looked apologetically at Lars. "Sorry about that."

Lars snorted in amusement and leaned in. "We could wait until he's—"

"Agatha!" Krosp's head appeared in the opening. "Come and fold down the bed!" He disappeared again.

Lars paused. "Normally, overly-protective cats don't bother me, but—"

"Agatha! Do we have any cheese?" Krosp peered down at them. "Bring up some cheese." He vanished.

They both stared up at the opening for a moment. Then eyed each other. "I'll bet he snores," said Lars.

"Not usually," Agatha sighed, "But I'll bet he starts tonight."

They both chuckled, and then looked into each other's eyes. They leaned in for a last kiss—

"Agatha! You missed a wet spot on my head! Bring the—" The flung towel struck Krosp in the face.

SEVEN

On this spot we will build a shield against the Heterodyne. A fortress so strong he cannot crack it. Like a mighty storm, he will rage and scream and throw himself against it. But here we will fight him, and here we will stop him. Because we will have a place of refuge. A place of strength. A place of hope. We will have Sturmhalten.

—ANDRONICOUS VALOIS, FROM THE COMMISSION OF
BUILDING DELIVERED TO THE WESTERN COALITION
AFTER THE BATTLE OF THE SIX SKIES

It was a crisp, frosty dawn. The weather up here at the pass was still meandering towards spring, but the drivers of the circus wagons were dressed in their performing finery, albeit over several layers of winter underwear.

They certainly attracted a fair amount of interest as they rumbled through the outskirts of the town. Technically,

Balan's Gap was still before them, constrained behind the city walls, but along the main road a ramshackle collection of businesses that existed to service, supply (and swindle) travelers had grown up around the various industries that had been placed outside the town for various health, space or aesthetic reasons.

Last night the circus had arrived at one of the staging areas that existed for arriving or departing trade caravans. While there were still plenty of other travelers who used the old roads, there had been enough excess space in the staging area that the circus had been able to put on a late night performance, to great success. Thus, this morning, they were buoyed along by a large crowd of well-wishers, and noisily escorted by a ragtag convoy of children who frantically waved at the drivers and the various characters who sat waving back wearing grins that didn't look forced at *all*.

Abner and Master Payne sat together on the driver's seat of the lead wagon, sharing a couple of mugs of stewed tea, and a large basket of freshly baked cardamom butter rolls.

To the amazement of a small girl, Payne drew an impossibly large handkerchief from Abner's ear, delighted her brother by blowing his nose in it with a sound like a rampaging elephant, and then scandalized their mother by stuffing it back into his long-suffering apprentice's ear.

The cart slowed to a stop. Before them were several other wagons, all awaiting the pleasure of the gate masters of the town. Each wagon was assessed an entrance fee based on the number of riders, number of horses, purpose of travel, and how much trouble you gave the gate keepers. Three wagons ahead, a stout, richly dressed merchant was making things expensive for himself by insisting that the animal pulling his cart was not, in fact a horse, but a rare, short-eared mule.

Both of the watchers appreciated natural comedy in the wild, and were mentally making notes for a future skit.

"So," said Abner, taking a sip of tea, "You really think this—" he glanced back at the wagon's door, "Is going to work?"

Payne looked at him askance. "Come now, Ab. It's far too late to say anything other than 'Yes.'"

With this cheery statement ringing in Abner's ear, the wagon eventually rolled to the head of the line and stopped at the behest of a guard in a grey woolen uniform and a non-regulation set of enormous fur mittens.

He sauntered on over. Payne offered him a steaming pastry. The guard accepted it as his due. "Welcome to Balan's Gap." He leaned to the side and quickly surveyed the line of circus wagons. "A Heterodyne show is it?"

Payne nodded. "Twenty-six wagons. Sixty-two horses, one clank, and three cows. Forty-eight people."

The soldier smiled. Tolls for large parties were always easier to skim. "Well, let me tot that up for you, sir." He began to assess the quality of their clothing. "Will you be stopping in town?"

The upper half of the wagon door behind Payne and Abner slammed open and Dimo, now sporting a jaunty cap emblazoned with a prominent Wulfenbach insignia, leaned out and snarled. "Hoy! Vat's der holdup?"

The young soldier reeled back in surprise and hammered twice on the door of the guardhouse behind him. This swung open and an older officer stuck his head out. The younger soldier muttered, "Jägers, Sir."

The older soldier swallowed and stepped forward. "We weren't informed you were coming." He eyed the wagon and frowned, "You don't look like one of the Baron's... *official* convoys."

Dimo guffawed and leaned on the door. "Nah. Dey vas just goink our vay, und dey's *fonny* guys."

Payne nodded rapidly. "It's been a great honor, having them travel with us, but surely the Prince could get them where they're going faster? Or perhaps we could just leave them here? Please?"

The older guard smiled grimly. "Oh, no. I'm shunting you to the military lane." He pointed to a different gate, which was still sealed. Unbidden, the younger soldier dashed off and moments later the portcullis began to grind upwards. He continued, "Once the Prince gives his approval, you'll be through the town within the hour and there's no charge."

Payne looked distraught. "But... supplies..."

The officer threw him a brass and beribboned token, which was stamped with the town seal. "Surrender that to the Quartermaster once you're past the city and he'll *give* you supplies. Our compliments to the Baron."

Payne tried again, "But—"

The old soldier interrupted with a curt, "Move along!"

Payne hesitated, and Dino smacked the top of his head. "Hyu heard de man, sveethot, ve iz schtill bunkies!"

The old soldier shuddered, but held firm and waved the caravan along, and then made sure the gate was lowered behind them.

Within the depths of Sturmhalten Castle, the seneschal, a tall angular man with elaborate moustaches, received the city gate report from a deeply breathing soldier. He scanned it and waved the man back to his post. With a sigh, he strode down through the elaborately decorated hallways, past the bustling domestic staff.

He stopped before an enormous door constructed of wrought

iron and blue enamel, and selected a large silver key. Once he'd gone through, he very carefully closed the door again and then stepped up to the little platform. Above said platform was a large raised area, which was cluttered with a bewildering array of devices, several of which meticulously tracked his every movement.

At the center was a large, dark, wooden desk, carved in the Jacobean style. Seated at this desk, in a tall-backed leather and gold ornamented chair, with his back to the door, was the master of Sturmhalten, The Gatekeeper of Balan's Gap, His Royal Highness, Prince Aaronev IV. The Prince waved to acknowledge his seneschal's presence, but did not look up, as he was engaged with something laid out upon the desk before him. His seneschal could not quite see what it was from this angle, but every now and again something twitched briefly into view, and he was just as glad.

He waited patiently until there was a thin squeal, which was suddenly cut off. The Prince sighed in annoyance and leaned back in his chair. He began to wipe his hands with a towel. "What is it, Artacz?"

The waiting man pulled out the report and cleared his throat. "It's today's report, sir."

Aaronev paused, reached out and tapped an elaborate chronometer sitting upon his desk. "It's a bit early, yes?"

Artacz nodded. "Indeed it is, sire. But to start at the beginning; we had an unusually large party of tailors through the Copper Gate—" he paused.

Aaronev drummed his fingers several times. "Hm. Challburg is celebrating the Feast of Saint Finnemede The Overdressed early this year... what else?"

"A fight with rather amusing consequences at the Rusted Swan—"

Aaronev interrupted, "*Again*? Mph. Tell the landlord that he is to stop trying to make change in base eight, or he'll be paying his taxes in base *twelve*."

Artacz smiled briefly. "Good one, Highness. And finally, a party of the Baron's Jägers have attached themselves to a traveling Heterodyne show. They have been shunted to the Military road, and are awaiting your clearance."

Aaronev waved a hand. "Ah. Klaus occasionally foists a few Jägers onto travelers. It lets him assess the safety of the roads while keeping them out of his hair. Well, I certainly don't want to keep them here, so if that's all, you may go."

Artacz bowed and stepped backwards until he reached the doors. Smoothly he opened them and was just about to exit when Aaronev shouted, "Wait!"

The seneschal looked up in surprise. "Your Highness?"

Aaronev had turned about in his chair. A look of keen interest was on his face. He leaned forward. "Did you say—A traveling *Heterodyne* show?"

Payne crumpled the note in a massive fist and slammed it down upon the table top. "*A command performance!*" His roar of despair reminded Abner of a dying rhinoceros. He shook his fist with the crumpled note at a cruel, mocking universe. "And he very kindly sent the Jägers on ahead—Just like we *asked*!"

Marie judged that the main explosion had passed and gently stroked his perpetually tangled hair. "Enough, dear," she murmured. "It was a good plan. And at least we haven't been searched. It seems that all he *really* wants is to see a show."

Abner dug into the paper bag on his lap with a rustle. A crudely printed label proclaimed that it contained genuine candied fish. This initially loathsome, but surprisingly addictive delicacy was one of the town's principal items of export. "It's not your fault that the Prince was bored, sir." He crunched down a lemony minnow.

After a moment Payne nodded grudgingly. "True enough." He leaned back and slid an arm around Marie's waist. "Well, we'll keep Moxana out of sight, and just give him a good show."

Abner swallowed a lime guppy and grinned mischievously. Yes sir! I was thinking *The Socket Wench of Prague*."

Marie stiffened in disapproval. Payne looked worried. "Um... that one's a bit *risqué*, don't you think?"

Abner sat back and balanced a chocolate carp on his fingertip. "Oh, yessir. They might even run us out of town tonight."

Master Payne and the countess looked at each other and began to grin. "Now *that's* a good plan," Payne conceded.

A brisk knock at the door announced Professor Moonsock, who carried a rather official-looking envelope as if she was afraid it might explode. "This just got delivered, sir. It's a note from the palace."

Marie took the envelope and sliced it open with a fingernail. "The Prince wants to see a specific show," she looked up with tired eyes. "*The Socket Wench of Prague*."

Abner's eyes bugged. Payne shrugged. "Okay—not so good a plan."

Marie cleared her throat. "P.S.—Tart It Up."

Payne slumped and rubbed his eyes. "Downright terrible plan."

"All right! I get it!" Abner leapt to his feet, crammed a last fish in his mouth and stomped towards the door. After but two steps, he gagged and spat it back out into his hand. Payne and Marie looked at him in astonishment. "Sorry," he said embarrassed, "Somebody slipped in a pollywog."

The Royal Theatre of Sturmhalten was small, but elegantly appointed. The architect that had been brought out from Paris had understood that the building itself should be part of the theatre-going experience. Red velvet seats and gilded carvings of extremely healthy young people in exceedingly impractical clothing were lavishly spread about. An afternoon rehearsal had revealed excellent acoustics, a Spark-designed-but-probably-not-*too*-lethal lighting system, and a concession stand serving a variety of drinks and local delicacies, from which candied fish was noticeably absent.

There was also a Royal Box, directly overlooking the stage, equipped with a gleaming machine cannon mounted upon a swivel. The caretaker had helpfully pointed out that it could cover almost any part of the theatre. He also emphasized that the Prince hated a dull show. This had led to a feverish rewriting session.

It was now evening. The show had started. Richly dressed merchants and government officials were drinking and applauding the antics onstage, as uniformed ushers glided through the darkness, escorting patrons with softly glowing crank-operated lanterns.

Up in the Royal box, Prince Aaronev had just allowed his servant to pour him another glass of tokay, when the door swung open and a richly dressed young man entered the box.

He was tall and broad at the shoulder. A little stockier than he should have been, but it was obvious that he kept himself in shape by the grace with which he moved. His reddish hair was cut full, and pulled back into a small queue, which was the current fad amongst the dandies in Vienna, and an elegant pince-nez perched upon his nose.

With a small motion, he dismissed the servant, locked the box door, made a small bow of familial respect, and seated himself in the next chair.

Aaronev smiled in genuine pleasure. "Tarvek. I was beginning to think you weren't coming." He glanced at the box's empty third chair. "Where is your sister?"

The young man shrugged. "Sorry, father, we had some late guests I had to see to." The Prince frowned. Tarvek continued, "As for Anevka, you *know* she isn't keen on anything that isn't grand opera. She begs your indulgence and says that she will join us later at supper." He looked down at the stage, where Dame Ædith was throwing knives with amazing accuracy, especially since she was continually being harassed by what looked like a demented bat. Tarvek wondered how they'd managed to train the creature. "What have I missed?"

The Prince had still been brooding over the news of the aforementioned guests, but at Tarvek's question, he visibly perked up. "Quite a bit! An excellent magician, some song and dance, a sword mistress you would have enjoyed, I'm sure, and a *hilariously* bad midget in a cat suit."

Tarvek eyed the stage. "Yes, I can see the bullet holes from the warning shots."

The Prince chuckled. "I was laughing so hard I could hardly aim."

Tarvek nodded as he spooned some caviar onto a cracker. "It's good to see you so happy, father. I've been worried for you of late."

The Prince sipped from his glass. "Thank you, my boy. Yes, this show is a welcome change of pace."

On the stage below, Master Payne was booming out the traditional opening of the main event. The audience grew hushed as his stentorian voice rolled over them, setting the scene. Aaronev quietly continued, "I must confess, son, I..." He breathed deeply. "I have felt—for some time—that our task may be... impossible." He sighed, "I—We have looked for so long."

Tarvek leaned towards him. "There *are* certain realities that are undeniable. No one could say you were disloyal, father."

Aaronev scowled. "They can! They have!"

Tarvek reached out and took one of his father's gloved hands. He spoke earnestly. "Anevka and I—We both know you have given this task your all. I know that if The Mistress were here, *she'd* say—"

"*KNEEL,* YOU MISERABLE MINIONS!"

Both of the men froze in terror, and then whipped about to stare at the stage. Below them, Agatha, in an extremely tight leather outfit, strode about demanding to know if various implements of torture had been prepared to her unreasonable specifications. After a moment, the younger man slumped back into his chair and chuckled.

"Ho! That gave me a bit of a turn! That girl they've got playing Lucrezia certainly has a commanding voice, don't—"

"Tarvek!" Aaronev's voice cut across the younger man's burbling. He had pulled a slim, metal box out from under his coat. Dials and small meters encrusted its surface. At the moment, all of the lights were flashing green. "It's her."

Tarvek stared at the glowing device like a bespectacled hamster looking at an approaching snake. "No!" He whispered. "Impossible!"

Aaronev thrust the device into Tarvek's hands. "Look at the meters! The harmonics match *perfectly*!" He rubbed his hands together gleefully. "It's her!"

Tarvek stared at the device. Viciously, he smacked it against the arm of his chair several times. The dials wavered, and then the needles swung back into the green. "The fuses must be old! This isn't proof—"

His father grabbed his coat, and with surprising strength, dragged him to the edge of the balcony and pointed towards the audience.

Throughout the entire theatre, the audience, as well as the ushers, had dropped to their knees, and were staring, enraptured, at the figure marching back and forth upon the stage.

Tarvek stared at the tableau below them for a moment and then slowly collapsed backwards into his chair. "Oh, dear," he muttered.

The curtain came down for the final time. The audience was on its feet. The enthusiastic applause was beginning to taper off, but was still satisfyingly loud to the cast filing off into the wings. The Countess took a final look at the audience through a chink in the side curtain, and signaled Captain Kadiiski to bring up the house lights. She then turned away and smiled. "Good show, folks."

Taki grinned as he removed the Baron's pants from his head. "We have *got* to do that one more often!"

André rolled his eyes as he handed the giant screwdriver to one of the prop handlers. "Don't be absurd! The catfight scene in the grease vat? That *alone* would get us jailed anywhere east of Bucharest."

Guntar smiled as he wiped off his construct stitching. "If I can play one of the grease monkeys? So worth it."

Pix sashayed over to Abner. Her diaphanous High Priestess outfit strained as she leaned in and gave him a deep kiss. He responded, but then realized that with this outfit, there were no publicly acceptable places to put his hands.

Pix murmured, "I was worried that this play might be a bit too…" She glanced over at Agatha. "Sophisticated. But she did just fine."

Abner smiled. "Yes, well, I had her rehearse her lines separately. She didn't know the context."

Agatha was peeking through the curtain at the exiting crowd. Lars stood beside her, giving her a gentle hug. "You did good."

"But I'm not sure what I did."

Lars coughed delicately. "Well, I suppose I'll just have to take some time and explain the nuances. For your own good, of course."

Agatha felt her heart skip a beat. "Yes," she said. "I think I'd like that." She turned to Lars and shyly smiled. They looked into each other's eyes, and leaned in for a kiss—

There was a brief clamor from one of the side doors, and an elegantly dressed retainer in a blue velvet coat and a powdered wig stepped backstage. He was met by Master Payne.

The retainer bowed his head respectfully. "His Highness

wishes to convey his pleasure in your performance." With this, he drew forth a thick leather purse, which he dropped into the circus master's hand with a satisfying "chink."

"How generous," Payne murmured. It was certainly a surprise. Usually a Command Performance meant that, as one old showman had famously put it, "They command, we perform, nobody pays." But this—

The retainer nodded and then continued. "In addition, the Royal Family was so taken with the young lady who played the Lady Lucrezia, your Madame Olga, I believe, that they have requested her presence at the palace for supper this evening." His gaze found Agatha. "A coach is waiting."

Several minutes later Agatha found herself the center of a great hum of activity. Several dressmakers were busy sewing her into a splendid lace confection colored a rather bilious sea foam green.

She critically examined a sleeve. "Um… I don't know a lot about fashion," she ventured, "but this color—"

"It looks terrible on you," the seamstress said around a mouthful of pins. She sat back and eyed Agatha critically. "It would look terrible on almost anyone, but on you? It's hideous."

Agatha stared at her. "That's good?"

The seamstress sighed. "It's tricky. We can't put you in rags, because that would be an insult. We have to put you in a good dress. But we want you to be subtly unappealing enough that you won't have to fend anybody off." She spit a pin into her hand. "Princes hate being fended off. So we go for an off color. Simple, yes?"

Her hair was being plaited and set by two hairdressers and the troupe's make up artist was delicately running brushes over her face. While this was going on, she was being given a crash course in court etiquette, which essentially boiled down to "Vaguely agree with everything, commit to nothing."

Finally everyone was done and nodded at each other in satisfaction. Agatha turned to look at herself in a mirror and gasped in dismay. She looked... not terrible... it *was* a nice dress. Her hair was stylish and her make up was flawless, but she looked... totally uninteresting.

Even as she understood what had been done and appreciated the artistry behind it, it was a terrible thing to do to a young girl.

Marie knew what was going through her head and patted her hand. "Just think of it as another part, my dear." Agatha tore her eyes away from the dull creature in the mirror and nodded.

Lars strode up and took her left hand. "Here," he said briskly. "This couldn't hurt." He slipped a gold ring upon Agatha's finger. She examined it. It was a wide band, seemingly constructed of smaller gold wires laced together. She looked up at Lars.

He grinned. "Tell him you're married. Some of these guys don't like to shop second-hand, if you know what I mean." Agatha blushed. Lars continued. "I use it to keep me out of trouble when I pass through a town."

Agatha looked at him askance. "What *kind* of trouble?"

"Unasked for romantic entanglements," he said frankly. "More importantly, it unfolds into a very serviceable lock pick that opens a wide variety of cell doors." Lars smiled. "Trust me on that."

Agatha leaned in and gave him a kiss. "Thank you, Lars."

As Master Payne escorted her to the waiting coach, a small frown crossed her face. "People keep giving me rings," she confided to him, "But I think a small death ray might be more practical."

Master Payne merely patted her hand and assisted her into the waiting coach.

This was a splendid-looking vehicle. A roomy, elegantly-styled black compartment, adorned with fenders and finials of gleaming silver. Silver caged lights festooned the surface, and the now-familiar sword and gear sigil was emblazoned upon the sides.

As the footman assisted her up into the plush, satin-lined interior, Agatha realized that there were no horses. Once the door was closed, the driver threw a lever, and there was a great hissing from the back of the coach. Through the small, leaded rear window, Agatha saw a sturdy little motor burble into life, and with a cloud of steam, the coach rumbled off.

Agatha took the opportunity to examine the passing scenery. Balan's Gap was a prosperous town, thanks to the pass, and had been so for quite a while. All of its streets were paved with cobblestone or brick, and the night was illuminated by hundreds of lights.

Not just by the traditional torches, gaslamps and incidental fires of the still bustling shops and taverns, but also by the startling blue-white glare of the new-fangled electrical arc lamps that were coming out of England. Overall, surface travel was certainly reduced from its glory days, but you'd never know it here. Travelers from all across the Empire wove through the streets of Balan's Gap.

But the town had its eye upon the future. They rolled past the airship docks, and Agatha could see that they were being expanded. Still brightly lit despite the lateness of the hour, teams of stevedores and balloonjacks were roaring and calling as cargo cranes groaned, swinging pallets loaded with cargo to and from the lines of waiting delivery wagons. The roads here were choked with carts and vans, their teamsters swearing and screaming at each other in a dozen different languages.

The driver of Agatha's coach relied upon his distinctive horn to clear the way, but when that failed, he did not hesitate to leave the roadway and send pedestrians leaping for safety by driving down the sidewalks without ever reducing his considerable speed. Occasionally, members of the city constabulary would hear the commotion, see the cause, and hastily drag themselves and anyone nearby to safety, stepping out again only when the royal coach had passed.

In this manner they approached the castle. This was a massive edifice, obviously built as a solid defense against a dangerous foe. Agatha realized with a start that this must be fabled Sturmhalten Castle itself.

Ancient battle scars covered its stone walls, but it stood unbroken. A wide moat, easily thirty meters across surrounded it, spanned by a single grand causeway, lined with lights. The coach turned onto this, and Agatha glimpsed the gigantic doors of the castle itself, opening to admit them.

They passed beneath the massive portcullis and into an interior courtyard that was brightly lit with electrical lights and alive with servants bustling about.

Here the coach slowed and actually took some care as it threaded delicately between the people and inner structures. It finally glided to a stop, hissing, at the foot of a broad marble stairway, which was flanked by two statues holding large, electrically lit globes.

Several steps up, idly tapping his foot, was a tall, elegantly dressed young man. Dark auburn hair was artlessly swept away from his eyes, which were adorned with a tiny pair of spectacles.

When the driver and footman saw him, they froze, and then leapt to the ground and frantically tried to get the coach door open while babbling. "Forgive me, your Highness!" Agatha then noticed the pin at the young man's throat, which was the same sword-in-winged gear that adorned many of the walls and lampposts in the town. "We brought the young lady as swiftly as we could, Prince Tarvek—the market—!"

The young man waved his hand impatiently, cutting the babbling off dead. His voice, when he spoke, was obviously amused. The sound of it sent an odd sensation down Agatha's spine.

"Yes, yes. *Calm* yourself." He stopped before the bowing servants and languidly motioned for them to straighten up. "My Royal father *insisted* that I meet the coach." The servants blinked and stood rooted to the spot. The young man sighed. "You may now leave us. *We* shall escort our guest to dinner."

He then turned to Agatha, who executed a perfect curtsey. "Your Highness," she said.

Tarvek focused his attention upon her fully and his smile faltered. *What the devil is she wearing?* he thought to himself. For a moment he wondered whether the circus had tried to send a different girl. This plain thing bore only a superficial resemblance to the fiery actress he'd seen strutting about the stage—

Actress... Tarvek stopped and forced himself to mentally step back and analyze what he was seeing. The planes of her hair, the lines artfully painted upon her face, the perfection of awfulness that was her dress… His breath caught in admiration. There was cunning here.

The Prince smiled in genuine appreciation at a work of art, and took her hand, "Enchanté," he murmured. He then folded her hand across his arm and they climbed the stairs, entering the castle.

They swept past rows of bowing servants. Several of these darted on ahead, no doubt to warn the rest of the staff, as wherever they went, they were met by downturned heads. Agatha began to wonder if Royalty was inclined to study phrenology.

"My father and my sister will be joining us." Tarvek said. "It will be a small, family meal tonight. You must forgive the impromptu informality of the occasion, but we know your troupe will want to leave tomorrow, and we quite enjoyed your performance."

The castle interior was magnificently decorated, with rich carpets and floor tiles arranged in intricate mathematical patterns. Grand tapestries depicting scenes of the Storm King's legend lined the hallways, and where they were absent, lavish paneling and cunning woodwork carved into fantastically interwoven geometric shapes were to be seen.

They entered a large open area, which was dominated by a grand fireplace. Agatha paused in admiration. Most fireplaces, in her experience, served as large, efficient heat pumps apparently designed to suck warmth from all other parts of the room. This one, however, had been overlaid with a fantastic arrangement of large glass pipes, filled with a slow roiling liquid, which swept out from the sides of the fireplace and curled around the entire room in a series of graceful arabesques. As a result, the large room was delightfully warm, even here at the doorway. Agatha was impressed.

"The heat is stored in the liquid, which is piped around the room, where it evenly radiates back out," she declared in admiration. She studied the liquid slowly moving through the nearest pipe. "This isn't water, is it?"

Tarvek had looked surprised at her analysis, then pleased. "Close. It's actually a super-saturated oil and brine solution of my own formulation."

"You designed this?" She surveyed the system and looked at the Prince with a new respect.

Tarvek shrugged diffidently, while standing a little taller. "Oh, years ago." He patted a pipe gently. "It has held up quite well though."

"Your Highness is a Spark?"

The prince nodded. "A family trait we've managed to endure for the last five generations." Warily he looked at Agatha. He saw that this news had not caused the usual reactions of visible fear, uneasiness or screaming. Indeed, and even more disconcerting, Agatha's attention had shifted to the spinet that rested in the center of the room. How refreshing.

"What a beautiful instrument," she exclaimed. It was slender and low. Its dark, varnished wood decorated with a splash of festive rosemåling. The top was open, and the mathematical perfection of the strings glinted silver in the light.

"Mademoiselle has a good eye. It's a Christofori[44]." At this news, Agatha snatched her hand away.

---

[44] Bartolomeo Christofori di Francesco was an Italian creator of musical instruments. He is credited with inventing the piano. This invention did not experience great success however, until two years later, when he invented the piano bench.

Tarvek laughed. "It's quite alright, this is certainly no museum." He paused, "Do you play?"

Agatha nodded, and looked at the spinet with longing. To play such an instrument...

Tarvek came up behind her and murmured, "I would very much like to hear you play something. Perhaps after dinner."

Agatha bit her lip. Tarvek really had a very nice voice. What Lars strove to create on stage, the Prince of Sturmhalten did naturally. The Countess had told her to try to get back as soon as possible, but surely, a little musical entertainment wouldn't cause any problems...

"Please, brother—" A new voice crackled from the doorway. An odd, metallic voice. "Save the flirtation for dessert. It will go well with the rest of the cheese."

The two of them turned. A small procession had entered the room. Leading the way was a grandly appointed lady, in a magnificent red brocade outfit. It was edged and looped by strings of gold beadwork that flashed in the light. Her retinue consisted of several maids, some of which were dressed in rather exotic outfits, no doubt gleaned from foreign traders that had passed through the city.

However, the thing that drew the eye, was a foursome of liveried footmen, who carried upon their shoulders a sort of palanquin that supported a large device. It was over a meter in diameter, and had been sculpted and adorned with flowers and assorted allegorical figures, which failed to hide the glowing dials and gauges covering the rest of its surface. On the back, a small engine chuffed quietly, powering a collection of filters and bellows, and sending out small puffs of blue smoke. Three thick leather pipes exited from the mouth of a carved serpent, and stretched down to connect to the back of the lady.

With a start, Agatha looked at her again and saw that she was not excessively made up, as she had first assumed, but was in fact, some sort of human-like clank, one whose construction reminded Agatha of nothing so much as Moxana. The clank girl continued. "During dinner itself, I really *must* insist upon intelligent conversation."

Agatha was so astonished at this apparition that her mind made the obvious connection and she spoke without thinking. "Tinka?"

Prince Tarvek gave a start at this and regarded her with amazement. "This, mademoiselle, is my sister, the princess Anevka Sturmvarous." Agatha quickly repeated her curtsey. Tarvek continued. "And this, Anevka dear, is Mademoiselle Olga. Her circus—"

He paused, and then clapped his hand to his head and laughed. "Of course! Master Payne's Circus of Adventure! I had forgotten their name! No *wonder* she knew about Tinka!"

Anevka's eyes had been examining Agatha. Darting about and focusing with a series of quick, audible clicks. Now she glided forward. The men behind her stepped forward as she did, maintaining their exact distance, as if they were connected to her by an invisible yoke.

"Extraordinary." Anekva's voice, while odd, was fascinating. Her face, it appeared, had only a limited range of expression. Her actual voice emanated from a small, decorated grill nestled in a jeweled collar at her throat. "Then it is to your wonderful circus that I owe my life."

Agatha blinked. "Do tell."

Tarvek shrugged. "An—" he hesitated. "Experiment of my

father's went wrong. As a result, my sister was dying. Her body itself was failing. I won't bore you with the details as they were quite horrifying, but the only thing that could save her was to remove her. Easy enough, of course, but the associated psychological trauma of no longer having an actual body was almost as deadly."

Anevka fluttered her fan. "I had just redone my entire wardrobe. The irony was simply too much to bear."

Tarvek ignored this. "Then a traveling show came along. And there, treated as just another sideshow novelty, was a Van Rijn! A real one! I've been studying them for years, and there was no mistake."

He shook his head at the memory. "Well, I took it. I'm not proud of that, but time was running out."

He straightened up and gestured at his sister. "And I did it. I was able to reverse engineer enough of Van Rijn's designs that I could build Anevka a working body that was more sophisticated than a hand puppet. I sent payment to the circus, but by then they'd quite sensibly left town."

Agatha stepped forward and examined Anevka's head in wonder. A frown crossed her face.

"And your brain fits in there? I would think the necessary mechanisms alone—" Belatedly Agatha realized what she was saying and her hand flew to her mouth in embarrassment. "Forgive me, your Highness! I... I was just—"

Anevka burst out laughing and lightly bonked the top of Agatha's head with her fan. "Don't be ridiculous, dear girl! You can't imagine how refreshing it is to have some honest curiosity. Most people do their damnedest to pretend that everything is perfectly normal."

She swiveled about and indicated the device the four retainers carried upon their shoulders. "That is where the corpus Anevka is located. My catafalque keeps me alive, and through these—" she indicated the leather hoses, "I am able to manipulate and control this clever little doll my brother built for me."

Agatha regarded the device and the obviously delighted Anevka with awe. "Your brother has done you proud, your Highness. It's a magnificent feat of medical engineering." She realized that this might be a bit abstract as far as compliments go. "And you wear it so well."

Anevka laughed. "He's very clever, for a boy who kept buttoning his shoes together."

Tarvek rolled his eyes. "I was four!"

"Four and a half."

Tarvek turned to Agatha. "Ignore her. As you can see, she still needs work." With his hand, he quite openly made the universal gesture that all mechanics made to declare "This is a dangerously crazy machine[45]."

Agatha tried to ignore this. "But what happened to Tinka?"

Tarvek immediately stopped smiling. "Ah. Once again my father enters the story."

"Hi—hihi—ness—ness—"

They all turned, and coming from another doorway was a second clank woman. She was dressed in a simple robe. But unlike Anevka, this was obviously an automaton. She moved in a distressing, jerky motion, and even when she stood in one spot, she swayed slightly, as if she was perpetually off balance.

---

[45] This useful little hand gesture tends to be made as surreptitiously as possible, since even crude, home-brewed clanks tended to be big, fast, and possessed of a fine sense of self-preservation.

"Tinka!" Tarvek quickly moved to the clank's side and helped steady her. "Tinka, why have you left the lab?"

The machine's face swiveled towards him. Her enormous eyes blinked with a click. "I—I—I heard—servants said—Ma—Ma—Master Payne's circus he—he—here?"

Tarvek nodded slowly. "Yes, it is."

The clank shuddered. "Would you—would you—I—I—I can—would you like to see me dance?" She jerked away from Tarvek and spun about in a graceful twirl that ended with her slamming into the nearest wall. Tarvek leapt to her and caught her before she fell. She looked up at him. "I—I—I require maintenance. Please please please—" This continued until Tarvek gave her a short smack on her shoulder, at which she stopped in mid-word.

Anevka tilted her head to one side and gently tapped her folded fan against her jaw. "This is very unusual," she confided to Agatha.

"What, her condition?"

Anevka shook her head. "Oh no, in that she is moving at *all*."

Meanwhile Tarvek had waved over a pair of servants, to whom he passed the malfunctioning clank. "Take her back to my lab. Tinka, I'll be there soon."

The clank jerked in the servant's arms. "The circus. I must—"

The servants led her away, still stuttering. Tarvek wearily ran a hand through his hair and turned back to Agatha and his sister. "As I was saying, my father couldn't resist taking her apart. I've done the best I can reassembling her and that is the result." He shoved his hands into his pockets. "She can walk and she can talk. But there is something seriously wrong and I cannot figure it out. I—feel like I owe her. Without her—" He glanced at his sister, who patted his arm before turning away and leading her entourage out through the far door.

"I *will* repair her." He glanced at Agatha, and with a small smile, again offered her his arm. "I suppose that sounds foolish. To feel obligated to a... a glorified clank."

Agatha covered his hand with her own. "Not at all," she assured him. "I think it's rather noble. Besides, Master Payne believes they were—*are*, more than just clanks."

Tarvek considered this. "Hm. I might want to talk to your Master Payne." A small bell chimed from the other room. "Ah, dinner."

With that, they went through the doorway into an elegantly appointed dining hall. Light was supplied by the ubiquitous electric lamps, which were hung in decorative clusters across the frescoed ceiling. The walls were lined with the castle's now familiar liveried servants, who stood motionless, their hands at their sides. A long table was covered in a snow-white linen cloth and another electrical display merrily buzzed and crackled down the center. Only four place settings were in evidence, each of them bracketed by entirely too many utensils. Agatha examined one, and upon hefting it, guessed that it had been cast from solid electrum.

Anevka was ensconced on one side of the table. Most of her retinue had been dismissed, except for the four men who carried her device. They stood quietly behind her ornate, open backed chair.

Agatha and Tarvek were seated together. Next to Agatha, at the slightly raised head of the table, sat the master of Sturmhalten, Prince Aaronev IV.

He was obviously Tarvek's sire, with the same blue eyes

frankly assessing her from behind an odd set of glasses. These contained several inset lenses, which he used by disconcertingly moving his head about as he studied her. Aaronev and his daughter were in a discussion as Agatha and Tarvek entered.

Anevka was leaning forward, her voice quiet, but intense. "But why can't you just *analyze*—"

Her father cut her off. "Enough daughter. This discussion is finished. Our guest is here."

When they reached the end of the table, Agatha again curtsied. *I'm getting good at this,* she thought.

Tarvek stepped forward, and made a small formal bow. "Father, may I present Madame Olga, of Master Payne's Circus of Adventure."

The Prince waved Agatha forward. "Do be seated, my dear."

Agatha settled into the chair that a servant held for her. A small swarm of them then descended upon the table, pouring wines and setting out various foodstuffs. Agatha's wineglass was filled from an elegant green cut-glass carafe. The wine was a deep purple and smelled of spices and green fields. Agatha took a cautious sip.

Agatha had not really had much experience with wine before she left Beetleburg. Her parents had not favored it. Once she had joined the circus, she had been given an instructional course in wine, beer, ale, and cider as well as a wide variety of cordials and homebrewed spirits. Partially, the Countess had explained, because a young lady should be educated about these things, and be able to converse about them knowledgably. Partially, Pix had explained, because a young lady should be aware of the effects of these things upon her and be able to recognize when she was being plied. And partially, Zeetha had explained, because sometimes a warrior needed to get really drunk, and like all worthwhile things, it got easier with practice.

This had lead to some rather amusing nights and some rather awful mornings. On the whole, Agatha had decided that alcohol was something that she could take or leave, and for the most part, left. This particular beverage, however, seemed tasty and of a rather low potency.

A server placed a small bowl of what proved to be a deliciously savory red cabbage and bacon soup before her. The others were similarly served, which precipitated a discreet clattering of spoons.

Anevka ate nothing, but merely sat with folded hands and chatted with her father about a few items of castle management. After a few moments, the Prince cleared his throat and turned to Agatha. "We very much enjoyed your performance this evening."

Agatha nodded. "Your Highness is most kind."

Aaronev raised his own glass and looked at her over the rim. "We knew the lady you played, you know." Agatha choked slightly on a spoonful of soup[46].

"Oh. I… I hope I haven't given offense," Agatha stammered. "It's difficult to remember that we actually portray real people." She thought for a moment. "Sort of."

Aaronev laughed. "Nonsense, my dear. Truth be told, you captured her perfectly."

This gave Agatha a bit of a pause, as she was still reconciling herself to the idea that Lucrezia Mongfish was her actual mother.

---

[46] In the Heterodyne plays, Lucrezia Mongfish was the ingénue, to be sure, but initially, she was always portrayed as a comically evil figure, who was vain, megalomaniacal, treacherous and an inveterate liar. She was always redeemed by the power of Bill Heterodyne's love sometime in the third act, but until then, she was an audience favorite.

Aaronev continued casually. "In fact, it's remarkable, really, but you sound just like her."

Agatha smiled gamely and took another sip of wine. The taste was growing on her. "Why, thank you, your Highness."

Aaronev slowly swirled the wine around in his glass. "Have you known many Sparks?"

Agatha waved her hand in dismissal. "Oh no!" She paused and then felt compelled to add, "Well, I did grow up in Beetleburg, so I saw Dr. Beetle, of course."

The Prince nodded. "Oh, of course. Did you see him a lot?"

"Almost every day. I assisted in his lab for years."

Aaronev's eyebrows went up in surprise. "Did you now?"

"Oh yes, I was there when he died."

Tarvek broke in. "We heard about that. A great shame. We had heard that this mysterious son of the Baron's killed him."

Agatha nodded. "Yes, but to be fair, Dr. Beetle *did* throw a bomb at him." She smiled. Gil would be happy she remembered that part. That made her happy, too.

Aaronev nodded as if this was a perfectly normal turn of events. "So you've seen the Baron and this son of his?"

"Oh yes, I saw the Baron a bit when I was abducted onto Castle Wulfenbach, and his son, Gilgamesh Wulfenbach wanted to marry me." Tarvek choked on a spoonful of soup at this, and had a small coughing fit. A servant stepped up and thumped him on the back. Tarvek waved him away and grabbed his wineglass.

Anevka leaned forward. "Did he now? But here you are."

Agatha shrugged. "I had to escape from Castle Wulfenbach when everyone found out I was actually a Heterodyne."

This time Tarvek actually sprayed his wine across the table.

EIGHT

The fifty families play a game
That all revolves around a name.
To play the game you must be skilled
The Game of Kings can get you killed.
They plot and murder, lie and sin
Determined no one else should win.
They'll turn Europa upside down
To try to claim the Lightning Crown.

—ANONYMOUS

(No, really, we don't know who wrote it. Honest.)

Over the next several courses, Agatha chatted away, cheerfully answering the occasional question, and recounting her experiences of the last several months. A small growing voice of alarm from somewhere deep within her head vainly tried to get her attention, but was

343

easily overridden by her mouth, which babbled on.

The only time she paused was when she was talking about Gilgamesh. She was giving the facts of her final encounter in a clear steady voice, but a distant part of her noticed that her eyes were streaming almost nonstop, and there was a discernible huskiness to her voice. How sad.

"I suppose I'll never see him again. If I'm lucky." She took a deep breath and smiled at the Prince. "And this is a simply lovely torte." She then collapsed face forward onto her dessert.

There was a pause, as everyone in the room waited to see if this was the end of the show. After a few moments, Agatha began softly humming some sort of waltz. The Prince impatiently waved over a server, took the decanter that had contained Agatha's wine, and gave it a sniff.

"Hmm. I think I used a *bit* too much on her."

Tarvek had pulled Agatha's face up and was gently cleaning it with a warm cloth that another servant had handed to him. "You *think*?"

Agatha's eyes focused on Tarvek and a wide smile spread over her face. "You're very cute," she whispered. "I hope you don't think *I* picked out this ugly dress." Tarvek's face reddened slightly as he finished up.

"Oh dear," tittered Anevka, "Here I thought she was telling the truth and now it's obvious that the poor girl's been hallucinating."

"Shut up!" Tarvek felt flushed. Within his head, plans and schemes were shattering and reassembling themselves into new configurations at lightning speed.

The rest of the family stood, and Aaronev ordered a pair of sturdy servants to hoist Agatha to her feet. "I feel very strange," she confided to one of them. "Zeetha will laugh at me."

The Prince was ebullient, dancing in place and rubbing his hands together. "Come! Bring her! I have everything prepared!" Tarvek and Anevka glanced at each other. The young man spoke hesitantly. "But father, wait. Shouldn't we—" he thought frantically for a second. "Shouldn't we send for some of the others? They'd want to be present for something so momentous."

Anevka chimed in. "Father, even if you're sure she is The One, this is a terrible idea. You could *kill* her."

Aaronev waved this away. "Bah! The others died because they were not her! It's as simple as that. I have manipulated every other variable and failed." He glanced at his daughter, and a brief flicker of remorse flashed across his face. "You should know that better than anyone, Anevka."

The clank girl's eyes clicked once. "I do, father."

They had been hurrying along the corridors of the palace. Servants scurried before them, lighting lamps and opening doors, but at the last set, they simply opened them and stood back. The royal party swept through, and Tarvek closed and locked the doors behind them.

The large room they were now in had once been the castle's chapel. Graceful lines arced upwards for several stories, and one could see where thin, arched windows had lined the walls. These were now bricked over, and the naves were filled with glowing banks of machinery. Dominating the central area was a tall, angular device. It had multiple rods and couplings that pierced the ceiling, without regard to the religious pictures that could still be faintly seen there. At the base was a peculiar looking throne. The seat was studded with contacts and a set of ominous-looking straps were attached to the armrests. From a rack overhead, a cluster of vaguely non-Euclidian crystal rods pointed straight down, directly to where the chairs' hapless occupant would reside.

Aaronev took a moment to examine Agatha. With a few deft movements, he removed the various ornaments and jewelry that had been placed in her hair, along with her glasses. "No, this time—" he muttered, "This time, it will work!" He spoke to the two servants carrying Agatha. "Strap her in!"

The two did so, with a quiet efficiency. Then, at Aaronev's quick dismissal, they bowed and quickly exited, relocking the doors behind them.

Tarvek moved closer. "Father. Don't do this."

Aaronev darted about the throne, checking settings and adjusting dials. "I must! Our family has been given a sacred task! I will complete it! I will prove that I am still worthy to lead The Order!" He made a final adjustment and turned to Tarvek, who was alarmed at the gleam he saw in his father's eyes. "And I will see her again," he whispered.

Tarvek tried again. "You can't be sure—"

Aaronev's hand whipped out and Tarvek found his coat clutched in an iron grip. When Aaronev spoke it was with the strength and assurance of a powerful Spark in full burn. "Of *course* I'm sure! The harmonic readings are perfect! The people *obeyed* her! She confessed to being Lucrezia's daughter! This *is* The Child!"

He released Tarvek and made a final adjustment. He turned to his daughter, who had glided up behind him. "Anevka, *you* know, don't you? Tell your brother that I am correct."

Anevka nodded. "I do believe that he is correct, brother. Therefore—" She reached out and clutched her father's head.

Aaronev didn't even have a chance to register surprise before a bolt of electricity arced through him. He jerked once and his clothes and hair burst into flame. The crackling blue discharge surrounded him for several seconds before it cut off, and he collapsed to the ground, smoldering.

Anevka's outfit and wig had been burned away, revealing a grey metal manikin. Various blobs of half-melted jewelry clung at her throat and wrists. She looked down at her carbon-smeared body and tsked. "That," she announced to no one in particular, "was my favorite dress."

This broke the spell that had frozen Tarvek. "Anevka, what the hell—!"

Anevka interrupted. "Do you know how many girls father's destroyed in that machine? Do you?" Tarvek shut his mouth. Anevka stepped closer. "I do! The only thing that could have possibly made it all worse would have been if he had actually succeeded. And make no mistake. He would have. She is the one!"

Agatha, who had been half-heartedly struggling against the chair's restraints, looked up at this. It was obvious that she was still disoriented. She peered down at the remains of Aaronev and a faintly disturbed look crossed her features. "Did you do that just for me?" She thought about this. "Should I thank you?"

Anevka strode up to her and tilted her head to one side. "Don't be silly, girl." She reached up and extended a finger, which she lightly tapped against Agatha's forehead. A short burst of electricity arced and Agatha collapsed. "I have my own use for you."

Tarvek felt an unexpected pang of concern. He knelt and

lifted Agatha's head, checked her pulse and gently rolled back an eyelid. "But shouldn't we—"

Anevka imperiously waved him into silence. "Come along, brother, the clock is ticking now, and we have much to do."

Several hours later, there was a frantic knocking at the door to Master Payne's wagon. After the show, the troupe had packed up and prepared to leave at a moment's notice. But Agatha had failed to return, and a growing unease had begun to permeate the group.

Eventually, Payne had insisted that the drivers, and anyone else who could, should try to get some sleep. He had ostensibly done so himself, but despite the fact that he and the Countess had burrowed beneath their comforters several hours ago, the instant the first knock sounded, Payne had bounded to his feet, still dressed, a small pistol magically appearing in his hand. The Countess' feet had yet to touch the floor, but the rifle she drew from beneath the covers moved without hesitation.

Payne moved up to the door and listened for a moment, shook himself, and suddenly appeared a lot more rumpled and sleepy. He slowly opened the door, concealing the pistol behind the door. "Yes?"

A few steps below him was a squad of Sturmhalten soldiers. Abner was bracketed by a pair of them. Zeetha stood to one side, next to Yeti. To anyone else, she would have looked merely nervous, but Payne could see that she was a fraction of a second away from drawing her swords. That wasn't good.

A Captain stood before him. The man stared a bit too long at the hidden hand holding the pistol behind the door. Payne switched mental gears. This required finesse. With a flick of his wrist he slid the pistol out of sight up his sleeve as he slowly—very slowly—brought his hand out from behind the door and scratched at his chin.

The Captain relaxed slightly. "Evening, sir," he said, while sketching out the half salute that soldiers gave civilians they were supposed to be polite to. "Are you the master of this circus?"

Payne nodded cautiously. "I am."

The Captain drew a small note from his pocket and scrutinized it in such a way that Payne knew he had it memorized. "You were traveling with one Olga Žiga?"

Oh, this definitely didn't look good. "Yes, but at the moment she is at the palace—a guest of your Prince."

The Captain nodded. "Indeed she is, sir." He paused, and ran an eye over the other circus members who were quietly collecting. "Were you aware that this 'Madame Olga' is a fugitive? Wanted by Baron Wulfenbach himself?"

This was unexpected, and Payne was honestly taken aback, which was handy, as it helped with the lying. "No! Of course not!"

The Captain nodded. "Yes, that's just what the Prince told me you'd say. Well you've had a lucky escape, sir. As have we all, I suspect. No telling what she's capable of if the Baron's after her, eh?"

Payne felt the jaws of the trap close. Intellectually he had to admire the way it was done.

The Captain continued. "Still, it's an ill wind that blows no one any good, eh?" He ostentatiously fished about in a courier's pouch at his belt and hauled out a leather pouch adorned with the seal of the royal family. It clinked as he tossed it from hand to hand. "Prince Aaronev has sent you this reward! Mighty generous says I, but 'no bless obli cheese,' says he."

Payne blinked. "...Does he?"

The Captain nodded as he handed the money over. "All the time." As Payne took the money, the Captain's hand tightened. Their eyes locked. When the Captain spoke again, the easy-going tone he had effected had vanished from his voice. "He also says that, for everyone's safety, he thinks it best if you and your good people leave town."

Payne licked his lips. "But it's—"

In his best parade ground voice, the Captain merely said, "Now." The rest of the soldiers present straightened and presented arms with a snap. "Your escort is waiting."

Payne knew when to cut his losses. "We're moving out," he roared to the half a hundred hidden ears he knew were listening. A part of his mind noted without surprise that Zeetha had vanished.

In a surprisingly short time, the circus was on the move. The streets of the town were empty. A mist had drifted down from the surrounding mountains, giving the electric streetlights a glowing blue halo. Along the route, soldiers stood quietly, watching the train of wagons as it rumbled towards the gates. In the lead wagon, Abner, Lars and Krosp sat glumly.

"Well, that could have gone worse," muttered Abner.

"Something's not right," said Lars, eyeing the soldiers.

"Of course not," snapped Krosp, his ears flattened. "That story about a reward is hokum. The Baron thinks Agatha is dead. If he thought otherwise, he'd come and get her. The Prince just wants us to leave, and this way, we daren't complain."

Lars looked lost. "But what will we do?"

Abner looked at him levelly. "We go down this road about fifteen kilometers and turn left at Mulverschtag. That'll get us on the road to Mechanicsburg."

"No! I meant—"

"Oh wait," Abner interrupted snidely. "Are you seriously thinking we should go back—into a hostile town full of armed soldiers—to try to rescue a girl from a madboy's fortress?"

Lars examined this statement. "Yes," he said simply. "Yes I am!"

Abner sighed. "There're a million reasons why that isn't going to work."

"Dun vorry," a low voice chuckled from above. The three whipped their eyes upwards. Dimo, Ognian and Maxim were lounging on the roof of the wagon. Dimo was staring down at them and indicated himself and the others. "Dere's three reasonz it *iz*."

Agatha blinked. Her mouth tasted terrible, her head was throbbing, and she felt like she was shackled to a table. This last realization snapped her awake. She *was* shackled to a table. Some sort of lab bench, and by straining her head, she could see that she was wearing remarkably little. This didn't look good.

She was in some sort of laboratory, racks of electronic devices surrounded her, and there was a pervasive smell of ozone and burnt insulation.

Suddenly a figure loomed up from her right. It was Anevka.

She had been cleaned and polished. Her wig was black and glossy, cut short in front and tied back with several gold chains. She was dressed in a red velvet lab coat and violet work apron with matching gold piping[47].

By rolling her eyes, Agatha could just see her retainers, with the ever-present device resting upon their shoulders. They stood motionless, eyes half closed.

"Oh good," Anevka said. "You're finally awake!" She glanced behind Agatha's line of sight and made a small adjustment to an unseen device. "Happy?"

That was an easy one. "Certainly not!"

Anevka nodded. "Very good!"

"No—Not good! How dare you people do this to me? Get me some clothes!"

Anevka actually rubbed her hands together. "Excellent. A lovely strong command wave." She looked back at Agatha. "Do you have any questions?"

Agatha had a great number of questions, as well as several strong opinions about Anevka, her situation, her lack of clothing and Anevka's preoccupation with whatever it was that was keeping her from setting Agatha free. After about a half an hour of this, Agatha began to wind down. "Are you even *listening* to me?"

Anevka made a final adjustment to the oscilloscope she'd been monitoring and nodded in satisfaction. "Oh yes, and you've been just *perfect*! I quite think you're done."

---

[47] From the description, it seems likely that the Princess Anevka was wearing something from Monsieur Oliphaunt of Paris' "Beautiful Abominations of Science" line. A perennial favorite amongst Sparky fashionistas with a taste for vivisection. As *The Journal of Paris Fashion* said in a favorable review "Très mad? Très chic!"

She shut down the device and then turned to a small cloth-covered ceramic tray. A delicate flip of the fabric revealed an array of gleaming steel surgical instruments. Anevka ran her hand above them, and then selected a simple scalpel.

"And now, let's hear you beg for your life."

Agatha's eyes bugged out. "What?"

Anevka twirled the scalpel around her fingers. "I've got my readings. Now I get to have a little fun."

A squawk from behind Agatha revealed that someone else was here. Tarvek strode into sight, flinging down a set of tools and grabbing Anevka's wrist. "Stop!" Agatha realized that she didn't know whether to be more relieved at his intercession or scandalized at her state of undress before him. Another glimpse of the scalpel in Anevka's hand helped prioritize things nicely.

Anevka rolled her eyes at Tarvek. "But why? We have all the readings that we need."

"Don't be a fool. We should test it first."

Anevka considered this. With a deft flick of her wrist, she tossed the scalpel back into the tray with a clatter. "You're right, of course," she said regretfully. "It would be unforgivably stupid to kill her before we're sure."

Suddenly a commotion filled the air and several people burst into the room. A cluster of brawny castle servants were restraining a lone Geiesterdamen. She was wearing an elegantly cut robe that had been thrown over little else. Her white hair was disheveled and chopped short, and her pearly white eyes glared furiously. The four men holding her had obviously had a rough time of it, as all of them suffered from bruises, scratches, and torn clothing.

When she saw Tarvek and Anevka, the captive woman roared furiously, in what, Agatha realized in astonishment, was perfectly good Romanian[48].

"What is the meaning of this? Where is your father, the Prince?" She saw Agatha for the first time and paused. "What are you children playing at?"

Tarvek stepped forward. "Good evening, Lady Vrin. There are things you should be made aware of—"

Vrin lunged at him, almost throwing her captors off balance. "Release me, you insignificant worm!"

Anevka crossed her arms. "Oh, I really don't want to listen to any more of *this*. Tarvek?"

Her brother stepped behind her and was making some adjustments to a control panel on her back. "I've made the adjustments to your voice box. Try it now."

Anevka stepped forward. "Release her." The servants stepped back. Vrin launched herself towards the mechanical girl, who again spoke. "Lady Vrin? *Kneel!*"

The voice that boomed out, artificially amplified, sounded remarkably like Agatha's. The effect upon the Geisterdamen was electric. She froze, and then dropped to her knees. "Lady?" she whispered.

Instantly she grabbed her head and screamed. The servants again grabbed her arms. She glared up at Anevka. "You are not her," she hissed in fury.

Anevka put her head to one side. "Tch. It appears you were

---

[48] Romanian was the official language of the Empire. However, most educated people in the sciences were conversant in Latin, Greek, and German, as well as English (the language of trade) and French (the language of diplomacy). Certain schools of mathematics are best discussed in Arabic, and Russian is always good for a laugh. At this time, thanks to her secretarial duties for the late Tyrant of Beetleburg, Agatha was conversant in all of them.

right, brother. We are not there yet."

Tarvek nodded slowly. He pulled a pad of paper from a coat pocket and began to scribble some notes. "Hmm. I suspect your speaker needs more bass. Maybe what I need to do is isolate the command harmonics, and then amplify *them*..."

Anevka patted him on the shoulder. "Yes, yes. You *do* that." She turned back and with a few twists, released Agatha.

Stiffly, she climbed down from the bench. At a sign from Anevka, two more servants took hold of her wrists. Anevka continued. "Take these two troublesome girls and put them in the cell with the others."

As they were being led away, Vrin rallied and called out, "You will pay for this! When your father and The Order—"

Anevka interrupted her. "My father is dead. And this pathetic girl?" She indicated Agatha. "She is your 'holy lost child,' for all the good it will do you."

This information struck Vrin like a physical blow, and she stared at Agatha in astonishment as they were led away.

As they moved through the deserted corridors, Agatha shivered. She realized that she was still in her underwear and turned to the nearest servant. "I want some clothes." All of the men chuckled at this.

"I'm sure you do," the one she addressed replied. Agatha glared at him and spoke again. This time her voice was loud and insistent. "I'm cold and I want some clothes. *Now*!" All of the servants blinked. And without a word, the man she'd addressed turned and left. They kept walking, but several minutes later, as they came to a thick armored door, he returned at a trot, holding a bundle that Agatha recognized as her outfit. As the lead servant unlocked the door with a complicated looking key, he handed it over. Agatha took it, and then she and a thoughtful Lady Vrin were shoved through the door, which could be heard locking behind them.

Agatha had been a tremendous fan of the Heterodyne Boys novels. On a fairly regular basis, one or the other of the heroic duo had been tossed into cells by cackling villains. Thus, the room before her was oddly familiar. Bare stone walls, a small slit of a window, several bunks covered with mounded blankets, and a plain wooden table were before her.

Agatha looked at the outfit in her hands. "I didn't expect them to actually get me my clothes," she remarked. A frown crossed her features.

Her train of thought was interrupted by Vrin coming close and staring into her face. Agatha tried not to flinch. "The Anevka-clank claims that you are The Holy Child. Why?"

Agatha found it difficult to look into the odd eyes of the woman before her. "I don't know. I don't even know what all this Holy Child nonsense is about. I'm not even a child. I'm eighteen, thank you very much."

Vrin blinked. "Eighteen..."

"Klazma? Klazma *Vrin*?" Both Vrin and Agatha turned in surprise. In the rear of the cell were several bunks, mounded with blankets. One of these mounds moved, and revealed two more Geisterdamen, sleepily rubbing their faintly glowing eyes. With quick movements, they slid from the bunk and began eagerly questioning the Lady Vrin in their own language.

Agatha was obviously the subject of a great deal of the discussion. Vrin's declaration, "Na fig seg unat plin," was greeted with exclamations of dubious surprise. Agatha tried to listen to the conversation as she set about stripping her dress of the ruffles and lace that inhibited her movements. She didn't know what was going to happen, but she suspected she would want to be able to move fast.

As she slipped her glasses back on over her ears, one of the Geisterdamen, who had been looking at her intently suddenly started and declared, "Zoy!" along with a lot of other words, the only one of which that Agatha could understand was "actors!"

This started a brief argument between the two, which only ended when Vrin slammed her hand down on the table. She took a deep breath and turned towards Agatha. Agatha could tell that Vrin was unsure about how to deal with her.

Vrin studied her for a moment, and then spoke slowly. "The Geisterdamen have long sought a child who was stolen from us."

Agatha shrugged apologetically. "I've never seen, or even heard of a Geisterdamen child."

Vrin nodded. "This was a pink child. It was the offspring of the persons you would know of as Lucrezia Mongfish and the Bill Heterodyne."

Agatha's felt an odd sensation in her stomach and face went blank. "Really."

Vrin's eyes never wavered "A female child. She would indeed be eighteen years old." Agatha bit her lip. Vrin continued slowly. "And it was said that she would have the Spark."

Agatha smiled brightly. "Well. That's fascinating. A lot of people have wondered what your people were doing for all those years. You were searching. For a Heterodyne heir. A lot of people were doing that."

Vrin continued to study her. Agatha felt compelled to continue. "Well *my* father was a blacksmith, and I think I would have noticed if he was some sort of legendary hero."

These were familiar lies, and Agatha felt herself relax as she told them. "As for me being a Spark, well that's just ridiculous!" She noticed about this time that Vrin was no longer looking directly at her, but instead, slightly to the left of her face. A quick shift of her eyes revealed her faithful little clank, which had crawled from her pocket, and was waving hello at the fascinated Geisterdamen.

Vrin nodded slowly and leaned back against the table. "A blacksmith, you say."

Agatha sighed. "A really good blacksmith." She put the little clank on the table and tried to change the subject. "So what happened back there? What's going on?"

Vrin took a final glance at the pocket-watch clank and then ignored it. The other two Geisters openly stared at it, and one of them actually poked it with her fingers and started making adorable cooing noises at it.

Vrin spoke seriously. "It appears that the royal children have staged a coup. They claim that our liaison, Prince Aaronev is dead."

Agatha interrupted. "That's true, I'm afraid. I saw it. The princess, Anevka, electrocuted him." She paused, and then added, out of a sense of fairness, "Prince Tarvek seemed surprised and rather annoyed about that."

Vrin raised her eyebrows at this, and then rubbed her brow. "Znug!" she swore.

She looked at Agatha and seemed to come to a decision. "We—" she indicated herself and the other two Geisterdamen, "—Are the priestesses of our Lady, our Goddess. Thus, we are able to command our Lady's... lesser servants. As you no doubt heard, the Royal Children appear to be trying to recreate the true voice of our Lady, which could compel not only these lesser servants, but us as well."

"But what does that have to do with me?" Agatha asked. "She was analyzing my voice. Do I really sound like that? Like your god—like your Lady?" She paused as the implications struck her. "What if *I* told you to kneel?"

Vrin actually smiled. "Why, I'd probably laugh so hard, I'd only slap you twice."

Agatha stepped back. "What?"

"The voice they seek is... very much like yours." She considered. "Especially when you are angry, I think. But even if you are the child we seek, a child is never exactly the same as her mother. Even with us—" Vrin stopped as she realized that she was getting off the subject. "But we can discuss this later. Now, we must escape this place." She looked over at the table. One of the Geisters had the little clank dancing on the palm of her hand. "Can your little device open doors?"

Agatha shook her head. "Not without tools, but—" Suddenly she remembered Lars' gift, and slid the ring off of her finger. She fiddled with it a moment, and suddenly, with a satisfying "pung," it unfolded. "—We do have a lock pick."

Vrin looked at Agatha with a new respect. "Impressive."

Agatha smiled. "Okay, now let's get out of here!" With that she knelt down and proceeded to tinker with the lock mechanism. After a few terse instructions from Vrin, all three of the Geisterdamen prepared to deal with the outside guards.

Ten minutes later, they were leaning against the table, arms folded, as Agatha continued to work at the lock. Vrin leaned in. "You have no *idea* how to use that thing, do you?"

Agatha sat back on her heels and blew a lock of hair out of her face. "Yes, well, they didn't cover this in holy rug rat school."

Vrin grabbed Agatha's shoulder and jerked her to her feet. "Speak with respect! I do not care who you are, you will *not* mock our quest. It is *all* to us."

Agatha bit back a retort, paused, and then said quietly, "Maybe you should explain it to me."

Vrin looked surprised, then nodded slowly. She sat Agatha down on one of the cell's beds, and then sat opposite her. She thought for a minute, and then started speaking. Her voice took on a storyteller's cadence.

"Since the beginning of all things, we have served our eternal lady. No matter how long her absence from our presence, we knew she would always return to us.

"From when I was a novice, she visited us frequently, always in the same lovely aspect. She helped us increase our crops. Helped us make stronger children. Those were happy days in the City of Silver Light." Vrin paused.

"But then the Day of Reckoning occurred, as we knew it must. As the Lady herself had foretold. She came to us in high distress. The Gods were at war, and as had been foretold, she carried within her own body the Holy Child.

"It was the Time of the Final Prophecy, beyond which even Our Lady could not see. We were to prepare for The Great Battle, even though we knew she would be taken from us.

"But still we had hope. For we had been given a task. Our only task, the reason we had been created. We were to protect the Holy Child. Protect her from those whom we knew would try to steal her away from us.

"We knew when they would come. We knew what they would do. We knew their powers and abilities—"

Vrin paused. Agatha could see that she was shaken by these memories. The two Geisterdamen reached out and touched her shoulders in support. She took a deep breath and continued.

"And yet, knowing all that, we still failed. We failed utterly. The enemies of our Lady were too strong. Our Lady was taken from us and the Child had been stolen. There were no more prophecies. It was The End of History. The end of our world."

Vrin stared bleakly at Agatha in silence. Then, astonishingly, she smiled. "But when your world ends, apparently a new one glides in to take its place. The sun rose. The stars wheeled across the sky. Sisters realized they were getting hungry. So… we sat down and ate. It was the last meal and the first.

"We bid farewell to the dead. We rebuilt The City of Silver Light. We welcomed New Children. We worshipped the Lady, because we had never worshipped anything else. Perhaps, wherever she was, our prayers would help her."

Vrin took a deep sigh. "And then, our prayers *were* answered. They were answered with rage and fury. With pain and fire. Our Mistress did indeed return. This time, she appeared in her most terrible aspect, The Lady of Sharp Crystal, who had not been seen for over fifty generations. She purged the High Priesthood with the burning light when she learned that we had failed to protect the Child. She purged the Commanders. The Artisans. We feared she would purge us all.

"After the burning, she embarked upon a Great Building. Nonstop we worked. Almost two hundred of our sisters died before she was finished. Then came the greatest punishment of all.

"Three thousand of The White Elite were selected. Warriors, scientists, adjudicators, facilitators—none of the clans were spared. We were assembled and then marched through the One-Sided Door and exiled here, to The Shadow World."

Vrin looked tired now. "Our only task is to search this wretched place until we find the missing child." The other two Geisterdamen again gently stroked her shoulders. Vrin reached up and softly patted their hands. "We have been here... through fourteen winters now, with no one we could trust but ourselves."

She released the other women's hands and leaned towards Agatha. "Even if we found her, I... suspect we will never be allowed to return to the City of Silver Light. No one ever returns through the One-Sided Door, though many swore they would try. We will die here." Suddenly, she straightened up and her gaze hardened. "But if we do succeed, our sisters back home may once again see The Lady in her Joyous Aspect, and once again live in happiness."

Agatha paused, but that seemed to be the end. "There's a lot of that I don't understand."

Vrin stood up, and a sardonic smile briefly crossed her face. "Hardly surprising. Apparently here in The Shadow World, one's Gods rarely show up on a daily basis." She glanced at the surrounding cell. "I cannot say I blame them."

Agatha thought. "But what does—*did* Prince Aaronev have to do with all this?"

Vrin hesitated, and then shrugged. "In this world, the Lady was known to the people as Lucrezia Mongfish." She paused, but Agatha resisted the temptation to interrupt.

Vrin nodded approvingly. "She had many allies. Some secret, some not. Prince Aaronev was always amongst the foremost of these. He was one of the leaders of a cabal of Sparks and their followers. All of them he pledged to Our Lady's service. As a reward, he was entrusted with her most sacred devices." Vrin paused. "He was really killed because of you?"

Agatha nodded. "He had placed me in some sort of machine. Anevka didn't want it activated."

Vrin shook her head. "I must confess," she admitted ruefully, "I had never fully... trusted him. Apparently I did him a great disservice. I know that some voices in his Order grumbled at serving Our Lady. They claimed that furthering her agenda was not a part of their original charter or some such. With Aaronev gone, I do not know whether the Order's loyalty will fade as well. Some embrace The Lady, but..."

She sighed and leaned back. "But his children are our biggest threat now. Anevka anyway. Tarvek is annoying, but spineless." She looked around the cell. "It would be simpler to stay in here forever."

Agatha puffed a lock of hair out of her face. "You may get your wish." She waved the lockpick. "Any of you want to have a go at this?"

Vrin shook her head. "None of us are artificers. I think you'd have better luck giving it to your little contraption."

Agatha sat back and looked at her. "That's not a bad idea!"

She squatted down before the little clank, which looked at her curiously. She held up the lock pick. "Here! Can you use this to get out of here?"

She handed the tool to the clank. The clank took the pick and examined it with interest. Then it dashed over to an iron drain grate in the stone floor. It jammed the end of the pick under the grate and with a twist, popped it off the floor. Then, with a sound that sounded suspiciously like "wheeee"—it dropped down into the darkness, taking the lock pick with it.

Everyone looked blankly at the hole, but nothing happened. Vrin looked at Agatha reproachfully. "I wasn't being serious," she said.

At that moment, there was a "chunk," from the door, which swung open. Standing in the dim light stood Tinka.

She stepped forward. "Mi—mi—Miss Clay must come— come—come with me now. Y—y—you others stay—stay here, please."

Agatha and Vrin looked at each other. "The guards," Vrin said carefully. "Where are the guards?"

Tinka's head jerked towards her. "They—they are sleeee— sleeping." Her head snapped back to Agatha. "Miss Clay wi— wi—will come with me n—n—now."

Vrin nodded reasonably. "Of course. Eotain. Shurdlu. Smanga tik tik."

With a sudden burst of speed, the two Geisterdamen bracketed Tinka and grabbed her arms. The mechanical girl swiveled to look at each of them in turn. "Oh. You—you—you are very fast."

"Zoda hoy," Shurdlu affirmed.

There was a bright blue flash and the two spider riders dropped senseless to the floor. Tinka snapped forward and her palm smacked against Vrin's forehead and delivered another electric shock before the woman had taken two steps. As she collapsed to the floor, Tinka turned to Agatha. A thin wisp of smoke came from her outfit. "Now they—ey—ey will sleep too." She stepped closer to Agatha. "Miss Cl—Cl—Clay will co—come with me now."

Agatha nodded. "All right. But first…" She deliberately took a minute to lay the stunned Geisterdamen into more comfortable positions before she accompanied the mechanical girl out of the cell. Tinka paused to twist the key in the cell door lock.

Agatha saw three uniformed men, who were obviously guards, slumped upon the floor. Tinka went to the far door, looked out, and then beckoned Agatha to follow.

Despite Tinka's jerky movements, they moved silently through the surprisingly empty halls. Earlier, there had always been a servant going somewhere or doing *something*, but now, it seemed like they were the only living things moving through the castle. Agatha regarded the Muse with a slight feeling of dread.

Agatha felt a rush of relief when they stopped at an ornate door and Tinka knocked softly. The door opened to reveal Tarvek, who beamed upon seeing Agatha. Tinka tried to perform a curtsey, but banged her head into the doorframe. "Hi—high—Highness. I—I—I have brought her."

They stepped into the room and Agatha gave a start as she saw—"Moxana!"

The automaton gracefully nodded towards her. Tarvek practically clapped his hands in glee. "Yes! Isn't she marvelous?" He gestured to the other mechanical. "Tinka went out of the castle, found your circus, and brought her back here—*all by herself*! It's *extraordinary*!"

Agatha looked at the malfunctioning clank with mixed feelings. "Tinka and Moxana were always close."

Tarvek nodded. "Having Moxana here will make repairing Tinka ever so much easier. Especially—" and here one could see that there was a very real possibility that Tarvek would combust from sheer glee—"She even brought me some of Van

Rijn's notes!" And to Agatha's shock, he produced the battered folio that Moxana had given her.

"That was in my wagon!" she protested.

Tarvek ignored her. "I'm going to find the other Muses. I'm going to rebuild them all!"

Agatha turned to Tinka. "But," she asked. "Why? Why did you bring him Moxana? Master Payne said you were stolen. These people damaged you."

The mechanical nodded. "T—th—that was unfortunat—t—te. But soon all will be—be—be well. Because while here I learned that Prince Tarvek issssszzz—erk! The one we—we—we were made for."

Agatha turned to Tarvek. "Made for?" She shook her head. "If they were made for *anyone*, they were made for The Storm King."

Tarvek paused, and then shrugged modestly. "Yes, well, I *am* The Storm King."

On the face of it, this was rather analogous to someone admitting that he was the White Rabbit of the Equinox. Agatha decided to treat Prince Tarvek the way that she always treated Professor Rollipod back at the University[49].

"Do tell!" She cooed. "That's very nice! Would you like some juice, your majesty?"

Tarvek looked at her with a tired annoyance. "Stop it. I don't think I'm old Andronicus Valois. But I *am* his direct descendant, through my mother, which is why my last name

[49] Cleonicus Rollipod, Ph.D, Order of the Steel Pen, etc., was a brilliant botanist, who single-handedly developed the universally popular "Meat Wheat," despite the fact that he was convinced that he was really a giant bumblebee (bombus megamaxillosus). Luckily, he was one of those people who looked good in yellow and black.

isn't Valois. The lineage has been guarded and preserved by the Sturmvarous family for ten generations, and if you keep looking at me like that, I'll make you sit through a recitation of the entire genealogy."

Agatha couldn't stop looking at him, but she tried to do so differently. If true, this was astonishing news. There hadn't been a Storm King for almost two centuries. Occasionally, one appeared in some of the more obscure Heterodyne Plays, but they weren't popular, if only because too many people found the idea of a new Storm King to be too implausible.

Tarvek continued, eyeing her carefully. "It's quite the family secret. You can imagine what would happen if it got out. But apparently these two—" he indicated Tinka and Moxana, "— Trust you, so I shall as well."

Agatha nodded slowly. "I think I know something about having explosive family secrets." She paused. The memories of what she talked about at dinner were weirdly distorted, but accessible. "That is, if I still have them..."

Tarvek looked embarrassed. "Of course you do. I won't tell, my sister wants you dead, and no one will believe the servants."

Agatha analyzed this, and was not completely reassured. Tarvek ran what he'd said through his head and came to a similar conclusion. "A living Heterodyne heir is too important to risk. But even if you weren't a Heterodyne, I..." He looked at her earnestly. "I'd want to get you as far away from my sister as possible."

Agatha nodded gratefully. "Won't there be repercussions from her having... killed your father?"

Tarvek looked uncomfortable. "Quite possibly. It depends

how perspicacious the Baron's Questor[50] is, but Anevka can be very...convincing." Seeing Agatha's face, he tried to dispel the mood. "But that is not your problem. My father's unexpected death has placed me under some obligations that I must deal with as soon as possible[51]."

Tarvek continued. "Tinka will guide you out of the castle." He pulled an official looking note from an inner pocket of his coat. "This will insure that you are conveyed safely back to your friends at the circus. My father sent them packing early this morning, but I managed to have them detained outside of the city walls."

Agatha took the note. "I'd better get there quickly. They'll be very worried. You won't have problems with your sister, will you?"

"Will I have problems with my..." Tarvek's mouth quirked upwards. "You *must* be an only child. My sister will be *furious*, of course. But she requires maintenance, and for that she needs me. She'll scream and throw things and demand that I let her kill someone, but the servants know to stay away from her at times like that."

---

[50] As much as he tried, Klaus could not be everywhere. Occasionally he empowered extraordinary individuals to act in his stead. The Baron's Questors were arguably some of the most powerful figures in Europa at this time. They could go anywhere. Demand to see anything. And at a moment's notice, demand co-operation or obedience from any of the Baron's people, as well as act as judge, jury and executioner. They were doubly annoying because they tended to travel incognito, so one always had to be careful about who you arrested (which was rather the point). They also tended to be damned hard to kill. However, the penalties for defying or incarcerating them paled beside what happened if you impersonated one. Naturally, they were the heroes of hundreds of folk tales, legends and stories.
[51] Being a Spark was dangerous. This was no secret. Many Sparks dealt with the ever-present possibility of death or defeat by constructing elaborate doomsday devices. Finding and disarming these was a popular staple in Heterodyne Plays. For Sparks, end-of-life counseling usually involved architects and demolitions experts.

"That's... good?" Agatha ventured.

Tarvek sighed. "In our household, that's as good as it gets." He stared at nothing for a moment, then visibly pulled himself together. Now, when he looked at Agatha, she was struck by the air of authority he displayed. "But by the Law of Succession and the Right of Inheritance, I am the Prince of Sturmhalten now. Protector of Balan's Gap and Defender of the East. My sister will be controlled. As for you..." He considered Agatha as if he had never seen her before.

Agatha found herself flushing slightly under his scrutiny. Then, to her astonishment, he bowed. "Allow me to be the first to formally acknowledge you as the future Lady Heterodyne. It is my sincere hope, when everything is settled, that you would consider returning to Sturmhalten."

Agatha's eyebrows went up. "Returning?"

Tarvek smiled. "Oh yes, with a Heterodyne back in power, we'll want to strengthen political ties with Mechanicsburg. But more importantly..." Here he faltered at bit and rubbed his neck. How annoying, he was acting like a tongue-tied schoolboy at his first dance. "I... um... I mean I *personally*... I would very much like it if you... came back... here... and wanted to aid me in reconstructing the Muses."

"Me?" Agatha was startled. "Why me?"

Tarvek gently patted Moxana's chair. "Moxana claims that you are a very strong Spark. I myself have found you intelligent, personable, quite comely—" Tarvek reddened as he realized what he'd said. "—And unlike my sister, or indeed most of the Sparks I have met, refreshingly sane." Most of the last of this came out in a bit of a rush.

Agatha regarded the young man. To her surprise, she realized that his recitation of her assets had pleased her excessively. Again she felt a tingle run down her back. Working closely with Prince Sturmvarous could be interesting. Any mechanic with a scrap of curiosity would jump at the chance to work with actual Muses. She frowned. She did have to consider the realities of the household however. There was no question that Anevka was very dangerous. Tarvek seemed to sense her thoughts.

"I'm not saying stay now. In fact, I insist that you get as far away as you can from my sister's influence for the moment. Give me time to work on her." He smiled. "You'd only have to come back when *you* thought it was safe. If you're really worried, I'll build you a... a death ray or something."

Agatha went slightly weak at the knees and she had to take a deep breath. "I... I think I might like that," she said carefully.

Tarvek beamed. "Wonderful!" He gently took Agatha's elbow. Another tingle ran up her arm from where his hand touched her skin. "But now, I'm afraid, you must be going, and I have things that must be done."

Agatha took a step towards the door and then stopped. "Wait! What about the Geisterdamen?"

Tarvek frowned. "What about them?"

Agatha paused, unsure how much she wanted to reveal. She spoke carefully. "They claimed to..." Oh dear. How awkward. The word "worship," while accurate, would no doubt lead to a very complicated discussion. A discussion Agatha realized that she would have to have, but possibly not when she should be fleeing for her life from a mechanical homicidal maniac. "... know my mother."

Tarvek frowned. "Yesss... I had heard a *little* about that, but I never really paid attention..." He looked at Agatha. "If Lucrezia Heterodyne was your mother..." He blinked. "Good lord. You must be this... child person they're always going on about. Fascinating." He pondered this for a second, and then forcibly shook himself, and again took Agatha's elbow. "Rest assured that I'll take good care of them. I'll definitely try to find out a bit more about this... mythology they've built up. But now you really *must* be going!"

Agatha saw the sense in this, and soon Tinka was leading her through the now gloomy corridors of the castle. Tinka carried an ornate hand-cranked electric candelabra, that served more to distort the shadows and keep Agatha on edge than light their way. She tried to make conversation.

"It's so quiet," she whispered. "Where is everybody?"

"Most of the ser-servants are con-confined to the servant wing-ing-ing. The old P-P-Prince is dead. There are... pro... pro... procedures that must be observed. Tinka continued. "Prince Tarvek will take care of it. All will be well-ell-ell."

Agatha had her doubts about the simplicity that Tinka seemed to take for granted. "I really think it's a good thing that I'm leaving."

"Our Prince agrees." Tinka nodded and her head fell off. Her body took another step, froze, and then toppled forward to the carpet. Agatha gave a small scream of surprise.

From a shadowed alcove, the three Geisterdamen stepped forth, Eotain casually wiped her blade clean on the curtain. "Forgive us for taking so long to find you," Vrin said with a slight smile.

The three didn't look like they were going to attack her. Agatha pointed at the Muse's head. The eyes blinked frantically.

"You didn't have to do that." She looked at them again. "How did you get out?"

"Thanks to you." Vrin brought her hand out into the light. Agatha's small pocket-watch clank cheerfully waved the lock pick when it saw her. "Your little automunculous apparently went down the drain, climbed back up outside the cell door, and opened it from without."

Agatha felt odd. "Oh good," she said weakly. "It worked."

Meanwhile Shrdlu had picked up Tinka's head and brought it to Vrin. Tinka's eyes were still blinking, and the mouth moved. Faintly, her voice could still be heard. "Miz-zirk—no—no—get away—zt! Now! Clax—!"

Vrin casually dropped the head to the floor. Agatha winced. "Where was this thing taking you?"

Agatha saw no reason to lie. "Out of the castle. Prince Tarvek wants me gone before the Baron sends someone to investigate his father's death." She paused. "He said he was going to take care of you too."

Vrin looked at her with an unreadable expression. "Oh, I can well imagine that he would have 'taken care of us.'" She nodded. "He is certainly correct about one thing. If The Wulfenbach Empire will be interfering here, then we must hurry." She turned away. "Come with us."

Agatha didn't move. "I hate to leave Tinka like this—"

Vrin cut her off with an impatient wave of her hand. "You must leave with us." She paused and visibly forced herself to be a bit less autocratic. "This is but a mechanism. We have permanently damaged nothing. It was already broken, and this is but another minor repair that Prince Tarvek can easily perform. You are the one that is in danger now, and I assure you, child, your safety is our chief concern."

Agatha saw the logic in this, and so the four headed off. "This isn't the way we were going," Agatha quickly pointed out.

Vrin snorted, but didn't slow down. "Sturmhalten Castle is not so much a castle, as a structure that contains secret passages. I don't know where the *tik tik* was taking you, but I know where we must go now."

Agatha followed for a moment, then asked, "So the late Prince Aaronev was a follower of... your Lady?"

Vrin frowned. "Supposedly. To hear him tell it, in his youth, they were... romantically involved." She shrugged, "Or so he claimed. Our Lady never deigned to verify it, one way or the other. But in fairness, he always spoke of her with the proper reverence." She was again silent, but Agatha could see that this was a topic she felt strongly about, and indeed, she shortly continued.

"But this entire family—" she shook her head. "All of them are as twisted and duplicitous as a sack of oiled snakes. One can never trust anything they say, even when they are speaking an obvious truth. *I* believe that Aaronev secretly hoped to learn how to use The Lady's *shk-mah* for his own ends!"

She eyed Agatha expectantly, and seemed disappointed that this revelation had less impact on her than Vrin had expected.

"Ah," Agatha said. "Her *Shik Whatzis*, you say. The impudence."

Vrin glowered at her. "I believe the *ignorant* call them Slaver Wasps."

Agatha stumbled, and only avoided slamming to the ground face-first because Eotain and Shrdlu grabbed her arms without breaking stride.

Agatha dug her heels in and dragged the whole group to a halt. "My mother was The *Other*?"

Vrin looked surprised. "You didn't know?" She nodded. "Oh. Well, yes. Lucrezia Mongfish was the being known to The Shadow World as The Other." She said this as if it as common knowledge[52].

This time Agatha did stop. "No! I can't believe it! The Other was responsible for the revenants. The death of... of thousands! All the destruction—!"

The Geisterdamnen circled her, and looked at each other in confusion. Agatha ignored them. "But wait—" She reviewed her histories. "No—The Other attacked Castle Heterodyne and *kidnapped* Lucrezia Heterodyne. That's how the whole thing *started*!"

Vrin gently clasped Agatha's hand and pulled her down the hall. "Really? How interesting."

Agatha's head was so a-whirl with this latest revelation that it was several moments before she was again aware enough to take stock of her surroundings. The room the party was now half way through was large and dimly lit.

"This looks familiar..."

Vrin interrupted. "It is the castle chapel. We do much of our work here."

Agatha shuddered as she remembered what had happened the last time she was here. "And what is it *you* do?"

Suddenly the three white ladies turned on her and forced

---

[52] The identity of The Other, who had destroyed Castle Heterodyne, wiped out over thirty of the Great Spark Houses of Europa and precipitated the Long War, was one of the greatest mysteries of this time. The Other never issued demands, ultimatums or justifications for her actions, leading some to wonder if she was a Spark at all.

her down into what Agatha realized was the same device that Prince Aaronev had strapped her into earlier that evening. She protested and thrashed mightily as she was buckled in. Vrin stood before a control panel. "We do what we always do. We serve the Goddess!" And she threw the switch.

A great cloud of electricity erupted around Agatha, enveloping the chair and its occupant. She felt a tingling dancing across her flesh for several seconds, and then, from behind her, the apparatus she was strapped into began to roar and vibrate. There was a great final scream of tortured machinery—and then only the sound of turbines winding down. Everywhere lights changed from red to green, and relays could be heard clacking down in sequence.

Agatha opened one eye. Nothing. She looked at herself. Nothing had changed. She looked around. She was still in the chapel. She was beginning to think it had all been some sort of pointless joke when she saw the three Geisterdamen. They were standing reverently, heads bowed, eyes closed, their hands intricately folded before their chests. Praying, Agatha realized. Next to them was a clock-like device. Its single hand was sweeping backwards and just as Agatha figured this all out, the hand hit zero. A great organ note boomed forth as a fresh wave of power cascaded down the device and poured directly into Agatha. Her head slammed back and she screamed as the energies swirled around her.

Suddenly the power cut off. Released from its grasp, she limply slumped forward. Throughout the apparatus, smoke poured from vents. Busbars had melted and fuses had overloaded.

The three Geisters opened their eyes and stared at the

motionless girl before them. Shrdlu sighed. "I think we have killed another one."

"NO!" Vrin violently shook her head in denial. "No! I was so sure! I *am* sure! *This was the girl!*" She looked at Agatha. "Have I erred? Can it be the machine *itself* that is flawed?"

A small moan came from the seated figure. All of the Geisters started in surprise. "She's alive!" Vrin smacked the other two into action. "Get her out of there!"

Quickly, the restraints holding Agatha were removed. But even when released, she remained limp and made no voluntary motion. Suddenly she gasped and her eyes flew open to stare blankly at the three women leaning in towards her. "Hfgm," she burbled.

Eotain looked distraught. "Well, at least she's alive. Surely that counts for *something*—"

"Silence!" Vrin snapped. She grabbed Agatha's jaw and pulled her face towards her own. "Can you understand me?" She spoke in the Geisterdamen's own language.

Agatha looked at her owlishly. "Gominal," she whispered. Vrin dropped her hand, turned away and sighed.

Shurdlu shrugged. "Another vegetable."

Eotain looked unsure. Agatha was staring at the three now and feebly thrashing about in her seat. "I don't know..." Eotain said slowly. "This one seems... different."

Vrin's head snapped up. Cold fury was reflected on her face. "No. She is gone." Agatha's hand twitched towards her, and clasped her sleeve. With a casual back hand, Vrin cracked Agatha across the face, spilling her out of the machine. "She is *useless* to us."

Without another thought, she turned away, her mind already

planning ahead. "Come," she said to the others. "We must leave this place quickly."

Shurdlu looked troubled. "You will leave The Lady's devices in the hands of those children?"

"For the moment, we must. But we *will* be back. And then they will—"

"You *did* it!" This declaration stopped all three of the women dead. They whirled in surprise to find Agatha standing tall.

But... they all hesitated. It... wasn't Agatha. The body language was all wrong. The girl before them looked directly at them and they involuntarily stepped back. A fire burned in her eyes that sent a shock of recognition through Vrin.

Agatha's face was set in a delighted grin as she jerkily examined her arms. "You did it," she repeated in delight. "I can't believe it! You actually found her!" The Lady Lucrezia twirled in place and hugged herself in glee. "I'm back!"

NINE

A secret shared is a secret known to the Baron

—FOLK WISDOM

In a dark alley near the center of Balan's Gap, a sewer cover lifted itself slightly. A guttural voice whispered, "Iz clear." Without a sound, the cover was lifted all the way up and gently set to the side. Quickly, Dimo, Maxim and Ognian flowed upwards and assumed positions equidistant from each other. The town was quiet. The mist had continued to roll down from the surrounding mountains, blanketing the streets. Most of the buildings were dark, with only the occasional light. The streets were empty.

After a minute, Dimo quietly whispered. "Iz goot."

A hand reached up from the sewer, clutching a stiff and unresponsive figure. Dimo grabbed it and examined it worriedly. It was Krosp. His limbs were stiff, his face set in a grimace of pain. He was filthy, and soaking wet. "Iz he any better?"

Lars levered himself up out of the manhole. "No."

Maxim scratched his chin. "I dun underschtand vy he iz like dis. He hef no problem mit goingk *into* der sewer."

Lars looked at the Jäger and shrugged. "I don't think he really understood what a sewer *was*."

The purple Jaeger chuckled. "Ho! Vell Hy guess he know *now*! 'Specially ven he fall in!"

Lars nodded. "Yes, he seemed fine until then."

Maxim corrected him. "No, he vas fine 'til hyu said dot he vould need a bath."

Dimo interrupted them both. "No, it vos ven hyu said dot he could giff *himself* a bath."

Maxim grinned. "Oh, jah! Dot vas it! Becawze he iz a kitty!"

At this, all four of them reevaluated the sodden, stinking mass Dimo held in one hand, imaginations running furiously. Krosp suddenly showed signs of life. One crazed eye rolled towards Dimo. "Kill me," Krosp whispered.

"I can't say I blame him," Lars conceded.

Dimo nodded. "True enough, but ve needs him." With that he strode over to a water barrel and plunged Krosp in fully and agitated his hand thoroughly. In less than a minute, a bedraggled Krosp clawed his way out of the barrel. He shook himself and glared at the others. "Never speak of this again," he hissed. "Or you will all die."

During this, Maxim and Ognian had vanished. They reappeared now from opposite ends of the alley. Both looked troubled. "Zumting is wrong," Maxim stated flatly.

Oggie agreed. "Jah. De streets iz deserted."

Dimo looked at Lars. "Iz dot normal dese days?"

Lars shook his head. "Of course not. This is a major caravan town. The Night Market is famous for its late night specials, and the Red Quarter *never* closes. We were supposed to come up right between them, so we could blend in with the crowds."

The group looked around. There certainly were no crowds now. Dimo scowled. "We moof qvick den."

Lars looked at a set of enameled street signs riveted onto the walls at the nearest corner. He nodded. "The castle should be this way."

Oggie grinned. "Hah. Ve valk in, ve valk out. Vill be piece of piroshky!"

It wasn't, of course. The castle sat tall and forbidding in its crater. For the first ten decameters, the sheer stone walls were bereft of windows, decorations, or indeed, handy projections of any kind. The massive drawbridge was up. But the final straw was the seething, crackling lacework of energy that surrounded the base of the structure.

Ognian slumped against the nearest railing. "Hy'm chust gunna shot op now," he muttered.

Krosp patted his arm. "Thanks."

"A lightning moat," Lars marveled. "I've never really seen one."

Maxim nodded sagely. "Yah. Iz hard to gets de insurance."

Suddenly a voice from behind caused them all to start. "About time you boys got here."

Sitting in an embrasure was Zeetha. She continued. "Krosp, I expected. The Jaegers are…" she looked at them and nodded. "—Not much of a surprise. But you, Lars—" Here her grin widened. "What are *you* doing here?"

Lars looked away. "Why? Well she is a member of the show.

I...we... we just couldn't leave her."

Zeetha looked at him fondly. "I see." She leapt down beside them. "Well I guess there isn't much danger—" She clapped Lars on the back. "Not if you're here, hm?"

Then she frowned. The muscles under her hand were tight with tension. When Lars turned towards her, she was forcibly struck by the rigidly controlled fear she saw in his eyes. "Zeetha—" Lars said quietly, "I have *never* felt a town as dangerous as this. Something is very, very wrong here. Do you know *anything*?" He gestured at the empty streets. "What is going on here?"

Zeetha's grin vanished. "Prince Aaronev is dead. A lab accident, they say, though there's a general feeling that there must be more to it. The town is officially in mourning. No one is allowed on the streets after dark. It's expected that the Prince's son, Tarvek, will be the new Prince, once the Baron's Questor is satisfied."

Lars looked intrigued. "A Questor? Here?"

Krosp nodded. "Balan's Gap is an important trade city because of the pass. Plus, The House of Sturmvarous is a major player amongst the Fifty Families[53]. The Baron has to be able to demonstrate that the succession here is legal and legitimate."

Zeetha nodded. "A messenger has already been sent off to the Baron. Because of the city's status, the Questor is expected to be here in time for the funeral. That should be in about three days. The bureaucracy is in a panic." She indicated a large, ornate

---

[53] The Fifty Families are a coalition of those families that used to rule Europa. Their ancestors were brigands and thugs who were so good at killing people that the remaining people started giving them things so they'd stop. This made them Royalty. These days their descendants never mention this, as it seems entirely too much like honest labor. While the Fifty Families can do nothing directly about Klaus, they still have enough influence that they can be an annoyance.

building which was doubly noticeable because most of its lights were still burning and if the evidence of its chimneys was to be believed, every fireplace in the building was going full blast. "Apparently there're a lot of files that need to be 'updated.'"

She continued with a grin. "The city is also *supposed* to be sealed. No one in, no one out, until the funeral. That's the local tradition whenever one of the Royal Family dies."

Dimo considered this. "Vot do dey say about Miz Agatha?"

At this Zeetha got serious. "Nothing." Dimo started to shrug, but Zeetha interrupted him. "No, you don't understand. Everyone is talking about everything because they're worried. I can tell you a whole lot of gossip about the Royal Family. The guards, the servants, who's looking after the royal horses—But about a young actress who was visiting the Royal Family when the Prince died? Nothing. Not a word. Not a *whisper*. It's as if she were never there at all."

Lucrezia's movements were already more sure and graceful. Shurdlu and Eotain knelt before her, weeping tears of joy.

"Oh, you dear girls," Lucrezia cooed. "You did it! I'm ever so pleased with you!"

This only sent the two into new paroxysms of joyful weeping. Lucrezia knelt next to them and gathered them within her arms.

"Oh Lady," whispered Shurdlu. "To have you back at last..."

Eotain continued. "We have worked so hard."

Lucrezia hugged them tighter in delight. "Shhh," she whispered. "Yes, I know. And I missed you as well." She released them. "Now pull yourselves together. I need you to be strong for me."

She gracefully rose to her feet. Eotain reverently offered her Agatha's glasses. Lucrezia looked at them blankly for a moment and then gingerly, with several attempts, slipped the loops over her ears. She looked around the room with a renewed interest, and paused as she saw Vrin huddled separately on the floor. She stepped over towards the prone woman.

"And you, Vrin, are you happy?"

"Of course, my Lady." Vrin raised her face from the floor, but seemed incapable of raising her eyes above Lucrezia's waist. Lucrezia realized that the woman was terrified. Interesting. She began to notice other things.

"Why is your hair cut?" Traditionally, the Geisterdamen never cut their hair.

"It... it is a mark of my shame, Lady." When Lucrezia said nothing, she continued. "When first you sent us here, your gateway, and most of your device plans were destroyed. I... none of us could rebuild it. Even I, your High Priestess had not the skills."

Lucrezia nodded slowly. This explained much[54]. Vrin continued. "We were cut off from you, and I couldn't even punish the...saboteurs."

This word caused Lucrezia to sharply draw in her breath. Vrin finally dared to look Lucrezia in the face. "But I remembered the name of Prince Aaronev. With his help, I kept our sisters safe. We rebuilt your machine—" Here she broke down and wept. Years of tightly held frustration and fear were finally allowed release, in this, her moment of triumph. "And I found the child! Everything worked! You are here and

---

[54] Most plans or devices created by Sparks tended to frustrate those non-Sparks who attempted to repair or duplicate them. Working on them excessively tended to drive those who did so quite mad. Disappointingly, this didn't help.

I can finally—*finally* beg your forgiveness!"

Lucrezia's eyes had gone cold. "Surely I sent adequate guards. Surely you knew how to utilize them. Who destroyed my gate?"

This was the moment Vrin had feared for years. "Oh Lady," she whispered, "It was one of us."

Lucrezia froze. "One of you?"

Vrin huddled prostate upon the floor. "Yes Lady," she whispered, "The Lore Mistress, Milvistle. She…" Vrin swallowed, "She doubted your divinity."

Fury filled Lucrezia's face. "Is she dead?"

Vrin nodded frantically. "Yes, Mistress! But…"

Lucrezia grabbed Vrin's hair and yanked her upright. "*But*—?"

"But there are signs that she did not act alone!"

"Traitors?" Lucrezia screamed. "*Heretics?!* Amongst *my* priestesses? How *dare* they?"

She released Vrin and stood there, a look of calculating rage upon her face. If Geisterdamen had arrived here ready to rebel, there must be rebels plotting back in The Silver City. Right below her very nose…

This line of thought was cut off by the trembling woman at her feet. "There are others about whom I have doubts, my Lady."

That caught Lucrezia's attention. An opportunity to work off some of the betrayal and indignation she felt would be quite welcome indeed. "Who? Tell me!"

A smooth voice, speaking in perfect Geisterese, cut Vrin off before she could speak. "I trust *I* am not on that list, Lady Vrin."

All four women whirled to see Tarvek Sturmvarous standing before them. Before they could react, he smoothly dropped to one knee and bowed in supplication. "Welcome back, My

Lady." He raised his head and smiled. "Allow me to be the first of many to offer you my service."

Vrin opened her mouth angrily, but was stopped by Lucrezia gliding forward, her face a picture of joyful amazement. "Wilhelm?" She reached Tarvek and he rose to face her, surprise and a touch of confusion in his eyes. Lucrezia studied his face and reaching out, sensuously slid her hands down his arms. Tarvek shivered.

"I can't believe it," Lucrezia breathed. "Why you're—" her tongue delicately licked at a corner of her upper lip—"You're looking better than ever!"

The light dawned. Tarvek cleared his throat. "Ah. Forgive me, my Lady. You have confused me with my late *father*, Aaronev Wilhelm Sturmvarous." He stepped back and made a slight bow. "I am Aaronev *Tarvek* Sturmvarous, his son."

This news caught Lucrezia by surprise. "Dead?" she whispered. "Faithful Wilhelm is dead?" She looked back up at Tarvek. "When?"

Tarvek sighed. "Just last night, I'm afraid. Like myself, he never faltered in his devotion to you, my Lady. But I'm afraid that actually finding your daughter precipitated a... crisis of faith in my sister, Anevka. One that proved quite fatal to my father."

Lucrezia closed her eyes and sighed heavily. She gently reached out and touched Tarvek's shoulder. "I'm so sorry for the loss of your father." Her eyes opened and they were as cold as space. "And now I really must kill your sister. Do bring her to me."

Tarvek shrugged. "I have already ordered some of your priestesses to do just that." He turned towards Vrin, who looked as if she would burst with barely suppressed rage. "That *was* the correct thing to do, wasn't it, Lady Vrin?"

Vrin stared at Tarvek and opened her mouth. Her gaze shifted towards the hand that Lucrezia had delicately laid upon young Sturmvarous' shoulder. She closed her mouth. "Yes," she responded through clenched teeth. "Yes, of course it was, Master Tarvek."

Tarvek raised a finger imperiously. "*Prince* Tarvek," he corrected her chidingly, "It is *Prince* Tarvek now, Lady Vrin. *Do* try to remember that." Vrin stared at him for several moments, and then nodded with a jerk.

"I would suggest," Tarvek said, turning his back to Vrin and addressing Lucrezia, "That the Lady Vrin and her retainers go and inform the rest of your priestesses that you have returned."

Lucrezia smiled. "They're here?"

Tarvek nodded. "A substantial number of them. When they first arrived, my father turned a cavern in the basement over to them. That is the Lady Vrin's domain."

Vrin reluctantly acknowledged this. "It is... a very comfortable place." She shook herself and addressed Lucrezia. "We are divided into three shifts, My Lady, two of which were always traveling the Shadow World searching for the Holy Child, while the remaining third rested and guarded your machines." A thought struck her. "We... we won't have to search anymore. I don't know where we'll put everyone—"

She gasped as another thought struck her. She turned to Lucrezia and dropped to her knees. "My Lady," she said, her voice quavering with emotion, "My Lady, our task has been fulfilled. May we... may we be allowed to return to The City of Silver Light?"

This question caught Lucrezia by surprise. She considered it. "Well, I don't see why not," she conceded.

The three Geisterdamen shrieked with joy. Eotain and Shurdlu hugged each other with almost bone-cracking force. Vrin stared up at Lucrezia with tears streaming from her eyes. Lucrezia held up an admonishing finger. "But not immediately, of course. I must repair the gateway and assemble other assistants as loyal as you have been."

"Impossible!" Vrin swore. "There will never be anyone who loves and needs you as much as we do, Mistress!"

Lucrezia smiled. "I shall just have to make do."

Tarvek leaned in. "Perhaps the Lady Vrin and her retainers should go to the caverns and let the others know the good news that you've returned, not to mention that they will be returning home." Vrin looked at him. Tarvek continued, "plus I imagine, you'd like to smarten the place up a bit for when The Lady comes to inspect it?"

Vrin shot to her feet. "Of course! We will prepare a feast for my Lady!" She paused. "Most of the food of the Shadow World is rather disgusting, My Lady, but we make do."

Tarvek nodded. "They've actually learned how to make a rather tasty cheese. We didn't even know they'd brought cows down there—"

Vrin stuck out her tongue in disgust. "Moo-cows? Those stupid fat things? Ew. We make our 'cheese' from the juice of our own cob spiders."

"Really?" Tarvek, who had eaten a lot of "cheese," looked ill. "How fascinating."

Lucrezia gave a snort of laughter and then looked startled.

Tarvek noticed. "Are you all right, my Lady?"

"There is so much that I have forgotten about this place," Lucrezia murmured. "There is always so much happening, and so much of it is so delightfully ridiculous."

The Geisterdamen formally bowed, and then darted off. Lucrezia looked after them fondly. She turned to Tarvek. "Vrin does not like you."

Tarvek shrugged and started to walk. "She has been touchy and suspicious about everyone ever since your machinery was sabotaged. Rather unfairly, I feel, since none of our people were involved." Lucrezia remained silent. Tarvek continued. "I shall have a suite set up for your use—"

At this point, Tarvek realized that Lucrezia was no longer by his side. He wheeled about and discovered a now naked Lucrezia delightedly examining herself in front of a large mirror. His strangled "glurk!" caught Lucrezia's attention.

"Oh *do* forgive me," she sang out as she turned and looked at herself over her shoulder. "It's been so long since I..." she paused, and gave a peculiar laugh that sent a small chill up Tarvek's spine, "Since I was really *human*, I suppose, that I have to get used to it all over again." She ran her hands down her sides and nodded approvingly. "Yes, I can work with this."

She turned back to Tarvek, who was resolutely facing away. Lucrezia smiled. This sort of thing was always fun. She sashayed over to him. "Now you were saying?"

Tarvek nodded. He turned, saw her lack of clothing and spun back, his face flushed. "Yes. Well. There are hidden parts of the castle. I'm afraid that you'll have to stay out of sight for the next few days. Until after my father's funeral. We can't risk having the Baron's people seeing you yet."

Lucrezia frowned with mock severity as she oh-so-casually took his arm. She noted that he was sweating slightly. "But surely these are *your* lands." She thought about this and continued more seriously. "What do you care about some Baron?"

That stopped Tarvek dead. He turned to look at her and to Lucrezia's surprise, stayed focused on her face. "You really *have* been out of touch for a while. Interesting. Baron Wulfenbach means *nothing* to you?"

Lucrezia stared at him. She tried to stall for time and regain the upper hand by going back and picking up the clothing she had dropped. However, despite the view she provided, she saw that Tarvek was no longer flustered. The young Prince was more formidable than she had first thought.

"A Baron Wulfenbach you say? My, that does take me back. His *father* meant quite a lot to me, but that was such a long time ago." She frowned in genuine annoyance now. "I wonder where *dear* Klaus was keeping his mother? I had thought him the last of his family."

Tarvek looked confused. "Well, there is a son, yes, but the one we're talking about—this is in fact the same Klaus Wulfenbach of whom I speak."

Lucrezia's jaw dropped. "HE CAME *BACK*?"

In Tarvek's opinion, the fear and astonishment he saw in her face was the first honest emotion she had displayed. He nodded slowly. "Yes Lady. A few years after he disappeared."

Lucrezia reeled. "Only a few—!"

She saw Tarvek studying her and caught herself. She allowed herself a small wistful smile and sighed affectionately. "That man."

With that she pulled herself back together instantly. Tarvek was impressed. She raised her chin and smiled. "Very well. Klaus is here. How droll. He is but a Baron, how much trouble can he be?"

Tarvek stared at her. He slowly removed his glasses and rubbed his eyes. "Please have a seat, my Lady. This... this may take awhile."

Meanwhile, aboard the flagship of the Wulfenbach airship fleet, Gilgamesh Wulfenbach faced his current opponent.

The last three months had seen a startling change in the young man. He was unshaven. His clothes had obviously been lived in for days, if not weeks. They were tighter as well. While he had never been out of shape, he had obviously been working hard in the interim, and his chest and arms had begun to resemble the proportions of his father. His hands had acquired new bruises and scars. More importantly, there was a grim and increasingly distant quality to his eyes that was worrying to his man servant, Ardsley Wooster, as he stood safely up out of the way on an overhead catwalk and watched the fight.

Below, in a large, empty machinist's bay, a chunky, crab-style clank clattered forward. It had obviously seen better days. Its shell was battered and coated with a patina of rust. Several of its multi-jointed arms were already out of commission, and the armor plating had been peeled back in several spots.

However, it still moved with a vicious speed and purpose, and the remaining knife-edged arms wove through the air with a determined malice.

Gil easily avoided several attacks, and then darted forward and thrust a long steel spike directly into a mass of exposed tubing. There was a bright blue flash, a gout of green fluid, and the clank collapsed to the deck, spraying a shower of gears across the floor.

Gil turned away. Wooster dropped gracefully from the catwalk and hurried over to a large metal dome which, when lifted, revealed an enormous stone tea pot as well as various condiments.

Wooster prepared a large mug for Gil and then turned with it in his hand. His smile faltered, and then gamely returned. Gil hadn't moved from where he'd stopped after delivering the *coup de grace* to the attacking clank.

Ardsley peered into his face. Gil looked lost. Ardsley gently but firmly insinuated the mug into Gil's hand. After a moment, Gil registered its presence with a slight raising of his brows, and took a long, slow sip before he dropped into a chair.

Wooster leaned in. "Impressive, sir. Although I believe that one actually had time to look worried."

Gil shrugged. "It was too slow. Even after I reworked it." Wooster shivered. Gil's voice was even more disturbing than his appearance. Over the months, it had deepened and the infrasound harmonics that warned listeners that its owner was enmeshed within the grip of the Spark were almost always present.

He tried again. "Indeed, I don't know why you bothered."

This actually provoked a response. Gil looked at Wooster and frowned. "It's one less killer loose in the Wastelands. Grantz brought another one in yesterday, yes? I'll take a look at it tonight."

Now, Wooster couldn't argue with the concept behind Gilgamesh's actions. The younger Wulfenbach had returned from his expedition to find the Heterodyne girl, determined to "clean up the Wastelands." He had even received the blessing of the Baron, who had seen the wisdom of letting his son work off some of the rage boiling away inside him by tackling a task large enough to absorb a Spark's sustained fury. Thus, he had allowed Gilgamesh to retain several of the extraordinary figures that Klaus kept on the Wulfenbach payroll.

In a world filled with monsters, there inevitably were people who enjoyed the challenge of taking them down. The ones who learned how to do this effectively, without having to be taken down themselves, found that the Baron was an excellent provider of weapons, transport, ammunition, intelligence and health insurance. Grantz was a fine example. While Gil had never met him, he always managed to drag back a steady supply of feisty monsters and rogue clanks who suffered from a minimum of damage.

What bothered the Englishman was Gilgamesh's follow up. "Taking a look at" the things retrieved from the Wastelands usually meant examining them, patching them up, repairing them and then beating them to their knees in single combat. The creatures that survived certainly became much more tractable, but Wooster could see that Gil's finer qualities were being burned away at an alarming rate. He had gone so far as to try to talk to the Baron, but the Master of Castle Wulfenbach had himself been locked away in one of his laboratories for the last several months, and had been incommunicado to someone of Ardsley's pay grade.

Wooster had seriously considered adding knockout drops to the young master's next cup of tea, but the last time he had tried that, he'd awoken two days later with a headache and a red rubber clown nose stuck to his face. The students aboard the Castle took their pranking seriously, and incompetence was harshly mocked.

Wooster sighed. "Very good, sir. Perhaps you'll actually manage to damage yourself this time."

He was startled when Gil looked directly at him and growled. "And who would care if I did?"

The act of speaking seemed to unlock something within him, and he slumped forward in his chair.

"All of the other students have either run off or got shipped back home. My father's been locked in his lab for the last few months." He looked up, and Wooster saw how despondent the young man before him was.

"I can't leave, of course. I've got no one to talk to. I can't do anything." He looked at the sparking heap of clank. "Can't do anything *important*, anyway."

Ardsley was at a loss. He had never seen Gilgamesh like this. Even when he had first been revealed to the Fifty Families and the world at large, he had seemed to regard the rash of subsequent assassination attempts as an exciting challenge, and had confided to Ardsley that he, "didn't take it personally."

"You still have me, sir," he ventured.

Gil glared at him fiercely enough that Wooster stepped back in alarm. "You? *You're* only here—" With a jerk, Gil stopped himself. He dropped his head and a small chuckle escaped him. Wooster was extremely nervous now. This was one of those situations where prolonged laughter would be a reasonable cause to evacuate the dirigible. But when Gil looked back up, Ardsley relaxed. Gil looked calmer than he had in days.

"I'm sorry, Wooster." He took a deep breath and leaned back in his chair. Ardsley could see the muscles on his arms start to relax. "I know I must make your work difficult for you." Ardsley gave a noncommittal shrug.

Gil took a deep pull from his mug and rotated his neck, producing a disquieting series of pops and crackles. "And I do appreciate having you here. Having someone I can trust…"

This was getting embarrassing, for a variety of reasons. Ardsley briskly picked up the pot and refilled Gilgamesh's mug. "Of *course* you do, sir." From long experience, Gil knew to hold his mug motionless as Ardsley efficiently topped it off with just the right amount of cream and sugar to maintain his preferred taste. "*I* know how you take your tea."

Gil rolled his eyes at this, but said nothing as he sipped. Wooster took a few extra seconds to neatly wipe down his spoons. He spoke carefully. "And I am concerned for you, sir. Ever since… Miss Agatha died…" Gil had closed his eyes now. "I had not realized that the two of you were so… close."

This was the first time he'd felt comfortable enough to broach the subject. The servants aboard the castle had been buzzing about it for weeks, of course. Even while in the infirmary, Captain DuPree had laughed about it within everyone's hearing. Wooster had been unsure about what aspect of it the Captain had found funnier, the idea that Gil had been knocked out by his fiancée, or that he had thought he'd had a fiancée in the first place.

Ardsley had met Gilgamesh while they were both students in Paris. Thus, he was aware of the unusual history that the Captain and Gilgamesh shared[55].

It was only after a rather brutal sparring session (where Gil had taken her down in two out of three falls), that the Captain had agreed to stop talking about it altogether.

Gil looked sad. "We weren't," he admitted. "But we would have been." He looked over at Wooster and impatiently waved

[55] Klaus originally sent Bangladesh DuPree to Paris to teach Gilgamesh how to fight a crazy person (though this was not what he told Captain DuPree). There have been tantalizing hints that their relationship progressed beyond this, but many scholars regard this as unlikely, since both were still alive.

him over to another chair. Ardsley knew better than to argue when Gil was in one of these moods. He sat, and because it was expected, poured himself a mug of tea. While he did this, Gil idly balanced his full mug on his index finger. As he talked, he absent-mindedly bounced it from finger to finger. Wooster was almost *certain* that this was just something Gil did to keep his hands busy, and was not, in fact, meant to terrify him. This didn't help.

"Do you know," Gil volunteered, "I had resigned myself to bachelorhood?"

Wooster almost choked on his tea at this. The dynastic implications of this simple statement could shake Europa. He was also concerned as a friend. "Don't be absurd. You're still young."

Gil looked down from the great height of his twenty-two years and rolled his eyes.

Wooster frowned, "And, if you'll forgive me, sir—in Paris, you had quite the reputation for being able to secure the company of…" Wooster tried to smile innocently, "any number of young ladies[56]."

Gil looked at him evenly. "Yes, I'll never hear the end of *that*." He paused. "Ardsley, do you know how *boring* it is to be with someone who doesn't understand a thing you're talking about?"

Ardsley flashed back to a rather one-sided conversation he'd had with the newest scullery maid, fresh from the countryside, about the proper placement of various forks. It had not ended well. "I believe I do, sir."

---

[56] Parisian scandal-sheets of the period in question do mention one "Gilgamesh Holzfäller" a surprising number of times. Usually in connection with assorted foiled robberies, captured rogue experiments, subdued out-of-control clanks, and exposed secret societies. In these exploits, he was invariably accompanied by a revolving cast of vivacious, under-dressed ladies who had required rescuing. This was really as close as Gil had ever got to "dating".

Gil looked him in the eye. "That's how I feel *all the time*." He paused. "I'd always hoped I'd find—not just someone to marry—but a real partner. I'd read about female Sparks all my life, but even in Paris—" he shook his head in disgust, "Paris, for pity's sake, forget about finding a female Spark, or any girl I could just really talk to. About things I was working on, or ideas, or—"

Gil ran down at this point and sat slumped forward for several moments. Then he slowly sat back, his eyes fixed on something in the distance. "But Miss Clay—" he grimaced, "Or Heterodyne, or whatever... she had The Spark." He looked at Wooster a touch defensively. "And she liked me. She did." He closed his eyes. "And I liked her."

Wooster felt that he should state the obvious. "She ran away, after giving you a slight concussion."

Gil shrugged. "I'm not saying it would have been an *easy* courtship. But I believe—"

They were interrupted by the far door being slammed open. A high-pitched squeal announced the arrival of Zoing. The miniscule construct waved its blue claws frantically from within its concealing coat.

From long practice, Ardsley could sometimes actually understand parts of what the excitable creature said, but not this time. It was hooting and piping so quickly that he was completely at sea.

Gil however, listened intently and nodded in satisfaction. "Excellent, Zoing, well done." He turned to Ardsley and a genuine grin crossed his face. "Time to work!"

Without pause, he followed Zoing out the door. Hurriedly, a concerned Wooster followed. "Seriously?" he demanded as he tried to keep up with Gil's long strides. "Between marathon sessions in your lab, and your excessive dueling with assorted monstrosities, you're already driving yourself to an early grave!"

They passed a large boiler that had several red lights blinking ominously across its front. As he passed, Gil casually flipped two switches and gave the side a thump. All the lights changed to green. "Well I certainly can't stop now," he said reasonably. "The next few days will be critical. Should I let them die just so I can get some sleep?"

Wooster frowned. "If your father finds out that you have them—"

"I don't give a damn!" Gil interrupted fiercely. "And you should have thought of that before you helped me hide them."

Wooster grimaced. He'd thought about little else for days. Gil continued, "Besides, with any luck, we'll be done and have them out of here before he even—"

"Master Gilgamesh! The Baron demands that you attend him! Now!" Expressions of shock and guilt raced across Gil's face before he damped them down and smoothly turned to face the Lakya that had appeared at the end of the hallway.

He was not reassured by the creature's appearance. Ever since Agatha's escape and death, the Baron had been subtly dispersing the Jägermonsters throughout the vast Wulfenbach Empire. As a result, the Lakya had been given more and more of the day-to-day duties that the Jägers had been entrusted with aboard the castle. This had resulted in an increased superciliousness amongst the dapper constructs.

There was no evidence of that now. The Lakya before Gil looked almost frantic, and was obsessively rubbing his hands together in a frantic dry washing motion that any casual observer of the footmen would have known was only a few steps below actual panic.

Gil tried to marshal his thoughts. "But—"

The hand washing increased in intensity. "Now! Right now!" The Lakya chattered its teeth together. "I have never *seen* him so angry!"

Gil tried again. "Um...with me?"

A frantic nodding. "*Especially* with you!"

A peculiar calm settled upon Gilgamesh. For years he'd imagined what would happen to him if he failed to measure up to his father's never-ending tests. Surely the reality couldn't be worse. Probably. He nodded. "Very well."

He turned to Ardsley and put a hand on the distraught man's shoulder. "Wooster, go on to the lab without me. Work with Zoing. Keep everything stable for as long as you can. I..." He swallowed. "I may be gone for some time."

Despite this acceptance, it was still a pale, nervous face that shortly peered around the slightly opened blast door to Klaus' laboratory. "Father?" he ventured.

"GET *IN* HERE, YOU *IMBECILE*!" Klaus roared.

Gil quickly threw the door open wide and was hit with a wave of moist heat. The lab was like an oven. Even his father, who was a stickler for formal dress most of the time, was clothed in little more than rolled up shirtsleeves and a foundryman's leather overall. Gil tried not to stare. His father was sweating, which combined with his unshaven face and the circles under his eyes, gave him a terrifying appearance.

Reflexively, his eyes swept the room and discovered it equipped with a baffling hodgepodge of chemical, electrical and medical equipment. Whatever it was that the Master of

Castle Wulfenbach had been working on, it had been tortuously complicated.

Gil took in the large camp bed and the various kitchen trays, which indicated that Klaus' residence here had been prolonged and that this project had required constant supervision. He felt a flicker of curiosity, which was then snuffed out under the force of Klaus' rage.

Klaus grabbed Gil's upper arm and dragged him towards the center of the room. Gil saw an ornate, and obviously handmade container, over three meters in diameter, somewhat resembling a steam boiler, but fitted out with a bewildering array of additional devices. Studying it, Gil was even more puzzled. He could identify almost all of the devices in play, but could not conceive of what possible project they could all be working on in concert.

Releasing Gil, Klaus strode up to the container and threw a knife switch on the side. A set of green lights on the bottom of what was revealed to be a fluid filled tank flared on. Klaus spun about and pointed to the tank. "Who the blazes is *that*?!"

Gil stepped forward. Within the tank floated a naked girl. Gil estimated that when she stood, she would be tall and full figured. A short, thick mane of curly black hair floated above her head. Her eyes were closed, and there was a curiously blank look on her face. Gil studied her intently, frantically searching his memory.

Finally he gave up and turned to his father. "I… I don't *know* who she is, father. Should I?"

This only seemed to further infuriate the elder Wulfenbach. "*That* is the girl who's *body* you brought back!"

Gilgamesh stared at her. "Girl? What girl? I didn't—"

Realization hit him. "Miss Clay?" He stepped forward. "That's *Agatha*?"

"No!" Klaus roared. "That's the girl you *told* me was Agatha!" He slammed his fist upon the container, which boomed in response. "*Weeks* of preparation! *Constant* monitoring! I'm finally set to decant her, and *this* is what I find!" He glared at Gil. "You *fool*!"

Gil felt his head start to reel. He stepped back. Not from the heat of his father's rage, but from the waves of realization that were battering him with successive bursts of insight.

"She's still alive!" Another realization. "The circus... they *tricked* me!" He looked at Klaus blankly. "Father—they *tricked* me!"

Gil hadn't believed that Klaus could get any madder. He was incorrect. "Am I supposed to feel *better* because the heir to my empire was duped by a pack of *carnies*?"

Gil wisely realized that there was no good answer to this. Klaus turned away in disgust. Gil felt the ambient heat begin to diminish. He considered breathing.

"Fortunately," Klaus continued, "I decided to attempt a revival."

Gil blinked. "But... her head was—"

Klaus waved him into silence. "Yes, the brain was a complete loss. But then, I thought, a Spark's brain can be such an obstreperous thing. But a *Heterodyne,* ah—*that* would be a useful thing to have in one's arsenal." He turned to look at the floating girl. "I *had* the body. If I could repair that, why then I could fill it with any brain I wanted."

Gil stared. It was an audacious plan. But what left him breathless was the medical miracle that Klaus had developed solely in order to implement it. Even after this fiasco, the Baron's scientists would be developing and refining this for years to come.

"But now—!" Klaus ended this speculation by again smashing his great fist onto the tank. "I want her back here!"

Gil felt himself nodding frantically. "I'll—"

"No!" Klaus fixed Gil with a look of contempt. "I will take DuPree and I will fetch her myself!"

Gil blanched. He thought desperately. "Do you know where she *is*? It's been months."

This checked Klaus. "True…"

Gil tried to sound reasonable. "You've done some astounding work father, but you must be exhausted. *You're* the one who always says that important decisions should always be made twice—once when tired, and once when rested."

Klaus hesitated, closed his eyes and wearily rubbed his great jaw. "I do, don't I?" He regarded Gilgamesh with an unreadable expression upon his face. "Perhaps you are—" he paused. "*Yes*, Boris?"

The four-armed secretary checked the knock he had been about to complete. "An important emissary from Sturmhalten has arrived, Herr Baron."

This was unusual enough that it piqued Klaus' interest. "Very well, show him in."

The Count Hengst von Blitzengaard, immaculately attired in a formal traveling cloak, stepped into the lab and kept from perspiring by sheer force of will. Gil was impressed. He crisply bowed and formally presented a large black envelope, encrusted with the winged sword and gear sigil of the House of Sturmvarous.

"Forgive the intrusion, Herr Baron. I bring most grave news[57]." Klaus accepted the envelope, snapped the wax seal with a thumb and unfolded the document within. He looked at his son.

"Prince Aaronev Wilhelm Sturmvarous IV, is dead," he announced.

Gil frowned. That meant that Aaronev Tarvek Sturmvarous was the next prince. He shook his head. There would be trouble there—

"A *lab* accident?" Incredulity filled Klaus' voice. He slapped the paper. "It says here that Aaronev died in a lab accident."

Gil shook his head. "Preposterous."

The Count cleared his throat nervously. "The Royal Family assured the medical—"

Klaus interrupted him. "There are many things I can say against Prince Aaronev, but in the lab he was the most meticulous and procedurally brilliant—" Klaus stopped dead. Within his uniquely convoluted brain, things were coming together. "It's her!"

Gil tried to understand. "Her *who,* father?"

"The girl! Agatha! I know it!"

"How could you possibly—"

Klaus waved his hands impatiently. He had enough confidence in his son's thought processes that he did not even bother with full sentences. "Circus! Passholdt gone! Balan's Gap! Time versus distance. Aaronev is a fan of Heterodyne shows—he was always Lucrezia's slave! Of *course* that's where she'd wind up!"

---

[57] Amongst the aristocracy, black envelopes were reserved for the deaths of nobility. Amongst the merchant class, it usually signified an everything-must-go sale.

He turned to his secretary, who was already poised to receive his orders, notebook in hand. "I'll be leaving for Sturmhalten within the next three hours. I'm assigning the Seventh Groundnaut Mechanical, the Fifth Airborne, a wing of Hoomhoffers and two Bug Squads to come with. They are to be fully armed and should be prepared to encounter moderate resistance. Captain DuPree is to be in Command. I shall travel on her ship. Inform her at once. Within twenty-four hours I shall expect to be followed by a full Inspection Team. I shall want Sturmhalten probed down to the bedrock."

Boris nodded. "Very Good, Herr Baron."

During this, Count Blitzengaard's face has gone white. "My Baron!" he broke in, "The people of Balan's Gap are completely loyal to the Empire! This is an invasion! You must allow me to contact—"

Klaus cut him off. "No contact." To Boris he added, "With anyone." The Count drew his breath in outrage, but before he could speak, Klaus verbally steamrollered him. "Whereas I am confident in the loyalty of the people of Balan's Gap, I suspect there may be a threat to the populace of the Empire as a whole. Under those conditions, I may send in an Inspection Team protected by sufficient troops to ensure their safety and insure compliance. Boris will cheerfully recite the relevant passages from the treaty that Prince Aaronev signed when the city was annexed, as he escorts you to your quarters. Good day."

With that, the Count felt several hands clasp his shoulders and gently but irresistibly pull him from the room. As the door shut, Gil looked at his father and spoke seriously. "Are you planning on *leveling* Sturmhalten?"

Klaus frowned. "If I must."

Gil felt overwhelmed. "This is all about Agatha, but she's done *nothing*!"

Suddenly Klaus looked tired. "There is a possibility that she has done *everything*!"

Gil paused. His father was not known as an alarmist. "Explain, please."

Klaus paused. He considered his son for a moment.

Encouraged, Gil continued, "Father, if you'd let me just *talk* to her—"

But this had been the wrong thing to say. "Absolutely not," Klaus declared flatly. "That family is utterly poisonous, and this girl may be the worst of all."

Gil was lost. "But you liked the Heterodynes! You worked with—"

Klaus paused in the doorway. "Not the Heterodynes. The House of Mongfish. Your Agatha's mother was the worst of them. I couldn't stop her, but if I act quickly, I may be able to stop another war." With that he strode off down the corridor.

Gil started to follow him when a frantic Zoing raced around the nearest corner and squealed excitedly. Gil impatiently listened, and several seconds later was running at full speed back down the corridor.

He burst into the lab to find a sweating Wooster desperately dashing amongst the various devices, trying to adjust them. He was failing most spectacularly. All of them were blinking red. Many of them were shuddering and venting great gouts of steam.

He saw Gil and waved his hands. "Gil! Thank goodness! I don't know what to do!"

Gil strode forward and began twisting valves and rerouting cables. "Bleed the pressure here! Counter the loss by heating here..." Both Wooster and Zoing leapt into action as Gil continued to shout directions while performing his own corrections. Within several minutes, green lights shone instead of red, and with a sigh, Gil replaced a final clogged filter. He slumped. Wooster allowed his shoulders to droop slightly, and Zoing fell over sideways.

"Nice one, Herr Boffin" Ardsley muttered and then looked mortified at the slip.

Gil smiled. He hadn't heard Ardsley use the phrase since college, when they were both students. He nodded, but otherwise ignored it. "Unfortunately, it's even more unstable than I'd feared. I'll have to monitor it closely for—" He stopped aghast. "I can't—" He stared at Wooster and the Englander could see that Gil was deeply distressed. "I... I can't leave!"

"Does Sir need to go somewhere?"

Gil's face took on one of those intensely blank looks that Wooster had come to recognize. Within his head, Gil was frantically thinking. Assessing, sorting, imagining and computing possibilities faster than his friend would have ever believed possible. Wooster braced himself. Whenever this happened, it meant that things were about to get very interesting and very nerve-wracking, very, very quickly. This time, Gil outdid himself.

He blinked, and swiveled his head towards the waiting valet. "It will have to be you," he said hollowly.

Wooster swallowed. "Me? Sir, what are you talking about?"

Even more worrying, Gil was again in deep thought. "But how to *ensure*..."

Wooster felt a prickle of fear. This was—

Suddenly, Gil was right in front of him. His face centimeters from his. His large, powerful hands gripping his upper arms. "Wooster," Gil said very intently, "This is very important. Do you fear me?"

Wooster had braced himself for any number of things, but this was not one of them. "Sir?"

Gil gave him a small shake. "No, really. Be honest."

Wooster considered the question carefully. Suddenly he realized that Gil was holding him so that his feet were not actually touching the floor. That helped clarify things. "Ah—a little, I confess."

Gil searched Ardsley's face. He nodded. "I can work with that." Then he grinned. "Miss Clay—Agatha Heterodyne— she's *alive*!"

Wooster's jaw dropped at the news. "Alive!"

Gil nodded in delight. "Yes! She found people to help her and she tricked me!" He paused as another thought struck him. "*And* Captain DuPree no less! Hee hee, she'll be *furious*!"

Wooster nodded. "But—that's *wonderful*, sir."

"Yes, but there's a problem."

"Your father," Wooster surmised.

Gil nodded. As he spoke he pulled down a large leather travel satchel and began placing useful things inside. "That's right. He knows, and he's going to go get her himself."

Wooster frowned. "That... could be bad."

Again Gil nodded and pulled open a cabinet containing maps. He sorted through them quickly and tossed a series of them into the bag. "Bad indeed. So I'm sending you to her."

"Me?" Wooster didn't even try to hide his surprise.

Gil pulled down a magnetic compass he'd been experimenting

with. He hesitated, and then gently switched it on. Instantly his entire body was forcefully spun about until it was facing towards Magnetic North. Regretfully, he switched it off and placed it back on the shelf. "Yes, I want you to get to her first. Warn her. Hide her."

Wooster looked lost. "Where? In my room?"

Gil sighed and closed the bag with a snap of fasteners. "Don't be ridiculous. After you reported that she had escaped, you were ordered, if the opportunity presented itself, to do everything within your power to get Agatha to England."

Wooster felt the floor drop out from under him. "I—Wh—What?"

Gil continued blithely. "This will enable you to do so."

Wooster stared at him.

Gil rolled his eyes. "Please. You don't work for me, you work for British Intelligence. You did when we met back in Paris. It's why I recommended you for duty aboard Castle Wulfenbach, it's why I made you my valet, so I could keep an eye on you. My father certainly didn't object. To be honest, for a while I thought you might be one of his little tests." Gil shrugged. "It's been an enjoyable game, and I'm sorry I have to end it, but this is quite important."

Wooster blindly reached back and found a chair. He slowly sank into it, shaking his head. "Oh, dear," he muttered. "You've known all along. They'll be so angry..." He looked at Gil and a touch of his old smirk crossed his lips. "I suppose I'll be in slightly *less* disgrace when I bring them Agatha Heterodyne."

Gil did not smile back. "Yesss—" he said thoughtfully. "About that." He leaned into Wooster and tapped his friend's chest. "I do not intend to have Agatha escape from one potential prison by entering another." His voice began to shift, and Ardsley grew alarmed.

"She will not be used as some political pawn against my father. She will not be enslaved for the 'good of the empire.'" He leaned back, grinned, and playfully slapped Wooster's face. "You knew me back at school, and perhaps you don't take me very seriously. That would be a mistake. You *must* understand this."

The grin turned into a snarl and Wooster found himself being hoisted into the air by his shirt. "When I come to her, she will be safe, unharmed, and free. Because I definitely *will* come, and if she is not—" Wooster felt his teeth rattle as Gil shook him once—"I will destroy 'Her Undying Majesty.' I will melt what is left of your miserable island into slag, and then boil the seas around you for the next thousand years!" This last was delivered at a roar. "Do you understand?"

Wooster desperately tried to see some trace of the man he thought he'd come to know over the last three years. What he could see was not reassuring. "You... you couldn't!"

"Couldn't?!" screamed Gilgamesh. "*Couldn't?* I am Gilgamesh *Wulfenbach*, little man, and there is *nothing* I couldn't do, had I cause!"

Again Gil grinned. This was even worse than him yelling. "And now... Now I *have* one!" Again he pulled Wooster up close. "Do. You. Understand?"

"Yes!" Screamed a terrified Wooster. "Oh God, yes! Yes, Master!"

Gil released him and he fell over backwards, but was instantly scrabbling back up.

"Much better," Gil purred. He flung the travel bag at

Wooster who clumsily caught it. "She is in, or near, Balan's Gap. Probably in Sturmhalten Castle. Take my flyer."

After Agatha had left, Gil had rebuilt the bizarre little heavier-than-air craft. Wooster had, out of curiosity, watched him closely enough to be able to fly it, but the basic concept had been so outlandish that he hadn't even bothered to pass the plans back to England.

"Watch out for the new Prince, Tarvek Sturmvarous. Around him, trust nothing you think you see." Gil clamped an iron hand on Ardsley's shoulder, checking his flight. "Do not fail me, Wooster. For if you do…"

"I won't, sir," the shaken man gasped. Gil smiled and released him. Wooster bolted down the corridor and out of sight.

As soon as he disappeared, Gil sagged against the doorframe. A deep sigh escaped him. "Goodbye, Ardsley," he whispered. "I'll really miss you."

He turned back to the room, and addressed the watchers who had observed everything. "Well," he said reassuringly, "I've done all I can. It should be enough. My sources say that he's one of Britain's finest agents."

"Thhh…" Gil's eyebrows arced in surprise. He stepped closer. From the medical slabs where they lay, cocooned within an intricate webwork of medical equipment, a rebuilt Adam and Lilith Clay looked at him with eyes that, although drugged, showed that they were aware of their surroundings.

Adam tried again. His new vocal cords rattling from deep within his patched throat. "—Thhank hhyuu."

Gil settled down and patted Adam's arm. "Thank me when she's safe."

TEN

SCENE; THE SEWERS BENEATH PARIS.

KLAUS; I can't stand this anymore! It's dark! It stinks! It's wet, and there are monsters!

BILL; Buck up, old man! At least fighting the monsters keeps us warm!

KLAUS; You cannot imagine how much I hate you.

—SCENE 2. ACT 2, *THE HETERODYNE BOYS AND THE MYSTERY OF THE MECHANICAL MUSKETEER*

The Empire was going to war.

In one of the larger docking bays of Castle Wulfenbach, a fleet of the Baron's heavy cruisers prepared for embarkation. The vast man-made cavern was filled with sound.

On a platform high overhead, surrounded by amplification horns, one of the Castle's marching bands kept people's feet moving quickly, drums and glockenspiels set the pace, as the brass filled the air with jaunty and patriotic marches.

Teams of longshoremen hoisted containers of food, fuel and ammunition. Riggermen swarmed over the exterior of the ships, freely slathering sealant upon the envelopes, checking cables, and testing exterior lights. Gasmen were checking gauges and, with a series of distinctive pops, disconnecting the gigantic rubberized canvas hoses that looped upwards towards the unseen tanks and pumps that supplied them.

A squad of overalled mechanics finished bolting down the cowling of one of the great engines and grinning, all three of them used their wrenches to beat out the traditional "Good to go" rhythm on the nearest support strut. A flagman on a nearby platform acknowledged their signal, waved them off, and then with a snap of his flags, relayed the availability of the engine to the ship's Chief Engineer. Within thirty seconds, the engine coughed, and with an escalating whine, the six-meter-tall propeller began to slowly turn as the motor went through its warm-up sequence. The large steel cables holding the great airship in place gave a groan, and a midshipman nervously checked the gauges on his quick-release buckle.

The metal decks thundered to the sound of hundreds of soldiers, all armed with rifles and assorted equipment being marched aboard. A pair of lieutenant-engineers blew their infamous three-toned whistles, and an aisle magically cleared to allow a squad of the tall brass fighting clanks, their fearsome machine cannons held at the ready, their tall red shakos newly brushed, to stride by in perfect lockstep with a hiss and a well oiled boom.

A lift whined, and from the shadows of the cavernous ceiling, a freight platform descended. Crowded around its edge was an unfamiliar squad of soldiers garbed in peculiar facemasks and long green cloaks. At the center of the platform was a stack of cages. From within could be heard high pitched growling and the occasional yip.

Unicycle messengers darted everywhere, their tin whistles piping a warning, usually followed by cursing and threats as they spun past within millimeters of the soldiers and crewmen.

One in particular shot out from between a pair of the tall brass clanks, leapt off his machine and snagged it in midair as he skidded to a halt centimeters away from Captain Bangladesh DuPree. As he stopped, the lad simultaneously pulled a flimsy envelope from the leather satchel over his shoulder and politely tucked his pillbox hat under his arm. Everyone was polite around Captain DuPree.

Bangladesh was the center of a small crowd of people vying for her attention. Those who only heard about the Captain's more egregious aspects would have been nonplussed. Despite the multitude of voices, she dealt with the cacophony around her, answering questions, signing papers, and receiving reports with an easy-going smile and a calm efficiency.

A radiohead, with its diminutive driver perched upon its broad shoulders, lumbered up carrying Bangladesh's air chest. She signed for it with a flourish and a pair of airshipmen gingerly hoisted it up and carried it onboard the dirigible.

Through this controlled chaos came the Baron's secretary. DuPree and Boris had a professional understanding. Boris disapproved of DuPree because her methods, while undeniably effective, were unnecessarily messy. But he acknowledged that she was an effective tool.

In the spirit of fairness, it should be pointed out that, when the subject came up, Bangladesh freely admitted that she also thought of Boris as a tool.

Mostly, they just tried to avoid each other.

Boris' presence here was unexpected. Whenever Klaus came along on a deployment, he turned over his considerable executive powers to his secretary. Boris usually wasted no time in using these powers to deal with the pressing bureaucratic business of the Empire without having to spend time waylaying the Baron.

"Hey, Boris!" she called out gaily. "Where is Klaus hiding? Tell his exalted crankiness that we are almost ready to ship out."

Outwardly, Boris ignored this over-familiarity, but with satisfaction, DuPree noted the small twitch in his left eye.

"You may tell him yourself, Captain." Boris pointed towards one of the enclosed observation decks that lined the walls. "He wants to see you at once."

Several minutes later, Bangladesh strode into the room. Dozens of people were vying for the Baron's attention. Klaus had the disconcerting ability to follow multiple conversations at the same time, and thus the noise level of the room approached that of a dull roar. Klaus himself was easy to spot, towering as he did above most of the other people present.

When the Baron saw her, he imperiously held up a hand to stop the other conversations and waved her over. Suddenly, there was a palpable edge in the room. Bangladesh realized that everyone was scared and nervous. Usually she was the cause of this, but now, there was something else... these people thought that something terrible was about to happen—

Without warning, Klaus' arms snapped out and grabbed her. One enormous hand easily trapped both of Bangladesh's hands straight up over her head. The other scooped her up and held her securely under his arm. "Quickly!" he roared.

Bangladesh had time for one startled thought. "*I never saw it coming.*" But instead of the expected blade, several small creatures were thrust at her. They looked like some sort of weasel, with short orange fur and thin, intelligent faces. This was so surprising that she didn't even struggle as they sniffed inquisitively at her. She noticed other things now. There were odd little devices surgically attached to the creatures' heads and they had no less than six short legs, tipped with delicate paws.

The handlers were more of the green-cloaked soldiers she had noticed in the hangar bay. At this point, all of the creatures gave a small squeal, and everyone relaxed. One of the handlers, who Bangladesh noted with a start of surprise had the skull-piece of a Slaver warrior attached to his cloak, pulled his animal back, and the others did the same. "She is clean, Herr Baron."

Klaus gave a nod. "Give us some room please." Instantly, a large circle of emptiness was created as everyone drew back from the expected explosion. Klaus gently placed Bangladesh on her feet, paused, and then withdrew quickly enough that her stiletto barely sliced the edge of his sleeve. Then to the astonishment of everyone, including Bangladesh herself, Klaus bowed in apology. "Forgive me, your Highness."

Bangladesh was always thrown whenever Klaus deigned to remember that she was a Queen[58]. She took another half-hearted swipe with her knife, but the moment had passed.

[58] A pirate queen, to be sure. But the aristocracy these days was feeling sufficiently under siege that they were prepared to overlook certain realities. As a result, many a formal banquet had been enlivened by someone foolishly inviting someone who was euphemistically referred to as "working royalty".

"Don't ever do that again!" she snarled. "What's with the weasels?" she demanded.

Klaus straightened up, collecting the Captain's hat from the floor as he did so. He presented it to her as he waved over the head handler, who approached warily. "They are known as 'Wasp-eaters.'" The little creature in the handler's hand obviously realized that it was being talked about. It looked at Bangladesh and smirked.

"We developed them to hunt down Slaver Wasps, but unexpectedly, it appears that they can also detect when someone is infected with a wasp."

Bang was unimpressed. "What, in case you don't notice the whole shambling, twitching revenant act?" She snorted. "Yes indeed, mighty useful."

Klaus rolled his eyes. "Yes, that was my initial reaction as well." He paused. "Until recently." He made a small sign to a group at the far door. This was opened, and the indignant person of Count Blitzengaard strode in.

"Herr Baron!" He began sternly, "I must vigorously protest this...this invasion!" He no doubt would have gone on for a good deal longer, but the wasp-eater nearest to him had snapped to look at him, then opened its mouth wide and hissed. The Count stopped dead and stared at the creature in astonishment.

Several other handlers had drifted close, and their charges reacted similarly. "What the devil are *those* things!" the Count cried out. Two more handlers darted forward and before the Count knew what was happening, his hands were secured behind his back. "What are you doing?" he roared.

"I'm afraid you must come with us now, Sir."

The Count stared at Klaus with wide, fearful eyes. "But I've done nothing wrong! I am a Royal Courier! No one is allowed to interfere with—We have Diplomatic Immunity! By your own decree!"

Klaus nodded. "You are correct, my dear Count. I assure you, we will do all we can to cure you."

"You must—!" The Count's brain belatedly analyzed Klaus' statement. "Cure? Wait!" But by then, he had been carried out the far door.

Klaus glanced at Bangladesh. Her face was a mask of amazement. There were many bad things you could say about Captain DuPree[59], but she was second to none when it came to assessing threats.

"You mean he's—"

Klaus nodded. "Infected by Slaver Wasps. A 'revenant' under the command of The Other. Yes."

"But he… he looks perfectly normal."

"Yes." Klaus lowered his voice. "As do the one hundred and seventy others we have uncovered aboard Castle Wulfenbach so far."

Bangladesh shook her head in denial. "But The Other is dead!"

Klaus shrugged. "It's possible that we're just discovering old infections." He paused, "But I was never sure. Did she die? Or did she just stop? There was no way to tell."

"But the Heterodyne Boys—" DuPree paused. The Pfennig dropped. "Wait…'She'?"

Klaus nodded. He placed one of his hands upon the Captain's back, something few other people would have dared to do, and indicated that she was to walk with him. They left the

[59] Gilgamesh had written most of them down in a rather thick book.

observation platform and took an otherwise empty catwalk out towards the flagship. Below them the embarkation proceedings were reaching a crescendo. Finally Klaus began to speak.

"You know that I've given standing orders to bring me The Other's creations." Bangladesh nodded. She'd transported a few of them. Those were some of the few times she'd felt nervous. There were things a Captain did not want on her ship.

Klaus continued. "I've studied them. The internal logics are familiar to me. Now these devices are very advanced, but their underlying principles are similar to those I saw years ago in the work of Lucrezia Mongfish. They were so similar, that I had long entertained the notion that Lucrezia was, in fact, The Other. This was despite the fact that, as gifted as Lucrezia was, she had *never* displayed this level of skill. It was almost impossible to believe she could have advanced so *radically* in just a few years." Klaus paused, and directly faced Bangladesh.

"But now I find that there is a daughter. Sired by Bill Heterodyne, no less. Styles do tend to run in families, and any offspring of those two—"

"Whoa! Whoa!" Bangladesh interrupted. "The daughter— That was the girl who was here. But she's dead now. I saw—"

Klaus overrode her. "You saw what you were *supposed* to see. You were tricked. The girl is alive."

Bangladesh thought back to the charred corpse they had exhumed. "Really? You're sure?"

Klaus nodded. "Yes."

Bangladesh shook her head in admiration. "Wow. She sure *looked* dead."

Klaus stared at her for several moments. He was at a loss for words. Bangladesh did this to him occasionally. Unluckily, it was never a condition Bangladesh herself suffered from.

"So she's The Other's daughter." She thought about this for a minute. "Big deal."

Klaus shrugged and resumed walking. "I fervently hope that is the case."

Bangladesh frowned. "You *hope* so? What else could she *be*? Klaus, what are you so worried about?"

Klaus turned and looked the puzzled woman in the face. "She could be The Other."

Bangladesh scratched her head. "Neat trick. She doesn't look like she was old enough to even be born back then."

Klaus nodded, and took a deep breath. This was going to be complicated, which was never Bangladesh's strong suit. "DuPree, do you remember where you first saw this girl?"

The Captain nodded. "Sure. That big weird hole in the sky."

"That's right. From your description of the incident, I believe those were... windows into... the future."

DuPree looked blank. "The future?"

Klaus plowed ahead. "Time. She will be able to manipulate time. She was looking at you from sometime in the future. Do you understand what that means?"

Bangladesh opened her mouth. She paused and then closed her mouth. Klaus was encouraged.

"What you saw might have been just a window. But what if it was a Gate? She could discover how to do this ten... *twenty* years from now, and *still* be the one who destroyed Castle Heterodyne nineteen years ago!"

He dropped his hands to his sides and looked at the Captain with raised eyebrows. It was then that Bangladesh shocked the Baron more than she ever had, or indeed, ever would again.

"But if I saw her... looking at us from the future...Then she'll still be running around in this future. If we're going after her now, then we're going to *lose*."

Klaus shrugged wearily. "And thus our predicament. I just don't know enough about the nature of time. Maybe she isn't The Other. Maybe The Future you observed can be changed. Maybe we do lose because you observed it." He spread his hands wide. "Maybe everything that has happened was some huge misunderstanding and we don't have to fight her at all. The problem is that while we know what it was that you saw, we did not see it in context. We do not know the larger story."

They approached the great airship. An airshipman who was winding a cable saw them and almost broke his back with the speed with which he untangled himself and snapped off a crisp salute. They moved along to the Captain's quarters.

Bangladesh's private suite was the standard size, two rooms, one little more than a large bunk surrounded by storage cabinets, and the other a ready room, notable for its generous size (almost twelve square meters) and the large set of floor to ceiling windows that covered one wall. This held the Captain's desk and dining table, and was again lined with racks and storage spaces. The ceiling overhead was covered with rope nets that on longer expeditions held bales and packages.

By tradition, Klaus should have taken the Captain's cabin, but as always, he insisted on sleeping with the other officers. No one blamed him for this.

Most Captains preferred to keep their quarters simple. Bangladesh, however, preferred a decorating style that Gilgamesh had once described as "Debauched Barbarian Princess." He had meant it as an insult, but once Bangladesh had learned what "debauched" meant, she had worked hard to live up to it.

The first surprise was the color. Everyone always expected red, but in fact, the room was painted a dark emerald green. This allowed any added red to really stand out. Which was a big help during clean-up. Most of the available wall space was taken up with mounted weapons, guns, knives, swords, all lovingly polished and oiled and ready to be grabbed. There was a great deal of ornamentation, every edge was filigreed with gold paint, and almost all of the fixtures were gold. The chains that held the hurricane lamps, the hooks that held clothing, every visible strut and rivet gleamed in the light. Those decorations that weren't gold were bones. They always turned out to be the bones of animals and monsters, but Klaus felt compelled to keep checking. Whatever they were, there were a lot of them. They had been cunningly fashioned into pieces of furniture, drinking vessels, chart holders, clothes hangers and lampshades.

The curtains gathered away from the windows and across the Captain's bunk were a luscious shimmering silk, with an intricately batiked design of skulls.

As always, the sight of the place gave rise to mixed emotions in Klaus. There was no denying it was tasteless, gaudy and ostentatious, but it did stir fond memories of his long lost wife.

While Bangladesh stowed her gear, Klaus continued. "Dr. Beetle's notes were very well encrypted, but my team finally cracked them. Unfortunately, many of them were lost in an ill-conceived fire, but some of the material we were able to salvage was about the Heterodyne girl.

"Barry and Agatha arrived in Beetleburg around twelve

years ago. Shortly thereafter he disappeared, leaving her in the care of the constructs, Punch and Judy."

He sighed. "Other notes clearly show that Beetle believed that she would be able to control Slaver Wasps. He planned to use her. Against whom is unclear, probably myself."

Bangladesh leaned back against the table. "I thought you and Beetle were, I dunno, friends. Beetleburg's listed as a friendly port. If you knew the Heterodynes so well, why didn't Barry tell you any of this?"

Klaus looked troubled. "That is the most disturbing part. Because of the fire, there is a lot that is only hinted at, but there's one place where he mentions that Barry Heterodyne claimed that *I* worked for The Other."

Bangladesh snorted at the idea.

Klaus shrugged. "But the notes don't say *why*. This does explain why Beetle didn't confide in me, or why Barry, Punch and Judy hid from me." He paused. "You would think they'd have *known* me..." He startled Bangladesh by slamming his hand down upon the nearest table, causing the objects thereon to leap several centimeters into the air. "Confound that fool and his fire!" he growled.

As a person who had set her share of fires, Bangladesh thought it prudent to change the subject. "So she can control Slaver Wasps? But when we had that outbreak on Castle Wulfenbach, people said they saw her fighting them with Gilgamesh."

Klaus allowed himself to be distracted. "One of the many mysteries that makes this so frustrating. One of the first revenants we uncovered was Mr. Rovainen."

Bangladesh hissed in a surprised breath. Mr. Rovainen had been one of Klaus' chief assistants for over a decade.

Klaus acknowledged her understanding of the situation with a nod. "He swore that young Agatha was The Other. That she was the one who gave him the order to activate the Hive Engine aboard Castle Wulfenbach, and that he was compelled to obey her.

"Therefore I must conclude that even if she is not the *original* Other, The Other's servants will see little difference. That alone makes her dangerous."

They headed toward the bridge. The corridors were filled with crew addressing last minute details.

Bangladesh considered all that Klaus has said. "So why haven't you announced this? You're the one who claims that the troops fight better when they're informed of the big picture."

Klaus looked embarrassed. "Because I want this girl alive, and even now, just the mention of The Other inspires fear and rage. Many people lost loved ones in the attacks. Few could properly control their emotions." He paused, and continued slowly. " Plus… I am not one hundred percent sure of her guilt. There are things here that do not feel right. I must treat her with utmost caution, I will bring her here, but I won't falsely accuse her."

They passed through a reinforced doorway into the main control room of the airship. This was the largest room onboard, easily four meters tall and almost ten wide. It was surrounded on three sides by enormous floor to ceiling windows. The remaining wall space was covered with work stations and various gauges and read-outs. In the center of the floor were two enormous ship's wheels, each manned by a burly airshipman.

Behind them was a low platform, circled with brass rails

containing a large, comfortable chair that had been bolted to the deck. As they entered, a lieutenant roared out "Captain on the bridge!" All of the personnel present snapped to attention, faced Captain DuPree and saluted. She returned the salute and dropped into her chair and attached the restraint webbing all ship-board chairs were equipped with.

Bangladesh's second-in-command, another "reformed" air pirate, stepped up and saluted before handing her the final check-list. Bangladesh didn't bother to read it. "Are we ready to kill people, Lieutenant Karuna?"

The Lieutenant shot a startled look at Klaus, who refused to rise to the bait, and continued to examine the view through the window. "Only if they refuse to listen to reason, Captain." It was a measure of her fear of Klaus that Karuna was able to say this with a straight face.

Bangladesh had selected her executive crew with care over the years. They were all ex-pirates, all ruthless enough that Klaus had determined that they had to be taken out, but smart enough to accept his offer of employment. They were all deadly fighters, and they were all women[60].

When they were again alone on the platform, Bangladesh leaned back and considered her employer carefully. "So why are you telling me? I don't even try to control my emotions. Gives you wrinkles."

---

[60] In the three years since she had joined Klaus' forces, Bangladesh's unconventional fight against the air force's traditional glass ceiling had produced a disturbing number of conventional casualties. Klaus did little about this, claiming that it was an internal problem that the service should work out itself. In truth, he had noticed that the newer officers, especially those who had helped bury their predecessors, tended to be a lot more open-minded about things. Plus, when he used female officers, a depressing number of foes of the Empire underestimated them—usually right up until they were blown from the sky.

Klaus glanced at her unlined face. "You are in command. These are things that you need to be aware of." He looked at the Captain seriously. "Besides—If I decide that she must die, I know that you won't hesitate to kill her."

A little frisson of pleasure ran down Bangladesh's spine. "Why Klaus, you sweet talking flatterer," she purred. She mulled over the information. "So who else knows?"

"Boris. The Bug Squad commanders, and the Deep Thinkers[61]."

Bangladesh nodded. "What about the Jägers? They're good fighters, and wasps won't—" she realized what she was suggesting. "I guess not. You might have to kill them."

Klaus nodded soberly. "I have considered this." He looked at DuPree with a hard look in his eye. "They have served us loyally and well these last years. Could you do it? Kill them all? Just because of their misplaced loyalties?"

Bangladesh sat back hard. "I don't know. It would be really tough." She shook her head and the admission was torn from between her gritted teeth. "I... I might need help."

Klaus rolled his eyes. "Keep the possibility in mind. I have taken pains, these last few months, to keep the Jägers busy in distant parts of the Empire. With any luck, this will be done

---

[61] Sometimes, when a madboy's schemes were not producing the desired results, they actually had sufficient insight to blame themselves. However, instead of addressing their numerous psychological problems, behavioral issues or basic inability to grasp reality, a significant number of them tried to solve their problems by making themselves *smarter*. The results never failed to be entertaining. If they survived, Klaus found them to be quite useful. Admittedly, the Deep Thinkers' ruminations were useless for day-to-day planning, but they were able to correlate vast amounts of seemingly unrelated data, and use it to predict future trends and outcomes, as well as enhance or prevent certain outcomes, usually by minutely affecting things that had no apparent connection. The downside was that Klaus grew weary knowing that every time he had oatmeal for breakfast, he was dooming humanity to a thousand years of war and slavery, and that this terrible fate was only prevented by his having a banana with lunch.

with by the time they get wind of it."

At this point, a Bosun stepped out onto the "ready" platform that was attached to the nose of the ship and blew his whistle[62], announcing that this ship was ready to leave. They were the first to do so, a fact that Bangladesh appreciated, and always rewarded on the first night out with an extra ration of schnapps.

They had only beaten the other ships by a few minutes however, and the other whistles sounded forth, each ship determined not to be the last to go. Indeed, to Klaus's ear, the last two whistles came simultaneously, a judgment that was verified by the grins that spontaneously broke out all over the control room. Simultaneous debarkation whistles were seen as a sign of good luck. Klaus smiled[63].

"Lieutenant Karuna, take us out." Bangladesh's First Officer acknowledged the order and within the minute, the airship was sliding out of the side of Castle Wulfenbach. They hovered in place as the great guide poles were retracted and the final lines were cast off.

---

[62] Every Wulfenbach Bosun's whistle was a marvel of acoustical engineering, and was tuned to a different pitch. These pitches were used to identify particular ships in fog and at night by dockhands as well as fleet commanders. While a Bosun might be transferred, the whistle itself was handed down within the ship. Particularly discordant or nerve-wracking whistles were a source of pride, and the sound of a dozen or so of them keening in the dawn air, growing louder as the great ships dropped out of the sky, had broken the nerve of more than one set of defenders.

[63] Mad Behavioral Scientists didn't get a lot of press, but Klaus had several of them on his payrolls. The morale of the forces of the Empire were often bolstered by statistically odd, but not all that uncommon occurrences that had been carefully woven into an efficient mythos of good luck. Similarly, things that were seen as bad luck tended to be things that happened because of sloppiness (uncoiled ropes), foolishness (not checking your safety line when outside the gondola), or terminal ignorance (lighting a match inside a gasbag). As a result, the Wulfenbach troops did better overall because they felt lucky, and as one surveyed the wreckage of those who went up against them, it was a hard point to argue against. If only because it was unlucky.

The remainder of the force, twelve ships in all, slid forth and began maneuvering away from the great mothership towards the rendezvous point a kilometer away.

Bangladesh nodded in satisfaction as her crew performed. She turned back to Klaus as a new thought struck her. "What about Gil? He'll have an opinion about this." She rolled her eyes. "He always does."

Klaus agreed. "At the moment my son is busy repairing and reanimating Punch and Judy, that pair of constructs he thinks I don't know about."

He settled back against the rail. "I don't want to disturb him, or them, more than I already have. If he can establish a sufficient level of trust, they will answer many important questions. They raised this Agatha girl, after all. But it definitely would be best to resolve this before he is ready to interfere. He would find some of these revelations to be... disturbing."

Bangladesh smiled wickedly. "Awww, c'mon. Let me tell him."

Klaus cleared his throat. "I think not. At this point, all Gilgamesh knows is that I want her here because, as the last of the Heterodyne family, she is a threat to the peace."

He sighed. "That's certainly true enough, and if a Heterodyne is all that she is, that's fine. But if I have to destroy her—" Klaus paused. "Well, he's very much in love with her. He is unlikely to be reasonable about all of this, no matter what I say, and I don't think he'd let me."

Bangladesh blinked and then looked at Klaus incredulously. "You don't think he'd *let* you? Gil?" She let out a burst of laughter that caused everyone in the control room to flinch. She spun about in her chair holding her stomach. "You're fretting about Herr Sensitive? Klaus, please."

Klaus frowned in embarrassment. "I assure you, if he allied himself with The Other, it would be very bad indeed. Not just for Europa, but possibly for the entire world."

Bangladesh tried to control herself and wiped a tear from the corner of her eye. "Oh, I understand, Herr Baron. Heaven forbid I have to face a put-out Gilgamesh." She broke into another series of giggles.

Klaus studied her in annoyance, but because DuPree was, in her own way, a valuable asset, Klaus felt he had to make an effort to warn her. "You knew Gilgamesh in Paris. While there, he tried to hide everything important about himself. Even from me." He eyed Bangladesh who tried to look innocent. It didn't suit her. "The Gilgamesh you think you know is not the real Gilgamesh. Do not underestimate him."

Bangladesh nodded, and Klaus could almost see his words slide free from her far ear and sail off into space. Mentally, he shrugged. He had done his best, and if worst came to worst, the boy could always use another test.

Lucrezia sat back and tapped the device that sat on the bench before her with a fingernail. The mechanism shivered, and began to spin gently.

She sighed in satisfaction. "There? You see? Place this in the control node, and the main device will be working better than ever."

Tarvek leaned over her shoulder, a look of rapt attention on his face. "Amazing!" he breathed. "I had no idea! You must teach me more!"

Lucrezia shrugged. The things she was revealing were, in

her opinion, elementary advances to existing mechanisms. Tarvek's reactions suggested that she had progressed more than she had realized.

"Well I certainly had the time," she conceded to herself. This was good, as it meant that she had more scraps to throw out that would keep the young Spark within her sphere of influence. To Lucrezia, it was patently obvious that Tarvek was an opportunist, one able to ideologically turn on a copper coin when circumstances warranted it, and she was well aware that she would command his loyalty only as long as she looked like she was going to win.

Lucrezia found that she actually enjoyed this. It was a refreshing change from the blind obedience of the Geisterdamen and she realized that once she started dealing with the various powers of Europa, they would be more like Tarvek than not. She was well aware that when it came to dealing with people, she was woefully out of practice.

She patted him gently on the cheek and smiled. He was also rather decorative. When she had the time, there were quite a few of the organic pleasures that she was determined to catch up on. "Of course, dear boy," she assured him. "You'll be ever so much more useful to me when..." she swayed, and Tarvek caught her by the shoulders.

"My Lady? Are you well?"

An alarmed Lucrezia shook her head. "I don't know. I... I feel terrible."

Tarvek sat her down, fished his watch from his pocket and took her pulse. He frowned. "Well, I can't say I'm surprised. Aside from a brief period of unconsciousness before you... ah... took over, this body has been without sleep for far longer than is healthy." He closed the watch with a click. "You're going to spoil it at this rate."

Lucrezia closed her eyes, and had to force them open again. "Oh, that tedious sleep business. I can't say I missed that. So silly of me to forget."

Tarvek kept his face neutral, but he had to admit that these little snippets of information about Lucrezia's previous state of existence were filling him with a burning curiosity, as well as a chilling sense of foreboding. What in the world had happened to her?

Lucrezia snapped back to attention. "But I am relieved. I had almost imagined that this body was rejecting me. Or even that the girl herself was fighting back."

Tarvek looked at her sharply. "That's impossible." He paused. "Isn't it?"

Lucrezia regarded him and frowned. "Oh dear. I do so mistrust it when 'impossible' is one's initial reaction to an idea."

She stared off into space for a minute. "Your sister—have they found her yet?"

Now Tarvek started to look worried. "No, my Lady. Your priestesses have not returned with her since last you asked, and you've already sent them all, so—"

Lucrezia felt a small jolt of fear. "When *did* I last ask?"

Tarvek again consulted his watch. "Ah—eleven minutes ago."

Lucrezia swayed in her seat. "Oh dear. I think I do need a dose of sleep." Then she sat up and delivered a brutal smack across her own face. "No! No, I must have this completed before Klaus' terrier arrives. It's such a perfect opportunity..." She turned to Tarvek. "Tell me, dear boy, can you mix me up some sort of stimulant?"

Tarvek frowned. "It's against my better judgment, medically speaking, but yes, of course, my Lady."

Lucrezia sighed in relief. "Good. Then I can—" and without any warning, she collapsed into a startled Tarvek's arms.

"My lady?"

A small, girlish snore was her only response. Tarvek sighed, and with a grunt, he hoisted her up into his arms. "Marvelous," he muttered. "*Now* what do I do with you?"

A hand reached up and grabbed his collar. He looked down to see Agatha glaring back at him. "Start by telling me what the heck is going on!"

Tarvek almost dropped her. "Agatha?"

The girl stared at him. "Yes?"

A wave of emotion crashed over Tarvek, catching him completely by surprise. He had accepted that Agatha was gone, gone forever, as he had been forced to accept so many other terrible losses in his life. Now that she was unexpectedly back, feelings that he had suppressed swept him up and threatened to overwhelm him. He hugged the surprised girl tightly to him, and whispered into her hair. "I thought you were gone."

Agatha realized that she took comfort from the feeling of Tarvek's arms around her, and relaxed slightly. "I think I was... asleep?" She pulled back and looked Tarvek in the face. "I was so... so angry. It was hard to wake up, but I knew I had to keep trying—what's been happening?"

Tarvek didn't even bother to calculate how this changed things. He gently set her down and answered honestly. "You've been... well, possessed, I suppose, by The Other."

Agatha nodded slowly. Things were making sense. "My mother. Yes, I still am."

Tarvek looked alarmed. "What? But—"

"She's still in my head... pushing." A disconnected look crossed her face. "Maybe I'm still dreaming..."

Tarvek grabbed her shoulders and gave her a shake. "No! This is no dream! You're only awake because Lucrezia fell asleep. *You've* got to stay awake! I'll help you!"

Agatha looked at him dreamily. "I don't think I can. It's so hard to think. Oh! Yes..."

With that she closed her eyes and began to hum a bizarre little atonal drone. A realization struck Tarvek that sent a shiver down his spine. "That's... you're *heterodyning*[64]," he whispered. "It's real? It works?"

Agatha's eyes snapped open. They were clear now. "It helps me think." She sagged. "But I can't do it forever."

At that moment, Agatha's little pocket clank stepped forward and chimed twice. Agatha looked at it and an idea burst into her head. "Yes! That would do it!" She scooped up the little device and gently twisted the little stem at the top. "Oh, you're wonderful!" The little clank reveled in the praise.

Agatha swayed, and Tarvek caught her. "My Lady?"

Agatha looked at him from the corner of her eye. "My Lady now, is it?"

Tarvek responded smoothly, "Well... yes, you are the Lady Heterodyne, right?"

There was something suspicious about this, but at the

[64] No other single attribute or talent of the Heterodyne family is so little understood, even today, as the ability they refer to as heterodyning. True heterodyning consists of producing an audible frequency that is the exact opposite of an existing audible frequency. These two frequencies ideally "cancel each other out." Agatha and other Heterodynes claim that they could produce a type of vocal "humming" that reduced or eliminated ambient noise, making it much easier to sink into a Spark enhanced fugue-state.

moment Agatha couldn't summon enough spare mental energy to care. "Whatever."

She selected a set of tools and flipped open the back of the little clank. Her knees started to shake. Tarvek moved closer and slipped his arms around her. "Here," he murmured. "Lean on me."

Agatha nodded her thanks and resumed tinkering with the clank. Tarvek looked over her shoulder and marveled at the way her hands moved. He blinked. "What is it exactly that you're doing?"

Agatha was silent for so long that he was afraid that she wasn't going to answer him. But finally, she whispered, "I don't trust you."

Tarvek considered this. He also considered the warm body he felt within the circle of his arms and realized, suddenly, that he wanted her trust, wanted it more than he'd ever wanted anything. He sighed. "Can't say I blame you."

More silence, punctuated by the sounds of tinkering. "You're working with The Other, aren't you?" Agatha whispered.

Tarvek shrugged. "I'd hardly be free or alive if I wasn't." Agatha said nothing, but he felt a slight shudder run through her. With a start, he realized that what Agatha thought about him was important. That he had to explain himself. "If I can learn what she's doing, I can learn how to reverse it. You must believe me... no one else can do this. No one else can stop her."

"I want to trust you." Agatha whispered.

Tarvek tried to sound sincere. He found it more difficult to do than usual. "You can."

Agatha looked back at him over her shoulder. "We'll see."

With that she flipped the case cover on the little clank closed. "Go on, you."

After a moment, it saluted and scurried off. Tarvek made a half-hearted attempt to grab it, but found himself hampered by the girl sagging in his arms. "Wait!" He looked at Agatha. "What did you do?"

Agatha looked at him and a grin oozed across her face as she slipped further down into his arms. "Now," she whispered, "You've got to trust me."

Tarvek glared and shook her. "No! Don't you go to sleep!"

Lucrezia opened her eyes and felt Tarvek holding her tightly. How interesting. "Ooo, Tarvek! You naughty thing! Are you taking advantage of a lady?"

Tarvek almost dropped her. "Of... of course not, my lady."

She settled a bit deeper into his arms and smiled at his obvious discomfort. "What a pity," She sighed. She frowned, and looked at him seriously. "Have they found your sister yet?"

Tarvek sighed.

Zeetha and Maxim trotted up to the rest of the group. Neither was breathing hard. "We ran around the whole castle." Zeetha said. "None of the gates are accessible."

Dimo scratched his jaw. "Gun be toff," he admitted.

Maxim nodded. "Kent turn off dot lightning moat."

Oggie felt he should contribute. "Kent fly."

Krosp lashed his tail in frustration.

Lars stood up and dusted his hands. "We'll just have to search for the secret passage."

He became aware that the others were staring at him. "...

What?" he looked at them in confusion. "They're in all the stories."

Several minutes later, they were, again, trudging through the city sewers. Krosp was miserably clutching onto Lars' vest.

"You didn't say it was in the sewers!" he hissed, his ears flattened.

Now that they could see them, it had to be admitted that as sewers went, the sewers of Sturmhalten seemed to be remarkably well-designed and maintained. Shortly after they had re-entered, they had found lanterns, as well as a collection of waterproof leather cylinders, which proved to contain well drawn, waxed maps of the system.

Large stone galleries were lined with walk-ways. There was no disguising the place's purpose however. If the omnipresent smell wasn't enough, now that they had sufficient light, they could actually see what it was that they were desperately trying not to step in.

Lars tried to ignore the more disgusting aspects of their surroundings, and looked for signs of secret passages. He felt a slight sinking feeling when he realized that subconsciously, he was expecting a small discreet sign with an arrow that said "secret passage."

"Every good story about rescuing the princess from the castle of the evil Spark has a secret passage scene. There's always an entrance in the sewers." He muttered.

The others looked at each other and shrugged. It wasn't like they had any better ideas. Lars halted and unrolled the map. He looked up and examined a small enameled metal sign that had been bolted to the upper wall. He checked the map again, and gave a small grunt of satisfaction.

"Okay, there should be something around here."

Krosp stuck his head over his shoulder. "What? How do you figure?"

Lars indicated the map. "Not too close to the castle. Not too far. Close to the city gates for escape. Close to the armory and the main barracks to rally the troops. This place is rife with dramatic possibilities. It makes sense to put it here."

Krosp stared at him and then waved his paws about in an impotent, but adorable, fury. "I can't believe I'm listening to this! You expect to find a secret passage because of some idiotic stories?"

He no doubt would have said more, but there was a dry scraping sound, and a section of the far wall shivered, sending a cascade of dried material to the floor.

Krosp felt a hand grab the back of his collar and he was jerked back behind a buttress where the others already waited. He felt lips tickling his ear, and Lars breathed, "The thing you have to remember, is that everyone has heard the same stories."

Zeetha sidled closer. "So what can we expect, story boy?"

Lars shrugged. "It depends. Could be a princess—"

The wall swung open and a clank, startlingly reminiscent of the long-lost Tinka stumbled out. Her eyes glowed with a blue fire. Immediately behind her came four worried looking retainers, carrying a bizarre container. "Hurry!" the clank whispered. "We haven't got much time!"

The carriers were obviously hard used, and were puffing and sweating. One of the rear men glanced back and shrieked, "Highness!"

From the open wall, five pale figures leapt to the ground. They caught sight of the princess and the lead Geisterdamen pointed. "Tikka zok!" she screamed.

"—Could be a monster," Lars finished.

The clank girl whirled and yelled back, "Voda za! Shibbak!"

Everyone looked at Lars. He shrugged. "Could be both." Then he shook his head. "But those are Geisterdamen. In a *town*. I've never even *heard* of that happening."

Dimo gnawed his lower lip. "*I* iz more interested in der doll gurl. She iz speakink like a Geisterlady, bot she hez miz Agatha's voice."

Krosp hissed. "They might know something about her. But which side—"

Oggie patted him on the head. "Ho! Dot's *easy*, poozy cot!" With that he straightened up and stepped out into the open between the two groups, who froze. He gave each a big smile and waved genially. "Hey dere!" he called out cheerfully, "Who vants to be my friend?"

Several seconds passed, and then all of Anevka's retainers shot a hand into the air and waved frantically. At this, all of the Geisterdamen raised their swords and with a yell, leapt forward.

Ognian nodded in satisfaction. "See? Now ve know who to fight!" Two of the pale women darted straight for the Jäger, who brought his halberd up horizontally and braced himself.

From the shadows behind him, Maxim and Dimo surged forward, leapt onto the halberd, and used it to boost themselves up and over the two attacking women, who were so distracted by this that Ognian was able to take out one with a vicious kick that broke the Geisterdamen's neck. The other quickly recovered and stabbed at Oggie in a blind rage, which was probably why she didn't see Zeetha slide from behind the Jäger and punch her sword through her.

The third Geisterdamen was closing in on Anevka when Maxim sailed in from above and cleanly decapitated her. Dimo landed between the last two and while managing to stab one, was unable to stop the last from driving her sword into his chest. The shock of the thrust threw him back and he dropped to his knees. The pale woman followed up swiftly, sword ready for the final stroke, when another Geister sword erupted from her chest. She froze and then dropped, while Anevka pulled the sword from her body.

She calmly examined her rescuers with evident interest. "Jägermonsters," she declared. "Of course. You must be looking for the Heterodyne girl."

For a horrible moment the Jägers and Krosp thought that the secret was out, until Lars nodded and said, "Yes! That's right! The girl from the Heterodyne show! Do you know where she is? Is she all right?"

Anevka's eyes narrowed and she nodded slowly. "I do. She is a prisoner in the castle. She was fine the last time I saw her..." Her head jerked. "But now you must all come with me! Quickly!"

Lars pointed towards the entrance through which she'd emerged. "Through here?"

Anevka shook her head. "That would be extremely foolish." She pointed at the dead women on the ground. "This was merely an advance party. Those tunnels will be swarming with Geisterdamen."

Dimo had been listening at the entrance, and he hurried up. "She gots dot right," he informed them. "Dere's lots of pipple and odder tings comink."

Lars looked stricken. "But—"

Anevka pulled him and the others began to move at her insistence. "I can get you into the castle. But not this way!"

Quickly they dashed down a short corridor until they found a rusty ladder. Behind them, they heard someone discover the dead Geisterdamen. Thanks to the efforts of the Jägers, they were able to boost up Anevka's container, and the rest climbed quickly. At the top, they pushed aside a large iron door and found themselves in a municipal storage vault that held spare paving stones. The only way out was an ornate iron gate, which was securely locked. As Maxim swung the heavy door closed behind them, Anevka fished a set of keys out from a pocket, and after some fumbling, found the one that snapped the ancient lock open. They darted through, slammed the gate shut and relocked it, just as the grate in the floor began to rattle alarmingly.

It was only when they had managed to dash around a corner out of sight did they pause. Zeetha stepped over to Dimo, who was letting Maxim examine his chest wound. The Jäger was obviously annoyed that he had been hit. "You going to be okay?"

Dimo waved his hand impatiently. "Iz honly a scratch."

Maxim smacked the wound with the back of his hand, causing the green Jäger to flinch and then curse. Maxim grinned. "She heet a bone. Iz mebbe cracked. Bot heez a tuff guy." He continued. "Iz gunna be a bit rough for a day or two, so dun go round tryin' to impress der ladies."

Dimo snarled. Zeetha smiled and headed back to the others, to find they were already talking.

"Okay, your brother killed your father. So that makes him the new Prince?" Lars summarized.

Krosp interrupted, "And you really think he's planning to take on Baron Wulfenbach?"

Anevka nodded sadly. "I'm sure of it. The Geisterdamen and their creatures were tools of my poor father. Tarvek controls them now."

Ognian shrugged. "Makes sense. Dere ain't been a decent rebellion against der Empire in vhat—two years?"

Maxim joined them. "Three. Dot magnetic prince guy. He kept der Baron busy for two whole months."

"Dot vas only becawz all der compasses got messed op and dey kept gettink lost," Oggie pointed out.

Both of the Jägers shook their heads. In their professional opinion, no one had come out of that conflict looking particularly good.

"But, jah, der Empire's due." He smiled ruefully. "A pity ve's gunna miss dot, dem Geisterladies might be fun in a schtand-up fight."

Zeetha scratched her head. "But, why did he kidnap Agatha?"

Lars looked at her askance. "Is that a trick question?"

Krosp nodded slowly. "Maybe it *is* a trick question." Lars looked surprised. Krosp continued, "But not for the reason the meathead thinks it is. If this Prince Tarvek is about to launch a rebellion against the Empire—well that's not something you do at the drop of a hat. It's complicated. You need a plan. The last thing you'd want to do is throw in a... a random kidnapping the night you set things in motion."

Zeetha frowned. "By that logic, the reason he started his rebellion today was because he had Agatha. *That* doesn't make any sense." She looked at Krosp and Dimo, who were looking at each other worriedly. "Does it?"

Anevka broke in. "There is always a use for a Spark. My father collected girls with the Spark whenever he found them. I imagine my brother is continuing this repellent practice. It does not help that your friend is rather good looking. I do so hope my brother can control his vile appetites."

She noted with satisfaction that her words had steered their imaginations into realms of speculation that were more alarming than accurate. That would have to do for now, but it was obvious that these people... especially the cat... person, were too dangerous to be allowed to live. But perhaps their deaths could be useful... if only one of them would drag their mind out of the gutter she'd suggested—

"You said you could get us into the castle," said Krosp.

Well done, faithful animal companion. "Indeed I can," said Anevka gratefully. "There are many tunnels under the town. We always kept a few hidden, even from the Geisterdamen, I doubt even my brother will be so reckless as to give them *all* the family secrets." They came to a corner and paused. The town was still eerily quiet, although there were a few dimly glowing windows now. They had to get off the streets.

"We will proceed to the home of my loyal friends, Lord and Lady Selnikov. They have long harbored fears of what would happen to the town were my brother to gain total control. I will be safe with them, and from there I will be able to secure you supplies and guides who will be able to get you safely through the sewers, into the castle, and lead you to the controls for the lightning moat."

"What about you?" the annoyingly smart cat asked.

Luckily, here she was back to the original plan. "I will rally the town and the army. When the moat comes down, we will take the castle. This evil must stop."

The cat stared at her. "The Baron is sending a Questor. Once he sees what's going on here, he'll send a fleet. Why fool around with storming the castle yourselves?"

When this was all over, she really hoped this creature was still alive. She'd keep it in a cage, poke it with sticks, and bring it to all of the planning sessions.

"The last thing I want is the Baron thinking that I cannot administer this town on my own. If I crush this rebellion myself, he has no cause to usurp my right to rule."

Krosp nodded and to Anevka's surprise, looked relieved. She realized that the cat, at least, must know that Agatha had no wish to encounter the Baron or his representatives.

Lars spoke up. "It'll all boil down to partisan loyalties then. Are you sure that the townspeople and the army will rally to you instead of your brother?"

Anevka gently touched her newly re-tuned voicebox. "Oh yes. Everyone in Balan's Gap *will* do what I say."

Several minutes later, one of Lord Selnikov's under-cooks was stumbling towards the back door of the kitchens. Before he got there, another set of blows landed on the far side, rattling the dishes.

"All right! All right!" he shouted. "Keep your hair on!" Grumbling mightily, he threw the great deadbolt, and heaved on the iron-bound door. "You must be new," he said as the door groaned open. "We don't accept deliveries before—"

The heavy door pushed into him and he stumbled back with an oath. Furious, he grabbed a broom and turned back to find a monstrous, green face leering at him from scant centimeters away.

"Bot dis iz a *very* special delivery!"

A jolt of fear surged through him as a crowd of people pushed into the kitchen. One of them called out, "Hey! Dere's food!" —And instantly, most of them fell upon the remains of last night's banquet. The under-cook was aghast, if only because, by tradition, this was the morning staff's breakfast that was being devoured before his eyes, and he knew who was going to get blamed for it. He raised the broom—

"Stop!" A tall girl with green hair snagged his sleeve. "I'd step back, if I were you. Those are Jägermonsters and animals eating there." Krosp waved his paw in acknowledgement. "How smart do you think it would be to get between them and food?"

The under-cook paused, remembering the face at the door. It was said that if you interrupted a Jäger at dinner, you'd be the dessert.

He saw Lars industriously carving himself a slice of roast swan. "Hey! What about that guy?"

"He's an actor."

This, the under-cook knew how to deal with. "I'd better go hide the silver."

He turned to go and found himself face-to-face with a bemused Princess Anevka, who was supervising her bearers as they gingerly edged her catafalque through the smaller doorway. In his panic, he executed a perfect curtsy. "Forgive me, your Highness!"

Genially, she waved aside his apologies. "It's quite all right, my good fellow. It's been awhile since *I* wasn't the strangest thing in the room. Now fetch your master."

With a quick bow, the under-cook took off like a shot.

Less than three minutes later, a very stout man clad in a lavish, ermine-trimmed dressing gown burst, huffing, into the kitchen.

He had been quite muscular once, and there was still some evidence of this under the fat that now swaddled his frame. He had a small dapper moustache that was sadly out of place on the broad, square face. His features revealed that he was obviously related to the Royal family from somewhere in the not-too-distant past. "Princess Anevka!" he gasped upon seeing her and her entourage. "It *is* you! Are you all right?"

The Princess shut the recipe book she'd been idly thumbing through, and tilted her head in amusement. "Quite well. Especially now that you are with me in all of your sartorial glory, Lord Selnikov."

The older man glared at her as he straightened his outfit. "Some of us were a bit rushed this morning."

"My apologies. But there has been a small shakeup in our plans." She took his sleeve and headed for the door. To the others she said. "Eat up, my friends, I must bring his Lordship here up to speed."

Lord Selnikov now saw what was depleting his larders (as the remains of the banquet had been quickly disposed of) and his protests and demands to know who and what those filthy creatures were easily kept Anevka from having to say anything until they reached his Lordship's private study, at which point she forcefully told him to shut up. He did.

"Last night my father found an actress with vocal harmonics identical to those we've been trying to duplicate."

Selnikov sat down in surprise. His mind considered the possibilities.

"She controlled an entire theatre full of people. They

responded just as though she were The Other. Once we had her, Tarvek was able to adjust my voice to match hers, perfectly."

"Astonishing." He thought for a moment. "And the effect upon the Lady Vrin and her people?" His Lordship may have looked like a carousing oaf, but he still had a sharp mind, when he was goaded into using it.

"Alas, my voice alone is not enough to control Vrin, and the effect on the ordinary priestesses leaves much to be desired."

Selnikov frowned, and pulled the head off of a stuffed hawk with a "pop," revealing the mouth of a bottle. He poured himself a large dollop of brandy. "That's inconvenient," he muttered before emptying half the glass with one swallow.

"Indeed, but there was no time to investigate the problem, as I barely escaped with my life."

Selnikov started. "What?"

"The Lady Vrin has decided that this girl is, in fact, their lost Holy Child, and thus my vocal experiments were, in effect, blasphemy. She was very touchy about it."

"What about your father? Surely he could talk—"

Anevka stared at him and then slammed her hand down upon the desk. "My father is dead! I cannot *believe* you are unaware of this! The town has been in mourning for hours!"

Selnikov reddened. "I was busy. Until quite late in the evening. I left orders that I was not be disturbed for any reason." The look on his face said that he regretted that particular order now.

Anevka considered him. "That's right, dear *Lady* Selnikov is in Paris, isn't she? Well I hope you enjoyed your little dalliance, and you're damned lucky that you weren't required."

Selnikov glowered, and took another drink. "Your brother?" he asked brusquely.

"My brother has denounced me to the Geisterdamen loudly and extensively. He ordered the guards to catch me, and immediately pledged fealty to this Holy Child and The Lady. He even shot at me as I was escaping."

Selnikov stared at her. "Good Lord."

Anevka nodded with a touch of pride. "Yes, he was *very* convincing. They will trust him. He will do his work, as we will do ours, and everything will work out beautifully."

She glanced out the window, and saw that the eastern sky was beginning to glow with the pre-dawn. "But now I *must* insist upon a change of clothes. It simply will not *do* to topple the Empire in our pajamas."

Several hours later, Prince Tarvek stumbled into the lab that now housed Moxana, as well as the deactivated Tinka. He collapsed into a chair and gazed at her in exhaustion. "Sweet lightning," he confessed to her, "That woman is going to *kill* me! I've *got* to get some sleep." He waved a hand. "She only stopped working because I refused her more stimulant. I... I'm worried it might damage her—well... that body." He paused, and shook his head in despair. "I don't even know if Agatha is still in there. I haven't seen her for hours, and Lucrezia's control of the body seems to be absolute. The machine she's working on is almost finished."

He scowled. "This will be trouble. The actual Lady Lucrezia is too much of a wild card. I probably should have killed her when I had the chance, but this opportunity was just too..."

He looked at the implacable face of The Muse. "This *will* work—won't it?"

Smoothly, the seated figure fanned out a large deck of cards face down, and gestured to Tarvek that he was to select one. Tarvek gingerly picked a card. He turned and examined it, a frown crossing his face. The picture showed a glowing funnel cloud bearing down on, or possibly being generated by, an intricate little device of unknown function. The number at the top read "XXX."

"*The Whirlwind*," he said flatly. "'Great power at great risk.' Or alternatively, 'beware of things underground.' Or possibly, 'expect an unexpected friend.' Or even 'learn a new piece of music.'" He flipped the card back onto Moxana's board with a sigh. "Thank you, oh Muse of Mystery." He dropped his head into his hands. "I suppose I'll just have to…"

He paused, as faint strains of… was that music? It *was* music, of a sort, and it was getting louder—or closer…

This latter proved to be the correct guess, as around the corner came a flowing tide of light. It was a horde of tiny machines. Tarvek realized that they looked similar to the small clank Agatha had worked on.

They were all producing a soft orange glow, and they were all humming a variant of the weird atonal melody that he had last heard from Agatha herself. And now, at the crest of the tide of machines, Agatha herself appeared. Her feet hidden by the adoring devices. To the electrified Tarvek, she appeared to be gliding towards him upon a seething river of light. Somehow, he could instantly tell that this was in fact Agatha, and not Lucrezia. With that realization, he tore his eyes away from her and focused on the machines at her feet.

"Your little clanks," he breathed, "They're reproducing the heterodyning music. Brilliant!" He listened briefly. Tarvek

considered himself a rather good musician, and he realized—
"The music is a little off from the stuff you produce yourself. Understandable, of course, but the effect upon your mind must be—"

Agatha's hands whipped out and Tarvek found himself caught up, his face centimeters from hers. Up close he could see that she was under considerable strain. Sweat was pouring down her face, and the pupils of her eyes were reduced to pinpoints.

"She's winning," Agatha rasped in a guttural voice. "I need your lab."

"Yes!" Tarvek gasped. "Yes! Of course!" He succeeded in pulling himself free of Agatha's grasp. "What are you going to do?"

She looked at him bleakly. "The only thing I *can* do."

Meanwhile, Agatha's rescuers found themselves trudging through the sewers of Sturmhalten for yet a third time. Their situation was improved however, in that this time, they had been supplied with guides, a pair of dour plumbers, who reluctantly admitted to knowing the sewers "as well as anyone."

They were also accompanied by one Herr Veilchen, who freely admitted to being an assassin in the employ of the Royal Family. The only ones who didn't feel nervous around him were the Jägers, who cheerfully tried to engage him in technical discussions about the best way to kill people in increasingly bizarre situations.

"I cannot believe how big these damn sewers are," Krosp groused for possibly the hundredth time. "The town isn't *that* big."

"You gotta remember," Sturvin, the first plumber said, "Balan's Gap used to be bigger. This is where the Western Coalition managed to hold back the old Heterodynes. There were a lot of armies bivouacked here for almost a decade before the Storm King whipped everyone into shape. The only reason the whole thing held together was because they had a proper sewage system." You could tell that this was a man who believed that his field of specialization was single-handedly responsible for dragging mankind down from the trees. In this case, perhaps a bit too *far* down, but you still had to admire his enthusiasm.

Lars carefully stepped over a bubbling green puddle. "So how did you two get to be such experts on the secret passages down here?"

Sturvin snorted. "We've worked down here for twenty-seven years, man."

The shorter plumber, Kalikoff, joined in. "When you're being chased and you need a place to hide, you learn what to look for."

Lars looked uneasy. "Chased? By what?"

"Duh—the usual. Giant cockroaches. Sewer serpents. Ghouls. It's a *sewer*. With tunnels connecting to the *catacombs*. What do you expect?"

Lars shivered. "Most sewers don't have any of that stuff."

Sturvin blinked in surprise. "What?"

Kalikoff looked at Lars skeptically. "Really? No albino squid?"

"No!"

The small man frowned. "How about rats? Everybody's *gotta* have them giant glowing rats."

Lars shook his head. "No. Little rats. Sixty centimeters. Tops."

The two plumbers looked at each other. Sturvin frowned. "That is one messed up ecosystem, man."

Kalikoff shook his head in agreement. "So in these other sewers—if they don't have this stuff, what do the *big* monsters eat?"

"What am I *doing* in here?" Lars screamed.

Zeetha patted him on the arm. "You're here to rescue Agatha, hero."

Lars closed his eyes and took a deep breath. "Right! Yes! Agatha! Beautiful girl held captive by depraved prince. Yes. Third act. Curtain going up." He took another breath and smiled at Zeetha. "Okay, I'm good." Krosp rolled his eyes.

Maxim turned to Herr Veilchen. "Hyu know de layout uv der kestle. Vere do dey keep all dere beautiful gurl captives?"

The assassin considered this. "Yes, of course, you'll want to rescue your friend first. I should have expected that. My priority is the shutting down of the lightning moat, but I don't see a conflict. Once we get inside, I will direct you to the dungeons, and then proceed on my own."

"Und vat if she iz not in der dungeons?"

"Then I expect you'll cause enough havoc looking for her that I'll have no trouble at all."

Maxim laughed. "Hyu gots *dot* right."

The cloaked man considered him for a moment. "I must confess to being surprised at the involvement of Jägermonsters in this matter. Is this Agatha of interest to the Baron?"

Maxim made a show of dismissing this idea. "Heh. Mizz Agatha, she help uz out avhile ago. She safe our lives. Ve gots to pay her beck. Hyu know how it iz."

"Hmm, I see." Veilchen answered like a man who did indeed

know how it was, but only on an academic level.

"Besides," Maxim continued, "Hit looks like dere might be sum goot fighting in dis. Dem Geistergurls iz pretty fast."

Veilchen waved a hand. "Oh, I try to avoid unpleasantness like that."

Maxim looked surprised. "Really?"

"Oh, yes. It's much more satisfying to kill without a fight."

Maxim stared at him. "Oh." Was all he said.

"Quiet!" This was delivered in a strained whisper from Kalikoff, who held up a hand to stop the group.

"What is it?" whispered Krosp.

"Listen," Sturvin muttered, "There're voices coming from the tunnel up ahead. Weird voices."

This was not the first time this had happened. Zeetha frowned. "But I thought you said these were the secret tunnels."

Sturvin shrugged. "Guess the Prince decided to share after all."

Kalikoff crossed a passage off on a map. There were a number of other passages marked in red. "This was the last of the routes that the princess suggested."

Veilchen leaned in. "But you know of others, don't you? Tunnels that can get us directly into the castle."

The plumbers looked at each other. "Well, yeah," Kalikoff replied, "But you don't want *those*."

"Why not?"

"Those are in the Deep-down. That's where the *worst* monsters are."

Veilchen looked interested. "Really."

"Yes."

"Monsters."

"Yes."

"Scary monsters."

"Yes!"

The assassin leaned in close. "Worse than *me*?"

Kalikoff stared at him for a second, swallowed and began releasing a set of bolts off of a nearby hatch. "Okay, down we go," he muttered.

Maxim looked at Veilchen with admiration. "It iz a pleasure to vatch hyu vurk!" he said sincerely.

Veilchen looked perturbed. "I can honestly say I've never heard *that* before."

With a sense of extreme caution, the party slowly clambered down a slime-encrusted ladder. The sewermen found a shelf full of lanterns and expressed a glum satisfaction when they were discovered to be still functional. The map was again consulted, a direction was picked, and off they went.

Zeetha found herself next to the taller of the plumbers. "So—if this place is so full of monsters, how is it you still know your way around?"

Sturvin sighed. "Well, we ain't been in the Deep-down for years, but it weren't always like this. We just started getting more and more of the big monsters, and there were a sight too many deaths down here. Finally Prince Aaronev had us close it all off."

He paused. "But ten, fifteen, years ago, before it got bad..." he smiled at the memory. "Well, it was an event if we had one of the Prince's experiments escape down here."

Kalikoff chimed in. "Heck, yeah! All the young bucks swarming around down here with torches, trying to impress the girls. And afterwards, when it had been caught and hauled up, why there'd be a celebration! A big bonfire, and lots of drinking in the streets! The Prince would make a speech, and hand out a reward to the feller who actually killed the thing."

Sturvin nodded. "Used to be kind of fun."

Kalikoff grinned. "And the girls would run around kissin' everyone in sight! Didn't even seem to mind the smell."

Sturvin dropped his voice conspiratorially, "Our old Guild-master used to say that the Prince cooked one up and let it go intentionally every couple of years just to liven things up some." He sighed for days gone by. "But these days—"

From a pool before them, a monstrosity that seemed to consist of nothing but eyes, tentacles and teeth erupted upwards in a geyser of filthy water. It screamed in triumph, whipped out a set of bright green limbs, grabbed a startled Kalikoff, and vanished, pulling the screaming plumber down into the murky depths.

Sturvin looked at the rest of the party, which was frozen in shock. "—*These* days, it ain't no fun at *all*!"

There followed a timeless period of running, screaming, crashing into various things and finally, with a grand sense of inevitability, tumbling over a precipice, and falling into an even deeper, darker pit.

Some time later, various groans filled the darkness. Eventually these groans turned into complaints. This was encouraging.

"Ug. What did we land on?"

"Hy lended on rocks. Hyu lended on me."

"Oh. Thanks."

"Who's got a lantern?"

"Er... dropped it."

"Terrific."

"Hey—Herr Sturvin, aren't there supposed to be phosphorescent crystals or fungi or something down here?"

"Oh, *those*. Yeah, we sold 'em."

"Figures."

"I have a firestarter."

"Great! Who's got the lantern?"

"...Look, I'm really sorry about that."

"Hey—wait... There's some kind of moss on these rocks."

"Moss? Naw, it's too dry."

"So what do you call this?"

"Huh. Okay, light it up."

There was the scrit-scrit-scratch of the firestarter, a gentle "fwomph" and Lars found himself holding a genially grinning skull with a head of burning hair. Reflexively, he shrieked and dropped it. It fell and went out, but before it did, everyone could see that they were in a cell, carpeted with mummified bodies.

In the privacy of the darkness, everyone gave vent to some screaming. Once equilibrium had been somewhat restored—

"Hokay! Der goot newz is dot der bodies vas not scattered."

"How is *that* good news?"

"Obivoulously dere ain't monsters attackink pipple from der dark and eatink dem."

"...That *is* good news!"

"Hey! I found the lantern!"

"Yay! Bring it over here."

"But der bad news iz dot anyvun who vind op here—dey *schtay* here."

The lantern's wick flared up, illuminating Dimo's grim face. "Befaw ve rezcue Meez Agatha, ve gots to rezcue *uz*."

* * *

Agatha dropped the wrench onto the floor and fell back into a nearby chair. "There," she sighed. "It's done."

Tarvek eyed the device before them. It was a slender column that stood over three meters tall. It was encrusted with various tubes and what looked like the bells of musical instruments. These increased in number and complexity towards the top, culminating in a great flowering of pipes, horns, and lenses.

Around the base, a swarm of Agatha's little clanks continued to tighten screws and industriously polish the brass casing.

"Good. Now will you tell me what you're going to do with it?"

Agatha wearily waved a hand. "I'm going to expose her, of course. If no one knows that The Other is back, if she manages to hide what your father was doing here, she could enslave most of Europa before anyone's the wiser. Then it would be too late."

Tarvek looked uneasy. "But, wait—"

Agatha interrupted. "You say you're innocent. This is a good way to prove it. Even if you told the Baron it was a lab accident, I'm betting he's still sending out a Questor.

"Now I imagine enslaving a Questor would be quite an advantageous thing to do, if she could. She'd have a powerful puppet with access to the Baron, and be in a position to directly threaten the Empire."

Tarvek nodded. "I... believe that's the idea, yes."

Agatha glared at him. "And you're helping her? Seriously? What kind of place do you think she'll make the Empire?"

Tarvek had the grace to look away. Agatha patted her device. "I can use this to let the Baron's man know what's happening before he lands." She frowned. "It's chancy. We have to get it to the roof without her priestesses noticing, and we'll have to make sure it goes off at just the right time. But at this point, it's all I can do."

Tarvek frowned. "But you're supposed to be hiding from the Baron. Once he knows you're here, he'll see to it that you're taken. He'll lock you in a lab and—"

"Good!" Agatha declared vehemently. "Maybe he can find a way to reverse this! Get her out of my head! The Baron might destroy me—but The Other certainly will! Me—and a whole lot of other people as well. I've been keeping the upper hand, but I've told you—It won't last. I have to make sure I stop her."

Agatha paused, and looked Tarvek in the eye. "I can... feel her... even now. You... you just can't understand how... alien her thoughts are. She's terribly mad. Stopping her... That's... that's worth giving myself up to the Baron." She shivered and looked at him pleadingly. "Don't you think?"

And seeing her there—seeing the fear in her eyes, alongside the simple raw courage, Tarvek realized that he would do anything. Move mountains, crush cities, toss all of his carefully laid plans into disarray, if that was what it would take to help protect this young girl who was willing to sacrifice herself in order to save Europa, who was standing there alone and helpless before him.

"No!" he whispered. "No!" This time he shouted it so loud that it rang throughout the vast laboratory. The clanks swarming about paused stared at him in astonishment. "No, I won't allow this!"

He pulled Agatha up from her chair. "You're still here. She hasn't won yet!"

"Tarvek, I don't even understand how she did this to me! It might be different if I had time to work on the problem, but I don't!" Agatha shook her head. "I've examined that throne machine. It's more advanced than anything I've ever seen before! I don't even know where to start. It's completely beyond me. I may be a Spark, but I was just a student, for goodness' sake!"

Tarvek rubbed his temples. "All right. Listen. I've actually had a lot of time to study it, and there are still parts that are beyond me. You're not stupid, it's just that your mother has achieved a level of technology we've never seen before.

"The truth is, Anevka and I have a plan. It's why we were trying to duplicate The Other's command voice. But we never expected father's 'Lucrezia' to actually come back!"

Agatha wobbled slightly on her feet, and a vague look crossed her face, which Tarvek failed to notice before he enfolded her in his arms. "I won't let her ruin everything!" he declared vehemently. "And I won't let her destroy you. To find you, out of nowhere—it's too perfect. Wulfenbach is a usurper—his empire won't last a day once he's gone!

"With The Other's technology, and you by my side, I'll re-establish the rule of the Storm King. We'll bring real stability to Europa! You must not give up!"

Suddenly, he realized that the figure in his arms was chuckling softly. He froze as Lucrezia flowed sensuously out of his embrace, and regarded him with amusement.

"My, my," she purred, "You *are* ambitious, aren't you?" She stretched languorously, and smiled as she noticed Tarvek's breathing speeding up. "So you want Klaus' little empire *and* this girl, do you?"

She made a show of examining herself. "Yessss... of course

you do." She smiled devilishly at him. "Well, I don't mind. In fact, this could work out even better than I'd thought, with..." she slowly shifted her weight from one leg to the other. Tarvek swallowed. "...benefits to everyone." She smiled again. "Shall we make a deal?"

Lord Selnikov entered the morning room and paused. "Why, your Highness! You look splendid!"

Anevka turned away from the window. "Don't I though?"

One of the latest fashion trends from Paris had been heavily influenced by a recent visit to the City of Lights by the Ice Tsars, who had swept in, camped in one of the finer hotels for three months, enriched a significant number of restaurateurs, artists and courtesans, and had measurably added to the city's annual revenue. They had behaved abominably, of course, as despotic, isolated Sparks tended to do when confronted by the wonders of civilization such as indoor plumbing, electric lighting and citizens who considered themselves to be more than slaves or mobile furniture[65].

Exciting times indeed, which the fashion trend-setters of Paris distilled down to; Cossacks may be cretins, but they certainly look snazzy[66].

Thus Anevka was dressed in a white uniform, adorned with lavish amounts of red and gold trim, topped with a massive ermine fur hat. "I must get the name of your dear wife's dressmaker."

[65] This led to even more exciting experiences with incorruptible gendarmes, state-of-the-art jail cells, and a once-in-a-lifetime-if-you-are-lucky meeting with the Master of Paris himself. When this was done, they were sent home with many exciting memories, several train cars full of purchases, and an assignment to read and write a report on Rousseau's "Discourse on the Basis of Inequality".

[66] Being French, they used better words than that.

Selnikov rolled his eyes. "Easy enough, I've certainly got enough of their bills around." He changed the subject. "Now, we've nearly finished gathering everyone—" He gestured towards the window.

Anevka glanced out. The crowd she'd seen earlier was already larger. Selnikov continued.

"Couldn't fit everyone in the square at once, of course. I figure it'll take three gatherings before we've got all of the important people, so you can begin addressing them whenever you're ready."

Anevka nodded and moved to a mirror to check her outfit a final time. "Very good. I want to move quickly."

His Lordship pulled a decanter from inside a hollow book and poured himself a small glass. "Oh yes," he spoke up, "I almost forgot. It took a bit of doing, but we've managed to isolate everyone who was at the theatre with your father last night." He waved a hand, "All except the actors, of course. I've talked to a few of them. They're not too pleased. My lawyer, Von Karloff, is one of them." He swirled his drink and pondered. "It was odd..." he sipped. "There was something... strange about them."

Anevka faced him. "Yes, I was afraid of that. They've imprinted on the girl. They belong to her now."

Selnikov looked as if the drink had soured in his mouth. "I see. I suppose we'll have to—"

"You will kill them."

Selnikov snorted. "Pft. That's hardly necessary. It's not as though that actress is the real thing."

Anevka slammed his hand upon the table. "Kill them."

Selnikov stared at her. "But... she... she can't..." He stared with a growing horror at the implacable face of the princess. "She isn't really... is she?"

Anevka folded her arms. "She can. She is." She turned away. "Kill them."

Selnikov gawped at her. "Wilhelm *did* it? He finally *did* it? The Mistress has *returned*?"

Anevka tossed up her hands. "So Vrin and the rest of the Geisterdamen believe," she conceded. "I heard that much before I fled."

Selnikov started pacing back and forth. He picked up his drink, stared at it and put it back down again. "But—but if she is back..." He looked at Anevka. "I swore to serve her! The Order swore!" He picked up his drink and put it down again. "If they find out I sided with you over her—" He stared at Anevka again. "If *she* finds out—" He grabbed his glass and downed it in one swallow.

"Calm yourself, uncle. The Order was created to serve the Storm King. My father and the Council may have been fools, but there are many in The Order who never liked how the organization was subverted. They will support us. By the time the Council learns of this, if they ever do, Lucrezia will be dead, her shrine destroyed, and the remainder of her machines and creatures firmly under our control."

Selnikov looked ill. "But... your brother..."

Anevka chopped the air with her hand, cutting off his objections. "You've assembled the people and the army with no interference, have you not?"

"Well, yes..."

Anevka nodded in satisfaction. "He is doing his part inside the castle. I am doing mine here. We must trust him."

The older man thought about this. "But you told those people with the Jägers that he—"

Anevka turned away dismissively. "What of it? It was a simpler story than the truth. Now their romantic imaginations are all fired up. They're probably having a marvelous time, dashing off to rescue their friend from the wicked prince!"

She turned back. "It's all moot anyway, as soon as they have served their purpose, Veilchen will take care of them. *We* must be ready to move when the moat is shut down."

Selnikov took a deep breath. "It will come down, yes?"

Anevka glanced out the window. The castle could be seen in the distance. "Oh, yes. Between Veilchen and my brother, there is no fear of that."

She turned back and gently patted Selnikov on the cheek. "It's a lovely plan, uncle. We should be able to smooth everything over before the Baron's people get here."

ELEVEN

The Storm King united all the land
He gathered the Sparks beneath his hand
He tamed the lightning and held the line
But then he met the Heterodyne—

—A BALLAD OF THE STORM KING
(UNKNOWN. POSSIBLY MONTCRIFFE OF
TOURS. THEN AGAIN, MAYBE NOT.)

A dramatic light flared in the darkness. Music, strange unearthly music, swelled. Suddenly, there was Agatha. Her face was tired, but determined. When she spoke, her voice was firm and compelling.

"I am Agatha Heterodyne. Daughter of Bill Heterodyne and Lucrezia Mongfish. I have discovered that my mother was... is—The Other. Her servants have captured me. They've done something to me, and as a result, her mind is trying to take over my body. I can't fight her off for much longer.

"Her forces have taken the castle at Sturmhalten. Prince Tarvek is helping me. Tell Baron Wulfenbach. Tell everyone. Someone needs to stop her. Please, I—" her eyes lowered and Agatha realized that she was still wearing nothing but the few scraps of clothing that Lucrezia had donned as a sop to Tarvek's sensibilities.

She gave a squeal and vainly tried to cover herself. "You could have *said* something!" she said hotly.

Tarvek sighed, and turned off the recording equipment. "I thought you said you wanted to get everyone's attention," he said weakly.

Agatha glared at him. "Gi—I mean, everyone's going to see this. Get me something decent to wear! Please!"

Tarvek nodded. "Of course." He thought for a moment. "I think I know what we need. Wait here." He took off. Agatha waited a few seconds after he had left, and then dropped her shielding hands.

"Quickly! We don't have much time!" From the swarm of small clanks, four moved forward from the rest. Agatha addressed them. "Did you record that?" A series of green lights flashed.

"Good. Prince Tarvek says that there's no way for us to contact the outside world. That seems... suspicious to me. I'm sure he isn't telling everything. But even if he's lying to me, this message has to get to Gilgamesh." She realized what she had just said, and blushed. "And the Baron, of course," she hastily amended. "You'll leave town. Find any airship coming in this direction. Play the recording. I don't know how long you can remain airborne, but I'm sure at least one of you will make it. You're my backup, in case something goes wrong here."

She swung open the window. With a final flash of green, the

four devices lifted off and flew out the window. "Good luck," Agatha called after them. "I don't know what's out there, so try to stay out of sight."

She saw a final glint of moonlight reflected from a lens, and then they vanished into the night. Quickly she shut and bolted the window and scurried back to the center of the room just as Tarvek returned, bearing a bundle in his arms.

"Here you go! This should be decent and look quite good for the message!"

Agatha smiled at him. "Oh, thank you, Tarvek! I don't know what I'd do without you."

Outside, up on the roof, a pair of Geisterdamen were huddled around a brazier, when their nighthunter, a shaggy bird-like creature, startled them by shrieking suddenly and launching itself from its roost. It had glimpsed a small flock of objects flying by. Time to hunt.

High overhead, a small airship of peculiar design droned through the sky. The pilot, one Ardsley Wooster, agent of British Intelligence, was hunched over the controls. Even after hours of flight, he couldn't help frequently glancing upwards, and suffering a quick stab of panic every time he failed to see the reassuring bulk of an overhead gasbag. The airship was an experimental heavier-than-air contraption put together by Gilgamesh Wulfenbach, and was held up by nothing but aerodynamics and its own engine. Wooster found piloting it one of the more nerve-wracking experiences of his career.

However, he couldn't complain about the craft's performance. His map and instruments confirmed that he was indeed over

Balan's Gap, hours faster than the quickest dirigible in the Wulfenbach fleet could have made the trip. He was already planning on trying to bring the craft along with Agatha and himself to Britain, where the Queen's Sparks could begin to tease out its secrets.

He banked the craft slightly, trying to ignore the heart-stopping aspects of the maneuver, and surveyed the town below. Definitely Balan's Gap, there was the squat immensity of Sturmhalten Castle, but it seemed awfully quiet. A flickering blue light caught his attention and he flew over the center of the town. He stared down at the roiling energies of the lightning moat. Something was definitely up.

For the hundredth time he wished Gilgamesh had given him time to do a little more research on what kind of situation he might be dropping into.

He did know that he wouldn't have much time. This aircraft was faster, but not that much faster than the oncoming fleet. He had gained no more than six hours on them, by his calculations. Not much time at all.

He began trying to find a level place to land, which was almost impossible in the dark. Luckily, there was just enough moonlight to illuminate the more unsuitable bits of terrain.

Suddenly, another set of glows from the ground caught his eye. Wagons. Camp fires. He realized that these must be the caravan staging areas. Most of them appeared to be unoccupied. This would be a perfect place to land. He swooped around once or twice before selecting his approach. As he did, he began to note the manner of wagons below him. There was a circus of some sort, he realized. Was it the circus that had aided Agatha? The laws of probability made the prospect likely.

With a more tangible line of inquiry before him, Ardsley began to bring the craft down.

But he had been seen.

Back inside the castle, Agatha dropped her hands and took a deep breath. She turned to Tarvek, who finished the shut-down sequence with a pleased look on his face.

"How was that?" she asked.

"I think that'll be perfect," Tarvek said with satisfaction. "Let's see how it looks."

"No!" Agatha stopped him. "Some of the connections are delicate. I don't know how many times it'll work."

Tarvek frowned. "True, you did slap it together pretty fast. But we should have time to go in and—"

A door slammed open and Vrin appeared. She was now clad in the traditional Geisterdamen raiment. When she saw the two of them, she bowed in Agatha's direction. "Mistress! The sentries have sighted an airship!"

Tarvek sucked in a breath with a hiss and checked his watch. "Blue fire! The Baron's man made *very* good time."

Vrin continued. "They said that it looked like it was coming down on the southeast side of the town."

Tarvek nodded. "Caravan field. Fire and oil! The circus is still there."

Agatha looked surprised. "I'd thought they were gone by now."

Vrin continued. "It was a strange airship as well. Small and very fast. It looked like a giant bird!"

Instantly an image of Gilgamesh's flying machine flashed through Agatha's head, and her heart skipped a beat. A shiver of anticipation ran through her.

She patted her device. "We've got to move this onto the roof now."

When the man before her didn't respond, she touched his arm. "Tarvek, it's time."

He turned towards her and she was surprised to see that he looked slightly ill. He fished a small device from an inner pocket and looked at her sadly. "Yes," he muttered. "I'm afraid it is."

He depressed a switch and a small blue light flared on the device. Every one of the small clanks that Agatha had created spat out a burst of sparks and froze, then toppled over, instantly stopping the underlying drone of the music they had been playing.

Agatha whirled. "What have you done?" she screamed. Tarvek looked at her pleadingly, but said nothing. "Not now! I knew I couldn't trust you! I—" She gave a violent shudder, and Lucrezia blinked, and then smiled.

"Ah! Tarvek, is it time?"

The young man nodded and indicated the waiting priestess. "Yes, my lady. Vrin says that an airship has been sighted, and it most likely is the Baron's Questor."

Lucrezia clapped her hands. "Excellent! Then we can—" Her eyes were drawn downwards as she realized what it was that she was wearing. It was a rather diaphanous gown that, stylistically, owed quite a lot to the Moravian artist, Alfons Mucha[67].

---

[67] Alfons Mucha is one of a handful of recognized Sparks who turned their talents to Art, instead of Science. He believed that aesthetically, nature was a superior designer and structural engineer, and so he produced a wide variety of man-made objects that looked as if they had been grown organically. These indeed proved to be stronger and more efficient, but tended to dry up and fall over in the autumn. Alfons also believed that beautiful women should wear as little as possible, and designed many outfits to prove it. Thus, while his architectural business foundered, its give-away calendars were extremely popular.

Lucrezia took a deep breath and indicated the outfit. "Tarvek... *dear*... what is this?"

The Prince grinned self-consciously. "Do you like it? Agatha wanted some different clothes, and that's an old Harvest Festival outfit that I designed for Anevka.

"Now I myself never really thought that she was suited for the art nouveau style, but the theme of the festival..." He realized that both Lucrezia and Vrin were staring at him with rather disbelieving expressions, and he stuttered to a stop.

Lucrezia smiled gently and patted him on the head. "It's lovely, dear. But now I'm going to change into something a *teensy* bit more practical."

She turned away and Tarvek let out his breath. Lucrezia paused, and looked back over her shoulder. "But we can play dolly 'dress-up' later, if you'd like."

With that she moved off, giggling, as Tarvek silently gritted his teeth. He swallowed his annoyance and turned back to Agatha's machine. The modifications he'd planned shouldn't take much time.

BY ROYAL APPOINTMENT
ANOTHER FINE OUBLIETTE FROM THE
ANCIENT AND HONORABLE GUILD OF
MURDEROUS DEVICE FABRICATORS.
TO VIEW OUR FULL LINE OF FINE GOODS,
PLEASE VISIT OUR MECHANICSBURG
SHOWROOM IN YOUR NEXT LIFE.

Lars read the small sign a final time and turned away in disgust.

"It iz very well dezigned," Maxim said with a touch of hometown pride.

"The walls are impossible to climb," conceded Zeetha.

Krosp sat back with mixed feelings of annoyance and relief. "There are drains, but they're so narrow that even *I* can't get through them."

"Can't anybody think of anything?" Lars asked.

Sturvin sat wearily down upon a collection of bones dressed in a ball gown from sometime in the last century. "I think we're really stuck here, folks."

Veilchen shook his head. "No—you're an old hand down here. Surely you have some trick up your sleeve? Some trade secret?"

The plumber snorted. "Wish I did. My partner now, he was always better at this sort of thing."

Veilchen sighed. "Well then..." He pulled a compact air gun from inside his cloak and fired it upwards. A small grappling hook soared over the dimly seen lip of the pit and out of sight. Veilchen pulled the rope, set the hook and then shimmied upwards. Before anyone else could blink, he pulled the rope up behind him as he disappeared.

The others realized what had happened and looked at each other in astonishment.

Sturvin sighed deeply. "You know, I keep meaning to get one of those things."

Zeetha looked upwards hopefully. "I don't suppose there's the slightest chance that he's gone to get help."

Maxim chuckled. "Ho, no vay! He left uz here to die! Vot a pro!"

Krosp snorted. "Yeah, well your 'pro' forgot something important."

A second passed and Veilchen's head popped over the lip of the pit. "Like what?" he demanded.

Krosp smiled. "Like why we're all down here in this pit to begin with."

A glowing tentacle dropped around the assassin's throat. "Whoops," Veilchen admitted. "Gotta go." And he was jerked from sight. A series of screams and roars erupted from above the pit.

"Now what?" Zeetha asked.

"Dependz on who vins op dere," Maxim replied cheerfully.

"How will we know that?" Zeetha asked.

Maxim patted a surprised Krosp on the head. "Dot's simple! Ven der noize shtops, ve toss de kitty op dere, and he'll tell us!"

"And if there're still monsters up there?" Krosp demanded.

"Jump down! Hy'm sure sumvun vill ketch hyu."

"At this point, I will be favorably disposed to some other plan," Krosp declared.

Ognian held up a hand. "Hey! Iz qviet," he announced.

"Is that good?" Lars whispered.

Overhead, about a dozen monsters leaned into sight and examined them hungrily.

"Guess not," Lars muttered. Above, the monsters surged forward trying to leap into the hole. This caused a blockage, and a small fight broke out amongst them. This was to be expected, as monsters have poor conflict resolution skills.

Ognian picked up his halberd and spun it about, limbering up. "Hey!" he said with a grin, "Howzabout ve keel enough monsters dot ve ken climb out over der bodies?"

"That's *your* plan?" Lars demanded.

Zeetha slid her swords from their scabbards and gave the

Jäger a nod. "Under the circumstances, that's a pretty good plan."

Lars shook his head. "I'm with Krosp on this, I want another plan."

"*I* got one."

Everyone jerked their heads up in surprise. A block in the wall about three meters up had slid aside, and Kalikoff waved at them before tossing down a rope. "Come on up! Hurry!"

Sturvin grinned. "Man, I wondered where you were!"

Several minutes later, they were trudging along a stone gallery. Along one side was a series of openings that revealed a large causeway below, illuminated by faintly glowing green spheres. These stretched off in both directions until they were out of sight.

Lars sidled up to Kalikoff. "So, no offense, but the last time I saw you—" he made chomping motions with his hands.

The shorter man waved a hand airily. "Oh that." He fished out a bizarre looking multiplex knife. "Thank my Official Sturmhalten Sewer Rat Knife." He flicked his hand, and a screwdriver appeared. Flicked it again, and a small saw blade slid out. Once more, and a small sword clicked into place. A final snap, and they all slid back.

"Wow," Lars breathed. "Where can I get one of those?"

Kalikoff shrugged apologetically. "Sorry man, you gotta be a Sturmhalten Sewer Rat. It's a union thing."

"I'll join."

Up ahead, Sturvin was studying his map, and frowning.

"So where are we?" asked Krosp.

"Not in a damn oubliette," the plumber snapped, "So I'd say anywhere is a big improvement."

Kalikoff chimed in. "I don't know either."

Ognian glanced out a window. "Hy s'poze ve could ask dem," he pointed.

Below, a procession of Geisterdamen marched silently by. There were easily hundreds of them. Phalanxes strode eight abreast, escorting heavily-laden wagons being pulled by bizarre animals that were like pale wolves, but with a dozen glowing eyes. Interspaced between these were troops of the gigantic white spiders. All of the ghostly women were fully armed, either with their slim curved swords, tall crescent-moon-bladed spears, or both.

Ognian found a half dozen hands covering his mouth.

"Where are they going?" whispered Lars.

Kalikoff whispered back. "Some of the old records mention ancient caverns, down beyond the Deep-down. There's supposed to be strange things living there—" he gazed at the passing ghost women. "I thought it was made up," he sighed.

Sturvin gazed down at them. "Man, there's gotta be hundreds of them. S'a damn army."

"Dey's actink like dey's guardink sumting," Dimo mused. "Sumting impawtent."

Below them, several wagons containing machinery trundled past. None of the group could have been expected to recognize the components of The Other's mind transfer device.

"So they had some sort of base under Sturmhalten," Zeetha realized. "A good place to hide. No wonder no one ever knew where they came from. But why are they leaving?"

"The old Prince is dead," Lars breathed. "I'll bet he was their protector or something."

Krosp was staring at the last wagon of machinery as it

moved on past. "There's something about that stuff that looks familiar," he grumbled. "I wonder what it's for?"

"Hy tink Hy know," said Ognian in a strangled voice, "And in der Master's name, keep qviet!"

The others looked back and shuddered into silence. A series of huge, misshapen creatures, larger than oxen and covered in spines and writhing tentacles, lumbered forward. Strapped to the wooden carts that groaned behind them were a series of large glass and metal spheres, covered with softly glowing dials and gauges. Behind the thick glass, undefined shapes roiled endlessly within a thick, oily liquid.

A squad of Geisterdamen marched grimly alongside each one, and a single pale warrior stood atop each sphere, easily high enough to look into the windows of the gallery. Instantly the group flung themselves to the ground and huddled beneath the openings as the great mechanisms rolled on by.

"Doze iz Slaver Engines," Ognian growled.

Lars spasmed in place. "Slaver—You mean like revenant wasps?"

"Ho yez."

Maxim sidled up to Dimo. "Der Baron gots to hear 'bout dis," he said grimly.

"Agreed."

"Ken ve keep Miz Agatha out uv dis?"

Dimo gave a single, silent laugh. "Ask me ven ve *find* her. Eef ve effer gets out uv here."

Maxim gave the green Jäger a light punch on the arm. "Patience, brodder. Soon ve gets lucky."

* * *

It was about a half an hour later. The procession had finally passed. The group had headed back up towards the way from which the Geisterdamen had come.

This had brought them to what could only be called a town. It was in a large cavern, stone facades and galleries were carved from the living rock, with the occasional incongruous wooden building. The rooms, as well as quite a lot of the rock wall, had been carved into sensuous, flowing designs, which had been painted in a variety of colors.

Most of the space seemed to be either communal living quarters or animal pens. A large central courtyard contained a fountain, which was adorned by a statue obviously representing a long-haired woman cuddling a child.

Ognian appeared at the entrance to the courtyard. "Okeh," he announced. "Hy followed dem a lonk vay down. Dey din't even leave a rearguard, and dey vas collectink all de lemps as they passed."

Maxim nodded. "Voteffer dey din take, hit looks like dey burned." He indicated a score of smoldering heaps littering the yard. "Hy dun tink deys cummin' beck."

Lars appeared. "Not only that, but it looks like any tunnel that might go upwards has been collapsed."

"They didn't collapse *everything*," Sturvin said pointing upwards. Small holes could be seen in the ceiling. "The smoke from these fires is gettin' sucked up somewhere."

"Effen if ve got op dere, Hy dun tink ve'd fit." Ognian scowled. "Mebbe ve better follow der Geisters."

"That's our last resort," Zeetha retorted. "It looked like they were heading deeper underground, and we're lost already."

Sturvin agreed. "We are so off our maps."

"Maybe we should just pick a direction," Lars suggested, pointing to a number of dark openings. "I mean how big can these tunnels be?"

Maxim let out a guffaw. "Hey, Oggie? Remember de Unseen Empire?"

The other Jäger's grin lit up the darkness. "Yah! Dose guys vit der lava cannons! Jeez, dot vas vot—a hunnert years ago? Mebbe more..."

"Ve vas mit der Red Heterodyne den," Maxim reminded him.

"Goot fighting!" Oggie remembered.

"Yah, but hit took uz two years to get outta dose caverns."

"Two *years*?" Lars gasped.

"Vell, hit should have taken vun," Maxim conceded, "But de Master, he develop a taste for bat sammiches."

"Dot nut," Ognian smiled wistfully.

"Hey!" Kalikoff called from another doorway. "Get over here! We found something!"

The "something" proved to be a large door. It was blocked off by a pile of broken furniture and other debris. "It was hidden behind all this junk," Kalikoff explained. "But there's a strong breeze coming from underneath it. I'm thinking it's a way out that they closed off."

Lars frowned. "All the other ways out they collapsed."

Dimo grinned. "Jah, but dis schtuff haz been here qvite awhile. Hy tink dey pile dis schtuff up here an' forgets all about de door." He shrugged. "Dey used to lose rooms and guests in Castle Heterodyne like dot all der time."

In short order, everyone had dragged away enough of the blocking material that Maxim and Ognian were able to drag the door open with a rusty squeal. Maxim wrinkled his nose.

"Fregh! Veird schmell in here," he reported.

The large stone chamber was filled with tall rusting metal pots, each of them easily two meters tall and several meters in diameter. The outer walls were coated with a layer of slime. Various tables and benches covered with bottles and dusty bits of machinery instantly identified the room's purpose.

"Iz an old Spark's lab," Maxim said.

"You think so?" Lars eyed it skeptically.

"Ho yez," Maxim assured him. "Hit's got dot feelink uv bad krezy." Lars looked at him. Maxim shrugged. "Hyu learn to recognize it."

"Man," Sturvin complained. "This place smells like a swamp." His foot crunched on a pile of broken glass. "Someone really trashed it, too."

Ognian frowned as he looked around. "Hy dun see nottink vorth barricading dis place over. Not ennymore, ennyvay."

Dimo stepped through a doorway. "Dere's anodder whole cavern back dere. Fulla more machinery, too… uh oh."

Instantly Ognian was at his side. "Someting is moffink out dere," he sang out.

From a large vat, a glowing bubble arose. It continued to expand until dozens of eyes cleared the lip and focused on the Jägers. When it saw them, tentacles slid over the edge and began to advance. Several similar creatures arose from nearby containers.

"And that's why the door was barricaded," Sturvin pronounced glumly.

Ognian eyed the slowly moving creatures skeptically. "Dose tings? Dey dun look like moch."

Maxim smacked him in the back of the head. "Oh now hyu iz just askink for it," he snarled.

"And he's got it," Krosp yelled. The group spun to see that the vats they'd strolled past were now disgorging swarms of smaller glowing creatures. They looked like small, fat, gelatinous pillows, with two stumpy legs. A single pale stalk sprouted from their heads.

"Aww," Ognian protested, "Dey iz cute." All the stalks swiveled towards him.

Zeetha moved away from him. "They closed the lab off rather than fight them," she reminded him in a soft voice.

"Hey! Hey!" Sturvin called out from the corner. "An elevator! Since the room was sealed off, it looks like they didn't disable it!"

"But..." Lars looked up the shaft. "Where does it go?"

"Anywhere but here is looking mighty good," Krosp snapped. "Everybody! Get on!"

Dimo watched as the creatures wobbled slowly in their direction. "Listen to der kitty. Hy dun like dese tings!"

Kalikoff examined the control panel and swore. "The controls are locked!" He snapped open his knife and attacked the panel. "Gimme a second."

Dimo looked back at the creatures. One of them shuffled ahead of the rest. It swiveled its stalk towards the worried Jägermonster. Instinctively, Dimo raised his left hand in front of his face, which was why the thin, barbed tentacle that shot from the stalk stung his hand, and not his face.

Astonishingly, Dimo screamed, and stumbled backwards aboard the elevator, just as Kalikoff wrenched a restraining bolt free. A fat spark jumped, and the entire elevator shivered.

"Everybody better be on," Sturvin yelled as he threw a lever, "'Cause we're going up!" With a jolt, the elevator cage began to rise. There was a soft pattering, as several dozen of the little barbed tendrils smacked into the bottom of the lift.

Ognian leaned over a kneeling Dimo, who looked up at him with agony on his face. "Dat ting got me mit poison," he spat.

Ognian bit his lip. "Iz bad?"

"Very bad," Dimo spoke through clenched teeth. "Hy ken feel it moffink op my arm! Hurry!"

Ognian stood up. With a flick of his fingers, the gigantic halberd spun in place, faster than the eye could follow. He then stopped it instantly, held out his hand, and caught Dimo's arm as it dropped from above.

Dimo's eyes closed and he let out a strangled scream before collapsing to the ground.

"You cut his arm off?" Lars asked horrified.

Ognian examined it critically. "Dis vas der correct vun, jah?"

Suddenly his face twisted as the severed arm began to liquefy, oozing out of the sleeve onto the floor. Ognian dropped it with a look of relief. "Yop. Dot vas it."

Meanwhile, Maxim was already applying a tourniquet to the stump of Dimo's arm. Ognian leaned in solicitously. "How hyu doink now, brodder?"

With a hiss, Dimo tentatively released the death grip he'd maintained on his upper arm. Maxim eyed the wrapping he'd applied, and gave a nod of approval. Dimo managed a shaky grin. "Better, Oggie, tenk hyu. Dot vas a goot cut."

Ognian let out a deep gust of breath and grinned back.

"Remind me," Lars said in a weak voice, "to never tell you guys I have a headache."

With a groan, the elevator came to a stop. Everyone looked out. A faint chemical light flickered, revealing an empty platform, and what they realized was—

"It's another elevator," Kalikoff declared. "This is just a transfer stage. We must be really deep if one elevator wasn't enough."

"Does it look safe?" Krosp tentatively patted a paw on the new elevator's dusty metal floor.

"Hy suppose ve ken dizcuss it vile ve vaits to see if doze poison-tings ken climb," Maxim said archly.

"Everybody get on!" Sturvin ordered.

"Let me give you a hand," Zeetha offered, then looked stricken. "Uh—sorry."

To her surprise, the Jäger laughed. "Ho! A joke!" He saw her distress and waved his hand. "Dun vorry, dollink. Hy iz not dead. Efferyting else ken be fixed!"

Sturvin threw the lever, and with a squeal, the lift began climbing upwards past endless walls of blasted rock.

"Fixed by whom?" Zeetha asked. "Lars once said that the Jägers don't let doctors near them, even if they're wounded. He says that you're waiting for a Heterodyne to fix you up."

Dimo eyed a preoccupied Lars. "Huh. Dot vun, he knows hiz stories," he conceded.

Maxim waved his mechanical arm. "Iz true. Sum uf uz have vaited for a very lonk time."

Ognian draped an arm over Dimo's shoulder. "Yah! But lucky for Dimo, ve got—"

Zeetha didn't see Dimo's arm move, but suddenly his fist was buried in Ognian's midsection. The Jäger gasped and dropped to the ground. "Hokay!" Dimo said brightly, "Right arm? Schtill feelin' goot! Tenks, Oggie!"

From the floor, Ognian wheezed, "S'okeh, brodder."

Sturvin called out. "Pay attention, people. We're nearing the top. We don't know what's up here."

As it turned out, there was disappointingly little. It was evidently just another platform stage, but the other elevator had been disabled by the crude, but effective, method of filling the shaft with large rocks.

"No way we can clear this," Kalikoff declared with finality.

"But—but we can't go down again," Lars said. "The lift is too noisy. Those things will be waiting."

"Ve could climb down," Maxim suggested.

"But Dimo—"

"Aw, he bounce pretty goot."

The subject of this discussion slumped to the floor, and gingerly rubbed his shoulder. "Eediots," he muttered. "Ve must find anodder vay. Miz Agatha—"

"—Is a Heterodyne?" Zeetha asked quietly.

Dimo froze, and then gave a forced chuckle. "Vot? Dot's krezy tok."

"One of you is always near her," Zeetha said flatly.

Dimo rolled his eyes. "She safe uz. Ve gots to pay her beck."

"And so you did. On the bridge to Passholdt."

Dimo frowned. "Dot vas for me. Maxim and Oggie gotta vait for dere turns."

Zeetha snorted. "Good one. You remind me of some of the people I knew back home." She crossed her arms. "I know you don't work for the Baron. Lars says that you wild Jägers are still looking for a Heterodyne heir. I think you've found one."

The two eyed each other. Finally, Dimo let his head thump back against the wall. "Iz hyu gunna expose her?"

"Of course not," Zeetha huffed. "She is zumil. My student. I protect her. So you can tell those elephants sneaking up behind me to relax."

Ognian and Maxim froze, looked at each other and then straightened up with embarrassed looks upon their faces. "Dose vere prime goot sneakin'-op moves, lady," Ognian muttered.

Maxim rolled his eyes. "Brodder? I vould just drop it, hokay?"

"Hey!" Krosp caught everyone's attention. He held his paw up and motioned for silence. "Does anyone else hear... singing?"

(It is here, with great reluctance, and a full awareness of how a chronicler should *report* a story without *being* the story itself, that one of your professors enters this narrative.

Surely the tedious whys and wherefores of how he came to find himself in this particular prison at this particular time have no significant relevance to the greater story, and thus, shall be ignored[68].)

Anyway, it was shortly thereafter that a lone prisoner, who had been attempting to lighten his pitiable fate by engaging in some heartfelt balladeering, was started when one of his cell's floor stones suddenly flew upwards, propelled by a hirsute green fist.

A few more stones disappeared, and an unshaven green face emerged. "Hello dere," it said cheerfully.

---

[68] Except to say that, when engaged in the perfectly legitimate art form known as Storytelling amidst the general public, one should always be aware of any and all local ordinances regarding slander, gossip, and defamation of character regarding a town's leaders, who usually regard freedom of expression as something reserved wholly for themselves. Just saying.

"Good grief," the prisoner replied in astonishment. "You're Jägerkin! Nov shmoz ka pop[69]?"

"Oho!" Dimo exclaimed as he hoisted himself up. "A home boy! So vere iz ve?"

Another Jäger appeared. The Professor offered him a hand up. "We're in a cell somewhere under Sturmhalten castle."

Dimo eyed the thick iron-bound door and nodded. "Vell— hit's been fun—" He reared back and with a vicious kick, smashed the door from its frame. "But ve gots to go."

The Professor stared at the door, and only slowly registered the parade of people climbing up from the floor and heading out. His attention was caught by a large white cat in an elegant coat, which paused long enough to poke him in the stomach. "I'd get moving, if I were you," he advised.

'I've just gotten excellent advice from a cat,' he realized. "At least the day can't get any weirder," he muttered.

This was when a large clawed hand swept him up in a hug, and a distressingly familiar face roared out, "Great-great Grandson!"

The crowd in the square shouted out a final sustained "Huzzah!" and then began a series of cheers that Anevka allowed to wash over her for several minutes before she pulled back into the room and closed the French doors. Even through the glass, the susurrus of the crowd could be heard, and Anevka hugged herself in glee as she gracefully stepped around her container's attendants.

---

[69] This is a phrase in the original language of the Mechanicsburg region, which roughly translates as, "Are you going to eat me?" Any long-time resident of Mechanicsburg will tell you that this is a remarkably useful phrase to know. Your Professor (for yes, this falsely incarcerated person was, in fact Professor Philip Foglio), is, despite the shrill claims of the local Chamber of Commerce, indeed a native-born son of Mechanicsburg.

"I could get used to this," she confided to Lord Selnikov. She looked at the list he was perusing. "And that crowd was the last of them?"

He looked up. "Oh, yes, your highness. The entire town should be under your sway."

Anevka hugged herself again. "Lovely. When the Baron's man sees how loyal the townspeople are to me—" She looked over and saw her uncle staring at the castle and frowning. "Why, whatever is wrong?"

Selnikov looked at her. "I fear for your brother."

Airily, she waved a hand. "Oh do relax. I promise I shall forgive him immediately." She thought for a second. "Almost immediately," she amended.

Selnikov shook his head. "Not from you, my darling niece, but from Lucrezia. He's all alone. Surrounded by her priestesses."

Anevka turned away. "Please. Tarvek could charm Klaus himself."

"But if she's enslaved him—"

Anevka spun and glared at the older man. "Your Lady's filthy wasps don't work on Sparks. That was part of the deal she made with those fools in The Order."

She studied Selnikov's face. "—But of course. There's something you've been keeping from me."

Selnikov looked at her, gave a small snort of amused resignation and sat down. He pulled open a desk drawer, and selected a glass. He then reached over to the ornate pen holder on his desk and pulled the pen toward him. A small spout popped out and a stream of brandy filled the glass. "No, he's safe enough from Lucrezia's wasps." He took a sip, and settled back deeper into his chair. "But there are others."

He looked at Anevka. "Your father may have been the Head of The Order, but there were others who were tasked with guarding some of The Lady's devices. She probably didn't trust any one person enough to own *all* of them, even someone as devoted to her as your father was."

He hoisted himself up from his chair and strode over to a map of the region. He poked a finger at a large red pin that was stuck through a town. "Remember Herr Doktor Snarlantz? The fellow with the unfortunate teeth? Over in Passholdt? He was the one entrusted with most of her hiver engine manufacturing secrets." He toasted the pin with his glass before drinking.

He turned back to Anevka. "To be fair, he was fascinated with them. He was always trying to improve them."

Anevka stopped him by raising a hand. "Wait—Passholdt? But—"

Selnikov drained his glass and drew another. "Oh yes, I see you've heard about how well *that* all worked out." He sighed. "Damned fool, that was an important pass. All to our short-term benefit, of course, but it's important to remember the bigger economic picture."

"Wasps?" Anevka said, tapping her foot.

"Yes, yes, yes. Anyway, Snarlantz occasionally got some amazing results from his meddling. This particular device, well, if we can believe his notes—"

Selnikov put down his drink and held his hands about ten centimeters apart. "It's a miniature Hive Engine. Capable of generating but a single wasp, but a wasp designed to infect a Spark."

"How very useful," Anevka purred. Then she started. "Wait. Are you saying this thing is in the palace?"

Selnikov nodded and gingerly picked up his glass. "Oh yes. The Jotun Brothers and I found it in Snarlantz's lab, after we lost contact with Passholdt. We had to remove all traces of The Order's involvement before the whole mess became public." He drained his drink. "It was quite a fire. We had a fine old time getting out." Astonishingly, one could tell that the old fellow had actually enjoyed himself.

Anevka leaned in. "Why wasn't I told?"

Selnikov looked at her blandly. "Because your dear father didn't trust you. I cannot imagine why."

Anevka looked away. "Does my brother know of this?"

The idea of Tarvek being considered more trustworthy than his sister caused his Lordship to snort in amusement. "No. My dear brother-in-law hid it away in a secret safe of his own design. I will show you where it is, but good luck getting it open."

Anevka drummed her fingers on the table for a second, then spread her hands. "A device Lucrezia doesn't even know about, hidden where she cannot find it, in a safe she cannot open? No, I think we have more pressing things to worry about."

Vrin frowned down at the small device in Prince Tarvek's hand. A small gaggle of Geisterdamen clustered around and tried to get a better look. It certainly looked like a diminutive Hive Engine, but—

She glared at the smirking young man. "And this will enslave a Spark? You're sure?"

Tarvek idly tossed the device up and easily caught it again. "Quite sure."

Vrin considered the device and the annoying fellow who held

it. "So, what, exactly," she said slowly, "Is keeping us from using it on you?"

Tarvek rolled his eyes. "And go against your Lady's wishes? Now that would be stupid. Besides—" He casually tossed the sphere to the priestess, who frantically caught it in midair and then glared at him. "There is only the one. She isn't foolish enough to waste it on me, since I'm already so obviously loyal to her."

Vrin ground her teeth together silently. Tarvek smiled and continued. "Evidently not everyone who gets infected stays sane, you know." He deftly reached out and plucked the sphere from Vrin's hand. "Or even lives. And since she still needs me..."

"For now," Vrin conceded. She eyed the device speculatively. "So she will try to use it on the Baron?"

Tarvek shook his head. "Not this one. Not at first, but in time. We still have to find out how it works. My uncle wasn't able to recover the creator's notes. A pity, that." He sighed. "But once we've relocated, we'll find a minor Spark and infect them with it under controlled conditions. With that data, and with the spent engine to reverse engineer, we should be able to duplicate it, and construct as many of them as your Lady wishes."

Vrin reluctantly looked impressed, and Tarvek spun the tiny sphere on a fingertip. "And then this little bauble will hand us the Empire."

Vrin looked like she had something to say about the word "us," but at that moment, another priestess entered and hurried up to them. "Lady Vrin," she said respectfully, "All of the Lady's devices have been removed."

Vrin nodded. She looked at Tarvek and smiled. "Excellent. Prepare the charges to collapse the tunnels. All traces of our

Lady's work must be erased. Bring in fuel for the fires, enough that there is no trace of this chapel."

"What?" Tarvek exclaimed. "A fire? In my family's castle? I think not."

Vrin gently placed her hand upon the pommel of her sword. "Putting your family's castle ahead of the safety of our Lady? You disloyal pig. A fire in the chapel will ensure—"

Tarvek interrupted her. "—That the Baron's Questor will examine the place with a fine-tooth comb! You couldn't *do* anything more suspicious!"

Vrin's grin faltered. "But we must hide—"

Tarvek rolled his eyes and strode over to a wall. Without even counting, he gently pressed down on a particular brick. "You people," he sneered, "Have all the finesse of a Jägermonster sandwich."

The room rumbled, and before the Geisterdamen's startled eyes, walls, floors and the ceiling split and folded, spun and dropped around them, and less than thirty seconds later, the chapel laboratory had been transformed into a rather neglected looking library filled with old books.

Vrin blinked in astonishment as the dust settled. Tarvek stepped up behind her. "We *have* had the Baron's people visit Sturmhalten before, you know," he said conversationally.

The chief priestess glared at him and then strode off. Tarvek watched her go and then, pocketing the sphere and humming a tune, he went looking for Lucrezia, whom he found dressed in traveling clothes in a small laboratory attached to one of the parlors.

When you had Sparks in residence, having quick access to materials and equipment became a high priority. Architects and decorators learned to just swallow their objections and expect the client to want a smelting furnace next to the master bedroom.

"My dear lady," he said as he entered. "I would appreciate it if you would have your servants refrain from trying to ignite parts of my house."

Lucrezia looked surprised. "Oh. Well, if you wish. I rather thought when we were done, you could just build another one. Besides, a fire can be so jolly on a chilly night."

Tarvek considered this and carefully removed his spectacles and cleaned them with a bit of silk. "Yesss—In a running, screaming, trying to save life and property sort of way…" he allowed.

"Anyway, we've been having so much fun!" She gestured, and Tarvek noticed the occupant of the nearest chair with a small start of surprise.

"Come, come," Lucrezia said, pulling at his arm, "I've been telling her our plans!" She turned to the chair. "This is Tarvek Sturmvarous, my dear!"

The occupant of the chair smiled. "Heavens! He *does* look like dear Wilhelm! Possibly a bit handsomer!"

Lucrezia grinned. "Isn't he though!"

Tarvek made a graceful bow. "Hello, my Lady. It is, as ever, an honor to meet you."

"Ooh, and so polite! Well, we always did have exquisite taste."

Tarvek started. Lucrezia laughed girlishly. "Oh, he's not *ours*, dear. Not like that." She sensuously brushed her fingers down her front. "*He's* gone all sentimental over The Girl."

"Pish," the other replied. "Between the two of us, we'll soon change that."

Lucrezia sighed. "Now, now, we mustn't be selfish. Besides, he still plays with dolls, and I'm not sure that he's ever—"

A scarlet-faced Tarvek executed a stiff bow. "If you'll excuse me, *ladies*," he said frostily. And strode off.

"Oh, now we've embarrassed him."

Lucrezia smiled devilishly. "Yes, he's so stuffy. Just like dear Klaus, remember?"

"Oh yes, this will be fun."

Tarvek stood next to a roaring fire in the fireplace of one of the smaller workrooms. He was emptying out a set of file boxes, perusing their contents, and then tossing the papers into the flames. A great many people on Castle Wulfenbach would have wanted to see those papers, and Tarvek took a quiet satisfaction in watching them blacken and curl before they ignited.

Suddenly, he raised his head slightly. "Ah, there you are, Veilchen. I trust you had a pleasant trip?"

There was a pause, and then the cloaked assassin stepped from behind the doorway, a worried look on what was visible of his face. "How did you—?"

Tarvek fished a small device from his pocket. "Please. You can't sneak up on me."

The assassin peered at the device and then glanced at Tarvek with a renewed look of respect. "I thought that was just your watch."

"Good." Tarvek smiled as he tucked it back into his waistcoat pocket. From another inside pocket he drew out a bizarrely shaped key. "This will allow you access to the controls for the lightning moat and the drawbridge. From what I've been able to observe of the crowds outside, Anevka should be ready to move." He glanced out the window and gauged the lightening sky. "We want everything done in daylight, so let her in when the tower clock strikes seven."

Veilchen took the key. Tarvek continued. "Now this is important. I believe that the Baron's Questor is already in Sturmhalten. We want him here at the Castle, but not too early. Try to keep him out until eleven."

"I don't suppose you know what he or she looks like?" Veilchen asked sourly.

Tarvek smiled. "Not a clue. But if it was easy, I wouldn't have you do it."

Veilchen shrugged modestly and bowed. "Thank you, your majesty." He paused. "You might be interested to know that there was a rescue party coming for some girl."

Tarvek paused. "I am interested."

"They were some of her companions from the circus you took her from. They saved your sister from some Geisterdamen in the sewers. They were an odd lot. A lover, I'm guessing, a female barbarian from somewhere I've never heard of, a talking cat..." he paused, "—and three Jägermonsters."

Tarvek frowned. "A *real* talking cat? How odd. I'm assuming that you took care of them."

Veilchen nodded slowly. "I did."

Tarvek turned back to the fire. "A pity. A real talking cat. I would have liked to have seen that." Veilchen shook his head and with a ripple of his cloak, was gone.

Tarvek stood nodding for several seconds after he was sure that Veilchen had actually left, then released a gust of breath. He took a tentative sniff and grimaced. "The next time you wish to sneak up on someone, my dear Veilchen," he muttered, as he checked his watch, "Don't come via the sewers."

* * *

The tops of Sturmhalten Castle were glowing with a rosy dawn light as the crowds began to form before the front gate. The crackling of the lightning moat could still be faintly seen, but the charged air kept everyone back behind the low stone walls. From an upper observation deck, Anevka and Lord Selnikov gave the crowd organizers their final orders. A quiet man sidled up to his Lordship and murmured quietly in his ear. Selnikov frowned and caught Anevka's eye. She leaned in.

"Highness," Selnikov reported, "A rather... unusual airship was sighted last night, and this morning my people have found it on the northern caravan grounds. It must be the Baron's man, but he has yet to announce himself to any of the cities' agencies."

Anevka waved at the crowd. "I was expecting that. No doubt he is assessing the town. Put out the word that any strangers are to be detained. Politely, of course, by someone smart enough to play stupid. We'll release them once Lucrezia is dead."

There was a sudden cessation of sound, and a few seconds later, the crowd gave a roar as they realized that the moat had been shut down.

The roar doubled in volume as, with a rattle, the drawbridge began to lower, revealing the great metal and wood doors. With a boom, it dropped into place. The crowd milled about indecisively, until the foremen whipped them up into action. A crew shoved a large wheeled battering ram slowly forward towards the waiting doors.

Lord Selnikov lowered a telescope and frowned. "They're not firing on us."

Anevka adjusted her hat. "I have never seen the Geisterdamen use anything but swords and pole axes, but I imagine with their backs to the wall, they'll find something suitably nasty to surprise us with."

The battering ram was now shoved up to the door. Part of the crew locked the wheels, while the rest released the chains that had kept the immense ram from swinging freely.

The crew chief called out, and the men swarmed to their positions, and as the chief began to chant, they began swinging the ram back and forth. With a final yell, they pushed the massive beam forward. With a crash, it smacked into the doors, bursting them open.

Selnikov blinked. "They weren't even barred."

The crew, who obviously hadn't expected the door to give so easily, milled about in confusion for a moment. Several braver souls peered into the courtyard, and then turned back to their fellows with postures that, even from a distance, easily indicated confusion and surprise.

The waiting crowd, seeing that there was no resistance, began to surge forward.

Selnikov swept everything he could see with his telescope. "Nothing! There's nobody in sight!" He collapsed the tube in on itself. "Something is not right," he declared.

Anevka turned to the runners by her side. "Find my brother," she ordered them. "Find him quickly!"

They darted off to spread the word through the increasingly chaotic crowd that was jamming into the defenseless castle.

About an hour later, a semblance of order had been restored. Anevka had ordered the cellar casks opened, and the majority of the crowd were standing about the courtyard with mugs of ale, congratulating themselves on a valiant attack.

Within one of the main dining halls, the early morning sun

illuminated the great table and caused the gilt-covered walls to glow warmly as a temporary staff served cold meat and cheese to a core group of soldiers and staff that reported to the princess.

One of these was finishing his latest report. "—And the rest of the castle appears to be completely abandoned, your Highness." Anevka listened to this with a growing nervousness. The sparse domestic staff that had remained behind after Anevka had escaped had been found dead in their rooms.

The tension was broken by the sudden entrance of one of the searchers. "We found him!" He shouted, "We found the Prince!"

Anevka nodded in relief. "Yes? So where is he?"

The searcher looked distressed. "Ah—"

She leaned forward. "Is he all right?"

The man was obviously at a loss for words. "We... we didn't want to move him. He's..." He gave up trying to explain. "You'd better come."

He led them down to one of the more isolated laboratories in the castle cellars. Racks of esoteric equipment hummed discordantly. Hanging from the ceiling, enmeshed in a nest of cables and tubes was Prince Tarvek. The large device he was connected to periodically rippled with waves of red lights. The crowd of searchers stared up at him.

"You see, your Highness? This is Spark stuff. We didn't know what to do."

Anevka nodded. She had to admit that she was at a bit of a loss herself.

Tarvek stirred, causing the onlookers to involuntarily step back. His eyes opened, and then focused on his sister. "Anevka," he whispered. "Thank goodness you've come."

Feeling the eyes of the crowd on her, Anevka warily stepped forward. "What happened, dear brother?"

Tarvek sighed. "Lady Vrin. She never trusted me, and she heard me talking to Veilchen."

Anevka nodded. "I knew she'd be trouble. But where is everyone?"

Tarvek open his mouth, paused, and then glanced at the listening crowd.

Anevka nodded, turned, and clapped her hands. A slight adjustment to her vocal apparatus, and everyone hung on her every word. "*All of you. Leave us. Shut the door. Do not listen in, and let no one disturb us.*" As one, the crowd turned and silently filed out. A small tug on her lines made her turn to her bearers. "*Not you. Stand there and don't listen.*" The four men assumed the bored, vacant expressions they habitually wore.

When the door closed, Anevka looked back up at her brother. "So where are they?"

"They're gone. All of them. And they've taken all of father's machines."

Anevka stepped back and made the small clicking sound that indicated annoyance. "She got away? How inconvenient."

Tarvek nodded. "They collapsed the tunnels behind them, and sealed the shafts to the Geister village."

"So we have nothing we can show Klaus' Questor? Nothing at all?"

Tarvek's eyes widened. "Is he here?"

Anevka waved a hand. "Probably, but he's keeping a low profile so far. I have people looking for him..." Her voice trailed off. She was obviously thinking hard.

After a minute, Tarvek cleared his throat. "Um... How

about getting me down from here?"

This refocused Anevka's attention upon him. She considered him for a moment. "No," she decided. "I think not."

Tarvek blinked. "Why on earth not?"

"Tarvek, be reasonable. The Baron's man will be here any minute." Anevka rolled her eyes. "I need someone to take the blame, and I'm afraid you're the only one left."

Tarvek's jaw dropped slightly and he stared at her. He then surprised his sister by laughing admiringly. Anevka tilted her head to one side. "I must say you're taking it well."

Tarvek chuckled again. "Oh, Anevka, you really are amazing. I can't believe how you've grown."

Anevka folded her arms. "Is maudlin sentimentality supposed to make me feel guilty about killing you? Because if it didn't work for Mummy—"

Tarvek shook his head. "Of course not. But I can assure you that you shan't have to worry about dealing with the Questor." Easily a dozen armed Geisterdamen stepped out from behind various devices. "Or anyone else, really."

Anevka whirled and saw that her band of carriers was surrounded, effectively trapping her. "What is this?"

Lucrezia stepped forth and grinned. "This, dear girl, is a change of plans."

Anevka ignored her, and spoke to her carriers. "Be ready to move, gentlemen."

Lucrezia smirked. "Oh surely you don't think they can stand up to my priestesses?" As one, the assembled Geisterdamen hefted their swords.

"Of course not. My boys are strong, but they're not dangerous." Idly her hand drifted up to the speaker at her throat and twisted a dial. "That would be me. *SLEEP!*"

This last command boomed out through the room, and with a sigh, every one of the pale women swooned and fell to the floor. The only exceptions were Vrin, who only kept her feet with visible difficulty, and Lucrezia herself. After a shocked second, Lucrezia whirled to face Tarvek. "You gave her my voice?" she shrieked.

Tarvek looked impressed. "And did a better job of it than I'd thought."

"Oh don't be so smug," Anevka hissed. "It still didn't take out Vrin."

That worthy arose from the side of the priestess she had been examining. "Of course not!" she sneered. "I am not some first rank priestess able to be manipulated by voice alone. I know my Lady!" She raised her sword and leapt forward. "And I know my duty! Die, monster!"

Her sword swept down, and was stopped dead when Anevka caught it in a steel hand. "I don't think I shall," Anevka said airily. Her other hand reached out and closed about Vrin's throat. "I am a very well-made monster." An electric blue flare crackled about Vrin's neck and head, and the Geisterdamen collapsed to the ground.

"Vrin!" Lucrezia looked furious as her ally toppled to the floor.

Anevka lazily examined her smoking hand. "Oh, don't worry. She's probably not dead. Yet."

She now looked directly at Lucrezia and took a step towards her. "So what do you think of my outfit? It's my 'Heroine of the City' costume."

She took another step, and Lucrezia took a step backwards. "Oh I'm sure you've heard stories like it: 'The Valiant Princess, who, when all seemed lost, rallied the people and took revenge upon her father's vile murderer?'" She took another step. "That's you, by the way."

Lucrezia retreated another step and discovered that she had backed herself up against a bank of machinery. Anevka shrugged. "The people love that sort of thing, you know. Why, I expect to see an opera based on the story within the year."

She took a moment to examine the white uniform she wore. She turned towards her sibling. "You're the one who knows about clothes. I think a large, dramatic splash of red will really set this off, don't you? Be honest now."

Tarvek looked at her over his spectacles. "A minute ago you were going to throw me to the Baron."

Anevka tilted her head. "That was then, brother, this is now. Do try to keep up. Father always said that if providence provides a convenient, powerless scapegoat, it is a sin not to use it."

Tarvek caught Lucrezia's eye and shrugged. "Father was not what I'd call an exemplary role model," he confessed.

Lucrezia darted sideways and snagged a sword from the floor. She hefted it experimentally.

Anevka paused, and rolled her eyes. "Another sword? Oh but you and your priestesses really are relics, aren't you?" She moved forward. "Well if that's the best a poor old thing like you can do—"

With a snap of her arm, Lucrezia threw the sword. Anevka didn't even have to dodge as it flew past her.

"That was truly pathetic," she said.

Lucrezia smiled, and crossed her arms. "Technically, I think the word you want is tragic. It'll make a fine opera. Probably the highlight of the third act."

A tugging upon Anevka's hoses made her turn in time to see the carrier, who had been skewered by Lucrezia's flung sword, begin to topple sideways, dropping the pole of her catafalque.

"NOOOOO!" she screamed as she lunged for the falling container. "Hold me!" She ordered the remaining retainers, who were already trying their hardest, "Hold me up!"

Anevka managed to stabilize the container and began to set it down just as Lucrezia, a new sword in hand, strode up behind her. "Stupid girl," Lucrezia gloated, "I'm doing you a favor! Don't you know that in all the best operas, the heroine *dies*?"

She swung the sword. Anevka felt a slight tug, but was still able to lash out with a backhanded swipe. It connected just enough to send a pulse of current into Lucrezia that threw her back into a pile of canisters, knocking her unconscious.

Anevka felt a small wave of dizziness, but she scrambled to her feet and grabbed the fallen sword. When she saw Lucrezia's supine form, she laughed as she strode towards her.

"Still breathing, eh? It's certainly time to fix that"

Just as she came within reach, Tarvek yelled from above; "Anevka! Voluntary disengage!"

With a shudder, Anevka found herself locked up in mid-stride, sword upraised. There was a panicky moment before her internal gyroscopes kept her from tipping over sideways.

"I can't move!" Her voice grew more strident as she began to panic. "Tarvek, what's happening? I can't move!"

"I know." From the corner of her eye, Anevka saw Tarvek twitch his wrist, and with a whine of servos, he was lowered to the ground. With a hiss, the cables and hoses attached to him fell away.

He took a moment to polish his spectacles. Anevka knew

that this was a sign that he was faced with an unpleasant task.

"Well, I can't say that any of this mess was part of my original plan," he mused as he gingerly stepped through the supine Geisterdamen. "But it's all working out so beautifully that I can't complain." He drew up to Anevka and looked past her. "One last thing before we get started; your attendants."

The remaining three men froze. None of them were terribly smart, but even so, they realized that the body count for the last three days was getting excessive. Even for the Sturmvarous family.

Tarvek raised a hand to calm them, and they flinched. He sighed. "Anevka, order them to go to sleep."

Anevka wanted to say many things, but found herself saying, "*Attendants. All of you go to sleep now.*"

With a sigh, the three men slumped to the floor and began to snore.

Tarvek leaned down and repositioned one of the men's arms into a more comfortable position. "Well I'm glad *that* worked. Replacing all of them would have been inconvenient."

"Tarvek!" Anevka screamed. "What have you done to me?"

Tarvek straightened up with a sigh. "When I constructed your body, I made sure that it would respond to my direct commands." He shrugged. "I never needed to utilize it, until now."

"But why do you need it now? I was about to kill this usurper!"

"That you were," he muttered as he began dragging the sleeping attendants off and leaning them against the closest wall.

"And what are you doing with my attendants? I need them!"

Tarvek straightened up. "Well, that's just the thing." He came up behind his sister. "You don't, really." He picked a limp hose up off the floor and showed it to the frozen girl. "Lucrezia cut your cables. She must have thought it would shut you down." He dropped the hose. "I didn't want your bearers thinking too much about the fact that it didn't"

Anevka's mind reeled. "My cables... But this body is just a puppet."

Tarvek nudged another of the cables with his foot. "Of course, I could tell those idiots you were powered by elf magic and they'd believe it."

"With my cables cut, I... I shouldn't be able to..."

"Although, all I really have to do is get you to order them to forget all about it."

"*Tarvek!*" Anevka sounded terrified. Unseen by her, he cringed and looked ill. "Tarvek, what's *happening* to me?"

He almost put his hand on her shoulder, but stopped himself with an effort. He grit his teeth. "I'll tell you."

As he talked, he began unfastening various buttons and snaps, and removed Anevka's fur coat. "After father put my sister Anevka through Lucrezia's damn summoning engine, it was clear he had failed yet again, and that she was dying."

His hands shook slightly as he removed her wig, and a note of remembered fury echoed through his voice. "Of course, *then* he was sorry. He almost went to pieces."

Tarvek paused, took a deep breath, and went on dispassionately. "I needed him rational, so I built you."

He removed her tunic, and folded it neatly. "Originally, this body was indeed simply a puppet run by my sister..." Tarvek paused, "But even from the beginning, you were something more than that."

He looked over at the catafalque, with its quietly humming

fans. "Nothing I did could save my sister. But you... learned from her, and as she faded, you did more and more on your own." He sighed and his voice shook slightly as he stared at a single glowing red light on the container's side. "In the end, you never even noticed when she died."

Anevka's voice was as plaintive as a lost child's. "You're trying to trick me," she whispered. "I'm not dead."

Tarvek came around and looked Anevka in the eyes. Tears rolled down his face. "I'm not lying," he said gently. "I am... I was very fond of my sister..." He gulped and took a deep breath. "I want you to know, that my father was not the only one who was comforted by your presence."

When Anevka spoke again, it was as if her voice was coming from a great distance. "I... I'm not... Anevka? Not your sister?"

Tarvek gently patted her cheek. "No."

"Then..." Her voice was faint now. "What am I?"

Tarvek's jaw firmed up. "A very good first try." His hand slid back around her head and flipped a small switch. "Goodbye, Anevka."

There was a burst of static from her voice speaker, and the light in her eyes faded out.

Tarvek slid to the floor and for several minutes, the young man was racked with sobs. Suddenly, he gave a final great sniff, and his crying stopped. "That..." he muttered shakily, "Was harder than I thought it would be."

He then rubbed his eyes, stood back up, and got to work. He had a plan.

TWELVE

One day The Baron was out a-walking, when by the side of the road, he found two injured constructs.

They possessed the faces and torsos of beautiful women, and the bodies of deadly serpents.

"Help us, kind sir," the creatures begged.

"Of course," said The Baron. He took them to his castle, and patiently nursed them back to health.

And when they both were once again sleek and strong, the first one bit him with her deadly, poisonous fangs.

"Why did you do that?" screamed the second construct. "He helped us!"

The first construct shrugged. "He shouldn't be surprised. He knew that we were monsters when he took us in."

"But we don't have to act like monsters," said the second. "I have chosen not to!"

"And that," said The Baron to the second construct as he revealed the armor beneath his clothing and drew forth his terrible sword, "Is why you will live."

—A TALE OF THE BARON/COLLECTED IN THE TOWN
OF BUHUŞI, ROMANIA

With a twist and a snap, Tarvek removed Anevka's head from her body. Tenderly, he placed it in a small cabinet. "Sleep well, Anevka," he whispered as he shut the cabinet door.

He then pulled out various tools and reconnected the hoses that Lucrezia had sliced free. When the catafalque was reconnected, he pulled a small key from an inner pocket and unlocked a metal canister that had sat, unnoticed, upon one of the room's shelves. The lid slid back into itself, and another clank head blinked in the light, and looked up at Tarvek with a grin.

This face was slightly different from Anevka's. It was more expressive, and Tarvek knew that it would take some getting used to. He reached in and pulled the head out. "Hello, Lucrezia," he said.

Privately, Tarvek had any number of reservations about this. He had been rather stunned when Lucrezia had explained that the Summoning Engine didn't transport a personality from some distant location, it received a personality blueprint, as it were, and built a new copy onto an existing brain. Theoretically, any number of additional Lucrezias could be thus created.

Overlaying a new mind upon an established personality was quite difficult. Lucrezia had designed the device to imprint upon her young daughter, which went a long way towards explaining why all the other girls who had been collected by the Geisterdamen over the years had failed to survive.

However, now that Lucrezia was here, she had demonstrated that it was but the work of mere minutes to recalibrate the device so that it would be able to download a new version of her personality into any girl at all.

Reconstructing a human mind onto a clank's cognitive engine had seemed like an insurmountable challenge to Tarvek, but Lucrezia had breezily claimed that she had prior experience transferring organic intellects to mechanical systems and vice versa. This disquieting claim was only made more so when she had demonstrated how easy it was for her to do, once Tarvek had constructed a new, untuned clank head.

The implications of this, and the realization that she had obviously already performed these experiments, had given Tarvek serious nightmares the few times he had managed to grab some desperately needed sleep.

The head in his hand smiled. "Tarvek, dear boy! I was beginning to think something had gone wrong."

"Sorry. Perhaps I should have put a clock in with you. You know, like a puppy."

"Father raised Sparkhunds[70]." Lucrezia replied conversationally. "They tended to eat clocks. We lost Auntie Skullchula's favorite grandfather clock that way."

Tarvek changed the subject. "This face is far more expressive than the last clank face. Some of my best work, really."

"Not *too* much better, I trust," Lucrezia said with a frown.

[70] Sparkhunds were a breed of wolf/mastiff hybrids, specially bred to hunt down Sparks. It was inevitable that some of the more perverse Sparks had found the concept amusing, and thus had made their own contributions to the breed. As a result, the Sparkhunds at the time of our story were enormous, semi-intelligent creatures with rudimentary hands and jaws that could tear through armor plating. Naturally, they still hunted Sparks, but now they enjoyed it.

"We don't want people to notice."

Tarvek smiled reassuringly. "You change your wigs, why not your face?" A thought occurred to him. "Actually, you could tell the townspeople this is how your face *always* was, and that's what they'd tell anyone who asked."

Lucrezia laughed in delight. "Oh, this *will* be easy! Now where is my sister?"

Tarvek tucked the head under his arm and threaded his way through the sprawled bodies on the floor. "She's knocked out, but she'll be fine."

Lucrezia's eyes darted about trying to see everything. Tarvek paused, and slowly spun about, letting her see the entire room. "Heavens," she remarked. "I seem to have missed quite the party."

They arrived at the frozen clank, and Tarvek quickly slotted the head onto the neck. "Nonsense," he said, as he grabbed the head and gave it a final twist, snapping it into place. "The *real* party is just about to start!"

The reintegrated Lucrezia clank gave a shudder, and she stepped forward. She raised her hands, patted her head, and gingerly rotated it about. "That felt most peculiar," she declared.

Tarvek turned away to get her wig. "Does everything work? Fingers? Toes?"

A sharp pinch upon his fundament caused him to whoop and leap upwards in surprise. When he spun about, Lucrezia regarded him innocently.

"I appear to have delicate motor control," she reported, while waggling her fingers.

"That almost makes up for your lack of overall control," he retorted.

504

Lucrezia stepped forward to retrieve the wig that had fallen to the ground and found herself pulled up short by the hoses connecting her to the catafalque.

She turned back to Tarvek. "Do I actually need this thing? It's most inconvenient."

Tarvek swallowed the lump in his throat. "No," He said huskily, "No you don't. But too many people outside of Sturmhalten know about it. In my opinion, we should keep it around until things die down, then we can come up with some story."

Lucrezia nodded slowly. "Yes, too many astonishing things at once would look suspicious." She looked over at the bearers stretched out upon the floor.

"That one doesn't look at all well."

"He's dead."

"Oh, yes, that would do it."

"A little surprise from your sister, when *my* sister proved a bit recalcitrant."

Lucrezia examined the wound and nodded. "Well, I do so love surprises."

Tarvek jerked a thumb over to the door. "There's a group of townspeople waiting outside. You can choose one of them to replace him. But we'd best get moving, they won't wait forever."

Lucrezia placed the wig on her head and delicately tucked it into place. "They will if I *tell* them to," she muttered. She turned about and allowed Tarvek to buckle the coat on around her hoses. "But you're right of course. The Baron's man won't."

She turned and delivered a nudge with her foot to the back of Lucrezia's head. "Wake up this instant, you *lazy* girl!"

Lucrezia's eyes blinked open and she dragged herself to a sitting position. Tarvek graciously helped her to her feet. She wobbled a bit, and then saw the clank examining her. "Lucrezia?"

The clank leaned in. "Lucrezia?" The two then blinked their eyes at each other in a swift pattern that Tarvek failed to follow.

A *mutual recognition code*, he realized. Lucrezia *had* planned ahead.

Lucrezia/Agatha clapped her hands in delight. "It *worked*!"

The mechanical Lucrezia nodded. "Of course!"

The two then hugged each other and gave a squeal of pure delight. "We're going to win!" They sang out.

"Mistress?" All three of them turned to see a shaken Vrin staring at the two women in astonishment.

Lucrezia/Agatha sighed. "Yes, Vrin. Oh, do close your mouth dear, it's unbecoming. I *did* try to explain this to you. *Both* of us are your mistress, now. You are to obey us both. Do you understand?"

With more assurance than she obviously felt, Vrin nodded once.

Lucrezia/Agatha continued. "Now, Vrin, Prince Tarvek, you, and the rest of your sisters will leave with me through the tunnels. As far as the rest of Europa is concerned, we were never here. We will catch up to the others, establish a new base, reassemble my machines, and get to work."

Mechanical Lucrezia continued. "I shall stay here. Everyone will think me the Princess Anevka, who has just rescued the town and driven off my traitorous, homicidal brother." She patted Tarvek upon the cheek. "Such a shame he got away after losing the fight with my attendants, especially poor, valiant—" She gestured towards the dead man, and then turned to Tarvek. "What *was* his name?"

Tarvek blinked. "I have no idea."

"—Augustine," Mechanical Lucrezia decided. "His name was Augustine."

"We had a dear pussy cat named Augustine," Lucrezia/ Agatha confided to Tarvek. "He also had to die. It was very sad."

Mechanical Lucrezia put the back of her hand to her head with a soft clong. "When brave Augustine impaled himself upon my wicked brother's sword, why, I almost wept because I was unable to weep for him." She paused, and turned to Lucrezia/ Agatha. "I think that last part needs some work."

Lucrezia/Agatha patted her on the head. "Oh, you'll be magnificent, darling. Klaus' man will swallow it whole, leaving Tarvek and me to work on the Hive Engines in peace."

Vrin and Tarvek started waking up the rest of the slumbering Geisterdamen. As they waited, Mechanical Lucrezia pouted. "Oh, I *do* wish I could work on that adorable little engine that's supposed to infect Sparks. That has *so* much potential."

"Now, now. We need you here being a good girl so you'll be able to actually *use* them when the time comes."

"Tedious, but necessary," Mechanical Lucrezia conceded. She leaned in and dropped her voice. "But it's *so* unfair, you'll also get to console poor Tarvek over the loss of his castle."

Lucrezia/Agatha gave a shiver of anticipation. "Mmm, yes, that will be fun. He still thinks he's going to learn all our secrets and rescue our daughter, you know."

Mechanical Lucrezia stifled a laugh. "Such a romantic. Those are so much fun to break."

Lucrezia/Agatha licked her lips. "I know. At some point I will have to let him think he's got her back." She fluttered her eyes. "She'll be *ever* so grateful, of course."

Mechanical Lucrezia slapped her on the arm. "You wicked, *wicked* girl!" and the two of them giggled. Tarvek heard them laughing. He didn't know why, but a shudder ran down his spine.

Several minutes later, all of the pale women were awake. Tarvek twisted a finial, and a door appeared in what had seemed to be a solid wall. The Geisterdamen trotted through to scout on ahead.

Mechanical Lucrezia waved them farewell. "This is where we must part company, dear. I really must awaken my attendants and tell them what 'really' happened before I let anyone else in, and that will be ever so much simpler when you're gone."

Lucrezia/Agatha nodded. "Of course. I'll contact you in a few months, when all the fuss has died down." The two hugged, and then Lucrezia/Agatha shooed Vrin into the passage and swung the wall shut.

That done, she went in search of Tarvek. She found him in a small bolt-hole room. It had been stocked with food, bottles of water, and a large armoire, from which the prince was selecting a new outfit. She leaned against the doorframe and watched him as he dithered about selecting a shirt. The prince should be an easy conquest, when she got around to it.

She ran a connoisseur's eye over the prince's naked torso and snapped out of her reverie. Now that she was paying attention, she saw the muscles that moved on Tarvek's back, as well as the ones on his arms. These were the result of determined exercise, and their patterns were similar to those she had seen on the myriad of fighting men she had leisurely examined as they slumbered beside her.

She felt a new layer of interest awakening within her. Prince Tarvek played the fop remarkably well, but his flesh unwittingly revealed a core of will and determination that he tried to keep hidden. He might be a more challenging conquest than she had assumed...

She cleared her throat. "Tarvek, it's time to go. We can play dress-up when we arrive."

There. A swift smirk flashed across his lips, which she never would have noticed if she hadn't known to look for it. And now, as he faced her, his face was a textbook combination of embarrassment and annoyance. Lucrezia shivered with pleasure. He acted the fop, and was dangerously good at it, but she was better. That made it the perfect game. "Surely you don't need much?"

Tarvek nodded and pulled a shirt off the shelf. She now suspected that he had selected it before he had opened the door. "True. The Geisterdamen carry everything important, and I do plan on coming back—" He paused.

"But?" Lucrezia asked.

Tarvek slumped, and selected a pair of boots. "But I don't really know when I'll be able to come back. This is my home, you know. My family's responsibility. It's surprisingly difficult leaving all this behind. Not knowing when or if I'll return." He pulled the boots on. "You ever get like that?"

If Tarvek had actually been looking at Lucrezia's face, he would have had much to think about, as upon hearing his innocent question, her face had involuntarily reflected a bleak terror that almost drove her to her knees. With a herculean effort of will, she gracefully clutched the doorframe and kept herself upright. She took a deep breath. "You have no idea."

Her voice was odd enough that it caused Tarvek to glance at her, but all he saw was a rueful smile.

He waited for her to say more, but when she did not, he shrugged and began the process of selecting a coat. Lucrezia rolled her eyes. This façade could get tedious.

She was saved from ennui by Vrin appearing at her elbow. "Mistress. The Baron is here!" Unbidden, she took Lucrezia's elbow, and pulled her over to a hidden window that looked out upon the courtyard. There was a crowd of townspeople there.

"His Questor, you mean? Well it's about time." She looked out, but everyone was staring upwards.

"What's happening? I don't see anyone—"

Shadows spread across the courtyard. The crowd began to seethe. Tarvek slammed himself hard against the dusty glass and craned his neck sideways to stare upwards. "Oh no," he whispered.

The sky above was filling with airships. Even as he watched, more of them dropped into sight from the clouds overhead, falling towards the town. As they began to slow, they seemed to fray about the bottom edges. This visual confusion was resolved when the dots bursting free from the airships got closer and were seen to be even smaller airships. These quickly spread out over the entire town while continuing to drop. There were dozens of them.

"Have my priestesses gone *blind*?" Lucrezia screamed. She turned to Tarvek, "Or even your sentries! How could they have not seen them coming?"

"They weren't *there* a minute ago," Vrin declared.

"There's always a bit of high altitude cloud cover that forms over the mountain at this time of the day. They must have known that." Tarvek muttered. "They could drift in with it, and then drop fast."

Lucrezia looked at him in amazement. "What—All of them? Flying in close formation? Within the clouds? That's extremely dangerous! Why would they do that?"

Tarvek looked at her and his face was grim. "It's part of the standard procedure for quarantining a Slaver-infected town! That's no Questor—that's the Baron himself up there and he's brought an army! He *knows*!"

Meanwhile, on a low rooftop, a grate was pushed upwards, and Krosp poked his head out. "It's clear!" he announced, and then he was pushed upwards by the flood of the others.

For several minutes, all they did was breath deeply, savoring the clean air.

As they were doing so, the Professor braced himself for the inevitable grilling. He was not disappointed.

"Zo!" Ognian gently punched him in the arm, "Hy gots any great-great-*great* grand cheeldrens yet[71]?"

The Professor sighed. "No."

The Jager frowned. "Hmf. Married?"

"No."

"Got's a gurl?"

---

[71] Many Jägers lose touch with their humanity. This should come as no surprise, considering they were recruited from the Heterodyne's army of reavers, pillagers, thugs and warriors, who were not chosen for their warmth and sensitivity to begin with. What did come as a surprise was that, to some degree or another, over time, they all regretted this loss. Many of them tried to develop interests and hobbies that tied them to normal people. The Jäger, Ognian, took an inordinate amount of interest in his descendants. He maintained records. He kept scrapbooks. He tried to set them up on dates. Thanks to his help the Professor's family, at the time of our story, was dangerously close to going extinct.

"No."

Ognian gnawed on his lower lip. "*Vants* a gurl?"

"*Yes.*"

Ognian's eyes narrowed. "Iz hyu steel on der road? Iz hyu steel lookink for dot 'perfect story'?" He snorted. "Get a job!"

The Professor snarled back. "Still looking for a *Heterodyne*, old man? Get a *life!*"

The Jäger bared his teeth. "Hyu vait und see, hyu young punk! Hy *vill*!"

The Professor rolled his eyes. "Shyeah. Fine. *I'll* get married, when *you* find a Heterodyne."

Ognian stood there with his mouth open. Then he gave the most alarming grin his hapless descendant had ever seen. "... Really?"

At that moment, shouts and screams from the courtyards below caught everyone's attention.

It was Krosp who glanced upwards. The sight of the approaching armada caused the fur to stand out from his body. He whirled and called out, "We have to find Agatha!"

Another watcher sat upon another castle roof and stared at the skies. It sat silently, except for a faint ticking. Its single eye slowly and methodically swept back and forth. An airship swam into view. The eye paused, and focused with a small whine. The emblem upon the side, the winged rook, sigil of the House of Wulfenbach, was examined, and matched against an image stored within. The small clank leapt to its feet and began to chime.

The sharp, clear tones were far louder than one would expect from a mechanism of this size, carrying far across the castle rooftops. After a minute, it paused. There was no response. The little clank looked upwards at a square keep that loomed in the center of the castle, but it saw no activity. It chimed again, astonishingly, even louder. Again, there was no response.

The device tapped its miniscule foot impatiently, and then scuttled forward. It slid under the nearest door, and found itself upon a staircase that wound upwards and downwards from where it stood. Unhesitating, it leapt up the nearest riser and began the laborious climb.

After several stories, it saw a window, the sill occupied by a lounging cat. The cat saw the small movement and instantly focused its attention on the device. It stared in fascination as the device approached, its muscles tensing, when the clank snatched the fluttering tail and gave it a quick bend.

The cat instantly rocketed off, the backwash of its departure sending the small mechanism skittering across the floor.

Grimly, it picked itself up and hauled itself onto the windowsill. It looked down upon the roof of the keep. To its obvious distress, the roof was empty. It was at a loss as to how to proceed, when it heard several people approaching while arguing. One of them was the man it was supposed to avoid. The other was the Mistress! But she had said to avoid her as well, until this task had been completed. But if the task was impossible to complete, surely it would be acceptable to report this?

The programming conflict swirled about its miniscule mind, as it ducked behind a drape and listened.

"But *what* does he know?" The Mistress asked.

"Stop asking me that! I don't know! I do know that this

changes everything! He'll tear this place apart! He'll find my secret labs! The tunnels!"

"That thing my daughter was building! Do we need to deactivate it?"

"Don't worry about *that*. She wanted it moved up to the roof. It's still in my lab. It's harmless."

"But what does he know?"

The voices faded as the small group moved off. The small clank peeked from behind the drape and seeing no one, leapt to the ground. Tarvek's lab then.

"I'll bet ten."

"Double."

"Three muses."

"Four sparks."

"Damnation!"

"Pay up."

Master Payne leaned back in his chair and reached inside his waistcoat. A look of surprise slid across his features as his hand felt around inside an obviously empty pocket. "My purse is gone."

Opposite him, a hard-bitten Captain of the Prince's Guard lowered his brows and deliberately removed his cigar from his mouth. A severe look came into his eye.

"Are you telling me…" he paused, "Sir—That you cannot pay your gambling debt?"

Payne looked at him owlishly for a frozen moment, and then chuckled appreciatively. "Nasty touch."

The Captain grinned and took a sip from the drink beside

his elbow and smacked his lips. "Aye, we get a passel of new recruits with that one."

Payne picked up the cards and examined them with professional interest. "Always said you can learn more about cheating from an old soldier..."

The Captain blew a plume of smoke. "Well, we get shot if we're caught," he said philosophically. "That sharpens the mind right quick." He saw Payne counting the cards, grinned, and pulled one out from his cuff. "Must say, I thought you'd do better than just stuffin' muses up your sleeve."

Payne paused slightly and a small expression of embarrassment flitted through his beard.

"Sir!" He said with offended gravitas, "You wrong me! I am but a simple entertainer. But wait—" His hand came up from underneath the table clutching a battered military wallet. "What is this, tucked into this wallet that you have so obviously dropped?"

The soldier's drink slammed onto the table and he frantically patted himself down in vain. "You devil! When did you—"

Payne ignored him and studied the documents he'd extracted from the wallet. "Oooh, a love letter from your commander's wife! Mighty spicy, I must say, sir! And this—my goodness! It's a layout of Sturmhalten's defenses! And look at this! It seems that *somebody's* been selling off army stores to the black market!" He tutted disapprovingly.

His last comment had caused the old soldier's face to go white. "That's a hanging offense! I'd never—!"

He saw Payne's slow grin and caught himself in mid-babble. The two men assessed each other for a moment, and then the soldier raised his glass and saluted the caravan master with a grin.

"T'cha! That's another one to you, you damn thimblerigger."

Payne was reaching for the cards, when the door to the wagon opened. Abner stuck his head in.

"Master Payne. Sorry to interrupt, sir, but it's dawn, and we have a visitor."

He was then pushed aside by a tall, determined looking man in a leather and fleece flying jacket. His hair was tousled and his face was coated with a layer of oil and dirt, except for two pale rings around his eyes, which had been shielded by the aviator goggles hanging around his neck.

"Good morning, sir." His accent marked him as English, and upper class English at that. "I'm looking for a girl."

While this was not at all what Payne had expected him to say, it was not entirely unprecedented. Many traveling shows were popular not because of the quality of their acts, but because of the quality of their actresses[72].

While Master Payne and the Countess turned a blind eye to the occasional sporting liaison various members of their troupe engaged in, they discouraged commercial prostitution per se, if only because the Baron taxed and licensed it, and mandated periodic medical exams for the entire caravan. This was a level of scrutiny they felt was best avoided.

"This is a respectable show, sir," Payne rumbled. "The girls here are not for sale."

The Captain leaned back and shrugged. "Astonishing, but

---

[72] Luckily, for all concerned, sometime in the past, an anonymous female Spark developed a quiet useful plant, known as "Trusty Maiden Weed". Due to its invasive qualities, it was now grown throughout Europa. When brewed into a tasty tea, and drunk on a regular basis, it prevented pregnancy, as well as a number of embarrassing diseases. Many traveling shows harvested it as they moved about and did a brisk business selling it in town. It was a rare woman who skipped her morning Maiden's Cup.

true, sir! Me and the lads have tried." He brought his chair down with a thump and he looked serious. "Now, sir, might I ask your business in Balan's Gap?"

Wooster rubbed his eyes. "I don't have time for this. There have been too many delays as it is."

He leaned on the table and addressed Master Payne. "I think you will know the girl I mean. Agatha Clay." Both Payne and Abner blinked at this, but gave no other indication. "You tricked the Baron into thinking she was dead."

Surreptitiously, Abner began sliding a leather cosh out from behind his belt.

Wooster continued. "But he's not fooled any more. He's coming for her." He tapped the table. "Here. Soon. I've been charged with getting her to safety. Where is she?"

The Captain blew out another plume of smoke. "And what does the Baron want with some girl?"

Wooster paused and then nodded. "Her real name is Agatha Heterodyne. She is the long lost daughter of Bill and Lucrezia. Raised in secret by the constructs Punch and Judy." They all stared at him in stunned silence. "At the very least you must have noticed that she's a strong Spark."

At this the Captain burst out with a guffaw that almost dislodged his hat. "A lost Heterodyne heir? You came to these people for a—" Again he laughed. Not noticing that in this, he was alone. "You daft fool! These people are actors! They do Heterodyne stories! They play Sparks! And you thought—"

Whatever he was about to say was cut off by the Countess appearing at the doorway, breathing hard. "Payne! Get out here! The Baron is invading! His airships just appeared out of nowhere! They're sealing the town!"

"What!" Instantly the old soldier was all business. He glared at Wooster. "You mean to tell me this fairy story is—"

With an elegant move that brought a look of approval from Wooster, Payne and the Countess, Abner leaned over and smacked the back of the soldier's head, sending him senseless to the floor.

Payne looked at Wooster. "Prince Sturmvarous took her. She's not here."

Ardsley frowned. In the town? In the castle? In the middle of an infestation sweep? This was going to be a tricky one.

A spinning metal disk bounced down a winding set of stone stairs, finally impacting upon the wall at the bottom before clattering to the ground. For several seconds, nothing happened, and then a small set of arms and legs unfolded from the main disk. With a snap, the small clank leapt to its feet, and then staggered slightly before its balancing mechanisms finally reset themselves.

It then set off at a run, dashing down several corridors and passing through a small courtyard, which was filled with anxious people staring upwards at the looming airships.

Up another set of stairs. Finally, it reached the door of Tarvek's laboratory. Executing a perfect third-base slide, it slid under the door. When it stood, it was confronted by a pile of deactivated clanks scattered about the room. Even more distressing was the Mistress' machine, standing in the middle of the room.

Frantically, the small clank spent almost a minute trying to move the heavy device by itself before it conceded the futility of trying.

There was nothing else to do. With the mechanical equivalent of a shrug, it reached up and activated the machine. Then it ran away. Very fast.

"Captain! Explosion in Sturmhalten Castle!"

Bangladesh was on her feet instantly. "Are they shooting at us?"

One of the other spotters lowered his scope. "No, Captain," he reported. "It appears that something actually exploded within the south tower keep of Sturmhalten Castle itself. A lot of the roof is gone."

The rest of the bridge crew continued to work, but Bangladesh knew they were waiting to see what she would do.

She frowned. No signals had come in from the other ships, and Klaus certainly hadn't ordered any of them to begin shelling. She scribbled a quick note and passed it to a messenger. "Get this to the Baron. He'll be with the marines."

The messenger hopped aboard his unicycle and sped off down the corridor. If the Baron wanted to—

"MISSILES!" screamed the spotter.

"Evasive action!" Bangladesh ordered even as she grabbed her own telescope and stared at the castle. The airship hove to one side, and began to rise.

"Belay that!" Bangladesh yelled. There were indeed missiles pouring from the ruined tower. Dozens of them. But they were travelling straight up for several hundred meters, and then detonating harmlessly.

The spotter confirmed this. "It... they look like... *fireworks*, Captain. It's too high for shrapnel. All it's producing is smoke."

There certainly was a lot of that. Before long it hung in a tall white pillar over the castle. He turned towards the Captain. "Maybe they're just happy we're here."

That snapped Bangladesh out of her momentary confusion. If there was one thing she was positive of, it was that no one was ever happy to see her. "It's some kind of Spark nonsense," she declared. "All hands, keep a weather eye out for anything unusual!"

In a small courtyard, Tarvek, Lucrezia and Vrin picked themselves up from the ground where they'd been thrown by the explosion. A few bits of rubble hit the ground around them. Tarvek stared upward in horror. "My castle!"

"Wasn't that your laboratory up on that top floor?" Vrin asked innocently.

"My lab!"

Missiles began shooting upward. Tarvek looked at Lucrezia, and his face went pale. "Uh-oh," he muttered.

"Tarvek!" Lucrezia grabbed him by the shirt and shook him until several buttons flew free. "The 'useless machine' that fool of a daughter of mine was building—What does it DO?"

Within the shattered room at the top of the tower, the last missile fired. From within the machine, a hidden array of lenses rotated into place and speaker vents opened. Lights flared.

Above Sturmhalten there was a sudden glow, a swell of unearthly music, and there stood Agatha. She was easily recognized by those who knew her, and was clad in the revealing festival outfit Tarvek had supplied. This would have drawn every eye towards her under any circumstance. At the moment, however, it was but a minor detail, as she was easily fifty meters tall, glowing, and slightly translucent.

The figure moved, and opened its mouth. "I am Agatha Heterodyne." The boom of sound blew out most of the remaining windows within the castle, and caused the stonework itself to vibrate.

"Daughter of Bill Heterodyne and Lucrezia Mongfish." There was a small hiss of static, and the figure jumped before continuing. "I have discovered that Baron Wulfenbach was—*is* The Other. Tell Everyone. I can' fight h—" More static, which increased as the message progressed. "—off much longer."

Static again. "—Servants have captured me. Done something to me." *Zzzt.* "—The castle at Sturmhalten. Prince Tarvek is helping me. Someone needs to stop—*Hzzzk*pop—Baron Wulfenbach. *Bzrt*—is taking over. *Kzzrrt*—Please. I need help."

The figure looked out, pleadingly, and then vibrated slightly, and the message began to repeat. "I am Agatha Heterodyne."

And everyone saw it.

On the town's caravan grounds, the circus members stared upwards in amazement.

"Sweet lightning," Abner whispered.

"Unbelievable," Payne breathed.

Wooster rubbed his head.

"Is going be devil tricky to pull off on stage," Otto muttered.

"What in the world is she *wearing*?" The Countess declared, scandalized.

The others stared at her. "Oh don't look at me like that," she said crossly, "You were all thinking it."

Payne clapped his hands and broke the spell. "Get everyone moving," he roared. "We're leaving! Now!"

Wooster watched the circus members scatter. "Aren't you being guarded and detained by the Prince's troops?" he asked.

"Nothing we can't handle," the Countess said as she reached into the nearest wagon and pulled out a large cast-iron fry pan.

"That's interesting."

"Oh yes." Marie turned and regarded the British agent closely. "And now, I want you to convince me you're not out to hurt Agatha."

Ardsley regarded her with a supercilious smile. "...Or you hit me with a frying pan?"

On a rooftop, the group of people who had ostensibly snuck into Sturmhalten to rescue Agatha, stared up at her image.

"She's a *Heterodyne*?" Lars asked in astonishment. Everyone else nodded.

"Glad you could join us, Lars," Krosp remarked.

Lars looked at them in bewilderment. "You all *knew* this?"

"The grown-ups knew," said Krosp.

"I just figured it out," Zeetha said defensively.

Lars stared upwards. "We have to help her!"

"Isn't that what we're already doing?" asked Kalikoff.

"Is there anything *else* I should know?" Lars demanded.

Maxim looked down. "I haff never luffed," he whispered.

Everyone looked at him in silence.

Krosp cleared his throat. "We really should get off of this roof."

As they headed for the door, Ognian glanced at the spot

where the Professor had been, and gleefully nudged Dimo. "Hy em goink to be a great-great-*great* grandpapa," he chuckled.

Dimo rolled his eyes. He knit decorative socks, but he didn't go around bragging about it.

Somewhere below them, Tarvek was again picking himself up off the ground. The initial soundwaves were so powerful that they had knocked them all down. He stared up at the endlessly repeating apparition in horror. "That wasn't supposed to go off now!"

"*You're* responsible for that?" Vrin screamed next to his ear.

Tarvek looked at her. "What?"

Vrin stared back at him. "What?"

"I can't hear you," Tarvek yelled back. "This damned music is too—" He did a double-take. The music? He whipped around, and indeed, there was Agatha, fleeing from the two of them as fast as she could.

Tarvek grabbed Vrin's shoulder and dragged her along. "The music!" He yelled. "It's freed her from the Lady's control!" Vrin nodded in understanding and raced along beside him.

Agatha frantically looked for an exit. She realized, however, that as this was supposed to be a hidden courtyard, it probably didn't have any easily identifiable entrances. She lunged around a likely looking corner and found herself in a dead end, used to store various shovels and brooms.

Tarvek appeared around the corner and stopped. He held out a placating hand. "Agatha! You've got to trust me!"

Agatha found herself pressed back against the cool stone of the wall. Her fingers frantically felt along the wall behind her, futilely looking for some sort of mechanism. "Don't be insulting. You're using me as much as... as she is!"

Tarvek looked at her steadily as he inched closer. He dropped his voice. "Can't you see I'm trying to get us both out of here alive?"

Vrin stepped out from around the corner and laughed. "I'm afraid that's not going to happen. Even if the copy within the clank Anevka is destroyed, my sisters have safely removed the Summoning Engine. Thus, I received permission to kill you both, if it became necessary." She jauntily flipped her sword into the air where it spun several times before she effortlessly caught it. "I was so worried it wouldn't become necessary."

Her blade lazily flicked out. Tarvek had already been moving to grab a broom, and thus didn't dodge in time to prevent the Geister's blade from slicing across his chest.

He slammed backwards against the wall. A line of bright red welled up under his hand and began to ooze down his chest. "That really hurts," he gasped.

Vrin ignored him, and facing Agatha she smiled and extended a friendly hand. "Now, girl—I don't have to kill you. You can still be useful. Come with me and I will kill this pig." Her sword flicked out, easily avoiding the broom handle Tarvek held defensively, carving a slice across his arm. "—Or spare him, if that's what you wish."

The new wound seemed to focus Tarvek's shocked senses. He stood straighter, and the broom, while still pathetic, was held with more authority. "No!" Tarvek interjected. "Agatha, just run!" He leapt towards Vrin. "You don't want to be trapped with them if I'm not there!"

With a satisfied smirk, Vrin batted away the broom handle,

knocking it from Tarvek's hands. "Wonderful! I do get to kill you!"

She stabbed Tarvek in the arm and held him fast. Tarvek turned to Agatha. "Go! I tried to get you out! Don't—AAGH!" He screamed as Vrin twisted her sword free.

"Oh I do wish I had the time to do this slowly." The Geisterdamen spun about and slammed Tarvek's jaw with her foot, sending the wounded man crashing against a wall. He slid to the ground. "But I'm in a bit of a hurry."

Tarvek made a supreme effort, and managed to roll over onto his back. Vrin placed her sword at his throat. "But before you die, I want you to admit that your machinations have failed. You thought you could betray my Lady! Use her for your own petty ambitions! Admit your defeat."

"Absolutely," Tarvek mumbled. "You're right. I failed, okay?"

Vrin glared at him. "You take all the honor out of *everything*!" she screamed as she raised her blade—

"*VRIN, STOP!*" Agatha yelled.

Vrin froze, and staggered back. "Your voice! You're not the Lady! I won't—"

The broom handle hit her on the forehead with such force that it drove the Geisterdamen to her knees.

"No. I'm not your Lady," Agatha agreed, "But it's hard to resist my voice, isn't it? *NOW PUT DOWN YOUR SWORD!*"

Involuntarily, Vrin's hand flew open and the sword clattered to the ground. Instantly, she snatched it up again. "You filthy changeling," she snarled. "That won't work on me! I'll kill you both no matter what you say—"

"*VRIN, STOP!*"

This time the handle smashed into Vrin's jaw, snapping her head to the side. Vrin fell over.

"Maybe it won't work on you. Not completely. After all, you know I'm not really her. But there's a part of you that *doesn't* know that. And that's the part that slows you down. So just give up, okay?"

"How dare you?" Vrin screamed in rage as she rolled to her feet. "I can control my own mind! You will die!"

"*VRIN, KNEEL!*"

The unexpected command froze the Geister as she was in mid-leap. As she teetered for a second, the broom handle hit her clean upside the head with the full force of the over-the-shoulder sweep that Agatha gave it, throwing Vrin back hard enough to lift her off the ground and drive her head into the stone wall. The Geisterdamen bounced back from the wall and collapsed in a heap.

Agatha stood ready, panting, but the woman warrior didn't even twitch.

"Give her another one for me," Tarvek said through clenched teeth. Agatha turned to him and sucked in a breath between her teeth. Sprawled against the wall, Tarvek was covered in blood.

"I should give you a smack of my own," Agatha said, shaking her broom, but Tarvek could see that her heart wasn't in it.

"Please don't," he said, in case he was wrong, "Bleeding heavily here."

A bemused voice from above sighed. "Ah, well, I suppose we should do something about *that*."

The two of them looked up. Staring down at them was a group of Wulfenbach soldiers, two of them clad in long, green cloaks with, Agatha realized with a start, Slaver Wasp skulls atop their heads. They were flanked by a pair of the tall brass trooper clanks, whose machine cannons never wavered from them.

The speaker was a short, plump, elderly soldier, with a meticulously cut, snowy white beard, who was casually sitting, his feet dangling over the edge.

"They say you can judge a person by their enemies." He pointed his pistol towards the still comatose Vrin. "So you two are lookin' pretty good right now. But I'm *sure* you could change my mind by doin' somethin' stupid."

Agatha dropped her broom with a clatter. The soldier smiled. "That's a good start, Fraulein. I'm Sergeant Scorp, First Vespiary Squad. Second Division. Second Army of East Transylvania."

One of the cloaked soldiers leaned in. "Sergeant, I believe that's the Heterodyne girl!"

The Sergeant's eyes flicked up towards the giant figure whose words were still booming out through the town. He then looked back to Agatha. "Really? She looks shorter."

"What? But of course she's—"

"—Jokin'," the Sergeant said gently.

The cloaked soldier looked at his superior for a moment and then nodded uncertainly. "Ah. Humor. Yes?"

Scorp rolled his eyes and sighed. "Yes, Dmitri, humor. Go check 'em out."

"Yessir!" Without another word, the two cloaked soldiers leapt the four meters to the ground, effortlessly landed on their feet, and approached the three. From large, wicker baskets at their sides, they produced bizarre, six-legged creatures, which they held up to each of them in turn.

Agatha—"Clean."

Tarvek—"Clean."

527

Vrin—The weasels shrieked and thrashed about in their handler's hands. "Revenant."

Scorp pushed the brim of his hat back and considered this. "Mighty interestin'," he declared. "Is that young fella ready to move out?"

The medic wrapping Tarvek's chest frowned. "He won't like it."

Scorp chuckled. "Trick question, son. He ain't really got a choice."

Agatha stepped up. "We need to see Baron Wulfenbach as quickly as possible."

The Sergeant nodded. "Oh, you will. Though he might not appreciate you accusin' him of bein' The Other and all."

Agatha's eyes bugged from their sockets. "What? That's not what I said!"

One of the Sergeant's eyebrows arced and he jerked a thumb upwards. "Oh, really? Ain't you been listenin'?"

For the first time, Agatha actually absorbed the words booming out from the colossus above them. "—Zzzk—Baron Wulfenbach was...is The Other—"

"Tarvek—" she began.

"Thought you said that boy shouldn't move," Scorp said.

"I didn't think he *could*!" the corpsman said in amazement.

"Live and learn," Scorp said cheerfully as he aimed his pistol.

A few minutes later, the squad was again on the move. The medic strode along, wiping his hands on a rag. "Did you *have* to shoot him in the leg?"

Scorp shrugged. "Figure I did him a favor. Iffin' she'd got to him first—"

In the arms of one of the large brass clanks, Tarvek writhed in agony. Partly from the pain in his leg.

"It's your own fault," a furious Agatha informed him for the twenty-eighth time, "And better than you deserve! Why did you alter my message?"

The effort of keeping his stories straight caused the sweat to pour from Tarvek's brow. "I didn't do it! Lucrezia did. She wanted it found after we left Sturmhalten. That way, even if you broke free of her, it would keep you and the Baron from talking."

"If you're innocent then why did you run?"

Any number of reasons, as well as convoluted definitions of the word 'innocent,' ran through Tarvek's increasingly chaotic brain. *I'm going into shock,* he realized. *Oh, that's just perfect.*

What he said was the simple truth; "You look very scary!"

Agatha opened her mouth, and then checked herself. If she looked anything at all like she felt—"I feel scary. In fact like I'm about to ignite! Why aren't I exhausted?"

Realization jolted through Tarvek, snapping him closer to coherence. "Oh dear," he muttered.

"*Now* what?" Agatha demanded.

Tarvek took a deep breath. "Listen—you're drugged. With a massive load of stimulants. Lucrezia insisted that her priestesses see her moving on her own."

"You're joking! She *wanted* to feel like this?"

"Don't hit me!" Tarvek bleated, "I had to give her a quadruple dose. Your body's been awake for *days* now. If you get excited, your brain could kind of short circuit. You've got to stay calm!"

"*Calm?*" She shouted, "I feel jittery and angry and… and I have a… a terrible pressure on my chest! Like I have a… a…" She paused, and then reached under her shirt and into her cleavage. She gave a start of surprise, and pulled out the miniature Hive Engine. "And what on earth is *this*?" she demanded.

Klaus had intended to join the troops in the initial foray into the town. If he was honest with himself, he'd been rather looking forward to it. *I've been hanging around the Jägers too much*, he thought.

But this plan had collapsed with the appearance of the giant apparition over Sturmhalten Castle. He trusted the even-headedness of his commanders, but many of the rank and file troops had lost friends and family to The Other.

A Lieutenant stomped into the Command center Klaus had established in the port hangar bay of DuPree's ship and saluted. "The townspeople are attacking us, Herr Baron."

Klaus drummed his fingers upon the desk. "That *is* to be expected when you invade them, Lieutenant."

The man had the grace to look embarrassed. "Yessir, but these people are unusually determined, sir. They claim we're…" he coughed. "Servants of The Other, begging your pardon, Sir."

Klaus' fist thumped on the desk, cracking it slightly. "Confound that girl!" He sighed. "Casualties?"

The Lieutenant consulted the notes he'd memorized. "Three of ours, fifteen of theirs, so far. They're determined fighters, but they're not very good at it," he offered. "The biggest problem is that it's tying up troops."

"Pretty smart." Bangladesh strolled in and casually leaned on the corner of the Baron's desk. "She 'asks' everyone to fight you, and they do, because she's The Other and they have to obey her, but since people aren't used to the idea of this new type of revenant, to any outside observers, it'll look like she's leading a popular uprising."

Klaus had been about to tell DuPree to remove herself from his desk, but instead he nodded. "Very astute." He studied Bangladesh and stroked his jaw. "Aren't you worried that I might actually *be* The Other, as she claims?"

Bangladesh snorted. "Nah."

"Really?" Klaus leaned forward. "Why not?"

DuPree rolled her eyes. "Klaus, you're *always* telling me—" Her voice grew deeper and she took on a rather pompous cadence—"Oh, DuPree, don't torture people. Don't burn their town down, it's not nice."

Her voice returned to normal. "Or whatever. So if *you* were The Other, *I'd* be a revenant, because there's no way you'd let me run around uncontrolled, and I'd have to obey you, even if a town really *needed* burning, y'know? But I can still act on my own better judgment, so I know everything's okay. It's all about free will!"

Klaus stared at her for a second and then slowly pinched his nose between his fingers. "And here I was foolishly hoping for an argument that would *reassure* the troops," he muttered faintly.

He straightened up and addressed the Lieutenant, along with the rest of the command staff.

"There will be no reprisals for attacks. No burning. No executions. As long as they continue to pose only a minor threat, our policy will be to contain them."

Bangladesh frowned. "They're revenants. Why can't we just kill them?"

Ah, DuPree, thought Klaus gratefully, *ever the easily-refuted, public voice of unreason.* "Because," Klaus said carefully, "This is something new. These people aren't shambling zombies. They aren't monsters. Without The Other or their intermediaries giving them orders, they're ordinary people. Perhaps they can still be saved."

He allowed this concept to roll over those assembled in the room, and was gratified to see the expressions of hope that began to fill their faces.

He gestured towards the giant apparition visible outside the portholes. "We simply have to find the girl. Once she tells them to stop attacking us, they will."

DuPree raised her hand. "And if she won't?"

Klaus smiled at her. "Then I'll let you make her change her mind."

Bangladesh squealed like a schoolgirl and dashed back towards the bridge.

Agatha examined the small sphere and a finger accidentally pressed a rocker switch. A red light lit, and a small jet of vapor puffed out from the top. Several meters away, the weasels paused, and then screamed in unison, to the bafflement of their handlers. This however, did put the unit on alert, so that when a crowd of townspeople poured around the corner, they were ready for them.

The chief Vespiary Soldier was astonished. "Amazing! They sensed those revenants all the way over there! They've never been able to do *that* before."

Tarvek, on the other hand was frantically whispering, "Agatha! Push the red button! The red button!"

Agatha saw his desperate face and made a decision. With a snap, she pressed the red button, and the device in her hands went inert.

"Form a firing line!" the Sergeant roared.

"No!" Tarvek screamed. "Don't drop me!" as the trooper clank dropped him onto the pavement.

"They're going to shoot them?" Agatha asked aghast.

This was obviously the case, as the crowd was surging forward. The soldiers coolly formed a line. The two clanks unshipped their massive machine cannons, and their motors began to whine as the barrels began to rotate up to speed.

"Fix bayonets!" Scorp ordered from the side. Smoothly the troops affixed the long steel blades to their rifles.

"But those people aren't armed!" Agatha cried. "Some of them are children! They can't—"

Tarvek grabbed her leg. "Stop them!" he said urgently. "You can control them. Tell them to stop! If they're not attacking, the soldiers won't shoot them!"

Agatha whirled towards the onrushing crowd and filled her lungs. "*LISTEN TO ME!*" she shouted.

"I think I found it, Captain."

DuPree took her hands off of her ears. "About time! The noise is killing me!"

The command ship had luffed over Sturmhalten castle, and the ship's observers had been told to find whatever was generating the colossal lightshow. They had been examining the grounds below ever since. One of them had thought to train her scopes within the shattered keep.

The image on the scope showed an odd machine, clearly operating, and throwing intense beams of light into the sky. The directional microphone also registered a significant uptick in decibels when the ship cleared the keep's walls.

"Yeah, that's gotta be it," Bangladesh declared.

"Orders, Ma'am?"

Bangladesh stroked her chin. "We should assemble a device team. It may be rigged to prevent tampering, so we'll want a gadgetman on a quick-pull return system. Once we shut it down, Klaus could study it or something."

Everyone within earshot stared at the Captain in astonishment. Finally Bangladesh couldn't contain herself any more and burst out laughing as she hit a lever. "Or we could just blow it up!"

The other crewmen relaxed. The scope operator wiped her brow. "You had me going there, Captain."

On the keel of the airship, a bomb-bay door fell open and a small dropedo screamed earthwards, landing within two meters of Agatha's projector. There was a satisfying explosion, and the giant image disappeared.

On the firing line, everyone blinked at the sudden cessation of sound. Even the crowd paused for a second, before continuing their advance.

"Eyes front!" Scorp roared. "The enemy is still advancing!"

Tarvek stared upwards at the smoldering keep. Suddenly, the ramifications of the silence hit him. The background music had stopped. Which meant—

He whipped around in time to see Lucrezia assess the

situation. He shouted to the soldiers. "Ignore the crowd! The Heterodyne Girl! You've got to grab—"

The gunshot echoed from the stone walls and froze everyone. Tarvek dropped to the ground as Lucrezia tossed the revolver away. "Such a waste," she sighed. Then she shouted. "*KILL THE SOLDIERS! KILL THEM ALL!*" And with a laugh, she vaulted over the nearest railing and darted off.

"Where'n the hell did she get a gun?" Scorp yelled.

The medic paled. "This... this is my gun, Sergeant."

"You and you!" the Sergeant pointed to two troopers. "Get after her! *Take her down!*" To the rest he roared, "Firing positions!"

He then faced the onrushing mob of unarmed civilians and grit his teeth. "*FIRE!*"

Lucrezia heard the boom of rifles, followed by the roar of the machine cannons from behind her and smirked. "That will keep them busy." She turned a corner and almost tripped over a wounded and shackled Vrin.

"Lady?" The Geisterdamen roused herself and smiled out from under the bruises. "I knew you would return!"

Lucrezia frowned. "You look terrible. I doubt you can run—" she examined the staple driven into the stone wall[73], "—even if I could release you."

A pensive look stole over Vrin's face. "Lady, please—"

---

[73] At this time, it was the practice of Wulfenbach forces during an invasion to shackle prisoners and then drive a large metal staple into a nearby wall, so they could be collected later. A territory as large as the Empire was always looking for trained soldiers, and very few of the rank and file were themselves driven by ideological ideals. Usually they were conscripts, draftees, mercenaries or such, and thus, when offered the choice of being cut loose with one month's pay or being allowed to join the well-fed, well-paid and well-dressed armies of the Pax Transylvania, many of them joined up without hesitation.

"I'm sorry, but I simply can't leave you here for dear Klaus to interrogate." She stepped close and fixed the trapped woman with her full gaze. "*Vrin—DIE.*"

The chained woman jerked and fell back, and with a look of agonized betrayal frozen upon her face, began choking and gasping as she thrashed upon the ground.

A pair of Wulfenbach troops pounded around the corner, saw Lucrezia, and raised their rifles.

She looked over her shoulder as she took off. "You wouldn't dare—"

Two bullets whipped past. One perforating her sleeve, the other clipping a few strands of hair. "Stop!" she screamed, "I surrender!"

She turned, hands raised, and saw the two soldiers taking aim at her heart. "Good." The left one said. "That'll make you easier to hit."

The unfairness of this statement so surprised her, that a Jägermonster dropping from above and slamming the soldiers' guns from their hands with a gigantic halberd seemed almost anti-climactic.

In seconds, the two soldiers were overwhelmed by a small crowd of people that included two more Jägers, a woman Lucrezia was able to identify as a Skifandrian, and a tall, good-looking fellow with a great deal of well-placed muscles.

They must be friends of my daughter, she realized. *They should be easy to fool.*

"You okay?" The voice was a bit odd, which was only fair, as upon turning, Lucrezia saw that it came from a white cat in a uniform.

To her embarrassment, she shrieked in surprise. This caused

the cat to leap in terror to the top of the tallest thing in the vicinity, which at the moment, was Lucrezia.

There followed a most undignified display of mutual screaming and thrashing that left the two even more entangled than when they'd started.

"What's the matter with you?" The cat demanded, "You almost scared me to death!"

The Skifandrian looked at her with narrowed eyes, "Are you all right?"

Lucrezia realized that subterfuge was worse than useless, and went straight to bewilderment. She'd always been good at that one. "Actually, I'm not sure. I think I've been drugged. I don't..." she took a deep breath. "Do I know you people?"

They all looked at each other. Apparently her being drugged wasn't totally unexpected. The tall man stepped forward. "I'm Lars. I'm... we're all your friends. We're here to rescue you."

Lucrezia looked up at the earnest young man and had to restrain herself from running her hands over him. From the look on his face, if her daughter hadn't done so already, then she had missed an obvious opportunity. "What a shame I don't remember you," she said softly.

The startled look on his face told her to dial it down a bit. However it had been a *pleasantly* startled look. Yes, there was fun to be had here when things had settled down a bit.

"So... Lars... what now?"

Lars glanced up at the hovering airships. "First? We get out of Sturmhalten."

The cat visibly drooped. "The sewers again."

"Hy go find us a vay in," Ognian volunteered, and shambled off.

Lars continued. "I'm afraid so. After that? I guess we get you to Mechanicsburg. It's only about three days away from here by horse if we ride steady."

Lucrezia froze. "Mechanicsburg?"

Lars looked at her. "Well, yes, of course." He took her shoulders. "We know you're a Heterodyne. We'll do whatever we—"

"NO!" Lucrezia pulled away from him. "I don't want to go there!" There were too many things that could hurt her there. "I *can't!*"

The Jägers stirred. "Iz best place for hyu. Keep hyu safe—"

"No! I won't go there!"

Lars looked at her helplessly. "But... but where will we go?"

Lucrezia desperately tried to think—

"*ENGLAND!*"

The firm voice came from above. They all stared upwards at the tall man in flying leathers who leapt down from the ledge overhead. He stood before Lucrezia and formally bowed. He appeared to have a large bruise upon his forehead.

"I am Ardsley Wooster, of Her Majesty's Secret Service. The Lady Heterodyne should remember me."

He glanced at Agatha and was perplexed to see the look of bewilderment upon her face.

Maxim stepped forward. "Right now she dun remember nobody, Brit."

Zeetha nodded, "She's been drugged."

"It's true." Krosp stared up at Ardsley. "She smells like a chemical lab. Trust me." He paused, "But *I* remember you from Castle Wulfenbach, you were pretending to be Gilgamesh Wulfenbach's valet."

"That was my cover." He studied Krosp. "I'm afraid I don't remember you."

Krosp smiled. "I'm sure most people consider you a pretty good spy, but they probably couldn't find the stuff you kept hidden in the linen closet air vent."

Wooster stared down at him and then nodded. "Lady Heterodyne, you are in grave danger here. I am empowered to extend an invitation to you to seek sanctuary in England, as an honored guest of Her Majesty. I have a flying machine at my disposal. It is parked back near your circus, so we must hurry."

Krosp frowned. "What guarantees do we have—"

"I accept!" Lucrezia declared.

A sharp whistle broke into the conversation. Ognian waved at them from around a corner. "Lezz go, keeds! Qvickly! Dere's soldiers all over der plaze!"

Shortly thereafter, they were once again clambering through the fetid pipes under the town.

Krosp scooted up to Lucrezia. "Agatha, are you sure about going to England?"

Lucrezia grinned. "Oh, yes! It's perfect! As long as Albia lives, England is closed to Klaus." A thought struck her. "Unless... Mr. Wooster, Albia *does* still rule, yes?"

The question caused Ardsley to stumble and he stared at Agatha with frank amazement upon his face. "Good heavens, yes. Why in the world would you think otherwise?"

This was a reasonable question, as Albia had been the reigning queen for a very long time[74].

"I... I've been out of touch," Lucrezia said defensively, "Anything can happen."

---

[74] A very long time indeed.

Wooster smiled and turned to continue. "Not in England, Miss. Her Majesty wouldn't permit it."

They turned a corner and daylight could be seen in the distance. They quickened their pace at the sight and soon encountered a rusty stormgrate. A shattered lock showed that the Jägers had preceded them, and they emerged, blinking, onto a streambed cluttered with debris. They waded ashore as Maxim and Zeetha reappeared from over a small hill.

"Hokay! Der circus is parked in the caravan staging area, and hy dun see any Vulfenbach troops."

Zeetha nodded. "They've got all the wagons hitched up, so it looks like they're getting ready to move out."

Krosp frowned. "No troops at all?"

"That's a stroke of luck," Lars said.

"I suspect that Sturmhalten is putting up more resistance than the Baron expected," Wooster said thoughtfully. "The whole giant lady thing, you know."

Krosp nodded. "That won't last though. The Baron's strength comes from paying attention to the details. We've got to get out before he gets here."

Wooster concurred. "But once *we're* gone," he said to Lars, "your people should be safe."

Lucrezia laughed. "Oh yes. Just tell him that I threatened to kill you all if you betrayed me."

Lars looked at her askance. "That seems a bit *much*."

They crested a small ridge, and below them lay the caravan grounds. The circus wagons were indeed all hitched up. The horses stamped their feet. A few tenders were busy in the distance checking harnesses.

Wooster stopped. "Where is everyone?"

Lars pointed. A crowd could be seen at the center of the array of wagons. "Pre-travel meeting. Whenever there's a possibility of trouble, Master Payne assigns places down the road where we can all meet up." He glanced back at the town and the airships floating overhead. "I think trouble on the road's a pretty safe bet this time," he said ruefully.

They came up to the three Jägers, who were looking uncharacteristically glum. Dimo was talking.

"Hyu two eediots gots to take care uf Miss Agatha, now."

"Yes, Dimo," the other two replied.

"*And* youselves!"

Maxim and Ognian looked even more miserable. "Ve try."

Krosp frowned. "Dimo? You're staying?"

The green Jäger nodded. "Yaz. Ve saw tings dot de Baron must know about. Geistervimmin in der tunnels. Hive Engines—"

"No!" Lucrezia snapped. "I don't want anyone going to Klaus!"

Dimo looked surprised. "But Lady, diz iz a lucky break for hyu."

Lucrezia blinked. Dimo continued. "Diz iz impawtent hinformation. De Baron may be after hyu, but he hates vasps and der revenants. Ven he hears dis, he'll go after der ghost ladies, not hyu."

Lucrezia thought furiously. "But... but he'll kill you."

Dimo frowned. "Vot? No he von't. Oggie vas de vun who ate all his—"

"Shoddop 'bout dot!" Ognian interjected.

"The Baron's troops are shooting townspeople! If they'll do that—"

Surprisingly, all of the Jägers grinned. "Ho! Iz dot all? Dun vorry 'bout dot! Dey's using stun bullets and 'C' Gas."

"What!"

Maxim nodded. "Ho yez! Hyu ken hear der difference ven dey shoots, eef hyu knowz vat to listen for."

Wooster broke in. "They *are* standard issue for police actions, M'Lady."

Tarvek might still be alive, Lucrezia realized. *How inconvenient.*

"So Hy vill buy hyu time—"

"*No!*" Lucrezia screamed in frustration. "You serve me and I *forbid* it! You'll tell the Baron *nothing*!"

The next question came only because Dimo had been a free agent for over ten years. As it was, it surprised him as much as it did Lucrezia. "But... vy?"

She stared at him. Furiously, she opened her mouth—

"Yes." The terrifyingly familiar voice said. "Tell them why."

From the wagon in front of them, Klaus Wulfenbach stepped forward. From the other wagons, doors slammed open and dozens of armed soldiers began to pour forth and encircle them. "*I* would certainly like to know."

Lucrezia stared at him, frozen by a cascade of emotions, of which both guilt and fear played a large part.

In the distance, Lars saw the circus members being quickly hustled off by a squad of soldiers.

Klaus stared down at her. He was used to reading people, but the reactions he was seeing on the face of the Heterodyne girl seemed inexplicable. "My spotters saw my son's flying machine, even though he is still back aboard Castle Wulfenbach. I can only assume that he sent his Mr. Wooster here to rescue you from me."

Klaus ran his eye about the scene. Unsurprisingly, the British agent had vanished. He wouldn't get far. Klaus turned back to the girl. "It seemed a reasonable guess that you would turn up here."

Klaus paused. "But perhaps you do not *need* 'rescuing.' At least, not from me." His features softened a bit. "You are Bill Heterodyne's child. You were raised by Punch and Judy, two of the best people I ever knew. My son... believes in you. Most importantly, you seem to have been raised away from the influence of your mother and her family." *That got a reaction. A small twitch in the left eye. Interesting.*

"If you are indeed innocent, then step forward now. It would be best for you—" Klaus paused, "—For everyone, if you joined me willingly."

A hush fell over the scene. The soldiers had paused. They were all watching and listening.

Klaus spoke gently, but clearly. "Yes, you will be guarded. This town is infested with a heretofore undiscovered type of revenant. Until I know what has happened here, until it is controlled, I trust no one." He firmed up his voice, and it rang out. "I can be ruthless, but I *try* to be fair. What is your decision?"

"I..." The fate of Europa teetered upon the edge of a knife. "I..."

"Agatha," Zeetha stepped from behind Lars. "This is the best thing we could have *hoped* for. Why are—"

"*YOU!*" The shout of surprise swung every eye back to Klaus, who was staring at Zeetha like he'd seen a ghost. "Djorok'ku skifandias von?"

Zeetha jerked like she'd been punched in the stomach. "Ah... ah...Zur bakken Skiff?"

"Kar!" The Baron roared, "Mor bakken Skiff!" He pointed a finger. "Braka na *Zantabr*—!"

What he had been about to say was lost, as at this point, a bug flew into his mouth. Klaus choked, and his eyes went wide. "Gak!"

Lucrezia smiled tightly and slipped the activated hive enginette back under her jacket. "*Got* you!" she whispered.

Up on the wagon, Klaus' face was turning red, and he dropped to his knees while clawing at his throat.

Lucrezia strode forward. "Why are you all just standing around? Can't you see he's *choking*?" A flustered looking soldier made a half-hearted attempt to block her. "Let me through! I can *help* him! He *wanted* us to work together!"

"Where's the damn doctor?" The trooper yelled. A Captain ran up. "They're all in that twice-cursed town!" He ostensibly drew his side arm. "Okay, Lady—" he hesitated, "—Heterodyne. He was giving you the benefit of the doubt... Earn it."

Lucrezia ignored him and knelt down beside the now convulsing Baron. Several of the soldiers leaned in.

"Get back! Give him air," Lucrezia cried. She began a showy, but useless massaging of the throat area, while under her breath, she was counting. On a normal wasp, the nerve fusion process only took seconds, if it successfully worked at all. There was no guessing how long this experimental specimen—

With a gasp, Klaus drew in a great lungful of air and collapsed. With a sigh, Lucrezia released the breath she hadn't even realized she was holding in.

Klaus began to breath normally. *Well done, Herr Doktor Snarlantz,* she thought admiringly, *requiescat in pace.*

"The blockage is gone!" she announced loudly. "He's

going to be all right!" She deftly loosened a few buttons on his coat. "Let's just give him a little more air and let him rest for a minute." The Captain nodded, but held his gun steadily upon her.

Lucrezia tried to ignore him as she continued to ease Klaus' breathing. His coat was definitely too tight here. She frowned, "What is this in your waistcoat?" She expertly picked his pocket and extracted a small metal case. It looked like a jewelry box—

"Why, it has the Heterodyne sigil on it. Was this for me?" She snapped it open. Within lay nestled a large, gold trilobite brooch. Lucrezia smiled in admiration. "Dear Klaus. You always thought of *everything*."

"Who *are* you?" The voice was ragged, but the steel behind it was unmistakable.

Lucrezia tried to smile like an idiot. "Why, Herr Baron. I'm Agatha Heterodyne—"

"No." Klaus heaved himself up onto his elbows and stared at her. Sweat poured from his face. "Speech patterns. Facial expressions. Body stance. I know you. Who?" He grimaced in frustration. "Arrgh. Something wrong with my head. Can't think!"

Lucrezia felt a frisson of fear. He shouldn't be this coherent, this *focused*, so quickly. She leaned in and smiled. "The confusion will pass. You were choking—"

"You did this."

Lucrezia abandoned the pretense. He was already hers. "Why yes, I did. And quite handily too."

Klaus' eyes widened. "Lucrezia!"

She flinched. "How did you know?"

"Heard you gloat too many times."

Lucrezia smiled grimly. "Well, you'll hear it a lot more often from now on."

"I think not!" Klaus' voice began to return to its full power. "I'll—"

"*Silence!*" Lucrezia hissed.

Klaus' voice failed him in midsyllable. His eyes bulged and he clutched at his throat. Lucrezia felt a wave of triumph roar through her. "It's working! My beautiful little wasp is controlling that magnificent brain!"

As the implications of this hit Klaus, he froze, and he stared at her. Lucrezia felt another jolt of fear from the expression on his face. With some effort, she shrugged it off. Klaus was harmless now.

"You should be happy, Klaus," she said. The Baron's mouth jerked upwards in a death's head grin. Lucrezia swallowed. What an impossible man.

"I'll give you what you want," she said soothingly. "A Wulfenbach/Heterodyne alliance, as civil and sweet as pie." She sat back on her haunches. "It'll just be controlled by me."

She stood up and leaned over him. "Let me help you get up," she said quietly. "Look grateful." Klaus jerkily extended a hand and Lucrezia once again experienced the sensation of a mountain rising beside her as Klaus slowly got to his feet. Around them, the troops cheered, and her daughter's friends looked relieved. She'd have to deliberate on what to do about them.

She waved at the crowd and spoke from the corner of her mouth. "Don't worry, I'll play the good little girl... in public."

She smiled and pulled out the trilobite locket. At the sight of it, Klaus' eyes widened and he stared at her with an unreadable expression on his face. "I'll even wear my little family sigil so everyone will know who I am! I'm so glad you thought to bring it."

With a giggle, she unsprung the pin and speared it through her collar.

With a snap, she closed it.

Her smile faltered.

There was a sound.

A whine. Like a mosquito. It was getting closer. No... not closer—

A clamp slammed onto her brain. "*NOOOO!*" Lucrezia screamed as she fell into the darkness.

Agatha blinked, and found herself facing an astonished crowd of people. She smiled in delight. "I'm back!"

Behind her, Klaus' greatsword reached the top of its arc and swept back down towards her neck.

THIRTEEN

People they say that the Heterodynes—
They will return.
They will come laughing and singing,
sheepish because they have kept us waiting.
They will smile and wink and
Show us marvelous things that will
Make the world a'right and then
They'll a'pat our heads and put us to bed.

But I thinks the Heterodynes—
They will return.
They will come with fire and smokes
and machines a'blazing in the night.
They will stare at us from bloodspattered faces
They will pull us up and roughly exclaim
"We bought you years, but you've done nothing

and now the monsters are a'snapping at our heels!"
—T. STORMBOY,
*LA REVUE PARISIENNE DES RÉFLEXIONS
CHAGRINES ET SANS MÉRITE, VOL. 2. ISSUE 3*

There was an explosion of movement, and Lars leapt forward. With a sweep of his arm, Agatha was thrown to the side, the Baron's blade slicing a few stray strands of hair from her head. She tumbled from the wagon, everything around her a blur. She realized she was clutched in Maxim's arms, but the Jäger wasn't looking at her.

Towering overhead was the Baron, sword dripping gore. He kicked aside a body at his feet. "Damn fool," he muttered. His eyes locked on Agatha's. "Kill the girl!" he roared. "Kill her companions, if you must. Kill them all!"

Maxim dropped Agatha to her feet, and with a hiss, pulled a slim rapier from its scabbard and with three strokes, cleared a space around them. "Time to fight!" he sang out.

Klaus made to leap, and a glittering flash of green and blue exploded before him as Zeetha attacked screaming. Klaus barely parried in time, and with an oath, leapt backwards to avoid the slicing *Quata'aras*.

Agatha darted forward and knelt at Lars' side. All of her medical knowledge delivered the same terrible answer. Lars' eyes opened and gazed at her blankly. "Agatha?"

"Don't move!" Agatha said desperately. She shucked her jacket and tried to tear off a strip. The heavy fabric stubbornly refused to tear. She whimpered in frustration.

Lars gently patted her hand. "It's amazing," he whispered. "I never even guessed. But it's so... so *perfect*."

"Lars, stop moving!"

His head fell back and he gave a ghastly smile. "Oh, that'll happen soon enough."

"NO!" Agatha gasped. "No, you're just in shock! I can—"

Lars cupped her chin. "It's okay, I can even promise I won't panic afterwards." He chuckled, and a bead of blood welled up between his lips.

Agatha wanted to scream at the helplessness she felt. "I don't have any instruments," she said, "I can't—"

"Shh." Lars feebly tried to move his hand. Agatha clasped it in her own. "'S probably for the best," Lars whispered. "A Heterodyne girl and…and an ordinary guy like me… probably lucky I lasted as long as I…"

Agatha waited for Lars to finish, and then saw that he had.

Around her the battle raged. The three Jägers ringed her with a shield of carnage. Always on the move, they mowed through soldiers. Never slaying, but leaving a trail of wounded who tied up even more troops.

On the roof of one of the wagons lay Ardsley Wooster, who had taken out one of the snipers and was busy finishing off the rest with their comrade's own rifle.

And at the center of the fight, drawing almost everyone's eye, were the Baron and Zeetha. Both were terribly fast. The Baron swung his greatsword with a deceptive ease that sent it screaming through the air. Zeetha couldn't hope to block its unstoppable force, but she danced between the strokes and at times seemed to fly. Klaus' coat was sliced in dozens of places, and not all of the blood that covered him was from Lars.

But fury and speed would not hold up in the long run against superior numbers. Even now the troops facing the Jägers were falling back and beginning to fire at them from a distance. From the surrounding wagons, a line of the tall brass fighting clanks strode forth. In unison, they raised their machine-cannons and fired a quick burst into the air. The human soldiers began to pull back. A bullet punched through Maxim's side, eliciting a howl of annoyance.

Klaus suddenly threw his sword at Zeetha. The green-haired girl dodged, and with a roar, Klaus tackled her and slammed her to the ground.

She began to bring her swords up and felt a knife at her throat. "Ni tok," the Baron snarled. The warriors last decision: Honorable surrender or death. She looked up into his face. "Ni tok!" he repeated. The knife pressed deeper.

Agatha leaned in and for the last time, gave Lars a kiss. "You were anything but ordinary," she whispered.

Wooster surveyed the battle. Not good. He aimed his rifle at the Baron. He couldn't kill him. The political ramifications of the Baron dying at the hands of a British operative would greatly displease Her Majesty, but *wounding* him—

A gun barrel poked against the back of his head. The fact that he was familiar enough with the sensation probably meant that he should get a new line of work. He was also rather impressed at his own calm. This evaporated when he heard the voice of the gun's owner.

"Please, try to resist." Bangladesh DuPree said hopefully. Wooster froze.

After it became evident that he was not going to resist, she sighed in disappointment. "Klaus always knows where the party is, but they're always so dull."

She raised her voice. "You are surrounded! Surrender and die!"

"I believe," Wooster said carefully, "It's supposed to be 'surrender *or* die.'"

Bangladesh cocked her pistol. "Dull, dull, dull."

Agatha slowly folded Lars' hands together on his chest. "Ordinary." She whispered. "But I *am* a Heterodyne!" She stood up and screamed. "*SHOWTIME!*"

The fighting paused. Bangladesh poked her gun against Wooster's head. "What is she trying—?"

With a groan, the wagon Bangladesh and Wooster were standing on began to tilt sideways. With a squawk, they lost their footing and slid off the roof, tumbling to the ground.

They stumbled to their feet, trying to avoid the wagon that appeared to be about to crash back upon them. They heard shouts from the other soldiers. Drowning these out were a series of snappings and grindings. All around them, all of the circus wagons were shuddering and warping. Wheels bent and slammed to the ground. Roofs broke and unfolded. Chassis' rearranged themselves, joints sliding into new positions. Springs and slats re-organized themselves into new configurations.

Klaus stared at the nearest wagon as it wrenched itself up upon two extended fenders, spoked wheels unfolding like flowers into crude hands at the end of their axles. From the under-carriage, a single great eye ground open, and with a whine, focused upon him. A shudder went through the giant clank, and it took a ponderous step towards him, shaking the earth.

"Clanks!" Klaus roared. All around him, the wagon clanks began sweeping their metal arms back and forth, scything down the human troops too slow to run.

A quartet of Wulfenbach trooper clanks strode forward,

purposefully lowering their great machine-cannons. Klaus pointed to the nearest wagon-clank. "Crossfire!" he ordered.

Immediately the four opened fire. Their bullets chewed away at the wooden structure and sent metal bits flying. Within thirty seconds, the ponderous clank had been reduced to fragments.

A Sergeant grinned at the Baron. "Haw! These things have no defenses!"

But Klaus was staring at the pile of rubble. It was shifting, heaving…

"There's something wrong here—"

Suddenly the rubble disgorged hundreds of miniscule clanks, none of them taller than thirty centimeters. They darted forward and then fanned out. Several dozen of them scurried towards the trooper clanks. The larger clanks seemed to be at a loss as to what to do. One went as far as to fire several rounds into a particularly slow specimen, but the rest easily converged around the larger clank's feet.

Several of the machines then began tossing their fellows at the trooper clanks. The small devices flew though the air and clung to the troopers with a magnetic "clang!" Before the clanks could react, the smaller machines detonated, blowing the troopers into fragments, which whistled through the Baron's forces.

Klaus picked himself up in time to see another lumbering wagon clank explode into a cloud of smaller clanks, which charged into the lines of soldiers.

He looked around wildly. The girl. The Heterodyne girl. Where had she gone? It was then that he became aware of the music that overlay the noise of battle.

Bangladesh DuPree and Ardsley Wooster stood side-by-side, their mouths hanging open in shock at the scene of chaos before them. They both remembered at the same time who they were standing next to.

Bangladesh raised her gun, but Wooster simply punched her in the face, and then ran away, which Bangladesh considered, in some undefined way, to be cheating.

"All right!" She roared. "I'm going to kill *somebody*, and I'm not picky about who or what it is!" A rumbling from behind caused Bangladesh to turn about and stare.

The newly repurposed merry-go-round focused its attention on her, took a step forward, activated its calliope, and began to spin.

Everywhere, Wulfenbach troops found themselves fighting clanks that minutes ago had been inanimate objects. The organized, by-the-numbers rifle volleys that had broken armies across all of Europa began to dissolve into random, panicky, free fire.

"All troops fall back!" Klaus roared above the din.

"Fall back to *where*?" a trooper shouted back. "We're surrounded!"

Another trooper pointed skywards. "Incoming cavalry!"

With a crash, a Hoomhoffer[75] slammed to the ground, crushing a phalanx of steadily advancing water barrels.

---

[75] Hoomhoffers were gigantic insects, the end result of some forgotten Spark entomologists' experiments. The original subjects had apparently been dust mites, too small to be seen by the naked eye. The experiments had been designed to "make those little rascals big enough that I get a look at them." They now required a small chugging engine to make sure they got enough oxygen throughout their enormous frames. This was a bit inconvenient, but their resistance to bullets, unearthly strength, newly-acquired ability to fly, and terrifying appearance made up for it. Plus, they ate a lot of dust.

Several more thudded to earth, and urged on by their mahouts, began to simply bulldoze their way through some of the encircling wagon clanks.

With a ragged cheer, the Wulfenbach troops rallied, and began a break-out action. Klaus took charge, and began directing the troops' fire.

"Don't shoot to destroy the clanks," he ordered. "Shoot to disable them. Concentrate fire on their legs!"

After several minutes, it was obvious that this strategy was working. Several of the lumbering wagon-clanks fell to the ground and began to clumsily drag themselves forward.

Suddenly, over the roar of battle, the ever-present music changed.

"Of course!" Klaus realized. "The music! She's directing the actions of the clanks through the music!" He paused and shook his head. "That's brilliant. I've got to remember that."

"Is 'brilliant' the same as 'trouble'?" asked a corporal who'd served with the Baron before.

"It is that," Klaus acknowledged with a grim smile, "We've got to find that girl and stop her before—"

There was a deep boom of sound, and one of the Hoomhoffers disappeared.

A scream from the mahout drew every eye upwards. Above the fray, the Baba Yaga flapped its enormous pinions as it dragged the Hoomhoffer skyward, clutched in its great metal claws.

The troops on the ground swung their rifles up and began firing just as the flying wagon swooped about and launched the captive insect toward the ranks of its fellows. The Hoomhoffer screamed in from above, its torn wings buzzing ineffectually, and smashed into two others of the tank-like creatures, crushing one and sending the other flying for several dozen meters. When it tumbled to a stop, it lay twitching, stunned.

With another loop, the Baba Yaga prepared to swoop down for another victim.

"The Hooms are scattering!" The corporal reported. An explosion sent shrapnel screaming through the air. "And that was the last of our clanks! We can't penetrate the enemy lines to find this girl, those friggin' little bomb things are everywhere!"

Klaus grit his teeth. *I underestimated her,* he realized. "Drummers," he roared. "Sound *Full Retreat*!"

The soldiers looked at each other in astonishment. Full Retreat? One of the drummers had a panicky moment before he could even remember how to play it.

They hesitated. A furious lieutenant kicked a wooden chest, which extruded a set of mechanical legs and began to pursue him, its lid snapping at him. That did it. The drums boomed out the unfamiliar refrain. With a step, then another, then several speeding up into a run, part of the greatest army that Europa had ever seen took to its heels.

Klaus loped up next to a Captain. "Have them form up on the other side of that wall!" He pointed.

"Not that great a defensive position, sir!" the Captain opined, eyes glancing up at the still circling wagon.

Klaus reached into his coat as he ran and produced an elaborate flare gun. He spun several wheels, aimed upwards and fired three times.

Overhead, various explosions bloomed in a variety of colors.

"I've called for reinforcements!" he said loudly. "Once they arrive they'll carpet-bomb the area, but we have to keep these clanks contained!"

This cheered the troops that heard it, and they ran with renewed purpose.

In a small clearing near-by, the circus troupe, as well as the soldiers who were guarding them, stared at the wall of trees that separated them from the various shouts, gunfire, music and explosions that filled the air.

A trooper gripped his rifle tighter and muttered. "What the hell is going on over there?"

A seasoned campaigner who sported a prosthetic brass nose tried to maintain an air of detachment. "That's Spark stuff. You manage to steer clear of it—you'll live longer."

The trooper looked resolute. "But they might need us."

This got him a mechanical sounding snort. "Oh? So you think you're smarter than the Baron?"

"What? No! Of course not!"

"Well, *he's* the one who told us to guard these mooks. So just do your job." This advice was accompanied by a metallic "click."

Suddenly the two soldiers realized that they were shackled to each other. As they stared at this, two more clicks caused them to turn, or rather to try to do so. They then discovered that their other arms were attached to nearby trees. Shouts of alarm from around the camp revealed that the other sentries were discovering similar constraints.

"What's going on?" the old soldier shouted. "How is this possible?"

A burst of fire and a plume of smoke revealed Master Payne standing before them. "A *good* magician never reveals how a trick is done," he intoned ominously. "An *evil* magician never leaves any evidence that there was a trick in the first place." He leaned in menacingly. "So which am I going to be *today*?"

The two soldiers stared at him and then dropped their weapons and huddled on the ground with their eyes firmly shut. "Good!" they screamed.

Abner shook his head admiringly as the troupe slipped past the prostrate guards. "That is such a great act."

The Countess looked at him in confusion. "Act? What act?"

At the keyboard of the Silverodeon, Agatha directed the clanks through her music. Strange notes spun away into the air and swirled around her.

"Agatha!" Zeetha stood at her elbow and yelled over the music. "The Baron's troops are withdrawing!" She pointed back towards Balan's Gap. "But there are airships heading this way! Your clanks can't fight them all! We've got to get out of here while we have the chance!"

Agatha waved her away. "You go!"

Zeetha blinked. "What?"

Agatha looked at her and Zeetha shivered at the expression on her face. "You go," Agatha said patiently, as one would to a child. "Get everyone away from here. Lars was a good person. He tried to help me. He cared about me. And for that, he's dead.

"He's dead, and I can't even try to fix it. Not out here, with nothing to work with—and the Baron is trying to kill all my friends, and—and there's other things… things wrong with my head. So you go, and I'll stay here and stop the Baron."

She turned back to her keyboards and the façade of calm reasonableness shattered as a maniacal grin smeared itself across her face. "I'll crush his whole army right here. Right now! And then he won't be able to hurt anyone else I care about. No one will. No one will ever hurt anyone else I love ever again or else I'll—"

And that was when Agatha's head exploded.

At least, that was what it felt like. Her vision went white. Well, actually, a sort of creamy, custard-like off white. She tasted an unexpected hint of lemon, and began to realize that it was, in fact, custard that was now dripping down her face.

Taki leaned in and scrutinized her. "So. How d'ye feel?"

Agatha considered this question. The answer surprised her. "Um...Pretty calm, actually."

Taki pumped his fist and twirled in place. "*Yes!*" He shouted. "*Extra* butter! *Less* nutmeg! I am a *genius*! Take *that* Brillat-Savarin[76]!"

A wave of water hit Agatha in the face, cleaning the remnants of the calming pie away. Taki whirled to face Ognian and Krosp, who held an empty bucket. "She was *fine*, you idiots! *Now* she'll—"

Agatha raised a dripping finger. "No, no... still calm."

Taki blinked. "Really? Um..."

Klaus Wulfenbach appeared from around a smoking wagon. In his hands he carried one of the great trooper clank's machine cannons. "*There* you are!" He swung the cannon up and fired. "DIE!"

---

[76] Jean Anthelme Brillat-Savarin was a French Spark obsessed with food and fine dining. His most famous saying was, "Tell me what you eat, and I will tell you who you are." He was devoured by a rather confused monster who had read his books and decided that what he most wanted to be was Brillat-Savarin.

Agatha took stock as hundreds of bullets screamed past her. "Astonishingly, still calm."

"Get *DOWN*!" Taki shrieked as he jerked Agatha back behind the bulk of the Silverodeon.

Huddled down, Agatha saw the organ begin to come apart as it was chewed up by the stream of bullets. She turned to the cowering cook. "Got a calming pie for him?"

Taki considered this. "I don't think I could bake one *big* enough."

At this moment, there was a small explosion, and the underlying bass notes that had been filling the air stopped dead.

Agatha's eyes calmly narrowed. "Uh oh."

Taki rolled his one eye at her in alarm. "What?"

"Well, I was using the organ to control all the wagon clanks. Without the music to guide them, I don't know what they'll do. They might run amok. It could be bad."

"Run amok—" Taki twitched. "More than they already are? It could get *worse*?"

Agatha calmly sighed. "It can always get worse." She shrugged. "On the other hand, they might just lock up."

Taki looked at her. "And that would be *good*, would it?"

The ground shook as a tremendous crash came from the other side of the fragmented organ. The machine-cannon fire cut off. After a few seconds, the two gingerly poked their heads up over the top.

Before them lay the shattered hulk of the Baba Yaga, which had evidently frozen in midflight, and crashed to the ground. Poking out from underneath was the twisted barrel of a smoking machine-cannon.

Agatha looked at Taki. "It could be helpful, yes."

Krosp popped his head up from behind a leaking barrel. "Oh No!" He leapt out and frantically tried to move the wagon, which didn't budge.

The three Jägers ambled up. "Get this thing off of him!" Krosp bellowed. The Jägers looked at him and then as one, looked towards Agatha.

"If the Baron is dead, there will be chaos!" Krosp declared flatly. "But if the Baron is dead, and *you killed him*, the Empire will hold together just long enough to exterminate you before it begins to tear itself apart!"

Agatha nodded. "Get him out!"

Without a word, the three Jägermonsters plowed into the side of the wagon, and it began to tip over.

As it went, it revealed the battered body of the ruler of Europa. Agatha leapt into the small crater and examined him. The others clustered around anxiously.

She leaned back on her haunches and looked up. "He's not dead, but I can't explain why." She looked down. "Or how much longer he'll stay alive. He needs medical attention. More than I can give him." She frowned and looked around. "Wulfenbach troops always travel with first-aid kits—where the heck are they anyway?"

"They retreated," Zeetha said. "But I kind of thought they'd come back when the music stopped."

"They're waiting," Krosp pointed skywards. Several airships that had been stationed over Sturmhalten were now noticeably closer. But much more alarming was a smaller ship that was now practically on top of them.

"The Baron's ordered a bombing run. They won't come back here until it's done." He looked grim. "But I imagine they'll be watching to make sure we can't get out." He looked at the Baron speculatively. "But if we haul him along with us, they'll have to let us through."

"NO!" Agatha said sharply. "The last thing we want to do is move him!" She slumped. "Gil is going to be so mad—" She started. "Gil!"

Krosp flattened his ears. "What about him?"

"He's here! One of the last things I remember from inside Castle Sturmhalten was that his airship had been sighted! His heavier than air flyer! I'm sure he's here, but I haven't seen him!" Her eyes widened. "I could've killed him myself—during this stupid fight!"

Ardsley Wooster, looking surprisingly unruffled, stepped out from behind a burning wagon and cleared his throat. "I can relieve your mind on that account, Miss. Master Gilgamesh is not, in fact, here."

Inexplicably, Agatha felt like she'd been kicked in the stomach. "He's not?"

Ardsley shrugged uncomfortably. "He suspected that you were here, but he said that he was quite busy..."

"Did he." Agatha felt her face going red. "Well. I guess he's found... something important."

Wooster paused, and then, nodded. "Oh yes, ever since his father began negotiating his marriage..."

"Fine." Agatha cut him off. "Let's just figure out how to get out of here."

Wooster nodded in silent satisfaction. If a wedge could be driven between the nascent Heterodyne and the House of Wulfenbach, it could only benefit England. He frowned to himself. So why did he feel like such a cad?

A rising sound interrupted his thoughts. At first he thought it was a sustained artillery barrage, but then he realized it was people.

"It's the troops."

Krosp got a worried look on his face. "Does anyone else smell something... odd?"

Zeetha leapt to the top of an overturned wagon. "They're advancing!" She paused. "But... their guns are down. They're... they're waving."

Wooster glanced upwards at the approaching airships. "At least they'll prevent the ships from bombing us."

Dimo took a deep sniff and frowned.

Maxim listened intently. "Doze are cheers," he said with a puzzled frown.

It was indeed cheering, which grew louder and more jubilant the closer it got. Words began to be discerned. Everyone seemed very excited that someone "had returned."

Soldiers could now be seen swarming onto the former battlefield. Waving their arms and tossing their hats into the air. The crowd got closer and closer and then broke and from within its jubilant depths emerged—

The Heterodyne Boys.

Agatha gasped. It was the Heterodyne Boys. It was the Heterodyne Boys looking just like she'd always imagined them. There was Bill, tall and broad, with a cocksure swagger and a disarming grin. Beside him was Barry, strong and solid, festooned with tools and gadgets that you *knew* could solve anything. On their arms were Lucrezia Mongfish, looking slightly villainous, but determined to put that all behind her for the sake of love, and beside Barry, the mysteriously exotic High Priestess.

Behind them, striding tall and proud, were their loyal servants, Punch and Judy. When Agatha saw them, she bit back a small shriek of surprise.

It was Adam and Lilith. They were alive. No, they were more than just alive. Their faces shifted slightly. They were whole and undamaged. They weren't her parents, the people she had lived with and loved, they were Punch and Judy, the Heterodyne's faithful servants. But she knew they were her parents—Their faces drifted out of focus—her head—

Something was wrong.

"Itz dem!" Ognian breathed.

"It *ken't* be!" Maxim said, "Bot Hy *seez*—"

"Ediots!" Dimo rasped. "Kloze hyu eyez and use hyu nozes!"

"No!" Agatha growled vehemently. "No! I don't... I don't believe this. It's... it's a trick!"

Krosp tugged her sleeve. "Don't believe it!"

Taki leaned in, "But act like you do!"

The group swept up to Agatha. Bill and Lucrezia opened their arms and cried out, "Daughter!"

Lucrezia advanced and Agatha shied away from her, until Taki surreptitiously shoved her forward. Instantly Lucrezia tightly enveloped her in her arms.

"At long last we have found her!" Lucrezia cried.

"Yes!" cried Bill enthusiastically. "Behold, Barry! We have found her!"

"Excellent, brother Bill!" Barry declaimed. "And now, we can return to the great battle! With Agatha, the newest Heterodyne at our side, we are sure to *triumph*!" The crowd again erupted into cheering.

Agatha had been trying desperately to free herself, but

Lucrezia was surprisingly strong. She grinned fondly at Agatha and hissed through her teeth. "Stop *struggling,* dammit." The voice was unexpectedly familiar.

Agatha froze. "*Pix?*"

"And now—" Bill sang out as he gestured theatrically skywards, "Our transport is here!"

"Yes!" Barry added, "Thanks to our good friend, Klaus Wulfenbach!" Above them, the smaller airship that had been bearing down on them began to descend. Barry surveyed the crowd. "I must say, Klaus has done rather well for himself."

The crowd roared in laughter. The ship's landing lights began to sweep about. A loudhailer crackled into life.

"Ahoy, Heterodynes! Prepare to come aboard!"

The cheering intensified as boarding ladders unrolled from several of the loading doors and fell to earth, where they were grabbed by dozens of soldiers.

They eagerly helped everyone onto ladders, although it was a slow process what with the number of soldiers who wanted to shake the Heterodynes' hands or just wish them well. But soon enough, they were all climbing upwards. Bill was the last to ascend. He paused to wave to the adoring crowd one final time.

"Goodbye, friends!" This was met with another burst of cheers. "We must—" Taki swung his ladder close and whispered urgently.

Bill started and called out— "The Baron! Our good friend Klaus lies injured!" He pointed towards the wreckage of the Baba Yaga. "His last order was for us to proceed without him, but you must see to him at once! We will return to get him as soon as we can!"

Below, a large contingent of troops had already begun to rush towards the wounded man, while the rest of the crowd continued to wave and cheer farewell as the airship began to lift away, carrying the ladders and their tightly clinging passengers.

Agatha watched as the earth dropped away below her. Her teeth were clenched and her fists were white.

'Lucrezia' leaned in, an enormous smile plastered across her face. "Smile! Wave! Look majestic."

"…Can't," Agatha said between tightly grit teeth.

Lucrezia looked anxious. "I didn't know you were afraid of heights."

"I'm not!" Agatha gasped. "But I've got cat claws in my butt! Let *go*!" She yelled.

Krosp looked at the rapidly receding ground and dug in tighter. "You must be joking."

Eventually Agatha managed to painfully pull herself up to the lip of the loading bay where Rivet waited with outstretched hands.

She suffered a final flash of agony as Krosp scrambled up her back and leapt from her head into the airship.

"Relax," he announced to everyone. "I'm safe."

Agatha rolled onto her back and blew out a great breath of air. Punch and Judy looked down at her.

"Are you all right?" Judy asked.

"You did great!" Punch said.

Agatha screamed.

Judy looked stricken. "Of course, I'm sorry! Here—"

She whipped out a small atomizer and sprayed Agatha in the face. There was a burst of cinnamon—and all of a sudden Agatha realized that it wasn't Adam and Lilith standing before her, but

Yeti and The Countess dressed in Punch and Judy costumes.

Agatha shook her head. "What?"

"It must have been quite distressing," the Countess said apologetically. "A delightfully hallucinogenic gas of my own devising," she said smugly. "One tries not to brag, but it makes the subject very suggestible. We always keep a large supply of it on hand, as it's proven useful in escaping from unpleasant towns in the past. They see what we want them to see.

"This time we just spread it around and yelled 'The Heterodynes have returned!'" She frowned. "I'm rather surprised at how easily that caught." She looked at Agatha. "I suppose your lightshow made it easier for them to believe it. I'll have to remember that." She held up the atomizer. "This is the antidote." She looked nervous. "I'm sorry we couldn't warn you."

"It did seem very real," Agatha admitted. "You were all amazing."

"Ha!" Gunthar puffed up a bit. Agatha looked at his outfit and realized that he had played Bill Heterodyne. "I always wanted to try playing Bill. Can't wait to hear what Lars thought. I'll bet I've got him worried," he chuckled.

He glanced around. "I'm surprised, actually, we thought he'd be with you."

Agatha felt ill. She opened her mouth—

"Lars is dead." Zeetha said. "The Baron tried to kill Agatha. Lars stopped him."

Everyone froze. They stared at Agatha.

"He... he jumped right in," she whispered in the silence. "I—I didn't *ask* him to. I—"

"No one asks anything like that." Abner stood in the

doorway. His voice was firm and filled the room. "But he gave it. Lars always played the hero." He put a hand on Agatha's shoulder. "You made him want to be the real thing." He faced the room. "And that's how I'll remember him."

Agatha took a deep breath. "Me too. Thank you."

The Countess nodded to herself with a sad smile. It looked like Abner's apprenticeship was over. She clapped her hands, breaking the mood. "All right, we'll talk about this later. Now we must deal with the present. We have an airship to run and know remarkably little about how to do it."

Ardsley stepped forward. "I might be of some assistance there, Madam. Ardsley Wooster, of Her Majesty's secret service. I am quite familiar with Wulfenbach engineering."

The Countess nodded. "Excellent. Yeti? Let's get Mr. Wooster here to the engine room. Captain Kadiiski will be pleased to see him, I imagine."

She turned to Agatha. "You should come with me."

On the bridge, they found Master Payne, sitting in the Captain's chair, as happy as Agatha had ever seen him.

Agatha looked around in amazement. "Is this really a Wulfenbach airship?"

The Countess sighed. "Oh, yes. It was *remarkably* easy to steal." She carefully didn't look toward her husband, while her voice gained several decibels without apparent effort. "But then, who would be fool enough to *try*?"

Ognian, who had been examining his reflection in some polished brass, turned to a stone-faced Master Payne. "Hey! Iz like hyu wife iz callink hyu a *fool* witout *ektually*—"

Payne glared at him. "You cannot *possibly* be as stupid as you *act*."

The Jäger considered this. "Ken if I *vants* to be!"

On the loading dock, Abner wiped away a tear and went to roll up the last boarding ladder, which, he realized with a shock, still had someone on it. He gingerly leaned out and Maxim's cheerful face greeted him from just below the edge.

"Hoy! Giff me a hand here. Hy gots sumtink hyuz gunna vant."

"Lars!" And indeed, the purple Jäger had him slung over his shoulder.

Maxim pulled himself aboard the airship. "Ho! Vell, now, dot's an interestink metaphysical qvestion." He gently lowered the body to the deck and then fanned himself with his hat. "See, hit's hiz *body*, bot Meester Lars ain't *uzin* it no more. So iz it *really*—"

"You brought him back," Abner said. "Thank you."

Maxim waved a hand. "Vasn't gun leave him." He patted Lars' shoulder. "Meester Lars—he vas scared to death. Ve could schmell it on heem. But he come to help Miz Agatha anyvay, und he sacrifice himself wit out tinkink. He fight vit the Jägerkin und die for the house of Heterodyne. Dot make him as goot as vun uf us, and ve dun leave our own behind."

Maxim stood up. "Ennyvay, hyu kin put him in der icebox and try to get him zapped back, but dot don't *vork* as goot as hyu'd tink. So ven hyu bury him—" Maxim gently placed his leather cavalry hat over Lars' face—"Hyu make sure he gots a hat."

Back on the bridge, Payne was arguing with his wife, though to a casual observer it would look as if he were merely explaining himself to an interested third party. No one was fooled, and they all tried to look very interested indeed.

"Ordinarily, stealing one of the Baron's airships would not be my first choice. But I want us as far away as possible, as quickly as possible."

Ardsley Wooster entered the bridge in time to hear the tail end of this. He shook his head. "It won't do any good. They'll hunt us down..." He paused and looked uncertain. "In fact... they should already be in pursuit." He looked back at the circus master with suspicion in his eye. "What did you do?"

With a theatrical sweep of his hand, Payne spun the ship's wheel, swinging the airship about in a tight turn. Below them the landscape tilted and with a rush, the city of Balan's Gap swung into view. Everyone gasped.

Pillars of smoke were rising from dozens of spots. The encircling Wulfenbach airships were obviously engaged in a battle with ground forces that had effective anti-aircraft capabilities. Several of the dirigibles were burning, and the observers clustered at the great tempered glass windows watched in horror as a dreadnaught slowly dropped to earth trailing a ball of blue flame.

Even from here, lines of troops could be seen engaging swarms of townspeople. Even more alarming, however, were the creatures that were bursting out of various wells and buildings.

Zeetha, Krosp, and the Jägers saw that these were reminiscent of the monstrosities they had fled from in the sewers. They seemed indifferent to the struggles of the people around them, and gleefully scooped up troopers and townspeople alike.

"*We* did *nothing*," Payne said. He kept the wheel tightly pulled and the beleaguered city slid away out of sight. When they were once again facing away, Payne relaxed his grip on the wheel. "But what with the fighting, and the appearance of those monsters from the drains, the Baron's forces have a serious battle on their hands. For the moment, no one will pay any attention to us." He looked at Agatha with an unreadable expression on his face. "No matter *who* we're carrying."

Agatha looked at him. "I didn't do that!" She paused, and continued uncertainly. "Did I?"

The side of Payne's mouth quirked upwards in a brief smile. "I should think not. Not unless you can command monsters to fight for you," he raised his eyebrows inquiringly.

Agatha blew a lock of hair out of her eyes. "Of *course* n—"

"Hey Dimo!" Maxim cried as he strode onto the bridge, "Hyu made it op dot ladder pretty fast wit only vun hand."

"Ha!" Dimo shrugged, "Dot becawze Hy used my brains."

The other two looked at him in amazement. "Eww," they said. "Messy."

Agatha threw up her hands. "What am I saying? Of course I can!" Realizations began to dawn. "The Other. She uses voice harmonics—and the Geisterdamen Vrin said I sounded like her!"

Zeetha looked apprehensive. She leaned into Taki. "I think we're gonna need more pie." The cook displayed empty hands.

Agatha grabbed hold of Krosp's coat. "I can talk to monsters!"

The cat squirmed in her grip. "Well, sure. But will they talk back?"

"The Slaver Wasps back on Castle Wulfenbach moved when I ordered them to. If *those* were her creatures, I'll bet these are too!" She turned to Master Payne. "Get me back there! I can stop them!" Payne and the others looked at her blankly. A Heterodyne was amazing enough. Now said Heterodyne was talking about confronting the monsters of The Other?

Dimo stepped forward, an apprehensive look on his face. "Dot iz not soch a goot idea, Lady. Hyu dun know dese monsters. Dey could be anybody's. Ve saw dem in der sewers.

"Eefen if hyu could use hyu voice to get dem all riled op, Hy dun tink hyu could get dem to calm beck down. Monsters like dot, ven dey gets goink, dey ain't nottink bot killink machines."

Ognian spoke up. "Jah, und not effen goot lookink vuns like uz."

Dimo stared at him levelly for a second and then just continued. "Hyu'z better let de Baron deal mit dis. Iz vot he dozz."

Agatha looked at him in frustration. "But I *squished* him with a *chicken house*!" All of the circus members gasped at this revelation. Agatha looked guilty. "Didn't I mention that?"

Dimo waved his hand reassuringly. "A leedle ting like dot? Oh shoo—" he conceded, "He'z a bit messed op, but he gun be fine! Hy giffs him de first aid!"

Everyone took a second to contemplate what a Jägermonster would consider to be first aid.

Agatha cracked first. "Turn this thing around!" She screamed. Everyone flinched. Agatha's voice was giving off harmonics that normally sent people racing for the hills. Combined with her increasingly frantic movements and overall air of barely contained fury, several of the more experienced performers seriously considered leaping from the airship.

Only Krosp stood his place. "Ain't gonna happen," he said firmly.

"It wasn't a request!" Agatha roared. She grabbed her head and stared at the cat with a look of dawning awareness coupled with a mounting rage. "Everywhere I go lately, there's chaos! I've got—I've got to try to *fix* something!"

She snapped upright and screamed in defiance. "I'm going to go down there and personally punch every monster in the snoot!" She focused back in on a suspiciously calm Krosp. "And don't try to stop me!"

Krosp casually put his paws behind his back and cocked a fuzzy eyeridge. "Wouldn't dream of it."

This was such an unexpected response that several circus members later swore that they could hear circuits snapping within Agatha's skull. Emotions flickered across her face almost too fast to discern. She settled for an icy rage. "Why *not?*"

Krosp took a deep breath through his nose. "By the smell of it, all of those chemicals they stuffed into you are burning off. It's also obvious that you haven't properly slept in days." He took another sniff and stepped back. "You're not going *anywhere.*"

Agatha's face went purple with rage. "*I'LL—*"

She froze, a peculiar look came over her face and she began to swoon.

"Hy gots hyu!" Dimo cried, and no doubt he would have, if he hadn't tried to catch her with his left hand. As it was, Agatha did a magnificent face-plant upon the deck.

Maxim nudged her with his booted foot and grinned at a chagrinned Dimo. "Should haff used hyu brains *dot* time, too."

Dimo glowered as he attempted to scoop Agatha up with one arm. "Shot op!" He shrugged his left shoulder in annoyance. "Hy gets a new vun soon."

Maxim nodded. "A new brain? Iz about time."

* * *

Agatha slowly awoke. The first thing she noticed was that the sky outside the porthole was dark. Obviously hours had passed. She realized that she was stretched out on a snug airshipman's bunk. The cabin was small and compact. The only signs of the regular occupant were a few framed tintypes of various women who apparently had trouble properly dressing themselves and a lovingly polished French horn hanging from a silk strap.

Agatha blearily raised her head and observed that she was clad in just a large, unfamiliar shirt. It said a lot for the state of her head that this observation, and the ramifications thereof, were processed without undo embarrassment. She considered this, and realized that she was more concerned about the indescribably odd taste in her mouth.

She was surprised that she didn't have a headache. Whenever heroines in the Heterodyne Boys novels awakened in similar circumstances, they invariably reported having them. Agatha however, was beginning to wonder if she'd ever have a headache again.

What she *did* have was a terrible thirst. She spotted a large canteen hanging from a bedside hook. With a bit of effort, she pulled herself up to a sitting position and, finding it full of water, took a deep drink.

She could hear the thrumming of engines. The ship was moving quickly, if she was any judge. She also heard voices. Many voices. As the murmur rose and fell, she realized from faint snippets that the discussion was about her.

She closed her eyes. It was going to be awkward, there was no denying that. They knew she was a Heterodyne.

A tear surprised her by rolling down her face. It was only the first of many. She would have to leave the circus now. They

574

wouldn't trust her, and... and she had gotten Lars killed.

Now the tears flowed freely and she sobbed quietly as she remembered the feel of his arms around her, the way he had smiled when she had delivered a line perfectly, the taste of his lips.

Gone. Gone forever.

Eventually she snuffled one last time and knew that she had to get up. She swung her legs onto the deck, and felt it vibrating beneath her toes. Master Payne really was driving the ship hard. That made sense.

She swayed to her feet. Shaky, but not incapacitated. Good. She looked about, found her glasses and slipped them on. Then she searched, but saw no other clothing. She blew a lock of hair out of her face in annoyance. She found a small tin washbasin, and poured in a splash of water from the almost empty canteen. She scooped the water over her face, and tried to imagine that she was washing away her old life.

She dried her face and slid her glasses back on. As she did so, she caught sight of herself in the small polished metal mirror bolted to the wall above the basin. A gleam of gold at her throat made her pause.

She blinked in surprise. It looked like—it was! It was her old locket! The one that Moloch's brother had stolen from her back in Beetleburg *months* ago!

But it *couldn't* be.

Well there was a simple way to settle it. The locket contained pictures of her parents. Her hand stopped halfway to her throat.

Her parents. These would be portraits of Bill Heterodyne and Lucrezia Mongfish. She had lovingly studied them for hours lying in her bed at night, or when she had been bullied at school. Wishing that the people in the locket would return from some magical, far-away place and tell her that she was a princess or some other squirmingly embarrassing fantasy.

Well, as far as fantasy parents go, she had hit the jackpot, and now she was terrified of what that meant. She had a sudden irrational thought: If the locket around her neck wasn't hers—If there was someone else's portrait inside, or even no portrait at all—then she could forget that she was a Heterodyne. It would no longer be real. It would be someone else's problem.

She stared at the locket in the mirror. But where had it come from? Of course it was hers. She recognized it in a hundred subtle ways and knew—*knew* that it was hers, and that it, and everything it contained and everything it represented—was hers and would always be hers. Even if she were too weak or scared to take it, it would still be there, around her neck and inside her head. Forever.

This realization flashed through Agatha's head in an instant. She looked at the girl in the mirror. The girl who had dreamed that she could run away with the circus and avoid her destiny. The girl smiled back at her regretfully. It would have been nice.

Then she set her jaw, and reached for the locket.

"DON'T *TOUCH* IT!" Zeetha's hand grabbed hold of Agatha's wrist scant millimeters from the clasp.

Agatha blinked. "What's wrong with it?"

Zeetha took a deep breath. "Something happened to you in Sturmhalten. You... changed."

Agatha nodded slowly. "Yes... The Royal family had this machine. I know you won't believe this, but because of it, I was possessed. My mind was taken over."

She waited for Zeetha to scoff. Instead the warrior girl looked like she was thinking. "What was it you were possessed *by*?"

This question was so unexpected that Agatha blurted out the truth. "My mother. Lucrezia Mongfish. They said she was The Other."

Zeetha looked troubled. "*The* Other? Then the Baron...This *will* cause problems."

"You *believe* me?"

Zeetha looked up from her introspection and saw Agatha's distress. She came over and to Agatha's surprise, embraced her tightly. Agatha found herself relaxing within Zeetha's embrace.

"We are Kolee-dok-zumil," Zeetha murmured into Agatha's ear. "We are a thing together." She drew back slightly and looked Agatha in the eye. "And in retrospect, I can see that the person we found in Sturmhalten was *not you*."

Her hand came up and touched the locket at Agatha's throat. "But when whoever *was* there put that locket on— *you*—Agatha—came back. I *saw* that."

The hand caught Agatha's chin and tilted her head so the two were looking into each other's eyes. "So you keep that locket on. You keep it on until you are strong enough to handle whatever is in that head of yours."

Agatha looked distressed. Zeetha frowned. "Is there a problem with that?"

Agatha glanced at the locket in the mirror. "My uncle made me this locket many years ago. It was supposed to protect me." She thought for a minute. "And I guess it did. It kept me from violently breaking through like most Sparks do, but it did it by keeping me... stupid."

She brought her hand up, as if she wanted to claw it away from her neck, but her hand hovered, centimeters away from it. Her face showed the conflict she felt. "It used to make me feel safe. Now whenever I think about it, it makes me *furious*."

She sat down hard onto the bed. "It's a symbol of how awful my life was. The headaches. The inventions that never worked. The people who treated me like an idiot. All of that was because of this locket." She pounded her fists upon her thighs. "This damned, stupid-making locket!"

She then slumped slightly and looked at Zeetha beseechingly. "But it *did* keep me safe. I *didn't* go mad. And now you say it made the thing in my head go away." She sighed and rubbed her forehead. "I really don't know how to feel about this," she confessed.

Zeetha nodded seriously and sat down next to Agatha. She slung an arm around Agatha's shoulders and gave her a squeeze. The two sat together in silence for a moment.

Finally Zeetha said, "You've been wearing it for a while now. You don't *sound* stupid. How do you feel?"

Agatha considered this. The answer surprised her. "I feel good. I think this thing—" she flicked the locket with a fingernail—"Has been off for too long." She paused again, "I... I can tell that my thinking has... slowed down a bit. I have to *concentrate* more when I'm thinking hard, but it's nothing like it was before. I think my mind has become too strong for it."

Zeetha nodded slowly. "So—it's something that you have overcome. Something that reminds you that you're stronger. But it's also something that is making you work harder to become even better? That's good!"

Agatha looked at her askance. "Really?"

Zeetha bounced to her feet. "Of course! Any warrior would cherish such a powerful symbol!" She touched the locket at

Agatha's throat. "You were meant to have this."

Agatha sighed deeply and stood up. "I sure hope so, because it looks like I can't take it off." She stretched. "That's something else I have to accept."

Zeetha nodded and declared in a ringing voice. "Think of it as a symbol of everything you've overcome, and everything you *will* overcome."

Agatha looked at her with a pained expression. "That seems a bit... precious."

Zeetha frowned. "When you're stuck with something onerous, make it into a positive symbol." She lightly smacked Agatha upside her head. "Unless you *want* to make yourself miserable."

Agatha smiled, and took a deep breath. "So where are we going?"

Zeetha smiled. "Are you kidding? Payne's been making a bee-line for Mechanicsburg as soon as we got the engines up to speed. The *last* thing they want to do is delay you."

Agatha nodded. She opened the door. "Let's get this over with," she muttered, and strode out.

Zeetha closed her eyes and counted to herself. At "ten," the door was jerked open and Agatha scuttled back in, slamming it behind her.

"Pants."

Zeetha said nothing, but silently handed over the bundle she'd brought with her. Agatha dressed quickly. Over her sturdy undergarments she wore a green linen dress that was expensive enough to command respect, but unimaginative enough to make it hard to remember. She laced up the pair of stout walking shoes with the unusual soles that had been constructed by the troupe's sparky leather worker and part-time cobbler, Sasho[77].

When Agatha finally appeared on the bridge, she found it packed solid. Everyone who was not actively involved in the running of the ship was gathered before Master Payne, who was standing on the elevated captain's deck.

The old showman looked unnaturally somber. The Countess stood beside him. Usually the two refrained from what the Countess archly referred to as "public indecency" and what everyone else called "holding hands," but now she was clinging on to her husband's arm as if her world was ending. And in a way, it was.

"This is it," Payne said in a voice that allowed no argument. "Master Payne's Circus of Adventure is finished." He paused as if he expected a reaction, but everyone remained deathly silent.

"By aiding the Lady Heterodyne, we have done what armies could not. We have humiliated the Baron and escaped to tell the tale." He shook his head. "No matter what we promise, he cannot afford to let us get away, and we won't—if we stay together."

This caused some murmuring, which stopped instantly when Payne raised his hands. "After we have dropped off the Lady Heterodyne, we will fly to Paris. Once there we will sell the airship if we can, but more likely we will have to abandon it. Afterwards, we must go our separate ways."

That provoked a sharper reaction.

"It cannot be helped!" Payne roared. "We have made

---

[77] They were easily the most comfortable shoes Agatha had ever worn. You could walk all day and not feel any fatigue. But if you stood still for too long, you had to pay attention, or else you found your feet starting to dance. They were great for weddings, but Sasho had been run out of his home town after the funeral.

our living by being fabulous creatures and thus, we are *memorable*. As a group we are even more so. We must change or we will die!"

The Countess gripped Payne's sleeve even tighter. "Payne," her whisper sounded loud in the silence, "Are you saying that we would have to... leave *show business*?"

Everyone's breath caught.

Payne shrugged uncomfortably. "We... might," he admitted. Sobs were heard from the crowd.

Suddenly, another voice rang out. "It does not have to come to that!" Ardsley Wooster, clad in engine begrimed shirt-sleeves stepped forward. "You don't even have to disband. Instead, you can come and perform for my countrymen. Come to England."

He indicated Agatha. "The Lady Heterodyne and myself will be heading there directly. If you come, you will all be guests of Her Majesty, the Queen. You'll be new! Exciting! A glamorous continental import with a stunning story to tell! You'll be the toast of Britain and will perform before Her Majesty herself!"

Payne frowned. "We'll be used as propaganda against the Empire."

Wooster paused. "Are we talking about the same Empire that will kill you if it catches you? Why, yes sir, I believe we are. Only you can say how firm a grasp said Empire still has upon your loyalty. For what its worth, it's not like you'll be asked to spread falsehoods."

Payne closed his mouth and looked at the rest of the troupe. "Your thoughts? This affects us all."

"I doubt we're worth an international incident," The Countess conceded. She brightened, "And I am a third cousin to Albia by marriage. Many, many times removed, of course."

"Performers to Royalty always looks good on the playbills," Rivet stated.

"Oh, yes," André said gloomily, glancing back towards Balan's Gap. "That worked out so *very* well the last time."

Trish turned to Gunthar. "I think getting Balthazar into a real school might be a good thing."

"Whoa!" the boy cried, "Hold on! They'd… they'd make me wear *shoes*!"

Dame Ædith stroked her chin. "I hear England is *crawling* with vampyres…"

Slowly, more and more of the troupe found themselves warming to the idea.

Finally, there was a call for a show of hands. The result was almost unanimous.

"Very well, Mr. Wooster," Payne announced, "We are loath to break up our company, and there is no denying that we will be safer for a while outside of the Empire. We accept your offer." He paused. "Do you… do you think Her Majesty would let us keep the airship?" He then winced at the fierce grip upon his arm.

"I think, for the good of diplomatic relations—" Wooster did not elucidate about whom these relationships were between, but he remembered that skillet—"We will have to return the ship, at least, to the Empire." The look in Payne's eyes forced him to add, "But if you tour the outer islands, I expect Her Majesty might put a ship at your disposal."

Payne and Marie looked at each other and nodded.

"I think you made the right decision, sir," Wooster said happily. "Let us examine the charts and we can plot the best course."

"Yes, we have about an hour and a half before we reach Mechanicsburg," Payne said.

Wooster checked himself. "Mechanicsburg?"

"Yes, Mr. Wooster," Agatha said, "They're dropping me off."

A touch of panic filled Wooster's face. "What?" The image of Gil's face filled his mind's eye. It was not a happy face. "No, back in Sturmhalten, you agreed to come to England."

"I most certainly did not!"

Wooster stared at her.

Agatha hesitated, and turned to Zeetha. "Did I?"

Zeetha nodded. "You did, but that was when you... weren't in your right mind." She continued thoughtfully. "In fact, it sounded like you'd rather have gone *anywhere* other than Mechanicsburg."

Agatha digested this information. "I see. That's... interesting." She turned to Wooster. "You think I should go to England with you."

"Indeed I do. Right now the Wulfenbachs want you under their thumb. In England, you'll be under the protection of Her Majesty. Once there, you'll be able to negotiate in safety."

Agatha thought about this and shook her head. "No. Right now, I'm just another potentially dangerous Spark. The Baron might not mind me being bottled up in England. He'd probably prefer not having a Heterodyne running around the Empire.

"Plus, even though they're at odds, I imagine that if his... fears about me are correct, then your Queen would easily be able to deal with me. Before the current rift, England aided the Empire when it was clearing the continent of revenants.

"But if I want to be treated as a Heterodyne, than I have to get to Mechanicsburg. Once I'm established, it'll be a different discussion entirely."

Krosp interrupted. "Oh, yes. You'll be a sovereign power

then. But that means that if you break the Pax Transylvania, he'll legally be able to roll in and crush you like he's done to hundreds of others." Krosp paused. "And I'll be honest, from what I saw, I wouldn't be surprised if he said to hell with the legalities and rolled in anyway."

Agatha nodded. "Krosp, you've studied military history. Has *anyone* ever taken Mechanicburg?"

Krosp paused. "No," he admitted. "But that was when the Heterodynes were in control. And, I'll point out, no one has ever successfully resisted the Baron."

"Sounds like it'll be an interesting fight," Zeetha said cheerfully. "But why are you willing to have it? I thought you were talking about just living a normal life?" She glanced at the rest of the circus. "Normal-ish." She amended.

"Yes," Agatha admitted. "That was the plan." She looked at Zeetha and gave her a lopsided grin. "But there's a serious flaw with that plan, one that ruins everything. I'm not really a 'normal person,' now am I? I'm a Heterodyne."

"But you don't have to fight the Wulfenbachs," Wooster insisted. "You can still be a Heterodyne in England."

"Yes, I imagine that's one of the reasons your government would like to have me. But I'm going to Mechanicsburg, and I'll tell you why. When my mother, Lilith, was about to throw me to safety, she said, 'Go. Get to Castle Heterodyne. It will help you.' She *knew* people, Klaus Wulfenbach amongst them, would be after me. But *that's* where she told me to go. Mechanicsburg."

She looked Wooster directly in the eye. "And since she was one of the two people in this world that I trust completely, *that* is where I'm going."

Wooster dropped his eyes and sighed deeply. "I see." He squared his shoulders and grinned. "Then I guess I'd better go with you." He turned to Master Payne. "My offer still holds, of course. But instead of going direct, I'll give you a letter to present to Her Majesty's ambassador in Paris. I expect you'll all be on one of Her Majesty's submersibles within the week."

Agatha nodded. "Very well, Mr. Wooster, I imagine you'll be quite useful, and I promise to visit your Queen eventually, if only to see how well my friends have been treated."

The agent smiled ruefully. "Perfectly understandable. I'd best find some writing paper so I can prepare those letters."

As Wooster left, Agatha turned to Master Payne and the Countess. "Thank you. For everything. I want you to know that I would have been happy working with you."

The Countess looked at her appraisingly. "I rather doubt it," she said frankly. "I suspect that in the end, we would have wound up working for you." She raised a hand to forestall Agatha's protest. "It's the nature of the Spark, my dear. We can't help it."

She looked Agatha in the eye. "But we *can* help how we treat those who fall into our orbit. Treat them with respect. See to their comfort. Reward their efforts—" She hugged her husband, "And allow them the illusion that they are in control of their destiny."

Payne nodded seriously as he patted his wife's hand. "Yes, as you can see, that's very important."

The Countess froze. "Hieronymus, you filthy commoner. Are you intimating—"

Payne glanced at Agatha. "Please, m'lady, don't argue in front of the Heterodyne."

Marie effortlessly switched gears. "Goodbye, my dear," she said with a tear forming in her eye. "Try to stay good." She enveloped Agatha in a tight hug and whispered. "But if you simply *can't*, at least remember to enjoy yourself."

Over the years to come, Agatha would often vacillate as to whether this was the best or the worst bit of advice she had ever received, but she had to admit, that she never regretted following it.

Payne took her hand, and a small, pleasantly heavy purse was placed there. Agatha tried to hand it back. "You've got to be joking. I... I destroyed all your wagons. Your possessions, your props, your books—I couldn't *possibly* accept wages."

Payne raised an eyebrow. "I know," he said delicately, "It's a bill."

Agatha hefted the purse, which seemed heavier. "Ah. Yes, of course."

Payne waved a hand. "Oh don't worry about it right away. Who knows? Perhaps we'll all become so fabulously rich from the new Heterodyne plays, that we won't need it, eh?"

"New plays?"

"Don't be naïve, my Lady. You'll be the subject of new stories before Wulfenbach's troops get their cook fires lit. We, at least, will be in a position of authority, for those that care about such things, and I promise you that we will devote as much care and respect to your tales as we do to the others."

Agatha turned to Gunthar. "I've never been in a pie fight."

He considered this. "Not yet," he conceded, "but the night is young."

Agatha turned back to Payne. "I'll repay every pfennig. I swear."

Payne looked shocked. "Why, I never thought otherwise." That said, he again turned serious. "At the moment, you're basically a good person, Agatha. Try to stay a good person, but don't let people take advantage of you. If you do, soon enough you won't *be* a good person anymore, you'll be a bad Heterodyne, and frankly, the world has had quite enough of them."

With that he offered her his hand, she shook it, and with a swirl of his great coat, he swept off. It was only after he left that Agatha realized that there was a smaller purse in her hand, with a small tag which read: "This, on the other hand, is a gift."

I wonder how he did that, she thought.

With Payne and his wife gone, the rest of the circus approached, and there was much hugging, and crying, and a great many questions about the Heterodynes and her life.

Agatha had thought that the others would be shy because of who she was, but soon realized that these were people who, on stage at least, hobnobbed nightly with figures of legend. To them, at least, she was still Agatha Clay.

All too soon, the landing gongs sounded, and Agatha, Zeetha, Krosp, Ardsley and the three Jägers were escorted to one of the launch bays. There they found several fully loaded horses, and a change of clothes.

"The horses are a surprise," Zeetha commented as she changed.

"They're good ones. Officer grade," Professor Moonsock said as she finished tightening the final saddle. "You should be able to get ten gold Pax-Guilders each when you sell them. Don't settle for less than five, or they'll think they're stolen."

"But they *are*—"

"—But you don't want people to *know* it!"

At last all the preparations were complete. The airship set down rather bumpily in a deserted field near a dilapidated farm house.

The bay door was rolled up and the Jägers leapt out and watched, as two of the roustabouts slid the ramp out and dropped it down with a dull clong.

A final round of embraces and goodbyes, and the three horses clopped down the ramp and began cropping the long grass as the group watched the ship close up.

Ognian took a deep breath of the crisp morning air and whooped. "Schmells like *home*, brodders!" The other two Jägers grinned. They all gave Agatha a slight bow, and trotted off to scout on down the road.

The ramp was slid back into place. The doors were rolled closed. The engines revved, the running lights of the airship blinked three times in salute, and it rose slowly into the sky. The figures waving from the windows rapidly dwindled and quickly became unrecognizable. Once airborne, the ship turned and headed off, away from the rising sun.

Part of Agatha felt that she should sit and watch it until it vanished from sight. She shook her head and sighed. They did that sort of thing in stories.

She pulled her horse around. The road into Mechanicsburg wasn't far. Zeetha and Wooster waited for her to take the lead.

Agatha sat up straight and touched the horse's flanks with her heels. She was a Heterodyne, and she was going home.

ABOUT THE AUTHORS

PROFESSORESSA KAJA FOGLIO is the current head of the Department of Irrefutably True History at Transylvania Polygnostic University. She first became aware of the power of Creative History while listening to the excuses of her fellow students who had failed to produce their homework. Her doctoral work brought recognition to the long-hidden Canis operisphagus, or "homework-eating dog," which, as we now know, infests most of our major schools and universities. She first became interested in the history of the Heterodyne family during the infamous "Nymphenberg Pudding Incident" when she was mistaken for Agatha by an angry mob of dessert chefs, from whom she barely escaped. Her subsequent research has brought her the grudging acclaim and jealous rivalry of many of her academic colleagues. She enjoys airship racing, Hyrulian Electro-Mechanical Shadow Puppetry, and illustrated novels.

PROFESSOR PHIL FOGLIO spends most of his time in the field, collecting legends, folk songs, anecdotes, and gossip pertaining to Sparks and their effects on village society and "folk science." This is a bit odd, as he was originally hired by Transylvania Polygnostic University to teach Modern Dance. He first became interested in Heterodyne stories while doing research on simple automatons, and was actually present when the Lady Heterodyne unleashed her "Battle Circus" upon Baron Klaus Wulfenbach. Through subsequent research, bribery, and rampant speculation, the professor has managed to fill in a great many of the narrative gaps in the early life of Agatha Heterodyne. He enjoys botany, mechanical illustration, entomology, and—in moderation—modern dance.

The ongoing adventures of Agatha Heterodyne can be found online, where they are updated every Monday, Wednesday & Friday at www.girlgeniusonline.com.